HIS KISS WAS FIERCE,

but Carolyn met him with a wildness of her own, clinging to his mouth and wrapping her arms tightly around his neck. Their highly charged emotions of a moment earlier had broken down all restraints, and Jason was lost to reason. His pent-up longing was now insatiable.

For Carolyn, there were no concrete thoughts, only the shimmering patterns of pleasure. She moved with him in a knowledge older than time, her body surging into this sensual realm she had never before explored.

* * *

Praise for Candace Camp's *Rosewood*:

* * *

"Candace Camp takes you on Millie's journey from spinsterhood to sensual awakening. I loved every delicious step."

—*Sandra Brown, bestselling author of MIRROR IMAGE*

CANDACE CAMP

LIGHT AND SHADOW

PREVIOUSLY PUBLISHED UNDER THE
PSEUDONYM LISA GREGORY

HarperPaperbacks
A Division of HarperCollins*Publishers*

HarperPaperbacks   *A Division of* HarperCollins*Publishers*
10 East 53rd Street, New York, N.Y. 10022

Copyright © 1985 by Candace Camp
All rights reserved. No part of this book may be used or reproduced in any manner whatsoever without written permission of the publisher, except in the case of brief quotations embodied in critical articles and reviews. For information address HarperCollins*Publishers,*
10 East 53rd Street, New York, N.Y. 10022.

This book is published by arrangement with the author.

Cover photograph by Herman Estevez

Quilt courtesy of Quilts of America, Inc., NYC

First HarperPaperbacks printing: July 1991

Printed in the United States of America

HarperPaperbacks and colophon are trademarks of HarperCollins*Publishers*

10 9 8 7 6 5 4 3 2 1

One

The bustling seaport of Antigua was as busy by night as it was by day. Long before dawn, fishing boats would leave the port, workmen shouting and whistling in the darkness of morning. By sunrise, the marketplace would come alive with merchants setting up their stalls of fruit and fish, breads and cheeses, burlap sacks of coffee beans and crates of tea. With the streets filled with shoppers, hagglers and bargain-makers, children, dockworkers and shopkeepers, Antigua had all the workings of a busy English city—except for the tropical heat that pervaded everything. In surrender to the piercing temperatures, the town would close up and take shelter from the beating afternoon sun. But Antigua would come alive again in the late afternoon, and by evening the taverns and streets, the dance hall and theater, captured a vibrant energy, rough and raucous, that lasted through the night.

Carolyn stripped off the chunky bracelets from her wrists and dropped them onto the dressing table. The glass gems were dull, shorn of their stage glamour, just like the cheap material of her medieval dress. It didn't do to look closely at anything connected with this acting troupe—including herself. Heavy makeup masked the clean lines of her face, making her look older than her twenty-six years. She frowned at her reflection in the spotted mirror above the table as she dipped her fingers into the pot of cream and smeared it over her face.

She had been good tonight. It was the best Juliet she'd done in her five years of acting. But there wasn't the elation one would have expected. It didn't matter here. The colonials would have applauded just as loudly if she had forgotten half her lines or stalked woodenly through the role. They were overjoyed simply to see such evidence of civilization as a Shakespearean play. At home, Carolyn mused, perhaps in one of London's fine theaters, the performance she had finished only moments ago would have met with the thunderous applause of a respectful audience. But here in Antigua, she knew that most of the men were more interested in the white curve of her bosom above the low-cut square neckline or a glimpse of her shapely ankles than in the eloquent lines she spoke. How the buffoons whistled and guffawed! And the rest of the crowd came in the hopes of finding a sophisticated mistress who spoke and looked like home. Well, they'd been disappointed in her, Carolyn thought with an inward grin. She wasn't about to give any one territorial rights over her. She was her own woman and had been ever since her husband died.

Kit Mabry. She had loved Kit's spontaneity, adored his boyish charm, but he lacked the stability to run their lives. It began as a joyous marriage, filled with the passion of young love, but as the realities of everyday life came to the front, it had been up to her to keep them clothed, fed, housed, and equipped with servants. It had also fallen to her to escape or cajole the creditors who dunned them. Kit's tastes had exceeded his pocketbook, and all of his lovely presents to Carolyn had to eventually be sold or returned.

"Lord, Caro, you're in a blue mood," Marietta Perkins remarked, reaching over from her dressing table to dip her fingers in Carolyn's pot of cleansing cream. As usual, she didn't bother to ask if she could borrow from her fellow actress.

Carolyn glanced at the thin-faced girl who had started out life as Mary Etta Weaver. Mary Etta wasn't a bad sort, though she was notorious throughout the troupe for her constant pilfering of supplies. But at least she wasn't catty or envious, as so many members of the company were. Few could forget or forgive the fact that Carolyn's well-bred tones were not the consequence of years of training and practice but simply the way she had always spoken. She was a British lady from a wealthy estate, cavorting about the British West Indies on rickety stages and in wretched inns, and few could understand why she was there at all. Rather than respect her immense talents (for she surely outperformed them all with every show), they resented her presence. She had been born to be a lady, and it showed in her carriage and voice, which defied the cheap clothes and dingy surroundings. "I guess it's because *Romeo and Juliet* is a tragedy. It's hard to feel cheerful when one's just been entombed," she quipped in a light tone.

"Really?" The girl sounded awed. "You mean, you actually felt like you was the girl what killed herself?"

"Well, not quite that sad," Carolyn admitted, flashing a smile that lit up her features. Her face was appealingly heart-shaped, with a delicately pointed chin. Her small mouth, with the upper lip a trifle short and the lower lip fuller, gave her a look that was a curious blend of vulnerability and seductiveness. Enormous eyes of a pure, deep blue dominated her face, gazing out upon the world with a tinge of cynicism and world-weariness. Across her nose and cheekbones lay the palest dusting of freckles, which seemed a reflection of the blazing red-gold color of her hair and gave her face a warmth often missing in fair-skinned people.

Carolyn had long been accustomed to the fact that she attracted men without trying. Even with Kit to show she was spoken for, other men had been drawn by her lustrous beauty and by the indefinable quality of her personality, the warmth and daring, the intriguing combination of lady and adventuress. She had never tried to lure men, yet they provoked Kit into jealous quarrels and even one duel. She had found out soon after her young husband's death in the Crimea that all male gestures of friendliness carried with them a high price tag—her presence in their beds. She was not about to sell her honor to obtain a man's comfort and protection.

Such an attitude had made her life difficult. This was the sixth acting troupe she had been with in four years, and the experiences she had would surely justify her somewhat cynical, and yet realistic, view of the world. Either she had refused to sleep with the troupe's star or manager and been kicked out for it or she had incurred the wrath of a wealthy patron who used his power to get her fired. She had been with this troupe the longest, primarily because the star and owner of the company, Florian McDowell, was too jealously guarded by his mistress Belinda to make many attempts to lure Carolyn into his bed. Lately, however, Carolyn had felt stirrings of doubt. Something was brewing, and it meant trouble for her. Florian had made a few improper suggestions to her when Belinda was not around, and though

Carolyn had put him off gracefully, his pride had been piqued. Florian liked to hold on to slights and magnify them until he believed that he had been gravely and unjustly injured. Moreover, fueled by the lies and rumors that ran rampant throughout the troupe, Belinda was unable to accept the fact that Carolyn had no designs on her place in the star's bed, and was constantly urging Florian to be rid of Carolyn and denegrating her talent as an actress. Balanced against Carolyn's advantages as a draw to the local males wherever the company played was the fact that invariably Florian had to deal with her rejected suitors' anger. While pride wouldn't let him yield to their demands, he wasn't above releasing her at another time to save himself future grief, Carolyn believed.

She knew her days with the McDowell Acting Company were limited. It didn't matter, she thought, she'd be glad to leave. Then she paused—what would she do if she was abandoned here, in dismal Antigua? The thought of looking for yet another troupe dismayed her, but would she be able to find any means of supporting herself without giving in to some man's offer of protection? She unpinned her hair and brushed it out at a furious pace as these thoughts raced through her mind. When she left her tyrannical father's house, she had vowed that she would never again be at the mercy of any man. She'd be a scullery maid—or starve.

She slipped out of her costume and hung it up on the rack for the wardrobe mistress, who was busy helping Belinda undress. As the female lead of the troupe, Belinda demanded this service, and Carolyn felt sorry for the already overburdened seamstress, who was responsible for cleaning, repairing, and making all their costumes, as well as packing, unpacking, and pressing the clothes before the shows. It was a demanding job, and the thin, hunched woman who filled it was always pale and strained. Carolyn helped her all she could, hanging up the stray costume, sewing the odd hems, without drawing Belinda's attention to either herself or the seamstress. As Carolyn brushed out her long hair, she heard behind her the sharp crack of a hand hitting skin, and she winced.

"You clumsy fool!" Belinda cried, her painstakingly learned upper-crust accent slipping in her anger. "You ripped the seam!"

The wardrobe woman bent her head to hide the anger flashing in her eyes, and Carolyn suspected she was hard put not to retort that it was Belinda's overeating that had caused the seam to rip, not her own lack of skill. Quickly Carolyn knotted up her hair and secured it with several hairpins, then slipped into her petticoats and pulled on a simple cotton dress. She turned her back to Mariette, to have her button up the long row of tiny buttons, which was almost impossible to do by oneself. "I don't know why you don't wear something prettier," Mariette sighed. "If I looked like you, I'd wear the prettiest clothes ever."

"I'm not interested in clothes any longer." That wasn't entirely true, for Carolyn still loved beautiful dresses, but her tastes were far beyond her price range. As long as she was forced to settle for something inexpensive, she preferred clothes that were serviceable and durable, not the gaudy, flashy things that Belinda wore and Mariette mooned over.

Mariette shook her head in wonder at Carolyn's attitude. "It must be your fancy upbringing."

Carolyn smiled wryly as she set a plain brown bonnet on her head and tied the ribbons beneath her chin. The gulf between her and the rest of the troupe was huge. Funny how she had never seemed to fit anyplace, with any group. Certainly not with the middle-class daughters and wives of the Indian officers she had lived among when she was married to Kit. Though her years in India had sated her hunger for worldly adventure, she had found that she missed the pleasures of her youth: the hunting, the excitement and the fast horses, the glittering balls and elegant dresses, the teasing and laughter and flirtations with eligible young men. Now, after years of traveling with actors, Carolyn found she even missed the deadly dull officers' wives' teas and the hot boredom of India. At least there she had been able to steal away and see something of the bizarre, fascinating foreign land.

She often longed for the pleasure of the rural aristocrats' life, but even when she had lived that life, she was a misfit. Her high spirits and taste for adventure had brought her into constant conflict with her stern father, and she had forever been in trouble for one indiscretion or the other—riding alone all over the place or waltzing with Johnny Fullingame before they were formally introduced (even though she'd known him all her life!), or playing a trick on Squire Moore with Kit. She had never been able to achieve her twin sister's calm, passive demeanor nor her well-bred response to every situation. When a glass light globe had toppled over and crashed against a housemaid's arm, slicing a long gash across her skin, Cynthia had fainted in the most graceful way possible, while Carolyn had jumped up and grabbed a white linen cover from one of the lamp tables and proceeded to bind up the poor girl's arm. Afterward, the maid had been dismissed for carelessness and Carolyn had been scolded by her aunt for a most unseemly display of quick thinking and a strong stomach.

Her final act of impropriety had been to elope with Kit

Mabry. Although Kit was from a prosperous family, he was the fourth son and therefore entitled to a mere sliver of the Mabry wealth. A kind and well-heeled uncle had bought him a commission in the cavalry, but it was not one of the prestigious regiments. It was obvious that if Kit were to rise in the army, it would have to be as an "Indian" officer, one of those less fortunate beings who earned his commissions by actively serving in India. Two black sheep in a world of "do's and mustn't do's," Kit and Carolyn found each other at age seventeen. When Carolyn announced that she wished to marry Kit, her aunt had thrown up her hands in dismay and cried that she couldn't, as she hadn't even yet made her debut. In a fit of rage, her father informed her that their marriage was out of the question and refused to listen to any of her pleas. Rather than fight the futile battle, Carolyn ran away with Kit to Scotland, where they married, and she hadn't heard from her father since. A tearful letter from her twin told her that Sir Neville had cut Carolyn's name out of the family Bible and refused to let her name be said in his house again.

Though she had been saddened, Carolyn was hardly surprised. She and Sir Neville had been at odds since she turned thirteen. He had tried forcefully to mold her into the image of her twin sister and her long-dead mother: quiet, retiring, obedient as dogs, and pleasant on command. There was no room in his vision of her for temper or spirit. All the joy and eagerness he had loved in her as a child he railed against in her as a young woman. Perhaps, she thought in retrospect, her love for Kit and determination to marry him had been as much a way to escape her father's dominance as anything else.

Carolyn shook the somber thoughts from her mind and

said her good-byes to the other women in the dressing room. She slipped out the side door of the theater into the hot, humid night. The stars shone clearly in the blue-black sky, but the midnight air was thick and oppressive, which was not unusual for the tropics.

Two local gentlemen waited at the foot of the stage-door steps, and as she exited, both straightened and swept their hats from their heads. "Madam," began one, while the other said, "Mrs. Mabry . . ." She gave them a vague, general nod and a formal smile.

"Good evening, gentlemen." Carolyn went lightly down the stairs, pulling on her short, threadbare gloves. The two men met her at the bottom step, each holding up a hand to help her down. She ignored both of them and managed to edge past the outstretched hands without touching either. One of the men touched her arm to detain her. Carolyn whirled and shot him a fierce glance. Surprised, he stepped back a little, his hand falling away. "Sorry, gentlemen, but I am not in the market for an escort. Please save your flattery and nosegays for a lady more disposed to them." She turned away.

"But, madam, please." The more persistent man pursued her. "I so admired your performance. I wished to give you these flowers as a token of my esteem."

Carolyn bit back the hot words that rose to her lips. She must not offend a theater patron by blurting out that the audience tonight had been interested only in leering at her and chatting among themselves. She could have been reciting nursery rhymes, for all they cared. "Thank you," she forced herself to say as she reached for the bouquet that the determined man waved at her. "Then I will accept them, of course." The bright, heavily scented tropical flowers were tied together by a thin blue ribbon, and the stems were crushed and warm from being held in his hand. Carolyn knew she would toss them away before she reached her room.

Her admirer fell into step with her as she started again, and she stopped again. "Really, sir, I must reiterate: I have no desire for male companionship of any sort. I am recently a widow. I'm sure you'll understand." She fell back on her much-used excuse.

The man hesitated, nonplussed by her forthright tone and words. "I'm sure your sorrow is great, but, please, grant me the privilege of comforting you."

Carolyn shrugged coldly. "There is no comfort for me. Excuse me. I must go now."

The man stood dumbly, and this time when she started forward he did not follow. Carolyn didn't look back to see his reaction, as she didn't want to encourage him with even that show of interest. She heard his footsteps starting across the street. He wasn't waiting around for the next actress to emerge from the theater. Surprising. Usually they were quite willing to settle for someone else.

Carolyn walked along briskly, not looking around her. In this area of town it was wisest not to catch anyone's eye. Sometimes merely a direct glance could be taken as an invitation. Her right hand was clenched around her satchel, which held her keys and some loose coins. It was only four blocks to the rooming house and Carolyn soon reached it. She slipped inside the outer door and closed it, then leaned back, recovering her breath. It was so hard to breathe on these islands. Even after all her years of living in India with Kit, then of touring the tropical colonies, she still was not used to the thick, heat-laden air. It was like trying to breathe soup, she thought.

Once inside the rooming house, she darted up the stairs. As she felt for the iron door key in her satchel, she thought of how good even her lumpy little bed would feel tonight, for she was exhausted. In the semi-gloom of the hallway, she found the keyhole and she stepped into her unlit room. Suddenly, as if a gust of cold air had swept over her, she felt it again—Cynthia!

With shaking fingers, Carolyn lit the wick of the lamp and then closed the door, locking it from the inside. Peeling off her gloves, she dropped them and the key on top of the chest and, deep in thought, she stepped urgently across the room to the open window. Moonlight illuminated the louvered shutters on either side of the window and fell in a bright square patch on the wooden floorboards. The glow from the oil lamp was low, and most of the room was in shadow, making her feel chilled and isolated, as if she were alone in the world. The bed, with its gauzy canopy of mosquito netting, was a formless, ghostly lump. Carolyn shivered and wrapped her arms around herself.

She knew she would sound like a madwoman if she tried to rationally explain what was happening to her. Her stomach tightened; her palms were sweating—she could describe it only as her "Cynthia feeling." She supposed it was something unique to twins, a sort of visceral linkage that carried over from infancy. As a child, she had experienced it often—suddenly she would "feel" Cynthia, and she would know that her sister was in trouble and needed her. She hadn't had the eerie sensation for years—until now. This was the fourth time since coming to Antigua that she'd had the feeling. She had thought that the vast physical distance separating them over the last few years had destroyed the bond. Then a month ago, as Carolyn was putting on her makeup before a dress rehearsal, the sensation was so strong and compelling that she had whirled around, half expecting to see her sister standing behind her, but there had been no one there.

Carolyn leaned against the windowsill and gazed at the night sky as worried thoughts raced through her mind. It had been eight years since she had heard from her twin, and it was painful to admit that she had caused the chasm that turned her family away from her, that kept Cynthia from corresponding with her. Not that they didn't try! The first year they were separated, their cousin Bella tried to help them by acting as a go-between, delivering messages from one to the other. But soon Bella's parents caught on and put a halt to their scheme. And Cynthia, so fearful of her father's anger and disapproval, made no attempts of her own accord to risk reprimand and contact her sister, not even daring to contact Carolyn through Bonnie, the girls' most beloved servant and companion all through their childhood. Years later, news of Cynthia's marriage to Jason Somerville had reached Carolyn, in a letter from Bella, who was now married and out from under her mother's thumb. She described the event in detail, and went on for two pages about the debonair Jason, his noble ancestry, his substantial fortune, and his brusque good looks. The letter, which had reached Carolyn in India, was yellow with age and was one of her few valued possessions.

After Kit died and Carolyn took up acting, she knew she had become an outcast from polite society and she had made no attempt to reach Cynthia, although she had continued to write Cousin Bella now and then to let her know where she was.

A shout from the street brought her back to the gloomy room—and her urgent dilemma. She had to find out what danger Cynthia was in, if any at all. Perhaps, she thought as she watched two young street toughs scamper off with the leather pouch of a drunk from the tavern below, she should find some way to make the journey home, to leave these islands and go back to her beloved England, despite her exile from her family. At least then she could track her sister down and look out for her well-being. But she wasn't even sure how she could find her sister's new home if she found a way back to England. Bonnie had told her that Jason Somerville was the heir to Lord Broughton's family estate in Kent. But for all she knew, Cynthia and her husband could be anywhere. . . . They probably had a home in London, as well. Or perhaps they were traveling on the continent, or visiting friends in Bath or Brighton.

Carolyn sighed with frustration and turned away from the window, slowly unfastening the long line of buttons down her back. It was impractical for her to rush to England to help her sister, but she couldn't ignore these dreadful premonitions. Cynthia had always turned to Carolyn when she needed help. Carolyn had been the stronger twin, the brave one, always ready to come to her sister's defense. She had been very protective of Cynthia, almost as if she were an older sister, but with the more intense closeness of a twin. On the few occasions that Cynthia had gotten into a scrape, Carolyn had rescued her, pretending that it had been she, not Cynthia, who had done the misdeed. Still, she knew she could do nothing for Cynthia here and now. She must accept that and simply continue her life. She hung up her dress in the wardrobe, slipped out of her crinoline and undergarments, and put on her thin gauze nightgown. Settling onto the low bed, she ducked under the mosquito netting and rearranged it around her.

Sleep would not come. She lay awake staring at the shadows and ghostly moonlit patterns on the floor, thinking about Cynthia and the stone house in the Lake Country, where the sisters had grown up. She remembered the mist hovering over the fields and lakes, enveloping the mountains, and the infrequent sunny days when trees and water and hills formed so lovely a picture it took one's breath away. A jumbled collection of scenes and stories from her childhood ran through her mind: noises, smells, people . . . a Christmas feast . . . a horse ride across the moors. . . . Recalling her most pleasant memories, she slid into sleep.

A winter landscape in twilight. The snow blanketed the fields and the mountains beyond. There was ice covering Shallowmere Lake, and she and Cindy were skating on it. Dressed elegantly in identical polka jackets and full skirts, they skated side by side. Suddenly, Carolyn was racing, outdistancing her sister, and Cynthia was struggling to catch up with her, crying out not to leave her behind. Then suddenly Carolyn was off the ice and in the snow, still wearing her skates. She staggered and stumbled, irritated that she hadn't taken off her skates. Yet she didn't stop to do so. She had to get there, had to. . . . She stumbled and went rolling through the snow. Strangely, it wasn't cold, but she couldn't breathe. Her face was buried in the powdery white stuff, and she struggled but couldn't get her hands and feet under her to rise, couldn't get her balance no matter how she tried. She began to struggle wildly.

Suddenly it was hot, not cold. She could smell the acrid scent of sweat, sense the pungent fear in the room, but she could not see. A heavy darkness weighed her down, smothering her. She couldn't breathe! In terror she lashed out with her feet and arms, scratching and kicking.

A man's voice swore, and suddenly two strong hands grasped her arms pinning her wrists down, but the pressure on her face was gone. Carolyn twisted her head to one side and gulped in air, then released a scream with all the volume her powerful stage voice could summon. The attacker released her arms and jumped off the bed.

Carolyn flung the pillow from her face and bolted up. A tall, masculine form blocked her doorway for an instant and was gone, his footsteps pounding the stairs. Then several doors opened, and the other troupe members poured into her room, with Florian and Belinda leading the curious crowd. "What the hell's going on?" Florian demanded.

Her words flooded forth in her terror and confusion. "He's—get him. He's gone. The stairs, Florian, the stairs!"

"What? Are you drunk?"

"No!" Carolyn jumped out of the tangled linens and managed to light the kerosene lamp, but her weak knees buckled and she sagged back onto the bed. Suddenly she began to shake. "Somebody—somebody tried to kill me."

"Have you gone mad?"

"It's obvious," Belinda smirked. "She's been having a nightmare."

"It wasn't a nightmare! I woke up and someone was trying to smother me with my pillow!"

Marietta Perkins gasped, but the other cast members looked nonplussed and disbelieving. One of the men looked heavenward and stalked back to his room. Florian was annoyed to have his sleep disturbed for this imaginary intruder. "Who?"

"I don't know! I couldn't see him; he had a pillow over my face. But I know it wasn't a dream."

"Who would want to kill you?" Belinda asked reasonably.

"Didn't you see him running down the stairs?"

"No. We heard you screaming, and then some thuds, but when we came out of our room there was no one in the hall or on the stairs."

"Well, those thuds were him running away."

"You ought to lock your door."

"I did."

"Maybe it was one of your disappointed suitors," Marietta suggested eagerly, and Florian frowned at her.

"That was probably it," Belinda agreed. "I've told you it's a mistake to be so particular, Carolyn. One of your men simply decided to use force instead of money."

"He wasn't trying to rape me," Carolyn snapped. "I think I know the difference, Belinda. There was a pillow over my face, and I was suffocating."

Belinda shrugged. "The man was simply stupid. He put the pillow over your face so you wouldn't recognize him, and pressed too hard."

"That's it," Florian agreed, happy to have the matter solved. "He won't be back tonight, at least. Just put that chair under the door handle and go back to bed." He yawned. "We'll discuss it in the morning."

"Florian, someone just tried to kill me! Do you honestly think I can drop off to sleep after that?" Carolyn shivered and wrapped her arms around herself, astonishingly cold in the warm night air.

"No, not, not murder," Florian began soothingly. "It was just a man trying to—"

"It should make me feel better if he was trying to rape me instead of kill me? He almost did both!" Carolyn exploded.

"My dear, you're going to have to learn to deal with these things without getting hysterical," Belinda cautioned. "No doubt, for someone of your background, it's difficult to live as we do. But if you intend to stay, you'll have to get used to it. You aren't in the ruling class anymore, 'Lady Carolyn.' You're just another one of us peasants."

Carolyn glared, the familiar irritation at Belinda's spite sweeping away some of her fear. Florian held up his hands placatingly. "Now, now, ladies. Let's forget all this and go to bed. It's the middle of the night."

The bystanders filtered out of the room, Marietta lingering behind a moment to draw in a last glimpse of the drama. Irritated, Carolyn closed the door on her and pulled the shaky little chest in front of it. Though it wouldn't do much to deter someone who wanted to get into her room, pushing aside the chest would cause a great deal more noise than prying open the flimsy lock.

Even shutting her eyes for a moment made her relive the scene again and again. So she settled herself into the chair and waited. She knew she'd never go back to sleep tonight. Florian was probably right when he doubted that the attacker would return, but logic couldn't prevail against the knot in her stomach. When dawn began to sift through the window, she rose stiffly and blew out the lamp. Closing the louvered shutters, she climbed into bed and, reassured by the light of day, went to sleep.

It was past noon when she awoke, and the room, bright with sunlight despite the closed shutters, was steaming hot and stuffy. Carolyn drew a deep breath and sat up. The incident seemed like an absurd dream. She padded to the window and opened the shutters. The sunlight glinted off the white stuccoed wall of the neighboring inn, and Carolyn winced with the glare.

There wouldn't be time for breakfast if she was to make the rehearsal at one. Quickly, Carolyn began to dress, her mind returning to the night before. It was hard to believe; that someone would really try to kill her. Surely no one hated her enough to do that. She had no money to steal. She supposed what Belinda said was possible. Perhaps one of her jilted suitors had been so stung by her refusal that he had tried to rape her. Still . . . most of her admirers were wealthy and respected members of the community, usually harmless and usually happy to turn to the company of one of the troupe's other women.

Carolyn shrugged. It didn't make any difference. Some lunatic was out to get her and no one would take her seriously. She tried to recall everything just as it had happened—the feeling of defenseless terror in her dream, her sudden awakening, her arms being pinned down as she gasped for air—but then she realized how pointless it would be to explain her case to the law. She could well imagine the colonial officials listening to her story, their lips curling in disbelief. No doubt they'd dismiss the whole thing as an actress trying to draw attention to herself and her company. She sighed as she pulled on her clothes. She would have to handle it herself, because those without money and influence had little recourse to the law. She'd probably wind up with one of *them* offering to make her his mistress. The only thing she could do to save herself was to somehow get off the island.

As she crossed the room to gather up her ankle-high boots, her bare foot came down on a hard object, and she cried out in pain. She bent over to get a closer look. It was a gold button, stamped with an image of a shield with a strange sort of animal lying before it. Carolyn stared at the button lying in her palm, puzzled, not realizing its significance. Then it struck her. In the struggle with her attacker, one of his buttons must have ripped off and fallen to the floor. It was from the sleeve of the man who had tried to kill her!

She closed her fingers over the button and walked evenly to the chest as her mind searched for new clues. She dropped the button into a small black lacquered box that housed her few keepsakes. It fell onto the letters she had received from Kit, which she kept bound with a blue ribbon, and rolled off to settle among the bits of her jewelry. She hid the box deep within her trunk, then sat down to pull on her boots, fastening them up the sides with a long buttonhook, while she thought about the button. It was an odd device on the front, which looked rather like a coat of arms. Perhaps she could trace the coat of arms and get some clues as to who had attacked her.

She sighed and shook her head. *No,* the thought of a nobleman creeping into this third-rate rooming house to smother a lowly actress was thoroughly absurd! Maybe he was a man of average means and less than noble lineage who had seen the device somewhere and liked it, and had it copied on his buttons. Or perhaps he was a planter who had pretensions and had invented a coat of arms for his family. Or maybe her attacker was merely a thief who had stolen a gentleman's coat. Looking up the seal in *Burke's Peerage* wouldn't help her, for the image was so small that it was impossible to tell what the animal was. "I might just as well comb the city and look for every man's jacket missing a button," she said to herself. Her clue wasn't really much help.

She slid the trunk away from the closed door, then took several moments to gather her courage before collecting her gloves and satchel and walking out to the hall. A quick glance at the corridor and stairs assured her that she was the only person around. She closed the door behind her and tried to lock it with her key, but whoever had entered her room last night had broken the lock. It didn't help her nerves to know that her room would be open to whoever chose to come in while she was gone.

She took a firm grip on her satchel, straightened her head and shoulders, and started down the stairs. The light outside was dazzling, and though the street was its usual dirty, somnolent self, it was curiously reassuring. Nothing had changed, except inside her, she realized. If she didn't allow herself to be frightened, she would be able to handle the situation.

The brisk walk to the theater helped clear her mind; nothing untoward happened on the way. Life seemed to be carrying on as usual, and the sights of the bustle of shoppers in the crowded and colorful marketplace, of children shouting and laughing as they played in the dusty streets, of dogs yapping and shopkeepers carrying crates of tea and carting sacks of flour into their shops—these common, familiar interactions of another working day dispelled her fears with every step.

When she walked through the side door and went to the wings of the stage, she saw that the company had not yet begun the rehearsal but was sitting around watching Florian as he walked about the stage considering its dimensions. He glanced up abstractedly and gave Carolyn an absentminded nod, then went on with his business. The cast members eyed her with varying degrees of curiosity, and Carolyn was determined to appear as if the events of the night before had not affected her as she took a seat with the company.

The rehearsal, a brush-up of a light comedy that the troupe had presented many times before, in many towns throughout the islands, was more boring than anything else. Carolyn had an excellent memory and needed only a little work to recall the lines perfectly. The purpose of these rehearsals was simply to block out the play on the new stage. The company put on a different play each week, playing one script at night and getting the next week's play into shape during the afternoon rehearsals.

They walked through the second act, Florian teaching them their new positions, and Carolyn went along, almost comfortable for the first time with the rest of the troupe. Here, in this familiar setting, with people she knew all around her, it was difficult to recall the terror she had known last night.

When the rehearsal was over, she hurried down to the docks to check the ship schedules before dusk settled in. There was a ship set to sail to Bordeaux the next morning. Deep in thought, Carolyn walked back to the theater. If she had the money, she could sail to France and there embark for England. After the strange feelings she'd had about her sister, then that attack last night, and now the availability of a ship to Europe, she was beginning to wonder if she was destined to be on the morning's ship. She didn't have the fare for passage to England, but perhaps she could get some money from Belinda, who would be happy to see Carolyn depart. She might broach the subject tonight.

Carolyn ate a quick, unappetizing dinner at the tavern next door to the theater, then rushed down the street to the theater and dressed for the play. Her performance of Juliet was far less satisfying than it had been the night before, but she couldn't work up any concern over it. She was far too occupied with her personal plans. After the play, she took off her makeup more slowly than usual, dawdling so that she could leave the theater with other people, for tonight she had no desire to be alone. Making casual conversation, she eased her way into the group of character actors who played the Montague and Capulet parents, and stayed with them for the walk to the rooming house.

When they reached their lodgings, one of the men veered off to a nearby tavern, and the others went to their rooms on the lower floor. Carolyn climbed the stairs alone, calming anxieties with the reassurance that she had only to scream and her companions, whose talk and laughter she could still hear, would come to her aid. Swallowing, Carolyn pushed the door and let it swing open. The hallway light illuminated the chest and bed, and suddenly she felt silly for thinking the room was anything but empty. Her shoulders relaxed, and Carolyn stepped into the patch of moonlight by her bed.

Suddenly the light from the hallway was gone, cut off by the closing door, and an arm went around her waist like a steel band, pinning her arms to her side. Before she could utter a sound, a hand clamped firmly over her mouth.

Two

"Don't scream." The low-pitched voice was harsh and threatening. She struggled, lashing back with her feet and straining against the grip of the arm around her waist, but her assailant jerked her back against him and tightened his hold. She felt the solid bone and muscle of a tall man against her back. Carolyn tried to scream, but the long, faintly calloused fingers of the hand across her mouth dug in painfully, stifling her gasps.

"Hush! You little fool! It is only I."

Even in his clipped, angry words there was the unmistakable accent of British gentility, and his tone suggested this was no stranger, but someone familiar from her past. . . . She stopped struggling. In turn, his grip loosened.

"Good." His voice was still low, but now sarcastic rather than urgent. "I'm glad to find that a few weeks' absence hasn't made you forget me entirely. But, then, seven years of misery would be hard to forget, wouldn't it?"

Carolyn stopped in amazed confusion. Who was this stranger? She started to speak, and she tasted the salt of his skin on her lips. His palm lifted tentatively from her mouth.

"You—" Her voice came out a croak, and she coughed and started again. "You must have made a mistake."

He made an exasperated sound and turned her around roughly. "Don't tempt me." He spoke in a snarl, his face inches from hers. "As it is, I'm barely controlling a quite compelling urge to beat you." He thrust her away and walked quickly and surely to the lamp and lit it. Carolyn knew she could seize the opportunity to run for help, but she stood rooted to the ground, staring at him.

The glow of the lamp he held cast shadows and light from the bottom of his face, giving him a satanic appearance and turning his eyes into pools of darkness. In the dim light, Carolyn could see that he was of better than average height, and the width of his shoulders hinted at a powerful build. Long fingers wrapped around the base of the lamp, and the tendons along the back of his hand were prominent and hard. They were strong hands. She remembered the feel of his faintly calloused fingertips on her cheek.

Carolyn faced him, certain that this was not the man who had attacked her last night. He had had more than ample opportunity to choke her, but he hadn't tried to. Instead, he had freed her as soon as she stopped fighting him. Even in this semi-darkness, Carolyn was positive that she didn't know him. She watched him silently as his eyes swept over her and his mouth pulled into a sneer. "Lord, you've been reduced to this so soon?"

Carolyn raised her chin at the contempt in his tone. "I don't know what you're talking about."

"An actress!" His voice was scathing, and he glanced around the room, in scorn of its shabbiness. "Were you really that anxious to humiliate me?"

"Humiliate you!"

He set the lamp down on the chest and crossed to the window to look out, as if he hated even the sight of her.

"Yes, humiliate me. I can't think of any other reason why you would stoop to selling yourself. Unless, of course, your fine lover has already left you flat."

It was all quite incomprehensible, but even so Carolyn was stung by his words into defending herself. "I don't sell myself. I act."

"You might as well parade around with *whore* stamped across your forehead."

"I never—"

He made a dismissive gesture. "Don't bother. I don't care. You can have had a hundred men. It no longer matters to me—until you pass the bounds of discretion."

"Just a minute. I don't know what you're doing here or who you think you are, but you have no right to come in here and insult me."

He turned in amazement, his sudden step toward her making her jump. "Right? I have every *right*. Haven't you any sense? I don't give a damn what you do, but you're my wife, and whatever you do reflects on the family. You should've thought about that before you ran off. I won't allow you to drag the Somerville name through the mud."

Carolyn blinked. Somerville. She had a glimmer of understanding. Jason Somerville was her sister's husband. Carolyn and Cynthia were identical twins, easily mistaken for one another. Was this Cynthia's husband? Had he seen her and thought she was Cynthia? "Jason?" she probed tentatively.

"What?"

It was Jason Somerville. And he wasn't a madman, but merely mistaken as to her identity. All she had to do was explain who she was, and he would leave her alone—and he would turn his wrath, which would double with *this* mishap, toward Cynthia. She pieced together that Cynthia had run away from him, but with a lover? It sounded so unlike Cynthia to follow her passions— That accusation must have sprung purely from jealousy.

Jason's outrage was barely containable. Carolyn couldn't tell this angry man the truth and set him loose on her sister. So much weaker than herself, Cynthia could be destroyed by this tyrant. She stalled for time to think the matter through. "How did you find me?" she asked meekly.

His laugh was harsh. "Your elopement was as inefficient as most things you attempt. I easily followed your trail to Plymouth, and it didn't take much greasing of palms to find out which ship you and Dennis had sailed on. He's a greater fool than you are; he booked passage in his own name. I took the next ship to St. Kitt's, and from there I traced you here. It didn't take much questioning in the hotels here to find out that a woman fitting your description was with an acting troupe. I saw your 'Juliet' last night—a laudable performance."

"Why, thank you," she retorted with equal sarcasm. "Surely you knew I had a talent for dramatics."

"Yes, I remember your excellent performance before we married."

He was as cold as granite, hardly the type for Cynthia. No doubt she had simply expected that her husband would love and cherish her as her family did. It must have been a great shock to Cynthia, with her cloistered view of the world, when she discovered how devoid of feeling this man was. No wonder she had run away. "Why don't you let me go?" she asked. "You can't expect me to believe you want me with you."

He smiled mockingly, not hiding his scorn. "No, you're

right. Any love I had for you died long ago. But let me remind you: Somervilles never let go of anything that belongs to them."

"I don't belong to you!"

"You are my wife. You're Lady Broughton of Broughton Court. I won't let you put a shadow on my name or shame my mother."

Carolyn drew herself straight, her eyes blazing. How dare he treat her sister like this! "You're a mountain of pride, aren't you? Well, prepare yourself for a shock, because I'm not coming back."

He crossed the room in long, furious strides, and grabbed one of her wrists, his fingers sinking into her flesh like talons. "Don't try me, Cynthia. You've pushed my temper to the limit. You will come back with me, even if I have to tie and gag you and carry you on board. I am your husband. In the eyes of English law, I own you. Your property is mine, and you are required to be obedient to my will. There's no court, no officer of the law who wouldn't support my right to take you home with me. Most of them would probably tell me I ought to knock some sense into your head!"

In the dim light his eyes were black, fathomless, and the lines beside his mouth were deep. With every jeering glance, his teeth flashed white, giving him a fierce, vulpine appearance. Terror flashed through her. She wasn't a coward, but this man frightened her. His grip on her wrist was alarming; it wouldn't take much for him to snap her arm as easily as a chicken bone. How had poor Cynthia ever endured his temper? Thinking of Cynthia having to live with this beast, she raised her eyes to meet his squarely, determined not to let her fear show. "You seem quite fond of beating. Is that the only way you know how to react, like a caveman?"

Carolyn felt the tremor of rage that ran down his arm, and thinking that her scornful words had thrust him over the brink, she shrank back, instinctively raising her free hand to shield her face. Somerville couldn't conceal his surprise. "So your fine lover has taught you to take blows. What a pleasant life you must have been leading." He released her wrist, almost pushing her away as if she were repugnant to him. "I fail to understand your reluctance to return to Broughton Court." He glanced pointedly about the room. "I would think you'd be quite happy to return to your comfortable life, now that Bingham has deserted you. What happened? Did the two of you discover that your sordid affair couldn't exist in poverty? Or did he learn that you're capable of loving no one but yourself?"

"You're despicable."

"I know your views of my personality. I'm cold, unfeeling, and possessed of only the basest drives. In short, a beast. You hate me. Now that that's established, let's move on to getting you out of here." His facial movements, perfectly controlled, showed no trace of his fury. He opened the closet door and jerked out the few dresses hanging there. He tossed them on the bed, then gathered the shoes and bags that lined the floor of the wardrobe and dumped them on the bed beside the gowns. With the same efficiency, he cleaned out the drawers of the small chest, and added these few possessions to the jumbled heap.

Humiliated, Carolyn watched him throw her garments together and give them a final encompassing look of disgust. She felt as if he had studied her life and heart and soul and found everything worthless. "Good Lord, Cynthia, did he abscond with all your clothes and jewels as well as your gold?"

"I—was forced to give them to the moneylenders."

"Even you couldn't have spent all that money this quickly. You forget, I know exactly how much you stole out of my safe the night you ran away."

"I never stole anything!" Carolyn denied heatedly before she thought.

He raised an eyebrow. "No? Perhaps you don't consider it stealing, since husband and wife are 'one flesh.' But it's been a long time since we were that, hasn't it?"

"Perhaps I considered it fair payment for what I suffered because of you."

He paused in surprise, then let loose a deep, unexpectedly rich laugh, which startled her. "You've changed a bit. Once you would have spent the whole time in hysterics. Bingham must have bestowed upon you a new courage and wit."

He was right. She hadn't been acting a bit like Cynthia. She would have been crying and repentant from the moment he seized her and clamped his hand over her mouth. Carolyn was amazed that Cynthia had found the courage to run away—but she had, and now she must help her sister any way she could. Carolyn knew that every moment she managed to delay him gave Cynthia more time to flee, which meant she must go along with the man's assumption that she was Cynthia for as long as possible. Surely she could keep him fooled for tonight, for in the dim light of evening, he wouldn't notice their differences. But she had to stop behaving like herself in order to carry it off. Calling on her strongest powers of concentration, she took a deep breath, then turned around and faced Jason. Outwardly the twins were indistinguishable, and now she had to *become* Cynthia in her every word and gesture.

Clasping her hands together tightly and assuming a look

of passive defeat, she submitted to Jason's domineering will: "What do you want me to do?"

"Pack these wretched clothes. You'll need something to wear on the trip, and I haven't time to purchase you anything here. We'll sail for France tomorrow."

"France?"

"Yes. The ship for Bordeaux leaves in the morning, which fits perfectly into my plans. I've asked Mother to meet us there. She had just left on her trip to Italy, so I put it out that you had decided to join her at the last minute, which I sincerely hope will lay some of the rumors to rest. Presumably I followed to escort the two of you home. We'll sail home from France with Mother, to give some semblance of truth to the story."

Carolyn began to pack her clothes in her worn carpetbag, then stopped short—Cynthia, who would undoubtedly have a maid do her packing, wouldn't know where to begin with the pile of clothes, whereas such organized use of space was second nature to Carolyn, after years of traveling. She glanced up—but Jason's back was to her as he stared out to the dark street below. She quickly stuffed her smaller belongings into a leather case, then sat, straight-backed and solemn, on the edge of the bed. She cleared her throat.

"I'm taking you back to my room at the Blue Oar." Jason stepped away from the window, then met her expression of concern. Jason sighed with disgust. "Don't worry. I don't plan to punish you by resuming my place in your bed. You've made it amply clear that my touch disgusts you, and, thank God, I no longer desire you. We're equally repelled, my dear, and we'll continue as before, with separate bedrooms. That's part of the bargain."

"What bargain?"

"The bargain we have for the future. You will resume your role as Lady Broughton. In public we will be the perfect, happy couple, at least for a few months, to quell the rumors, while in private we can be mutually indifferent. I don't care whether I have your company at any time. However, servants talk, so I presume we must share our meals. I'll try to go on business to London as often as I can. When the rumors have died down, we can establish separate households."

"Within the bounds of propriety, of course," Carolyn murmured.

"Of course."

"Then why must I return to your room tonight?"

"Because I want you under my eye. By the way, I have booked separate cabins aboard ship. I trust we can manage to avoid each other as much as possible as we sail."

"I'll make every effort." Carolyn's voice was tinged with irony. What a loving husband, she pursed her lips in sarcasm. She saw the whole story clearly now. Cynthia had so eagerly sought acceptance and love; this beast must have driven her to desperation.

"I'm sure you will." His tone matched hers.

Carolyn lifted her bags from the bed—again, she noted too late, a typically Carolyn gesture. To her surprise Somerville took them from her, then opened the door and stood aside to let her pass, reminding her of the polite conventions of society from which she had been separated for so long. She certainly hadn't expected such gentility from Cynthia's husband, but she guessed she should have known. That was all he was concerned about, after all—the appearance, and not the reality, of a pleasant marriage.

The Blue Oar, the oldest and most elegant hotel in Antigua, stood at a distance from the seedy waterfront. Pale blue in color, and accented with sparkling white louvered shutters, the elegant stucco building had upper and lower porches that encompassed three sides of the building and were also made of white wood with filigree and fretwork atop the slender columns. The many tall windows allowed the breezes to drift in and the guests to visit the verandas easily. White-painted cane furniture, cool and refreshing to the eye, rested on the lower porch, which was shaded by tall bushes and flowering plants. Jason and Carolyn climbed the porch steps in sullen silence, Carolyn glancing around secretly to take in the beautiful building.

Inside, Carolyn ignored a curious stare from the rather haughty-looking desk clerk. Not a single pleasantry or polite comment was exchanged as they were shown to the suite upstairs. The door opened onto a small, tasteful sitting room, which led to the master bedroom. Jason left her alone in the bedroom and spent the night on the long couch in the adjoining room after locking the door from his side. Carolyn walked out onto the veranda. She knew she could escape by the veranda if she tried. But instead she leaned against the porch railing and looked out at the night, pensive, alone at last.

As she had walked to the hotel beside Jason Somerville, Carolyn had designed a plan. Every day that she could fool Jason would give Cynthia another day to escape. If she could carry off an impersonation of her sister until they were aboard ship, it would be weeks before Jason began a new search, and by then Cynthia's trail would be cold. Then why not, she mused, carry on the masquerade and live Cynthia's life at Broughton Court? She could enjoy the luxury she had known as a child, wear elegant clothes, dine on sumptuous food. . . . Returning to England was the best thing that could happen to her.

Even as a child, her acting ability had always enabled her to copy Cynthia's mannerisms and speech almost perfectly. They had more than once pretended to be the other in order to fool Bonnie, their nurse. When Cynthia's pony had wandered into Mrs. Durkes' prize flowers and eaten several, Carolyn had ridden back to Mrs. Durkes' cottage to apologize, sparing Cynthia the ear-ringing lecture Mrs. Durkes delivered on the carelessness of children.

What little difference remained could be accounted for by the time she and Jason had been apart and the experiences she had gone through. The only thing that could be wrong with her appearance would be the cheap, ill-fitting clothes and her hair, but a different style could be accounted for by not having her maid along to tend to her hair.

Jason had assumed, after all, that she was Cynthia. Carolyn had learned in her years in the theater that people believe only what they want to believe, see what they want to see. Jason wouldn't be likely to examine her words and manner for much dissimilarity to Cynthia, especially if they disliked each other as much as he had said. And he had already promised that he would avoid her on the ship. It shouldn't be too hard, Carolyn thought, to carry off the charade for as long as she had to.

Carolyn doubted Cynthia had actually taken a ship to the West Indies. Her sister might be shy and retiring, but she was too sharp-witted to leave such an obvious clue. It was more likely Cynthia had booked passage in her lover's name simply to lead her husband on a wild goose chase. It worked,

Carolyn thought wryly, watching from the veranda Jason's shadow in the distant sitting room.

Carolyn had no idea what had happened to drive Cynthia off, but she was certain Jason Somerville was at fault. Her first encounters with Jason showed her he was capable of driving anyone to desperation. He seemed to hate Cynthia, whom everyone else always loved, and that alone was enough to indict his character.

No wonder she had been feeling her "Cynthia feeling" so strongly lately. Rescuing Cynthia would cause her no trouble except for having to put up with the foul-tempered Lord Broughton. After all, since her scare last night, she had planned to leave the island anyway. Florian might curse her for leaving him without a Juliet, but Belinda would be quick to soothe him. Carolyn had nothing to bind her to the troupe and every reason to go. For years, it seemed, she had longed to breathe the cool, moist air of England again, to see the calm, green beauty so different from the violent colors of the tropics. She was weary of her life here and wanted to go home. She would have left long before now if her sister hadn't lived in England, for she hadn't wanted to embarrass Cynthia. But now the scandal of Cynthia's sister being an actress would only add another ripple to the scandal already caused by Cynthia's running away from her husband. Cynthia would no longer be there to be embarrassed.

Considering her excitement to return to England, it seemed a most satisfactory plan. She was heartily glad that Lord Broughton had promised not to intrude on her bed, for that was the thing that made it possible for her to embark on this masquerade. Otherwise she wouldn't have risked it. Even to think of enduring that cold man's caresses made her shudder.

An unusually cool breeze made her shiver, and she went inside to undress for bed. She had made up her mind. For a while, at least, she would be Cynthia Somerville, Lady of Broughton Court, wife to Jason Somerville. Confident that her plan would work, and feeling more peaceful than she had for days, she slipped into a deep, contented slumber.

She was roughly shaken awake the next morning, and she blinked and stared at Jason Somerville in sleepy confusion. "Get up. We must leave for the ship."

"Now?" Carolyn glanced toward the open window. Dawn had barely lightened the sky.

"The ship sails early, and I intend to make sure we're on it. Now get dressed."

Her mind cleared, and she remembered who the man before her was and what they were doing this morning. She brushed back the loose hairs that had escaped her thick braid during the night, and yawned. "All right," Carolyn told him sleepily. "I'll get dressed—as soon as you leave the room."

He turned on his heel and walked out of the room. Carolyn rose and hastily made her morning ablutions, then slipped into her chemise, stockings, and pantalets, all of a lightweight material. She wore no petticoats beneath the cage of her crinoline, another way of combating the heat of the tropics. The dress she chose was white and plain, with elbow-length sleeves and a high neckline adorned with a crisp white collar. At the center of the collar she fastened the shell cameo brooch Kit had given her when they were first married.

She brushed out her thick hair, then made two lush

braids, which she coiled over her ears. With her modest bonnet tied under her chin and her unadorned dress, she looked very prim. Carolyn smiled at the thought; for all her good moral intentions and despite the fact that she had never given herself to anyone but her lawful husband, she was tarred with the same brush as prostitutes and adulteresses, all on account of her profession.

But she could leave the false reputation behind her now, for she was no longer a lowly actress but Lady Cynthia. She smiled at her image in the mirror. The excitement of performing put a pulse in her veins. The prospect of deceiving Jason was made even better by her rewards. Home, Cynthia's happiness, and—her smile took on a slightly wicked glint—the satisfaction of taking Broughton down a peg or two.

One of the hotel servants came in to fetch her luggage, and Carolyn made one last check in the mirror before pulling on her gloves and striding confidently into the sitting room, where Jason awaited. She was itching to get a better look at him, but lost her courage each time she tried. It wasn't until they were settled in their hired carriage, jouncing along toward the docks, and Jason was staring fixedly out the window, that she was able to observe him at her ease.

In the glaring morning light, she could see that he was a much handsomer man than she had thought last night. His thick hair was black and shaped well to his head. While most men of fashion sported thick, long sideburns, Jason's face was clean-shaven. Nothing blurred the straight, uncompromising lines of his face, his strong jaw, and his prominent cheekbones. His deep-set eyes were not dark, as they had appeared last night, but a startling silvery-green, rimmed with thick black lashes as straight as the eyebrows above them, which darkened his light eyes, and added a hint of smoky sensuality. With his well-shaped nose and broad mouth, he would have been a handsome man, Carolyn decided, if it weren't for his rigid expression and the deep lines that were set beside his mouth. A strain of hidden anger and discontent clearly marred his face. More likely, she mused, his look was simply an indication of his wicked temper.

The moment the carriage rumbled to a halt, Jason opened the door and jumped out as if he couldn't wait to exit. He reached up to help Carolyn down, but she stubbornly used only the door frame of the carriage to steady her as she climbed down the narrow steps. She was pleased to see Jason scowl at her rudeness. Majestic and still, the ship awaited them at the end of the long wharf; seeing it, excitement gripped Carolyn's stomach. She was going home! But she remembered to restrain her glee. No woman being forced to return to her husband would look so elated. She lowered her face to hide her expression.

"Come along," he said in a harsh whisper. "You can't put it off any longer."

Carolyn didn't bother to answer him. She merely walked along beside him and hoped that whatever jumping of her nerves Jason sensed would be put down to fear rather than excitement. He guided her up the steep gangplank and introduced her to the captain of the ship, a small Frenchman whose eyes swept over her with a cool lack of interest that was at odds with his countrymen's reputation as connoisseurs of women. He gave her a slight bow and tersely welcomed her aboard. Carolyn replied in his language, but hoped he wouldn't say anything further. She wasn't as adept in French as Cynthia was.

Jason swept her across the deck and down to her cabin. She would have liked to stand on deck and watch the ship pull away from shore, but no doubt Jason would think she might make a run for it at the last minute. Well, it was better that she stayed down here alone, anyway. Otherwise, Jason might see the light of eagerness on her face as they left. That would give her away immediately.

So Carolyn stayed in her tiny room alone, hands knotted in her lap. As she felt the tug of the ship as it moved from the wharf, she allowed a grin to break across her face. She'd done it! It would be weeks before they reached France, and even if Jason found her out, he could do nothing about it. She had outwitted him. Suddenly fear overshadowed her thrill and terror filled her heart at the challenge that lay before her. For, as certain as the light of day fades into cool evening shadows, this scheme had its dark side, too: Now there was no turning back.

Three

When the port was a good hour behind them, Carolyn took off her bonnet and set it on the small washstand built into the wall. She removed her hairpins and unbraided her hair, which fell in a vibrant mass over her shoulders. Then she drew her nightgown from one of her bags—it was mashed and wrinkled from being stuffed into the bag last night. It was also too thin to be proper, and she wished she had a dressing gown to wear over it. But it would have to do, for now she had to settle comfortably in her narrow bunk, don a pale, sickly look—and pretend to be seasick.

From the time they were young, seasickness had affected both children. Over the years, however, Carolyn had grown out of it, due to her frequent sailing between the West Indies and the American States. Now she felt no more than a slight uneasiness the first day they were under sail. Without having experienced as much sea travel as Carolyn she felt sure Cynthia would not have outgrown the illness. At the most, Cynthia would have crossed the Channel a few times, which further supported her notion that Cynthia had not really sailed to the West Indies as she had led Jason to believe.

This would be an important test of Carolyn's charade.

Although she longed to explore the ship, watch the busy crew at work, breathe the clear sea air up on deck, Carolyn knew she must feign illness and remain bedridden, should Jason check in on her. Taking to her bed did have its benefits, she decided: Pleading seasickness, she could remain alone in her cabin for several days, away from Jason's cold sarcasm and pretentious politeness.

Carolyn pulled the sheet up to her shoulders so that the thin nightgown was completely concealed. Closing her eyes, she let the gentle bobbing of the ship lull her to sleep.

Hours later the squeak of the door opening awakened her, and she blinked at the dark form of a man outlined in the low doorway. Drowsy and momentarily confused, she gave a better impression of being ill than her acting skills could have produced. "Cynthia?" Jason hesitated, then moved into the room and shut the door behind him. "I'm sorry. I had forgotten how easily you take seasick. May I fetch you anything?"

Carolyn shook her head listlessly. She spoke in a flat, drained voice: "No, there is nothing that helps but time."

"Silent suffering? Now, that's a new role for you."

"Jason, please . . ." she sighed weakly.

He had the grace to look slightly abashed. "I apologize. That wasn't fair, was it, taking a shot at someone already laid low? I'll leave you so at least you won't have to put up with my company. Shall I have any lunch brought to you? Soup? Porridge?"

"Perhaps I can keep it down." She hoped her rumbling stomach wouldn't betray her. She felt half starved, since they forgot breakfast in their haste to reach the ship.

"If you need anything, just yell out, or—knock on the wall. I'm in the next cabin."

With closed eyes, Carolyn nodded her understanding and looked as if she was drifting off again. After she heard the door shut, Carolyn sighed with relief. "Well, that should ensure my solitude for most of the day," she said to herself. "Lord Broughton doesn't seem overly concerned with his sick wife's condition." She fluffed up her pillows and leaned back, crossing her arms over her head. She was thankful for the solitude; she needed some quiet time to think about Cynthia.

Suddenly, it all seemed more difficult than she'd thought last night as she conceived the plan on the veranda at the Blue Oar. In the years since Carolyn left home, no doubt many things had changed about her sister: her opinions, her fears and hopes, her hairstyle, her taste in clothing. Her voice could have changed, her expressions, her gestures, her laugh.

The seven years that had separated the twins suddenly felt to Carolyn like an insurmountable obstacle. She had no idea who Cynthia's friends were or where they lived. Perhaps she liked to visit London frequently—or maybe not at all. Or maybe she preferred entertaining friends at—what had Jason called it? Broughton Hall? No, Broughton Court, she thought. He had called her Lady Broughton, so her father-in-law must have died and her husband had come into the title. But when? How had the older man died? How many people lived there now, and what were their names? And what were the servants' names? There seemed to be a million things she didn't know, any one of which might expose her as a fraud. Jason might not notice a few minor imperfections, but he couldn't ignore it if she didn't recognize the name of her housekeeper or one of his relatives. But at least there was no way he could chastise her for this charade without bringing light to the scandal, and she knew he would avoid that at all costs.

She spent all morning working on Cynthia's voice, calling upon all she could remember from seven years ago. One of the major differences was their laughs. Carolyn toned down her laugh, usually louder and more boisterous and worked on Cynthia's light, musical giggle. Cynthia's speaking voice was softer and more tentative, with a little upturn to the end of many sentences that made them almost questions. She rarely raised her voice—Carolyn could remember more than once seeing Cynthia's eyes blazing with anger while her voice still sounded smooth as butter.

That poised restraint, Carolyn knew, would be most difficult for her to mimic, for she was usually quick to express her emotions. All too often, everything she thought and felt was clearly written on her face. Cynthia, on the other hand, had managed to cultivate a demure social mask to cover temper and other unsuitable emotions for a lady.

She worked softly on her speech and laugh, ready to resume her sick posture should anyone intrude. She heard nothing except the creaking of the ship around her, but didn't raise her voice as she practiced.

To her surprise, it was Jason himself who stepped into the room carrying a tray at lunchtime. "Are you up to eating?" he asked disinterestedly. Carolyn thought that he probably would have been more concerned about a sick dog.

"Yes, I think I can."

"Do you want the tray here or in bed?" He asked, indicating the small table and chair.

She didn't want to get up in front of him in only her thin nightgown. "Bed, please." He set the tray down on the table and, taking her by surprise, slid one arm beneath her back, and with the other hand arranged her pillows against the wall at her head. Then he pulled her up in the bed until she reclined on the pillows. His hands were competent and unexpectedly gentle, but his manner was as remote as a stranger. The sheet slid down, and the curve of her breasts was plainly visible through the thin material that did nothing to conceal the dark circles of her nipples. Flushing, Carolyn grabbed the sheet and pulled it up to cover her chest. Although nothing in Jason's passive face indicated that he had seen her exposed breasts, Carolyn thought the avid, lustful stares of the men in the audiences on the islands were less shaming than this impersonal glance of the man who thought himself her husband.

Why, Carolyn wondered, did he hold Cynthia in such contempt? Perhaps his pride was so unbreakable that he couldn't bear the humility of Cynthia's running away. He never really loved her sister, she reasoned, so perhaps he had pursued Cynthia for her money, a fair trade for his lineage. Although, admitted, Cynthia's attitude carried something more than dislike for her husband; she detected tremendous scorn and contempt behind her sister's bold departure. What could have possibly caused this alarming chasm between them?

Jason turned back to the bed, placing the tray carefully on her lap. "Do you need anything else?"

"No, this is fine. I—appreciate it very much."

He shrugged. "I have no plans to starve you, you know. All I require of you is a civilized arrangement. We can manage, I hope, to be polite to each other in public, and in private we shan't have to meet."

"I wonder how far you'd go to protect your precious name," Carolyn murmured, and he frowned.

"As far as living out this sham of a marriage I so foolishly made."

Carolyn didn't know why she was prodding him this way. It was dangerous to goad a wild animal, and she suspected that underneath the polished exterior there existed a very primitive nature that, if angered enough, would turn on her. "You could insist on your marital rights. Many men would."

He quickly restrained his surprise. "Are you trying to tempt me, my dear? I'm long past that, you know. You no longer entice me. Even if you did, I haven't a taste for rape. I didn't enjoy taking you inch by grudging inch."

Carolyn did not look at him for fear her expression would betray her. She knew she'd made a mistake in pursuing this subject. Poor, dear Cynthia must have had to endure with wifely acceptance a touch she despised, all to marry into a name to please her father. . . . Carolyn warned herself not to speak, but she couldn't hold back. "Then again, a man can seek his pleasures elsewhere, can he not?"

After a long silence, Jason growled, "Yes, and so apparently can a woman, though for years I wondered if you knew the meaning of the word pleasure." His voice sliced through the air, as fast and stinging as a whip. "Were Dennis Bingham's caresses tame enough for you? Did you find at last the proper 'respect' in bed?"

Carolyn turned her face away, her cheeks flaming. Behind her Jason slammed his fist against the table. "Damn you! When I think of all the years of guilt and torture and self-doubt you put me through, then to find that you had bed down with—You're goddamn lucky I didn't take a whip to you."

Carolyn glared at him. "Am I supposed to be grateful to you for that? Should I grovel in thanks that you didn't beat me or whip me or resort to your other primitive, violent—"

He lunged at her, shoving the tray, and pulling her up until her face was level with his. "You blushed and were shocked if I so much as said the word *sex* to you. You were horrified because I wanted to possess my wife. Because I loved to look at you naked. And God forbid that your eyes should be assaulted by the sight of my bestial body! Yet all that time you were cuckolding me."

His blazing eyes were almost silver in his anger, and she wanted to look away, but it was as if he held her captive, mesmerized. Trembling with fear, Carolyn wet her lips and whispered, "Please, I—I—"

He released her with a gesture as harsh as his grasp. "Damn you, I didn't mean to get into this. Just stay away from me the rest of the trip. Just stay away."

Carolyn felt a surge of anger—as if his foul temper and abusive words were her fault! But she had already strayed too far from Cynthia's character. So she bowed her head meekly, letting her hair fall down to hide her face. In his disgust, Jason stormed out of the cabin. Carolyn lay still, shaking over the scene that she just endured. She was surprised her sister had been able to endure it for seven years. Even knowing that she wasn't the real object of his anger, Carolyn was a mass of quivering nerves.

She managed to avoid contact with Jason for three days—after that first lunch, he had been careful to send a cabin boy with her meals. But soon she thought she would go crazy if she spent another second alone in her little room. She had nothing to occupy her mind—no book to read or play to memorize or even sewing to do, and no one visited her. So Carolyn put on one of her worn dresses and climbed the narrow steps to the deck. She had to shield her eyes for several moments before they adjusted to the sunlight. Squinting, she took in the endless horizon of blue water and the brilliant azure that surrounded her. A breeze whipped around her, tangling her skirts and blowing her hair every which way. She put a hand on her crinoline to keep it in place, and when she glanced across the deck, she caught sight of Jason.

He was leaning casually against the railing, his face turned toward her, too distant to read his expression. Carolyn turned back to the railing, ignoring him. He *would* have to be standing there when her skirt caught the wind. The other day he had accused her of trying to tempt him; now, no doubt, he would think she had deliberately exposed her legs to him.

Neither of them moved for a long moment, then Jason strolled over to her with a forced casualness, stopping a few feet away. "Good afternoon."

"Hello." She felt awkward speaking to him, and it seemed unnatural not to address him by a title, but as informal as calling him "Jason" seemed to her, "Lord Broughton" or "milord" would be absurd coming from a wife of seven years.

"I take it you have recovered from your illness?"

"Yes, I'm feeling a little better. I thought a breath of fresh air might help me."

"No doubt."

They were silent. Jason had come over to speak to her, she knew, simply to give the impression that they were close, happy, affectionate. But under the circumstances, she saw no reason why she should try to continue the conversation. She stared glumly out to sea. Broughton spoke without looking at her. "Would you care for a stroll around the decks?"

"With you?" Carolyn asked.

He cocked an eyebrow. "Yes, of course, with me. It is not, I believe, an abnormal thing for a husband and wife to do."

"And we must keep up appearances, mustn't we?"

"Once that seemed a matter of great concern to you."

She cast him a sideways glance. "Perhaps I discovered that happiness was more important."

His face was stern. "Acting in a second-rate troupe made you happy?"

She couldn't suppress a grin. "I think you overestimate the ability of the McDowell Company."

"And you, it seems, don't take yourself quite so seriously."

Carolyn's mouth curved into a wry grin. "Experience is a good teacher, they say."

"You didn't answer my question, however. Were you happy living in seedy hotels and parading yourself on a stage?"

"It was novel. I had barely started on the career."

"I see you're still as clever at slipping out of any question you don't want to answer." Jason turned to face her.

"No! No, I wasn't happy. Does that satisfy you?"

"Then tell me what exactly your little escapade achieved. Was this some kind of prank that you connived to send me rushing across the Atlantic after you?"

"I had no desire for you to follow me, if that's what you're implying. Believe me, I don't want to be hauled home like a child who's misbehaved."

He closed his eyes briefly, drawing in a breath to restrain his temper. "Do you want me to escort you around the deck or not?"

"No, thank you. I'd prefer to be here by myself."

"Then I shall intrude on you no longer. Good day, madam."

She nodded the barest of good-byes, and watched from the corner of her eye as his arrow-straight form disappeared around the stern of the ship.

As Carolyn had hoped, she and Jason managed to avoid each other for the remainder of the voyage, except at meals. Jason escorted her to the dining room, where they joined the captain and two other passengers, French businessmen who spoke little English at their table. The captain was a man of few words, and the silence around the table was suffocating. Carolyn dared not say much for fear of exposing herself as a fraud, and Jason ignored her. She wondered what the others thought about their stiff, formal manner.

For the rest of the time, she strolled around the deck every morning and every afternoon, and spent the hours before dinner writing or resting quietly in her cabin. She found herself almost hoping they would meet unexpectedly up on deck again, though the chances of that were slim. He was a bully and foul-tempered. Jason seemed to make quite an effort to not be present when Carolyn went walking. Carolyn was used to being with people and had always had a gregarious nature. Now she was lonely and bored. She ached for conversation, for contact with the outside world—even that of Jason Somerville. Their encounters, though full of conflict, had at least been stimulating.

The ship finally docked at Bordeaux, although after a night at a hotel there and a bone-jarring carriage ride to Paris that took three days, she almost wished she were back on board the vessel. It was excruciating to be confined in a carriage all day with Jason sitting directly across from her. He said very little and spent most of his time staring out the rolled-up window at the countryside. But now and then Carolyn would glance up to find him watching her, his eyes narrowed, intent and unreadable. She never failed to feel a prickling down her spine. Always, in the back of her mind, loomed her greatest fear: Jason was on to her charade. He was planning his ruthless and brutal revenge. But then she would let the events of the last few weeks run through her mind, and she would assure herself once again—there was no way he could be on to her game.

Carolyn's curiosity about Lady Broughton would not be satisfied for a while after they arrived in Paris. Jason's mother would not return from Italy for several days, but then she planned to join them at their fashionable hotel. Carolyn hoped her heart was warmer than her son's. Up in their suite, an elegant sitting room with two bedrooms opening off it on opposite sides, a chambermaid unpacked Carolyn's small bags, and Carolyn was washed with embarrassment at the idea of the girl pulling out her clothes with a mingling of shock and amusement. She doubted that anyone quite so poorly dressed had ever arrived here before. Jason settled down in a stiff brocade chair in the sitting room, and Carolyn went to her bedroom to lie down for a rest after their journey.

For three days Jason never left the hotel suite without her. Carolyn suspected he locked the door of her bedroom at night after she went to sleep. It was almost as unpleasant as the trip in the carriage. At least here, though, she was able to slip away to her bedroom.

She had just emerged from her room after a nap one afternoon when a well-groomed woman swept into the suite. She was tall and regal in stature, and her white hair wound into a twist at the back of her head. Discreet emerald earrings matched the dark, rich green silk of her dress, which billowed out into a wide circle. The collar of the dress rose up her slender throat and ended in a ruffle, enhancing her dignified appearance. Three wide flounces of black lace shadowed the jewel-like color of the dress, and in one hand she carried a black lace fan.

"Mother. How good it is to see you." Jason smiled and embraced her briefly.

The older woman smiled slightly and her eyes flashed with wicked amusement. "I suppose I should return the favor and say I'm delighted to see you. However, quite frankly, it ruined a very pleasant holiday when I received your message from Bordeaux."

His smile, the first genuine expression of warmth Carolyn had witnessed, faltered. "Sorry," he murmured. "It was an emergency."

"So I gathered. Now, would you mind telling me what's the problem?" Her eyes fell on Carolyn. Coolly she greeted her daughter-in-law. "Cynthia."

"Milady." Carolyn quaked inside. What was she supposed to call this woman? She didn't even know her first name.

Lady Broughton's eyebrows rose slightly. "My, it must be serious to go from 'Selena' to 'milady.' "

"I think Cynthia would prefer not to be part of the Somerville family in any way." Jason's eyes flashed steel at Carolyn.

"I—I'm sorry, Selena," Carolyn stammered.

Selena seated herself on the love seat, and Carolyn hesitated, uncertain whether to remain or return to her room. Jason's mother knew nothing of what had happened, and she suspected Jason would prefer to tell her in private. However, Jason motioned at Carolyn to sit down, so she perched uneasily on one of the stiff-backed chairs. Jason clasped his hands behind him and walked over to the window. He cleared his throat.

"Mother, I need your help."

"So you indicated."

"I would like for you to pretend Cynthia was with you on your vacation in Italy."

"What?"

"That's what I've told people, and I'll need you to back me up."

"But—" Lady Selena's sharp, dark eyes flickered from her son to Carolyn, and Carolyn noted that they were green like her son's, but much deeper in color, and without the silvery tinge—unlike Lord Broughton's, these were warm eyes. "Very well." She turned to Cynthia. "Tell me, did you join me later, or did you leave with me?"

"Does it matter?"

"Of course. For one thing, your dates must coincide with mine. For another, Lady Emmeline Harrington was on the same boat with me all the way to Venice. Even given that poor Cynthia could have been in her cabin being ill the whole trip, I would have been bound to mention her at least."

"Yes, of course." Jason agreed. "Well then, she joined you in Venice or Florence."

"Florence, I should think. I met Miss Jennifer Soames in Venice, you know, Sir Richard's daughter, the one with teeth like a horse. She was there with her married sister— thank heavens, I didn't have to meet her, too, for she was laid up with some sickness or the other. But I did feel obliged to invite Miss Soames up to tea. But in Florence I was fortunate enough not to see a single soul I knew."

"I was beginning to wonder if that was possible," Jason commented wryly, and Carolyn couldn't suppress a smile. Selena was nothing like her son. Gracious, pleasant, and good-humored, she even seemed to exert a good influence on Jason.

"May I inquire as to why we are performing this little charade?" Lady Broughton asked gently.

Jason's lips narrowed. "Cynthia and I quarreled. I—frightened and angered her, and she ran from me. It took me some time to track her down and convince her to return. During that time she was alone and unchaperoned, of course, without the protection of her husband. You know what a scandal gossips could brew from that."

Selena shot him an assessing glance, and Carolyn guessed that she gave his story little credence. But she pursed her lips and nodded to her son. "Yes, of course."

Carolyn was surprised that Jason had not told the story in his usual harsh tone. He had, Carolyn reasoned, shielded his mother from knowledge that he knew would wound her. Lady Broughton was probably fond of Cynthia, and it would have upset Selena to learn that Cynthia had left her son for another man. That was most likely the case. Otherwise, Jason would never paint a rosy picture of Cynthia.

Selena studied Carolyn for a moment, then said, "I think the first priority is to purchase you a suitable traveling dress. We shall go shopping tomorrow."

Before Carolyn could say anything, Jason exclaimed, "For heaven's sake, Mother, this is not an excuse for a shopping expedition. We need to return to London."

"Surely a few days won't hurt. After all, one doesn't rush

home from a vacation in Italy. Do you have business that is so pressing?"

"No, but—" He hesitated, and Carolyn suspected he was searching for a more polite reason for hurrying back to England than his reluctance to spend any more time with his wife in the narrow confines of a hotel suite. "—there is no need for it, surely, and I do have matters that need my attention."

"Honestly, Jason, think. If you want people to accept this charade, you can't let Cynthia arrive in England looking like that. Everyone would know immediately that she hadn't been with me. And can you imagine anyone believing I would deliberately reroute my trip to include Paris and not visit Worth's establishment?"

Jason sighed. "You're right, of course. How quickly can you get it done?"

"Well, it won't be Worth, of course, but I suppose I could bully an acceptable dress out of a seamstress in two days. I'll need to visit Worth's and order a few frocks, but of course they can be shipped to me. I'd say three days, four at the most."

"All right. I'll leave it in your hands." Jason was happy to place Carolyn in someone else's charge.

Selena dined with them in their suite, and the mood of their meal was greatly lightened as she talked gaily about her trip and queried Jason about the latest gossip in London. Carolyn found her easy to talk to, though she tried to steer her conversation into the safe topics of the places and events of her childhood. Selena encouraged her to talk about the Lake Country, and Carolyn's eyes sparkled as she described the beauty of her native countryside. Selena laughed at several of her quips, and once even Jason let out a chuckle at her description of the squire whose land had neighbored Gresham Hall. She carefully avoided any mention of her family—the less she said about an identical twin, the better.

As they sipped brandy after the meal, Selena sighed and smiled at her daughter-in-law. "What a pleasant little chat. You know, my dear, I don't believe I've ever heard you talk about your childhood before. I take it you were an only child?"

Carolyn felt flushed and nearly gasped aloud. Before she could contrive some quick response, Jason carelessly replied, "Oh, yes, Cynthia's a one and only. I'm not even sure— who's your nearest relative, your Aunt Elizabeth?"

Carolyn nodded demurely, trying hard to keep in character. It seemed impossible that Cynthia never spoke of Carolyn, yet what reason could he have to lie to his mother about Cynthia's twin? In the few early letters she had received from Cynthia, her sister had told her that Papa had cut her name from the family Bible and forbidden all servants and family to speak of her. When they went to London for Cynthia's debut, no doubt Aunt Elizabeth had cautioned Cynthia not to mention Carolyn to anyone, for fear the scandal would mar Cynthia's first season. So Jason hadn't even known of her existence. . . .

A pang of hurt stabbed her—the thought that Cynthia was so ashamed of Carolyn's actions that she had never told her own husband about her was humiliating. But at the same time she was swept with relief, for if Jason had no idea that Cynthia had a twin, it was unlikely that he would be watching her closely, suspicious of her words and deeds. He might be puzzled by her, but it would take a large error indeed for him to think that the woman posing as his wife was not really his wife at all!

Selena returned to her rooms soon after they finished supper. Carolyn didn't hurry straight to her bedroom as she usually did, but went instead to the love seat Selena had occupied earlier. After Jason's revelation, she was no longer as concerned that she would slip up and reveal herself. He hesitated, then took his usual place in the brocade chair. "You were very pleasant to my mother tonight."

"Am I usually unpleasant?" she countered.

"No, of course not. You are always quite . . . polite, but more reserved, not as friendly."

"I was probably carried away by being with someone who doesn't hate me." Carolyn met his gaze challengingly, and for a long moment they stared at each other. His eyes trailed to her mouth and then took in her breasts and legs. Suddenly, she thought of his promise not to bed her, this man who *thought* he was her husband, who thought he knew all the secrets of her body. What if he came to her and began to kiss her with all the possessiveness of a husband? Panic filled her, and her heart pounded.

Carolyn shrank back as Jason rose, breaking their stare. "If you'll excuse me, I shall retire early tonight." His voice was clipped and hard. "Good night, Cynthia."

"Good night, Jason."

Four

True to her promise, Lady Broughton took Carolyn on a shopping spree the next day. They purchased an entire outfit, from a ruffled bonnet of cobalt blue to soft kid boots with tassels at the top to gloves to ribbon-trimmed pantalets and camisoles, even new white cotton stockings. By the time Selena was finished, there wasn't a piece of clothing on Carolyn's body that wasn't new, and of the finest quality. Selena even managed to cajole and bribe a fashionable dressmaker into sewing up two traveling dresses for Carolyn immediately.

It had been many years since Carolyn had been able to choose freely, without any concern to money as she walked through elegant shops, choosing fabrics and styles. It was all she could do to restrain her impulses and limit herself to the small amount of clothes she would need for the trip to England. After all, there would be Cynthia's things for her to wear when they reached Broughton Court, and she couldn't let Selena spend more money on her than necessary. She felt guilty for deceiving Selena. It was easy for Carolyn to justify her charade when she was around Jason, with his stern face and cold, fathomless eyes, but much harder to lie to this white-haired woman who linked her arm companionably with Carolyn's and whisked her through fashionable stores, treating her to expensive presents.

Carolyn was also grateful for the quick lesson their tour gave her in current fashion. After years in India, then in the Americas, she had grown out of touch with the current modes, and she had been afraid that she would show her fashion ignorance as soon as she encountered English high society. But after a day at Worth's with Selena, who ordered several outfits for the approaching fall and winter, Carolyn knew that tassels and fringe were the new rage, showing up on almost everything. Skirts were no longer perfectly round, but were gored to make them flatter in the front and pushed out behind, often with a small train. Cashmere and paisley shawls had lost much of their popularity, though they were still worn, and clever slippers with perforated tops that allowed one's colored stockings to show through were now the fashion.

Shopping with Lady Broughton was a real treat: not only did it release Carolyn from the silent, disapproving company of Jason, but it gave her time to relish the companionship of Selena, whose witty conversation was a pleasure to share. There was a mischievous glint to her blue eyes, and she observed the world with a wry sort of humor that was compassionate rather than cynical, and her calm demeanor invited confidences. Over coffee and pastries in a small Parisian café, Carolyn studied the lovely face and wondered how Selena could have raised such a grim, cold son. Perhaps the boy resembled his father in his harsh character. Selena must have led a more difficult life than showed on her serene face, forced to live with both a husband and a son who were uncompassionate.

Jason usually joined the two women for supper, either in

the suite or in one of Paris's excellent restaurants; now that Carolyn was properly clothed, she could engage in the fantastic nightlife of the city. Selena also had her maid alter two of her own gowns to fit her more slender daughter-in-law. They were a trifle old for Carolyn in design and color, but their quality enabled her to go to the finest places.

Jason continued to be silent and sarcastic, but rather than growing angry, Selena gazed at him with gentle concern. For her part, Carolyn did her best to ignore him, but neither woman's attitude improved his temper. He grew more taut, more sullen every day, and Carolyn was glad when her two elegant traveling dresses from M. Dumond's were delivered to their suite. They would leave Paris for England, which, she hoped, would improve Jason's temper.

"Not the most beautiful dresses," Selena said as she studied the new arrivals that Carolyn modeled, "but quite appropriate for traveling. Brown is such a dull color, but at least it doesn't show the dirt and soot. And they're good quality. I'll have Isabelle do your hair each morning, and you won't look a thing amiss. By the by, I'm glad you've decided to abandon those feathery curls around your face. Very pretty, naturally, but I think a bit of severity suits you. Makes you more striking. Don't you think so, Jason?"

Selena appealed to her son, who sat reading a back copy of the London *Times.* He had not glanced up when Carolyn paraded first one and then the other dress through the sitting room. Now he lowered the paper and spoke disinterestedly: "Yes, Mother, I agree. But, then, your taste is always impeccable."

Carolyn refused to let his sour comment spoil her pleasure of wearing the custom-made gowns of muted brown and green. Their excellent cut set off her fine figure, and the rich material enhanced her skin tones.

Jason folded his newspaper and rose from his chair. "I assume we are able to travel now, Mother?"

"Why, yes, I suppose so."

"Good. I'll make arrangements to depart tomorrow. Excuse me."

Selena sighed and shook her head as she watched her son leave the room. Carolyn knew Selena was on the verge of asking questions. The older woman turned to face her, and Carolyn looked away, and the moment was broken. "Then I must set Isabelle to packing my things."

"Of course. Thank you for the dresses. They're lovely."

Selena waved her hand and smiled warmly. "My pleasure, my dear. You know how I enjoy buying clothes."

Carolyn trailed back to her bedroom, not eager to confront Jason should he return. She packed the things Selena had purchased for her here in Paris, leaving her old clothes behind. The small black lacquer box of treasures was all of her old life that she would take back with her. Before she placed it in the new leather bag, she sat on the end of her bed and opened the shiny box. Among her bits of jewelry and memorabilia, the gold button gleamed up at her.

Carolyn rubbed it thoughtfully between her forefinger and thumb. If Jason had wanted to kill her, he had had scores of opportunity since that night on the island. Yet he fit so perfectly the shady outline of her attacker. Carolyn frowned. Perhaps it was Jason, not herself, who had the upper hand here. Perhaps she was going home with a man who had tried to kill her.

She dropped the button back into the box and closed the lid. Surely it couldn't be true; she had left her attacker on

Antigua. The only danger she faced was exposure as a fraud. Burying the box under a pile of new silk scarves, she resolved to leave her life on the islands behind her and begin anew— as Mrs. Jason Somerville of Broughton Court.

The threesome took the train to Calais, where they crossed the Channel. In the cabin she shared with Jason's mother, Carolyn again took to her bed, feigning seasickness. Fortunately for her, Selena hardly noticed Carolyn throughout the crossing, for she lay turned to the wall on her bunk, fighting the queaziness herself.

They spent the night in Dover and boarded the train the next morning. Carolyn closed her eyes, and soon the heavy rhythm of the train lulled her to sleep. When she awoke an hour later, Carolyn cast a surreptitious glance to the two seats beside her. Jason was not there, and his mother had nodded off. She could gaze at the English countryside to her heart's content without arousing any suspicions.

She watched the tended green fields roll by, the meandering roads, the little streams across which the train thundered on wooden trestles. Everything was so beautiful, she wondered how she stayed away so long. She had never been in Kent before, for it was far from her own Lake Country home, but the lush greenness, the cool, gentle beauty were unmistakably British. Once, she was sure she would never see the country again. Now, she ached to be outside, to feel the dewy air on her skin and smell the faintly flowery scent of the English countryside.

Carolyn knew only that the Somerville family home was somewhere in Kent. Selena would, she determined, continue to her London house from there. She had also pieced together that Jason and Cynthia preferred their country home to London's cosmopolitan bustle. That suited Cynthia, who no doubt was essentially a country girl, like herself.

However, neither Jason nor Selena had mentioned the name of any town near Broughton Court, and Carolyn had no idea when they would reach their destination. It was hard to hold back her eager questions, just as it was hard to pretend not to be thrilled at returning home.

Jason returned just as Selena awoke, and he smiled down at his mother. "We're approaching Barham."

"Oh, thank you, my dear. Heavens, Cynthia, have I been a dreadful bore? It must be a sign I'm getting older."

"I hope not. I slept most of the way, too."

Jason handed Selena and Carolyn their bonnets, and since Selena tied hers on, Carolyn followed suit. Maybe Barham was where they would disembark. . . .

"Is Broaddus meeting us?" Selena asked.

"Yes. I sent a wire from Dover telling him to meet us with the carriage. It will be an easier journey when they finish the spur to Hokely."

"Not nearly as pretty, though, with these iron monsters smoking through the countryside. Don't you agree, Cynthia?"

"Yes. It's so lovely here, it seems a shame to spoil it with progress." Hokely—another name to store away in her memory; apparently it was nearer Broughton Court than Barham.

The train slowed down and pulled into a small town, hissing to a halt at the station. Jason escorted the two women through the small station to an elegant carriage that awaited them. A lad dressed in livery was walking the horses, and a middle-aged fellow in the same uniform waited by the door of the station. He snapped up straight when Jason emerged from the station. "Milord!" A grin spread across his leathery face. He motioned to the lad walking the horses and hurried toward Jason, pulling the hat from his head.

"Broaddus. Good to see you."

"Milady, milady." Broaddus nodded toward Selena and Carolyn. He opened the door of the carriage, and pulled down the metal step. The three travelers climbed into the coach while the coachman supervised his lad and the porter as they loaded the luggage. Broaddus climbed up onto his high seat, and they started forward. Carolyn clenched her gloved hands together in her lap to control her excitement.

She could not see the town of Barham, for Jason left the window coverings closed. But soon the darkened coach was overly warm. "Shall we let in a little air?" Jason asked. "It seems stuffy."

"Yes, please," Carolyn was quick to answer. He rolled up the curtain beside her and, hoping she appeared merely bored, Carolyn studied the landscape passing by. Everything was shrouded in a lush gray mist, unlike the sultry humidity of the tropics. They passed orchards laden with heavy red apples and fields of some low crop Carolyn didn't recognize. She wondered what it was, and as if in answer to her question, Jason commented to his mother, "The hop harvest looks good this fall, don't you think? Another week or two and the pickers will be streaming in."

Selena wrinkled her nose. "They're as bad as gypsies. I'll make a point to have left for London by then."

Jason laughed and returned his gaze to the fields. In the distance, Carolyn caught a glimpse of water shimmering in the sun. As they drove, they sometimes lost sight of it; at other times, they pulled nearer. It was a river, and the road ran almost parallel to it. Late in the afternoon, they topped a rise, and the wide river was suddenly in full view. "Ah, there's the Teise!" Jason exclaimed with a broad grin.

He loves this country, Carolyn thought. With the name of the river, she had found out another fact. Perhaps if she could store all the various facts and dates and names in her mind, it wouldn't be difficult.

Soon they passed through the village of Hokely. As the sun began to set, they left the main road, taking a narrow path bordered by apple orchards and a few humble cottages. Seeing Jason in the passing coach, the children playing in front seemed cheerfully excited to see the familiar face. At the third cottage, a woman stood in the doorway, sweeping. When she saw the carriage, a wide smile burst across her face and she ran down the walkway to the road. Jason signaled to Broaddus, who pulled the carriage to a halt.

"Milord! Oh, milord, I wanted to tell you that Jamie is coming home next week!"

"Is he? Excellent." Jason leaned out the window to speak to her, and she bobbed a slight curtsy to him. "I trust he's feeling all right."

"Oh, yes. He'll never be as good as he was, but the doctor told him he would have died, most like, or at least lost the leg, if you hadn't sent him to that doctor. Clyde and me'll never be able to thank you enough. You're the kindest man ever set on this earth."

Carolyn gaped at her words. This was not empty flattery from this family, who, Carolyn suspected, were tenants on his land. This woman showed genuine gratitude and warm admiration. As the carriage continued on, Selena glanced back at the woman standing beside the road and asked, "What was that all about?"

Jason shrugged. "Not much, really."

"It sounded like a lot to Mary Fenton."

"Yes, I suppose it was. Her son Jamie fell off the roof of one of the oasthouses when he was repairing it and broke a leg. He developed an infection, and I had him taken to Tunbridge Wells to a doctor. Apparently he's doing better."

Carolyn hid her amazement. How could Jason have pity for others, people who meant little to him, and yet have no compassion or understanding for his own wife?

They drove up a pleasant tree-lined drive, which soon gave way to a vast green lawn and a large house that Carolyn knew must be Broughton Court. Built of gray-brown Kentish stone, it stood on a slight rise. Its lines were clean and uncluttered, the front perfectly flat, without columns or decorations. It rose three stories high, its shape a simple rectangle, with four chimneys resting on top. dormer windows were spaced along the front of the slanted roof. It was not as large or as old or as ornamented as many houses Carolyn had seen, including her father's home, Gresham Hall, but its unadorned lines expressed a majestic elegance and dignity that needed no embellishment.

Carolyn had imagined it would be a dark, somber place, an ancient abbey restored, perhaps, or an old Norman castle, stark and stern, jealously guarded and added onto throughout the centuries by the proud Somervilles. But this elegant structure was as warm and inviting as it was classical. With a sigh that she tried to make casual, Carolyn wondered how Cynthia could leave this lovely, perfect home.

Broaddus pulled to a stop in front of the house, and the lad jumped down to open the carriage door. Before he could get the step lowered, the double front doors opened wide, and a stiff, white-haired man stepped out. "Milford, welcome home."

"Barlow." Jason stepped out and turned to help the ladies down the small step.

"Hello, Barlow." Selena smiled and started up the shallow steps to the house.

A smile creased Barlow's wintry countenance. "Milady, it's so good to see you. We hadn't realized you would be coming."

"Yes, now Mrs. Morely will have to hustle the maids about, setting up another room."

"It will be a pleasure, milady."

Jason extended his arm to Carolyn and she took it gratefully, needing every bit of support she could get to make it through this nerve-racking homecoming. She would be expected to know the names of all the servants. Barlow ushered them into the house, where a line of servants awaited them. Carolyn swallowed. There were so many! How could she manage to keep them straight? They would be lined up according to rank, she knew, so the first one must be the Mrs. Morely Selena had spoken fondly of. Carolyn smiled at her and said hello to the woman's stiff, "Welcome home, milady." As she traveled down the line, she noticed that she was given a stiff courtesy noticeably cooler than the greetings received by Jason and his mother. The staff, she reasoned, was first and foremost the servants of the Somerville family, and Cynthia had gravely insulted the family by leaving. Whatever lies Jason had put out about Cynthia's joining Selena in Italy, he couldn't fool the staff of the house that Cynthia had left in haste.

Carolyn would not be shaken by the quiet disapproval of the servants. Suddenly, among the crowd of white-frocked domestics, she saw a blessedly familiar face. "Bonnie!" she cried softly and reached out to clasp the woman's hands.

"Milady." Bonnie patted her hand comfortingly. She was a narrow woman with a set expression, and a small, pale mouth. As a child, Carolyn had once seen Bonnie with her hair down, and it was thick and lush. But she kept its glimmer tightly restrained, braiding it in a tight knot atop her head. There was no indication about the short, solemn woman of the padded, loving nanny, but that in fact was what she once was. Bonnie had remained to take care of the twins all through their childhood. She was a strict woman, but she had loved them fiercely, though her love for Carolyn had often been tempered with exasperation. But she was familiar, a woman from her past, the first person she recognized on this mad adventure. Her faint northern accent was thoroughly familiar to Carolyn. "You looked tired, milady."

"Yes, I'm afraid I am," she said, hiding her glee.

When they had finished the line of servants, Bonnie rushed to Carolyn's side. "Let me take you up to your room, milady, and help you out of those clothes. Then I'll bring you a nice cup of hot chocolate. Eh? That would be the ticket, wouldn't it?"

"Yes, please. Jason, if you'll excuse me?"

"Yes, of course." His voice was impatient, and he was eager to be rid of her.

Bonnie led the way up the stairs to Cynthia's room, and Carolyn was grateful to have Bonnie there to show her the way, for in the maze of hallways, she never would have found the room on her own. When Bonnie stepped aside to let Carolyn by, she entered the large room, lit only by the red glow of the dying sun. The ornate furniture, massive and carved, seemed cluttered to Carolyn, who had become used to sparser furnishings. The frilled blue bedspread, heavy blue velvet drapes, the wallpaper splotched with huge, limpid roses, and the cavernous pieces of furniture looked cumbersome, even in the spacious room.

"You sit down right here," Bonnie pointed to the chair before the vanity table, "and I'll undo your hair."

"That would be nice, Bonnie. Thank you."

Carolyn set her bonnet on the table, and Bonnie removed the hairpins with swift, competent fingers. She untangled Carolyn's braids and began to brush them out. "All right, Miss Carolyn, tell me exactly what you think you're doing."

The words and tone were so familiar that it took Carolyn a moment to realize the import of what her old nurse had said. She stared at Bonnie in the mirror. "What did you call me?"

"Your name, Miss Carolyn. Come now, you didn't think you could fool your old Bonnie, did you? I always knew the two of you apart." She touched a faint white line near Carolyn's hairline. "You got that the time you fell and hit your head on your grandmother's sideboard when you were less than three. Besides, your hair's too light and your skin's too dark, from living in the sun."

Carolyn studied herself in the mirror. She hadn't thought about that. She had tried to protect her skin with wide-brimmed hats and parasols, but her face inevitably reflected the tropical sun. It showed in her hair, too, that had bleached a little, even through the hats. "Bonnie, you were always too clever for me."

"Thank heavens! Otherwise, you'd have led me a pretty dance. Now, are you going to answer my question or not? What are you doing here, pretending to be Miss Cindy?"

Carolyn sighed with the relief of telling someone, and especially Bonnie, who would be on her side and keep the news to herself. "I'm not sure. But I appreciate your not letting on down there."

Bonnie sniffed. "As if I'd have said anything in front of *him.* Whatever's going on, it's no business of his."

"Lord Broughton?" Carolyn smiled. "I imagine most people would think it very much his business that someone was pretending to be his wife. I guess you knew Cynthia ran away."

"Of course. My heart sank when his lordship sent word that he was coming home with Lady Selena and Lady Cynthia. At first I thought you were her, but then I sensed you were different, and as soon as I took down your hair and saw that scar, I knew it was you and not her. But where is she?"

"I wish I knew. I'm more in the dark than you are." Carolyn rose and pushed her fingers through her hair. "I was in Antigua when Lord Broughton accosted me in my room. I had no idea who he was or what he wanted from me—remember, I was an exile from this family long before Cynthia's wedding. Finally, I realized he must be Cynthia's husband and had mistaken me for her. He said he tracked her down to the island—along with a man named Dennis Bingham. Is that true, Bonnie?"

"Yes, and a fine gentleman he is, too," Bonnie retorted. "Not at all like his lordship. That one's a brute."

"You don't need to tell me that. Anyway, I realized it would be a great service to Cynthia if I let him continue to think I was she."

"That's true." Bonnie pursed her lips, thinking. "You were always fond of getting into trouble, but I think this time you did the right thing. It'll throw a spanner in the works, all right."

"Good! Then will you help me?" Carolyn turned around to clasp the woman's hands.

"Of course. I'd do anything to help her escape his lordship. But what can I do?"

"You can give me what I need most: information. I know nothing about my sister's life the past few years. I don't even have any idea where the rooms are in this house. I need to know everything about her life to keep from making a slip."

"I'll tell you everything I know."

"First explain to me what's going on. Why did Cynthia run away? Jason accused her of having an affair with this Bingham.

"It wasn't wickedness," Bonnie hastened to assure her. "Cynthia is a proper lady. But an angel couldn't have stayed with *him*. She never loved him, only married him because her Papa wanted it. She wanted to please Sir Neville, especially after you ran off with young Master Mabry. He'd rant and rave about how selfish his daughters were, and he'd implore Cynthia to not desert him like you had. So she wed Lord Broughton—though he was only Jason Somerville then. His father died three years ago. Anyway, his lordship put on a fine show for her. He acted like a lovestruck young man, bringing her flowers and candies. But after they were married, he turned into an animal."

Carolyn wasn't surprised that the intricate courtship traditions could mask the young man's true character. They may have flirted and danced at parties, or sat together at tea on their best behavior, but Cynthia would have never been left alone with her future husband nor had any serious discussion with him. Between Cynthia's naivete and her father's pressures on her, no doubt she would have married Jason without really loving him. At eighteen, with no experience of the world, Cynthia would have had little idea what love really was.

"Poor child," Bonnie continued. "I wasn't with her then, you understand. Later, she told me about what had happened—as best she could, for she was too much a lady to speak of the things his lordship did."

"Things? What kind of things?"

Bonnie's eyes narrowed. "Bad things, miss. In bed. She told me that he demanded she do dreadful things, sinful acts. Miss Cynthia was humiliated. He'd laugh at her, or else he'd throw a fit or ignore her. You don't know him, but he can turn you to a block of ice with one look. He's a terrible, hard man."

So Broughton had forced Cynthia to satisfy his appetites by sexually abusing her. For Carolyn, it was only after she joined the acting troupes that she was told quite a bit more and much more forthrightly by fellow actresses about the perversions of such demanding and self-centered men. But for her sheltered sister, these discoveries must have been devastating.

Kit's lovemaking had been a warm, loving act, always pleasant though never as exciting for Carolyn as it seemingly was for him. He had taught her to please him and take pleasure in what they did, but he had never rushed her or treated her with anything but affection. How awful it would be to have a husband who was neither gentle nor considerate, and for whom force, not desire, was a prime motive.

"Miss Cindy was overjoyed when his lordship stopped coming to her room at night. It was three years ago that he told her he no longer had any interest in her. She told me she thought she would never know love or happiness, but at least she wasn't forced to be hurt and humiliated. Then she met Mr. Bingham. He was a rare, fine gentleman, a friend of Master Hugh."

"Who?"

"Hugh St. John, his lordship's cousin. He lives up at Greyhill Manor. He's a good man, even if he is a friend to his lordship. That's only natural, them having grown up together, like, and being related."

"And Mr. Bingham—Cynthia fell in love with him?"

"Oh, yes. She came up to see me one evening, her eyes like stars. 'Nurse, I've found love!' she said. 'I was beginning to think it didn't really exist, but then I met Dennis.' I knew who she meant, and though it wasn't proper, her being married and all, he was good to her and loved her terribly—what a difference after all these years and the pain his lordship's given her! So when she made up her mind to go away with Mr. Bingham, I helped her pack her bags and sneak out to meet him. And I made sure no one went in early to wake her up the next morning, either."

"Wasn't his lordship furious with you?"

Bonnie shrugged. "He didn't know I'd helped her. I told everyone that her ladyship had said the night before that she didn't want to be awakened, so they figured she'd lied to me, too. And his high-and-mighty lordship never paid enough attention to Miss Cindy to know she was that close to me."

"Do you know where she went?"

The nurse shook her head. "No, she was too canny for that. If I knew, then I would have had to lie to his lordship, and she wanted me to be able to answer truthfully."

"It isn't likely that she'd have gone to the West Indies, is it?"

"Cynthia? All that way on a ship? Not likely. I'd say she'd

head to France or maybe Germany. She always liked the spas there."

"That's what I think. His lordship apparently followed her to a port and there found she and Bingham had booked passage on a ship to Antigua. He thought they'd been so incompetent Bingham had booked it in his own name, but I suspect Cynthia engineered it to lead him astray. It was sheer good fortune that I happened to be on the island at the time and Jason stumbled into me."

"She's protected, that's what," Bonnie nodded shrewdly. "The good Lord's giving her a chance."

Carolyn had never been able to grasp Bonnie's seemingly contradictory faith. Often, Bonnie had shaken her head and warned Carolyn that she was a heathen and destined for damnation in the life hereafter. "I hope He is," Carolyn said diplomatically. "Now, I need you to tell me about this house and the grounds."

"There's a garden out back, beautiful thing it is, too, though most the flowers are gone this time of year. The river runs behind the garden."

"The Teise?"

"That's right. There's not much else around except fields of hops. His lordship owns excellent farmland."

"What are those strange houses with the roofs like dunce caps?"

"Oasthouses. It's where they dry the hops in kilns. Oh, you should know about the Keep."

"What is that?"

"Hemby Keep. A defense fort it was at first. Then the family died out; they were somehow connected with the Somervilles, who lived at Greyhill Manor at the time. The Keep fell into ruins, and in the sixteen hundreds the Somervilles built this house. A lot of the stones of the ruined Keep were used in building this house, but the ruins are still there. It's south of here on a knoll, not too far to walk. Miss Cynthia used to go there often. She said it was peaceful, a good place to be alone."

"Tell me about the village and the people who live around here. I saw a woman not far from here today. I think Lady Selena called her Mary Fenton."

"She'd be Clyde Fenton's wife. They rent from his lordship, always have. The family's been here as long as the Somervilles." Bonnie went on to name the people of importance in the area as well as many of the tenants and some of the other workers around the grounds of the house. At Carolyn's request, she drew a rough sketch of the first two floors of the house, naming each room. When Carolyn asked about the third floor, she shook her head. "It's not in use, miss, unless they're having a big party with lots of people staying here. Most of the time, the furniture's kept covered. The attics are where the servants' quarters are. You wouldn't need to know about them. I doubt Miss Cynthia ever went up there."

Carolyn rose and stretched. "I think I've had about all the information my brain can handle at the moment. You were right when you said I was tired. I think I'll nap until time to dress for dinner."

"Very good, Miss Carolyn. Just call when you need me."

Carolyn explored the room after Bonnie left. She opened the drawers and closets, where an overwhelming array of clothes was stored. There were nightgowns and undergarments of lace and silk, stockings of all colors, ruffled petticoats, lace-trimmed pantalets, and chemises decorated with thin pastel ribbons. There was a high stack of linen handkerchiefs, monogrammed and edged with lace. Berthas and fichus and gauzy scarves to drape over bare shoulders were piled by the dozens. Jewelry boxes overflowed with earrings of pearl, ivory, jade, and other stones of unsurpassed beauty. There were ropes of pearls, necklaces of jet, lockets, and brooches of enamel, coral, and gold and silver set with precious jewels. One chest contained furs packed away for the summer—fox and chinchilla muffs and hats, a mink stole, a sealskin coat, and a sable-trimmed coat. Parasols of silk and taffeta decorated with lace and fringe filled another chest. Kid and cloth gloves in different lengths and colors lay beside a collection of painted vellum fans with ivory sticks and mother-of-pearl guards.

On the vanity table sat a row of glass bottles filled with sweet-smelling perfumes, and in the drawers were hairpins, beautiful combs, and hairnets, some of silk, some of velvet ribbon, and one of scarlet chenille with a ruche of black lace, obviously for evening wear. Another drawer held Cashmere and Paisley shawls and light shawls of black Chantilly and Maltese bobbin lace. A cherry wood armoire was lined with shelves on which sat hatboxes. One by one Carolyn took them down and peered inside, finding a wide-brimmed straw hat for summer wear in the country, a beaver bonnet for winter wear, hats of all different colors and designs to match her dresses. There were almost as many shoes lined up below the hatboxes: boots of all lengths, soft brocade slippers for at-home wear, and heeled silk slippers for evening wear.

The wealth and profusion of clothes and accessories was astounding, and Carolyn felt small and insignificant amidst this luxury, which seemed to take on a life of its own. Finally, turning to the huge mahogany wardrobe, Carolyn swung open its heavy doors and saw an array of garments beyond her wildest dreams. There were evening dresses, day dresses, ball gowns, walking dresses, all in the most beautiful fabrics she'd ever seen—poplin, muslin, silk, taffeta, brocades, in a wealth of colors. Many were of pastel colors: pale yellows, blues, and pinks, ruffled and flounced. Carolyn passed them by for she was instantly drawn to the jewel tones of the dresses of burgundy, emerald and midnight blue at the end of the wardrobe.

Hungrily, Carolyn fingered an evening dress of rich turquoise satin. With its scooped neck and wide taffeta sash, the garment shimmered in its beauty and elegance. It had been so long since she had seen and touched such clothes; she felt starved for this beauty and grace. She had always been attracted to beautiful things, but for years had been too poor to purchase them. It was sheer vanity, she knew, but she couldn't pass by these benefits that Cynthia had rejected. For the time being, at least, she would let herself wallow in the luxury. She would wear these soft, rich clothes and be lovely in them.

Carolyn napped for an hour and was awakened by the girl she had met earlier, whom she guessed was Cynthia's personal maid. Polly? Pamela? . . . she searched frantically for the girl's name. Ah—Priscilla! "I'm sorry to awaken you, milady, but it's nearly time for dinner."

"Yes, of course. That's quite all right." Carolyn sat up, stretching, refreshed and eager to get into the dress she had selected. "Is there time for a bath, do you think? I feel so grimy from traveling."

"Yes, milady, if you'd like. I'll draw one immediately."

Carolyn smiled. "Thank you, Priscilla."

The girl bobbed her a curtsy and scurried off. Moments later she returned with one of the other maids; together they pulled the short metal bathtub in front of the fire and carried in buckets of water to fill it. Next, Priscilla brought in a steaming kettle of water and poured it in until the temperature was comfortable. Carolyn released a sigh of pure sensual pleasure, as the hot water lapped around her. She thought she could have stayed in the tub for hours.

After she toweled dry, Priscilla helped her into her silky undergarments, then tied her into her corset, diminishing Carolyn's waist with every tug. Next came a petticoat, followed by the unwieldy cage that held out her skirts to their proper width. Priscilla twisted Cynthia's hair in an elegant pile, then tied a black velvet ribbon holding a mother-of-pearl cameo around her neck and set matching cameo earrings in her ears. When Carolyn rose, Priscilla carefully dropped the turquoise evening dress over her and buttoned it up the back.

"Oh, milady, you look ever so beautiful," Priscilla breathed in awe.

Standing before the room's sweeping mirror, she had to admit she looked lovely. The rich material of the dress and the excitement of wearing it put color in her cheeks and a sparkle in her eyes. Her blue eyes were enriched by the deep turquoise, and the excellent cut of the dress showed off her figure to perfection. She smiled, feeling imbued with confidence and courage. *Let* Jason Somerville be on his worst behavior, for tonight she felt more than equal to facing him.

Five

Thanks to Bonnie's crude map, Carolyn was able to find the dining room without incident, trying all the while to notice all sorts of details on the way. Just before she reached the dining room, she saw Jason, his back to her, standing in the drawing room, where, no doubt, the family gathered before supper, as had been the custom at her father's house. She walked in quietly, knowing she was challenging the man. Jason turned around, and suddenly the room was charged with tension. Jason's stare was fierce and compelling. He took a step toward her, and Carolyn, feeling the force of his magnetism for the first time, swayed forward, strangely drawn to him. She remembered the feel of his bone and muscle against her back that first night when he grabbed her from behind. When she thought of him taking her in his arms and kissing her, she experienced a sizzling rush of emotion, part anticipation, part dread.

"Jason?" The word came out breathlessly.

He started, jolted out of his thoughts, and he frowned darkly. "Damn you!" he growled.

"I—I beg your pardon?"

"Did you think to soften me toward you by wearing that

dress? We've gone long past that point, Cynthia. I'm not fool enough to believe you want to wear something I gave you."

Carolyn's stomach dropped. Of course! Why hadn't she realized it? Cynthia would never wear those bright, richly colored clothes. That's why they were shoved into the far end of the wardrobe. Cynthia loved pastel colors, lace and ribbons, quite the opposite from Carolyn's taste in clothing. Apparently her husband had bought Cynthia the vivid dresses, and she had rarely worn them.

Jason's sarcastic, biting tone angered her, and Carolyn's first instinct was to snap back a retort. However, she knew she must not answer him sharply. She had already made a serious slip in her role as Cynthia. With great effort, she lowered her eyes demurely and softened her voice, "Perhaps I have changed."

His jaw tightened. "You'll never change." He turned and strode to the liquor cabinet. "Would you like a sherry?"

She didn't know if Cynthia even drank sherry; was it commonplace for Cynthia to have a sherry before dinner? Or was this a trick to foil her charade? "Yes, please." She'd take the chance.

Without any expression, he poured her a small glass of sherry and, as if she might infect him with leprosy, handed it to her carefully. That Jason dreaded touching her hardly fit with the brief flame she had seen in his eyes when she came into the room. She couldn't have been mistaken about that.

Carolyn sat down in a brocade-covered chair and sipped slowly at her drink, trying to ignore Jason's prowling about the room. He finished his drink, poured another, and drank it quickly, too. Suddenly, he spoke: "I don't suppose you've been to see Laurel."

Laurel? Bonnie hadn't mentioned any neighbor or servant by that name. "No. I—lay down for a nap."

"Naturally." His voice dripped with contempt.

Obviously Jason thought she should have visited Laurel, whoever she was. A relative? A neighbor? He couldn't expect her to call on someone outside the house as soon as they arrived. She decided to squeeze some information from him. "Have, uh, you been to see her?"

"Yes, of course."

"And how is she?"

"Very much as usual."

"Good." Would it seem strange to ask if she would join them for dinner? Yes, if she was some old, beloved servant. Whoever she was, she must be ill, or else she would have come down to greet them when they arrived—"Did she ask about me?"

He shot her a black look. "You seem to have reached new heights of cruelty while you were gone."

She had made another misstep—but what? "I'm sorry. I didn't mean to be unkind. I was simply interested in—"

"You have never been interested in her!" He roared, and his eyes turned cold and steely. "For God's sake, at least don't pretend that. You used to be honest about your aversion to her, if nothing else. What sort of game are you playing? Do you want to convince me that now you're the perfect mother, the exemplary wife? Believe me, it won't work. I know you haven't an ounce of love for either one of us in that ice-cold heart of yours. You're the most unnatural mother I've ever seen. An animal cares more for her offspring than you do."

Carolyn stared at him, unable to make a reply. Her wits were suddenly scattered to the four winds. Jason glared at her and swung away, striding to the door and into the hallway. At that moment Selena entered the room, almost colliding with him. She stepped back hastily. "Jason! Whatever is the matter?"

He pulled up short, visibly struggling to contain his anger. Finally he answered in a clipped voice, "Nothing. I had merely forgotten something and was about to go get it."

"Oh." Selena glanced into the room and saw Carolyn's stunned expression. "Of course. Hello, Cynthia."

"Selena." Carolyn stood and greeted her, though her mind was still whirling from Jason's words. Jason had called Cynthia an unnatural mother. Mother! It was unthinkable. Impossible! Perhaps Jason had been married before, and Laurel was Cynthia's stepdaughter. Jason might think Cynthia mistreated his daughter, though Carolyn couldn't imagine Cynthia's not treating a child well.

"Shall we go in to dinner now?" Jason escorted his mother and Carolyn trailed behind them. Jason held out a chair for each woman, then sat at the head of the vast table, with Carolyn on his right and Selena on his left, as if they huddled together for warmth and security in this huge room with its long table meant for at least seven or eight times their number.

Dinner was long, with course following course. Carolyn thought it would never end. Jason was silent, and Selena carried most of the conversation. Carolyn was too preoccupied tonight to make small talk. Eventually Selena gave up and they finished the meal in an awkward silence. Carolyn soon begged to retire, using her travel weariness as an excuse.

When Selena bade her goodnight, Carolyn hurried up the stairs. She rang for her maid, and moments later Priscilla appeared to help her undress. Carolyn tried to sound casual:

"Priscilla, when you leave here, please tell Bonnie I would like to see her this evening."

"Of course, milady." Priscilla carefully hung up the soft satin gown, then undid Carolyn's stays. Carolyn slipped into the lacy nightgown Priscilla had laid out on the bed earlier, then wrapped a satin dressing gown around herself, belting it with its soft tie. Priscilla knelt to slip the pliable brocade slippers on Carolyn's feet, then rose and began to expertly take the pins from Carolyn's hair.

Carolyn closed her eyes, letting her mind wander as Priscilla brushed out her hair with long, even strokes. When she was done, the girl put the silver-backed brush on the vanity table. "Anything else, milady?"

"No, thank you."

"Then, goodnight, ma'am. I'll give Bonnie your message." The maid bobbed a curtsy and left the room. Minutes later there was a light tap on the door.

"You wanted me, milady?" she asked formally, closing the door behind her.

"Yes!" Carolyn went to her, reaching out her hands nervously. "Bonnie, who is Laurel? Lord Broughton called me an unnatural mother tonight! Does Cindy have a child?"

Bonnie snorted. "It's more like my sweet girl has an unnatural child! Sometimes when I look at that Laurel, I think Miss Cynthia's not far from the truth, when she called him a devil. That one's a devil's child for sure."

Carolyn gasped. "Bonnie, what are you talking about?"

Her old nurse glowered. "She nearly killed poor Miss Cindy when she was born, not that *he* cared. He was only concerned about his heir. Well, it served him right to get what he did, but it nearly broke my baby's heart."

"Why? What's the matter with her? Is the child ill?"

Bonnie tapped her head significantly. "Her mind is where she's sick. She's an idiot."

"Oh, no!" Carolyn groped for a chair and sank down in it. "Poor Cynthia."

"She lay in her bed and cried and cried. 'Course his lordship didn't think about how bad she felt. All he considered was himself. The baby was his, so she ought to love it, ought to want to cuddle it and sing to it, just as if it weren't a monster."

Carolyn swallowed. "A—a monster? You mean the baby's deformed?"

Bonnie shrugged. "It's not missing anything except a mind, if that's what you mean. But you know Miss Cindy. It gave her the shudders to be around abnormal things."

What Bonnie said was true. Cynthia loved beauty and perfection. She had always been horrified by anything ugly, ill, or abnormal. It was more than disgust; it was almost terror. She couldn't bear to see cripples or beggars; they made her ill. Unlike the other children they had played with, Cynthia had not enjoyed the fairs that traveled through, with their odd characters and freak shows. When Carolyn had caught the measles, Cynthia had taken one look at her and burst into tears, running away and locking herself in the nursery playroom.

It wasn't really unkindness on Cynthia's part, Carolyn knew. She was never cruel to those who were deformed or different. Carolyn thought it was that Cynthia's sympathetic emotions were overwhelmed by their affections. And now she had a child who was not normal. Carolyn could imagine her sister lying in her bed for weeks after having given birth, unable to cope with her daughter's problem. She could also envision her sister rejecting the child completely. Even though it was her own flesh and blood, she wouldn't have had the strength or courage to take care of someone who repulsed her so.

"Were you here when she gave birth to—to Laurel?" She had to stop calling the child "it." She was a human being, her niece, her sister's daughter.

"Oh, yes. She wanted me to be here from the first to care for the babe. Of course now the child will need a nurse as long as it lives. She'll never be able to take care of herself. Six years old she is, and can't do anything for herself."

"Can she talk? Walk?"

"She started walking when she was almost four, and now she gets around fairly well. Of course, I have to keep my eye on her like a hawk, because she doesn't have any more sense than a babe. She'll stick her hand into the fire, anything. She makes some sounds, not what you'd call talking exactly, but she makes a noise when she's hungry and she makes another sound when she sees his lordship."

"I see." She was filled with clashing emotions. She felt sorry for Cynthia, yet, as always when her sister displayed weakness or fear, she felt a rush of irritation. She was eager and happy at the thought of having a niece, a relative on whom she could lavish her affection. Yet from what Bonnie had said, Carolyn had a flutter of fear that she, too, might feel revulsion when she saw the child. "I—I want to see her, Bonnie. Is she already in bed?"

"No. I was about to put her to bed when Priscilla told me you wanted me."

"Then take me to her, please."

"Are you sure, Miss Carolyn? You'll be here only a little while. You don't have to see her. No one will think it odd. Miss Cindy rarely went to her, and then only because he forced her."

Carolyn summoned up a tight smile. She and Bonnie still

had trouble getting along, it seemed; the nurse's words irritated her. "Come now, Bonnie, you me. I'm neither delicate nor timid. Laurel is my niece, and I'd like to meet her."

Bonnie thinned her mouth. "Yes, miss."

The nursery rooms lay in the opposite end of the house, on the third floor. Bonnie led the way, through the turning hallways, and all the other doors along the way were closed, giving the area a gloomy, almost ghostly appearance. Bonnie opened a door onto a playroom where porcelain dolls and a multitude of toys lined the shelves. It was obvious that no money had been spared in furnishing this nursery. A door at the rear of the room led into a girl's bedroom, pink and white, full of ruffles and frills. The bed was a normal size but with high sides like a crib. It was odd looking, almost like a coffin, despite its white trim. Carolyn shivered at the thought.

Carolyn saw her upon entering. The child was sitting in a small rocking chair in the corner of the room, dressed in a long white nightgown with ruffles around the cuffs, neck, and hem. She held a little knitted blanket in one hand, and the other thumb was planted firmly in her mouth. Tears sprang into Carolyn's eyes. Laurel was not ugly or monstrous-looking at all . . . just the opposite, in fact. Her coal-black hair was the only resemblance to Jason; the cornflower-blue eyes, the graceful arch of her brows, the delicate ivory skin, the slightly short upper lip were clearly from her mother. She could have been a picture of the twins when they were children, except for the flat expression and vacant gaze, which made her a distorted image of her mother and aunt.

Laurel looked up at her, and a wondrously sweet smile spread across her face. Carolyn smiled back, making eye contact, wanting to scoop up the little girl and hold her tight. "Hello, Laurel."

The child opened her mouth and out came a noise that sounded like "Mog." A sweet sadness swelled inside Carolyn. She walked over to the child and squatted down in front of her. Laurel's eyes widened as if in surprise, and she reached out to touch Carolyn's bright, red-gold hair.

Bonnie came forward, saying, "No, Miss Laurel, now don't you go poking her ladyship."

Carolyn motioned Bonnie away. "That's all right. I don't mind." She smiled encouragingly at the girl. "Go ahead, Laurel."

The girl had drawn back her hand when Bonnie had spoken, but now she held it out again to run her fingers down the smooth fall of Carolyn's unbound hair. She touched the shimmering satin dressing gown and the creamy skin of Carolyn's cheek. Carolyn's throat tightened painfully, and she slid her arms around the girl, moving cautiously so as not to frighten her. But Laurel seemed not at all taken aback. Instead she threw her arms around Carolyn's neck and squeezed hard. Tears slid down Carolyn's cheeks in a silent stream of pity, regret, and love.

After a moment, she released Laurel and stood up, then reached down to take the child's hand in hers. "Shall I rock you for a little while? I see you're all ready to go to sleep."

They walked past Bonnie, who stood with arms folded, obviously disapproving of the whole scene. "It's all right, miss. She's not used to her ladyship doing that."

"I don't think she'll object, though, do you?" Carolyn asked curtly. "I want to do it."

Bonnie shrugged and left the two alone. Carolyn sat down in the rocking chair beside the bed and pulled Laurel into her lap. The little girl leaned trustingly against her chest, blanket still clutched in one hand, thumb firmly in her mouth. Carolyn rocked slowly, her arms around her, and now and then she smoothed one hand down the long black hair. How pretty she was. How could Cynthia not have loved her? She was so sweet, so obviously delighted at the sight of her mother. There was nothing grotesque, nothing even abnormal about her, beyond the disquietingly vague look in her eyes. Even Cynthia should not have been repelled by her. Cynthia had had a difficult birth, Bonnie said, and perhaps that was enough to turn her against her daughter. Carolyn remembered an officer's wife in India who seemed to hate her child for the pain it had caused her at its birth.

She kissed the top of Laurel's head and softly began to sing a lullaby Bonnie had sung to them as children. As she sang, an old pain returned, compounding the bittersweet emotions swelling in her. When she had been married a year and a half, she had given birth to a child, a delicate little boy. He was the light and joy of her life, but she knew from the very first that he was doomed, for he was weak and sickly from the day he was born. His fragile condition and the blazing heat of India had been too much for him. He died in her arms one night, and Carolyn had wept for days, lying curled up on her bed, feeling as if her whole life had been taken away from her. Eventually, the tears stopped, and the memories grew less vivid, less consuming, until finally she thought of him rarely.

But her silent grief had never entirely died. She had longed for a child, and hers had been taken. Now, rocking, singing the lullaby she had sung to her own baby, it seemed as if that need was being filled. Now Carolyn could love and care for the child Cynthia rejected. It was fate, she thought, that had brought Jason Somerville to her and made him believe she was her sister. Now she looked upon her role with new insight. This was more than a chance to help her sister: This was a God-given chance to give this child a loving mother and to give an empty mother back a child. She, Cynthia, and Laurel had been given a chance at a new life. With renewed vigor, she knew she would carry on this masquerade for as long as she had to. She would do anything—anything at all, to remain here with Cynthia's daughter.

She felt a sudden chill and turned her head—there stood Jason in the doorway, one hand resting on the doorjamb, watching them. His face was dark and brooding, his mouth slightly twisted. He looked away, and then he opened his mouth to speak. Carolyn raised a finger to her lips to silence him. Laurel's body was limp with sleep. She tried to lift the child, but could not. Jason quickly stepped forward to take the girl from Carolyn. He raised her over the side boards and settled her into bed, pulling the sheet and coverlet up to her chin. Her face placid against the pastel linens, Laurel was beautiful.

Carolyn was nearer to Jason then she'd been in weeks, as the two stood beside the bed. Suddenly Jason's fingers gripped her thin wrist, and he dragged her into the hallway, closing the door against Bonnie's sharp and curious stare. "What kind of game are you playing?" he hissed.

Even in the dim light of the hallway, she could see the anger burning in his eyes. His fingers dug deeper into her wrist. Carolyn lifted her chin haughtily. "I don't know what you're talking about. Let go of me."

"What were you doing in Laurel's room?"

"I was rocking her to sleep, as you could see."

He made an exasperated sound. "What on earth possessed you to go to her?"

"You told me I should, didn't you? I don't see why you are upset about it. Isn't that what you wanted?"

He frowned. "You've never done it before. Why start now?" He released her wrist, but he didn't move back. "Do you think you can win me back? Are you trying to deceive me into loving you again? It won't work, so you might as well not bother."

"I can't imagine why I would try to make you love me. I don't care about your opinion of me, one way or the other." In character or not, her pride wouldn't allow her not to refute his words.

"I can't believe you've really changed."

"Then don't. It's quite immaterial what you believe." With a shrug of indifference, Carolyn swung her hair back from her shoulders, the silky mass rippling across the pale ivory satin of her dressing gown. Jason's eyes followed the glimmer of her beautiful hair.

"Your hair is lighter."

"The tropical sun," Carolyn said nervously.

Jason lightly stroked the back of his fingers along her hair. "As silky as ever, though."

Carolyn stood perfectly still, hardly daring to breathe. Jason seemed almost dreamy, as if his mind were far away, bemused. He placed his hands on her arms gently and slid them over the sleeves of the dressing gown. She could feel the heat of his skin through the cloth, the infinitesimal tug of his rough fingers against the satin. Moving his hands up to her shoulders and gliding over the ridge of her collarbone, he grasped the lapels of the robe and eased them apart. The sash unwound and her robe fell open, revealing the thin, lacy nightgown beneath. Carolyn's breath grew quicker as he lowered his eyes to her breasts.

"All of you is as lovely as ever." His voice was hoarse.

Carolyn felt her nipples hardening and knew he would see it through the filmy material. Suddenly, Jason straightened and, with quick, sure movements, pulled her dressing gown closed and retied the sash. His eyes glittered, but his face was set and harshly under control. "But it isn't enough, my dear. Not any longer. Your beauty is a commodity too many men have had for me to be interested."

Carolyn gasped and went to slap him, but he grabbed her hand and held it away from him. "I know you don't want me in your bed. You've made that plain enough. And I've discovered that's the only part of you I ever wanted. So there's no point in these little charades you've been playing—wearing the dress I gave you, holding Laurel. It won't make me love you. Nothing can do that. You can't create again that nice, chaste relationship we had once, with me banished from your bed but still loving you, wanting you, pursuing you. Give it up, Cynthia."

"I don't want anything from you!" Carolyn retorted, holding the lapels of her robe together with trembling fingers. His knowing eyes had disturbed her more than any man's advances had. She hated him, despised his nasty, sarcastic tone, yet for an instant, when his eyes had caressed her breasts, she had lingered on the thought of his hands removing her robe, exploring beneath her gown. . . .

"Good," he snarled. "Then we feel the same way. Good night, Cynthia. I'm going to bed." He stalked past her and ran lightly down the stairs. Carolyn stood still until he disappeared. Then she glanced at the gloomy surroundings and sighed—why did they have poor Laurel stuck up here, away from the rest of the house. No doubt the proud Lord Broughton was ashamed of his daughter, and kept the girl hidden from his many guests and friends.

Carolyn belted her sash more tightly and resolved to

change that sort of thing around here. Gradually Jason would find out that Cynthia was no longer the meek mouse she had been before. She wouldn't put up with the kind of bullying he'd just shown her, nor was she going to let Laurel be completely ignored. On that thought, she marched down the stairs and into her room.

Inside, she locked the door, leaving the key in it, then took off her dressing gown and draped it across a chair. She wondered uneasily where the side door of her room led, and figured her husband's bedroom must be beyond it. A prickle ran down her spine. She didn't like the idea of her and Jason sharing such close quarters. Softly, she walked across the room and turned the knob. Praying that it wouldn't make any noise, she opened it a sliver and put her eye to the crack. She could see only a slice of a large bedroom—the foot of the bed, part of a window, a shaving stand. That meant it was a man's bedroom, surely. So it must be Jason's. Just then she caught a flicker of movement and Jason crossed her view, confirming her suspicion. She eased the door closed, then fetched the key from the hall door and tried it. It fit, and turned with an audible click. From beyond the door she heard a man's harsh laugh and knew that Jason had heard her locking the connecting door. She grimaced and returned the key to the hall door. What did she care what he thought? At least she felt safer now.

Priscilla had turned back the covers of her bed, and Carolyn climbed into it. It seemed strange to sleep in a bed without mosquito netting, but oh so nice to put one's face upon a soft, sweet-smelling sheet. She stretched and closed her eyes and was instantly asleep.

Carolyn did not awaken the next morning until late. Yawning, she tumbled out of bed and opened the curtains to find the sun was already high in the sky. She started about the business of getting dressed, then remembered where she was and who she was supposed to be. Ladies did not dress themselves. She yanked the bellpull and sat down to brush her hair, waiting for Priscilla. The young girl was soon there, a small tray with a pot and empty cup upon it. "Good morning, milady," she said cheerfully. "I brought you a little tea."

"Ummm, sounds delightful." Carolyn poured the tea and sipped it, while Priscilla took over the brushing and arranging of her hair. Thirty minutes later, dressed in a pale-pink dress that Carolyn was sure would be Cynthia's choice, Carolyn went downstairs, but found no one in the drawing or dining room. Carolyn supposed Jason and his mother had already eaten their breakfast. Chafing dishes along the sideboard in the dining room held still-warm eggs and ham. Carolyn served herself and sat down alone at the long table. A footman appeared soon after she sat down and served her another cup of tea. She looked out the window as she ate. The dining room opened onto the side yard and the stables beyond, and as she ate, she watched a groom lead a magnificent white horse out of the stable. Carolyn gazed at the horse, awed by his lean, high-strung beauty. How she longed to go off into the countryside on a horse like that! But Cynthia wouldn't go near the stables. That, she knew, would be the most difficult part of her disguise.

Jason walked into her view, dressed in boots and riding pants, stroked the horse's nose, and offered it a treat. Watching him take the reins from the groom and swing up into the saddle, Carolyn knew he was an excellent rider. He'd have to be, to control that horse. It had power, nerves, and will; Carolyn could see that even at a distance. She felt a distinct pang of envy—if only she could go riding.

She finished her tea and rose from the table. What should she do now, she wondered? Carolyn walked through the house in an aimless manner, trying to absorb the layout of the house and its contents without appearing obvious. Whenever she came across a servant, she experienced a moment's panic, not knowing their names, but she soon realized that there was no need for her to greet each one by name. They nodded or curtsied to her, and she nodded back, and the matter ended there. She cautioned herself to go slowly. She must not rush, must not start asking a lot of questions to gain knowledge. She would learn gradually, pick up on bits and pieces of things said and put them all together. It would be a difficult task for her; patience was not one of her virtues.

She wandered to the nursery, and she walked up the stairs to the third floor. It wasn't as dark now, but there was still the eerie look of unused rooms. Carolyn tapped softly on the playroom door and entered. Bonnie was seated near Laurel, who, sitting cross-legged on the floor, played with a rag doll, smoothing its yarn hair. Laurel was dressed as any girl of wealth would be, in a miniature of adult women's clothes. She wore a printed cotton dress with pinked flounces around the skirt. The bodice was long and the skirt short, ending about her knees. A bit of lace-trimmed pantalet showed below the skirt, which was puffed out with petticoats. She wore soft slippers and white cotton stockings. Her ebony hair was pulled back into two braids. She looked, Carolyn thought, like a dressed-up doll.

She didn't glance up when Carolyn entered the room, but Bonnie rose and took two quick steps forward. "Miss Carolyn, there's no need for you—"

Carolyn raised a hand to stop her flow of words. "Bonnie, I know there's no need to see Laurel. I want to. I think everything's turned out perfectly. Cynthia is free, and I would like to be the mother to Laurel that Cynthia couldn't be. I see no harm in that. Now I'll thank you not to try to dissuade me from being with Laurel."

"Well, you're the fine lady all of a sudden, aren't you?" Bonnie spat. "Seeing as how I know who you really are."

A faintly amused smile curved Carolyn's lips. She knew how to act the grande dame if she had to, and she knew she must make Bonnie her servant, not her confidante, whatever Cynthia's relationship with the woman had been. "You're threatening to go to Jason and tell him that I'm Cynthia's sister and that she's still out of his clutches? Even if you could convince him that you were telling the truth and shouldn't be put away in a lunatic asylum, I don't see how that would help you or Cynthia. Nor can I see why you should object to my treating Laurel as my daughter."

Bonnie lowered her eyes, too long a servant of aristocrats not to bend to the authority in Carolyn's voice. "Because she's not your daughter, that's why. Anything you ever wanted, you took. Miss Cindy always got second choice."

"That's not true!" Carolyn flared. "Yes, sometimes when we were children I took a toy from Cynthia, as all children will do. But I never preyed on her, as you're suggesting. In fact, I was the one who protected her from other children and from adults, too!"

"Maybe so, but it don't seem right, you taking over her child and husband and house and clothes and enjoying them like she never could. Pretty soon you'll probably have that devil eating out of your hand."

Carolyn laughed. "Come now, Bonnie, no one could charm Jason Somerville. You're just being sour. Look, I know we often didn't get along. We can't have the same relationship that you had with Cynthia. But we need to cooperate. We want the same thing for Cynthia. There's no harm in my loving Cindy's child when we both know she couldn't accept it."

Bonnie sighed. "All right. I give up. I know you'll get your own way, anyway."

"Believe me, there have been plenty of times I haven't."

While they talked, the child on the floor looked up and saw Carolyn. Beaming, she stood up and hurried to her with small, clunky steps. Carolyn knelt beside her, again flooded with warmth. She hugged Laurel, and to her surprise, Laurel quickly pecked her cheek with a tiny, shy kiss. Carolyn chuckled. "Well, how have you been doing, little one?"

"She can't understand what you say, miss," Bonnie sniffed. "There's no use trying."

Carolyn shot her a meaningful glance, and Bonnie rose, shrugging her shoulders. "I'll just go have a spot of tea in my room while you're here with her, if that's all right with you, milady."

"That will be fine."

Carolyn spent the next hour on the floor with Laurel, crawling about in a most undignified manner, playing finger games that made Laurel laugh and clap her hands with delight, reading to her, and singing little songs and nursery rhymes. When she finally stood up to leave, Laurel's face fell and she grabbed Carolyn's hand, saying "Mog" again and again.

"Are you trying to say 'Mama,' pet?" Carolyn mused, smoothing the child's hair. "Don't worry. I'm not going away forever. I'll come to see you again this evening, if you'd like. Good-bye." She bent and kissed the top of her head.

She left Laurel looking a trifle sad and popped her head into Bonnie's room to tell her she was leaving. At one she went downstairs to the dining room to find only Selena there. "Hello, dear." Selena rose and placed a peck upon her cheek. "Settling in again?"

"Oh, yes. I slept late this morning, and it quite refreshed me. I think I'll walk around the gardens a bit this afternoon. Would you like to join me?"

"Perhaps, for part of the way." The two women sat down at the table, the butler and a footman holding their chairs for them. As the butler began to serve, Selena turned to Carolyn. "By the way, we received a dinner invitation this morning."

"Really? From whom?"

"Jason's cousin, Hugh."

"Oh? Inviting us to Greyhill Manor?" How lucky that the name had stuck in her mind.

"Yes, Friday evening. He'd heard we returned yesterday, so he sent a boy round this morning with the invitation."

"That should be pleasant." Everything was a challenge to her, Carolyn thought, even a simple thing like a dinner invitation. No doubt she was supposed to have visited Greyhill Manor before and should know her way around it. She should also know Hugh and his background. Bonnie said he and Jason grew up together, but it was the social chitchat one carried on at such occasions that could be a disastrous obstacle course for her, not knowing the people, places, and events the others discussed.

From Selena's liberal talk as the two strolled through the elegant gardens behind the house, Carolyn learned that Hugh was two years older than Jason and was the son of Jason's father's sister, Lillian. Selena never mentioned a wife or children during the course of the conversation, so Carolyn assumed Hugh must not have either one. She also received the impression that Cynthia liked Hugh. Carolyn remembered what Bonnie had said about his being a fine gentleman and also the one who had introduced Dennis Bingham, Cynthia's love, to her. Cynthia no doubt had held him in high regard for that, if nothing else.

The gardens were lovely, and Carolyn soon gave up pumping Selena for information and simply enjoyed the walk though the carefully trimmed hedges, bushes, and trees. Late summer flowers were still in bloom, and the banks of hardy chrysanthemums were beginning to flower, glowing yellow and gold and white in their intricate arrangements. Many of the trees were starting to change colors, and even in the middle of the afternoon there was a slight nip in the air. Carolyn wrapped her light shawl around her shoulders.

The river flowed behind the gardens. Placed at the rear of the garden, overlooking the Teise River, was a graceful white folly. "When I first met Jason's father, the Somervilles still had a maze here, with the folly at the center," Selena remarked. "It was a matter of pride to them, for it had been planted by Charles Somerville over a hundred years before. It was a pretty thing, and all we courting couples enjoyed it. It gave us an opportunity to slip away and be alone with each other." She smiled at Carolyn. "I hope I'm not shocking you. Things were freer then, before our gracious queen."

"No, I'm not shocked. I'm interested. What happened to the maze?"

Selena gave her an odd look. "Hasn't Jason ever told you?"

"No, I don't believe so." She'd made another slip, she supposed, but it was better to brazen it out than get herself all tangled in explanations and excuses.

"He got lost in it when he was a small child, three or four. Of course, the children weren't supposed to play in it, because it could be quite confusing even to an adult who didn't know it. However, Jason and Hugh decided to explore it—

you know how boys are. Well, they got lost. We searched all over the place before anyone thought of the maze. By that time it was getting quite cold. We found Hugh sitting in the folly, but the boys had gotten separated. Finally we discovered Jason huddled up in one end of it. He was freezing and scared, though of course he wouldn't admit it."

"Of course not." Carolyn smiled what she hoped was a wifely smile to soften the flatness of her statement.

"They were both given quite a lecture, and the next day my husband had the maze cut down. They moved the folly to the edge of the garden, so that one could sit in it and gaze at the river. An improvement, really—" her eyes sparkled merrily "—though I had a sentimental attachment to the maze."

Carolyn thoroughly enjoyed Lady Selena's company and would be sorry when she returned to London. Selena acted as a buffer between her and Jason. Their worst scenes were always when the two of them were alone together. She thought about their bitter words last night; Jason's sneering avowal that he had been interested in her only for her body had hurt. It was silly, really, because the insult had been aimed at her sister, not herself. Besides, what did she care what a boor like Jason Somerville thought of her? His dislike of her was a compliment! Still, his remarks had left an emotional bruise, and she was afraid there would be more scenes like that after Selena left. Parodoxically, she realized that there was as much anticipation in her as dread.

Six

riday evening their small party of three set out in the carriage. Carolyn, in a light-blue dress trimmed in blond lace, looked icily beautiful, like a waxen doll. Her complexion was pale, and her blue eyes looked huge and captivating. Selena's dignified loveliness was enhanced by a dusty-mauve dress. The two women's wide skirts ballooned out, filling the carriage with the rich sheen of taffeta and silk. The faint scent of attar of roses mingled with Selena's heavier jasmine fragrance. Jason sat beside his wife, not touching her at any point, though that was difficult to do in the close confines of the carriage. In his black suit he struck a sober, almost ascetic note among the women's rich beauty.

Greyhill Manor was ablaze with lights to welcome them, a pleasant sight in the gathering gloom and evening mist. A somber butler opened the door and stepped out to help the party down, then led them into a drawing room where Hugh St. John awaited them. Carolyn cast a cursory glance at the house. It was lovely and gracious, though far smaller than Broughton Court. What Carolyn guessed was the original house, the half-timbered center portion, was an unlevel, quaint building, while the haphazard wings built off from it in three directions had a faded, graceful look warmed by the spread of ivy. The drawing room where they found Hugh was also gracious, but again with a certain warmth and lived-in quality that Carolyn found missing at Broughton Court, where everything seemed too well-done and too recent. Unlike the house itself, the furnishings had no sense of history or family.

But Carolyn liked Greyhill Manor immediately, as well as the lanky, smiling man who rose from a rose damask chair to greet them. He clasped Jason's hand warmly, murmuring a low hello, and placed an affectionate kiss on Selena's cheek. "Aunt Selena, how are you? Did you enjoy Italy?"

"Both Italy and I are doing wonderfully well," Selena returned with a sparkling grin.

"I can see that you are. You grow lovelier every day."

Selena laughed and tapped his arm lightly with her folded fan. "Liar. But I love you for it."

Hugh turned to Carolyn and took her hand in his, lightly brushing its back with his lips. "No need to ask how Italy affected you. You positively glow."

Carolyn smiled. It was difficult not to with this man. The resemblance between the cousins was startling—both were tall and dark, with the same firm jaw and long, slender fingers. But Hugh radiated a charm and warmth that were missing in his bitter, silent cousin. Carolyn wondered if Jason had once resembled Hugh more, if time and unhappiness had twisted his personality. If Hugh's brightness and conviviality outshone his cousin, he was careful not to emphasize it—he even managed to bring a smile to Jason's face more than once. The bond between the two was obviously strong, and Carolyn wondered how Hugh had handled

Cynthia's leaving Jason for one of Hugh's friends. It was a difficult situation to be in.

Later in the evening Selena played the piano for them, while Jason stood at her shoulder, turning the pages. The woman played with a polished talent that was a surprise. Carolyn sat down on an odd chair that had a back and one arm, but left the other side empty where an arm should be. It had been designed, she had been told, in the last century for gentlemen who constantly wore their swords at their sides. But it was quite a comfortable chair for women nowadays, allowing them more room for their wide-spreading skirts. Hugh chose a red velvet sofa near her.

For the first few minutes of Selena's playing, they were silent, but then Hugh leaned toward Carolyn slightly and murmured, "I am sorry, Cousin Cynthia."

Carolyn looked at him, startled. "I beg your pardon?"

He smiled, and there was a kind, sad look in his eyes. "You needn't pretend. Jason has told me the truth. I regret very much that I was the one who brought you and Bingham together. I never dreamed Dennis would—but, then I suppose I should have foreseen the possibility."

"I—well," Carolyn cast about wildly for something to say. She found that she very much disliked Hugh's thinking she was an adulteress.

"No, don't be embarrassed, please. I shouldn't have brought it up. But I wanted to tell you how much I regret whatever role I played in this unfortunate incident." He paused, studying his well-groomed hands. "Cynthia, I know my cousin can be a trifle difficult to live with at times. But he's a good man underneath. Please don't judge him too harshly."

"I don't think it's a question of my judging him," Carolyn retorted. "It's rather the other way round."

"What I mean is, don't let what he has said and done recently set you against him. Don't let him frighten you. Oh, I realize he may seem angry enough to kill you. He has a fierce temper, and his first reaction is to lash out when his pride has been wounded. But eventually he cools off. Then he can be persuaded to see reason. I'm sure that will happen in this case. After a while his temper will cool, he'll become resigned to what happened, and then he will be willing to . . . reconcile."

Carolyn looked down at her lap. That was the last thing she wanted. The farther apart she and Jason were, the better it was. "I don't think that will happen."

"Don't give up on it. Don't give up on him. Please."

His expression was so earnest and grave that Carolyn had to smile. Despite his faults, Jason seemed well-loved by his relatives and workers. There must be a better side to him, one he didn't show to his wife. "Very well. Since you ask it of me so sincerely."

He stiffened slightly. "Perhaps you think I'm overly concerned for my cousin."

"I think you're very kind," Carolyn told him truthfully. "I didn't mean to sound flippant."

"It isn't like you."

Another mistake. "I'm sorry. Sometimes people change—events harden them, make them cynical."

"Surely not you. I can't imagine you either hard or cynical. Sometimes I wonder what would have happened if I had met you before Jason."

Carolyn turned to him, startled. "What do you mean?"

He shrugged. "Nothing." He turned his attention back to

Selena, who was just finishing a Mozart piece. "Ah, Aunt Selena, a beautiful demonstration, as always."

"Yes," Carolyn chimed in. "Thank you. It was lovely." There was so much she should know about these people that she didn't. She might easily have asked Selena if she played the piano, which, given Selena's ability, would have been ridiculous from someone who had known her seven years. Everywhere she turned there were pitfalls. Fortunately, she had managed to pick up a bit about the family tonight through the others' conversation. If she was slow and careful and given enough time, perhaps she could pick up everything she needed to know.

Tired after her recital, Selena asked Jason to call for their carriage shortly after. Selena and the threesome set off into the night. Carolyn leaned back against the padded squabs, closing her eyes in exhaustion. The worry of carrying off her impersonation was draining in a social situation such as tonight's. The talk of relatives had set her thinking of her own pitifully small family. Even Cynthia had left her father now, and she wondered about him, how much he had aged, the state of his health. Perhaps she could go visit him soon. No matter how much they had fought or how bitterly they had parted, Carolyn had a love for her father deep inside. When she was a child, they had been very close, and she knew she would always carry that child's love with her.

She opened her eyes and looked at Jason. He was gazing blankly into space. "Have you heard any news from my father?"

Jason turned to her in surprise. "He is doing no better, the last letter I had from Dr. Jepson. It should be only a matter of months."

A chill ran through her. "A matter of months." Until his

death? That was usually what such a statement meant. Carolyn caught her lower lip between her teeth. Sir Neville couldn't be dying. He wasn't an old man—but, no, by now she guessed he was. "Perhaps I should visit him," she murmured.

Jason snorted. "Don't be absurd. Sir Neville is hardly a forgiving man. I doubt he'd let you in the house. It's too late now, dear wife; you can't break something, then expect to miraculously mend it just because you want to. Some things are past repair."

Carolyn felt the tears pricking at her eyes, but she forced them back, not wanting to let Jason see her sorrow. She knew far better than he how unforgiving Sir Neville was. His rigid morality wouldn't let him love a daughter who had committed a sin—or even a folly. No doubt when Cynthia left her husband he had written her out of his book, as well. Now he was ill and would die alone. It was his own fault, of course, but that didn't ease the stab of sadness in her heart. "Poor Father," she sighed, not caring if Jason saw her unrestrainable tears.

The next day, Selena and Carolyn went out in the carriage to pay several duty calls, and Carolyn was grateful for Selena's unwitting guidance in learning about her friends and neighbors. When people were out, they left calling cards, and at another house or two they were forced to sit through a tedious visit. Carolyn hoped she would not have to make these visits often. The following day, Carolyn was in the sitting room with Selena, idly chatting, when the butler entered. He gave Carolyn a bow and intoned gravely, "Reverend and Miss Nelson are here, milady."

Selena sighed with distaste from across the room, and Carolyn grinned at her mother-in-law's expression. Reverend Nelson was the vicar who had the living at St. Francis in Hokely, and Carolyn remembered that Selena had let out a heartfelt sigh of relief when they discovered no one at home yesterday. Selena had said something about his "dreadful lump of a sister." That must be the Miss Nelson in question. "Show them in, Barlow."

A moment later, Barlow led the couple into the room. Carolyn extended her hand, smiling. "Reverend Nelson, how pleasant to see you."

"Milady. Your presence has been sorely missed here. I'm sorry I wasn't in yesterday when you called."

Carolyn murmured a polite reply as she silently assessed him and his sister. They were so similar in looks that it was almost laughable. Their faces were round, their features ordinary—small, prim mouths; narrow eyes of an indeterminate shade of brown; no sign of cheekbones. Thin black hair topped their heads, though the reverend was balding. They were plump and soberly dressed, reminding Carolyn of sparrows. Even the clergyman's movements were quick and nervous, as he moved on to greet Selena, and Carolyn nodded to his sister, smiling. "Miss Nelson, how are you?"

"Fine, I'm sure. And you?"

Though her words had been conventionally polite, the young woman's face had been as stiff and cold as a mask. If there was any expression in her granite eyes, Carolyn was sure it was dislike, and Carolyn wondered if it was directed at her specifically or if the woman was generally soured on life. Miss Nelson turned from her so quickly it bordered on rudeness and joined her brother at Selena's side. "Milady, it's so nice to see you again." There was a trace of warmth in the colorless voice now.

"Millicent." Selena inclined her head. "Please sit down and tell us what's been going on in the parish."

Nelson cleared his throat and perched on a spindly chair. His sister took the love seat behind him and was silent as the reverend launched into a detailed description of the events of the church for the last several weeks. Carolyn struggled to repress a yawn. When he reached the subject of the Ladies' Bazaar two weeks before, he turned to his sister, beaming encouragingly. "You ran the show, Millicent, why don't you tell them about the bazaar?"

"It was quite a success." Millicent looked straight at Carolyn, her eyes bright with hostility. "It's unfortunate that you weren't here, Lady Broughton."

"I'm sure you managed quite well without me," Carolyn returned with a falsely sweet smile. She couldn't understand the woman's open antagonism. Even if Millicent Nelson disapproved of her—or rather, Cynthia—it was foolhardy to show it. After all, Cynthia was the wife of the most powerful man in the neighborhood, the lord who gave them their living. Well, whatever the reason for her hostility, Carolyn was sure she could handle it. A vicar's sister didn't seem much of an enemy after dealing with jealous actresses.

"Yes. And I'm sure you enjoyed your trip to Italy much more."

"Italy is quite pleasant." Carolyn refused to be ruffled.

"It was rather a sudden visit, wasn't it?"

Carolyn raised her eyebrows slowly, pinning the other woman with a cool, aristocratic stare, until finally Millicent had the grace to blush. Then Carolyn said mysteriously, "Yes, I'm quite impulsive at times. I find it makes life much more interesting, don't you?"

"I'm afraid I wouldn't know."

Nelson chuckled hollowly. "Millicent is never impulsive, milady. Everything runs according to her schedule at the vicarage."

"It's an admirable quality. No doubt I could use a little more of your sister's practicality."

"Indeed, we all could," Selena joined in, smoothing everything over. "Dear Cynthia would have found the packing far less hectic, I'm sure, if she had come with me when I first invited her instead of rushing to join me in Florence. But, then, she had such a difficult time deciding to leave Jason and Laurel even for a few weeks."

"Of course," Nelson agreed, while his sister shot Carolyn a look of supreme disbelief.

There was the heavy thud of booted heels outside, and an instant later Jason appeared in the doorway. "Ah, Thomas, Barlow told me you were here. And Miss Millicent. How kind of you to visit us." He shook the reverend's hand, then lifted Millicent's hand briefly to his lips. Carolyn saw Millicent's set face melt into a fatuous warmth, and she understood Millicent's antagonism: She was jealous, pure and simple. Millicent Nelson was in love with Jason.

Jason stayed with them for a few minutes, claiming that he was too dirty to be seated, having just come in from riding through the fields. "And of course, you felt impelled to stop and do a little digging yourself," his mother commented dryly.

Jason laughed. "Actually, it was a cart that was stuck. Rob Marsh's. I dismounted and put a shoulder to it." Amusement lightened his features, smoothing out the deep creases of discontent around his mouth and eyes. He was quite handsome; it was no wonder Millicent mooned about over him, the poor, stupid girl. There wasn't a bit of hope for her, even if Jason weren't already married. If she could have him, she wouldn't know what to do with him—Carolyn would have laid odds that Millicent was far too weak and inexperienced for someone like Jason Somerville. Standing there in his riding clothes, dusty and smelling faintly of horse and sweat, he exuded a masculine vitality, a potent virility. A line of dampness ran down the center of his shirt, which was open at the neck to reveal a browned, corded throat. Even Carolyn felt the visceral tug of his sexuality.

She blushed at the turn of her thoughts. What an awful thing to be wondering about!

Jason listened attentively as Nelson described the poor condition of the vicarage roof, which Carolyn felt sure he was hoping his wealthy patron would repair. He showed none of his usual impatience, and Carolyn was also surprised at the way he treated Millicent, speaking to her kindly but without being so attentive as to raise any false hopes. Carolyn found it hard to imagine Jason displaying such consideration. She had yet to see him be as rude or angry with anyone as he was with her.

Jason promised to look into the matter of the vicarage roof, then excused himself to go clean up. The vicar and his sister rose to take their leave shortly after. Cynically, Carolyn thought that they had accomplished their purpose and were now ready to go. When Selena and Carolyn heard the front door close after the couple, Selena let out a comic groan and rolled her eyes at Carolyn. "Thank heavens! Yesterday I was fool enough to think I would escape the Nelsons."

Carolyn chuckled. "I suspect there's no way to escape them. Under all that flittering and flapping, I think our dear reverend is a determined man."

"Why, Cynthia! I'm surprised to hear you say so. I thought Thomas Nelson was one of your friends."

"The vicar is always a friend of the lady of the manor. Didn't you know that?"

"Such cynicism." Selena shook her head and smiled. "You know, my dear, despite everything, this is the most pleasant visit I've had. I'm almost tempted to delay my journey home."

"Then why don't you? I'd love for you to stay longer." She dreaded the idea of being alone in the house with Broughton and his loyal servants. Selena seemed to be her one friend here, except for Bonnie—and she was not so much Carolyn's friend as Cynthia's loyal minion.

"Well . . . I could stay until next Thursday, I suppose. But I'm duty-bound to attend Kitty Thrasher's dinner Saturday evening. Her son's married some sort of merchant's daughter, and Kitty's trying to ease her into society. She's dreadfully afraid no one will attend."

Carolyn smiled faintly. A merchant's daughter. No doubt her father was quite wealthy and Crossley had married her to keep up his aristocratic style of living, but they were so ashamed of her they must sneak her into society at a small dinner party of friends. Carolyn wondered what Selena would say if she knew that her presumed daughter-in-law was really a stage actress fresh from the colonies.

As the days passed, Carolyn settled into the routine of the house, although there seemed little enough for her to do except dress in the morning and dress again for dinner. Bonnie told her that Cynthia left the running of the house to the housekeeper, Mrs. Morely. She did no more than approve the weekly menus, which Mrs. Morely presented her each Monday. Carolyn cared little for the needlework

Cynthia had done to occupy her time. Moreover, if she attempted it, her lack of skill would quickly give her away. Cynthia hadn't ridden. That left her with almost nothing to do except read, pick flowers and arrange them, and call on their neighbors.

Compelled by boredom and natural inclination, Carolyn found herself spending more and more time with Laurel. The girl was delighted when she came to visit. She loved to snuggle against Carolyn and listen to her sing. Carolyn lavished her with the affection that had been untapped since the death of her own child. As she grew more familiar with Laurel, it seemed to her that the child was capable of more than anyone had given her credit for. Her ability was below average, certainly, but Carolyn gradually became convinced that she could be trained to do a great deal more than she was doing now. It was obvious to her that no one had attempted to teach the child. Bonnie merely saw to her physical needs—dressing her, feeding her, bathing her, and making sure she didn't hurt herself in her sometimes wild, aimless movements. The rest of the household largely ignored her, and isolated and unstimulated as she was, there was no hope of her progressing. However, after only two weeks of Carolyn's attention, she was sure that Laurel was able to do more than she had when Carolyn arrived.

"She's simple, Miss Caro, and that's all there is to it," Bonnie insisted. "She can't look after herself. You think his lordship didn't take her to all the finest doctors? They all agreed that she's an idiot. They say it was that long, terrible hard birth Miss Cindy went through. It hurt Miss Laurel's brain."

"I didn't say she was normal. Of course she's not. But she's improved in the past weeks. See how she imitates the block fort I built?" Carolyn pointed at the girl: Laurel's tongue was clamped between her lips in concentration as she piled block on block in a semblance of a line. Just as she spoke, Laurel reached out and tumbled all the blocks over, beaming. Bonnie shot Carolyn a meaningful glance. "Oh, I know she does that sometimes. Her attention span is short, and she gets as much enjoyment out of tearing them down as putting them up. But that doesn't make her efforts at building with the blocks any less."

"Yes, milady, if you say so." Bonnie was clearly unconvinced.

Carolyn continued to work with her, concentrating on teaching the girl how to dress herself. Carolyn showed her how to pull on her pantalets and chemise and petticoat, praising each effort Laurel made, though progress was slow. But Carolyn was certain that Laurel understood, that the girl wanted to learn.

Although the nurse resented her intrusions into the nursery, Carolyn wasn't easily intimidated, and she ignored Bonnie's hints and disapproving looks. She had no trouble putting Bonnie in her place when the woman became too vocal in her complaints. It became a running battle, but Carolyn was determined to win. There was the risk, of course, that Bonnie might reveal her true identity to Jason, but Carolyn believed Bonnie's concern for Cynthia would keep her from taking that step. Even if she did, Carolyn wasn't about to let the nurse keep her away from Laurel—nor would she let Jason do it, even though he had clearly told her to stay away from Laurel. She kept her visits to the nursery quiet and learned the times when Jason might be there so that she could avoid him.

When his mother returned to London, Jason escorted

Selena and stayed there several days on business. Though Carolyn hated to see Selena go, she was glad that it provided an opportunity to have Jason out of the house. She was able to see Laurel as often and for as long as she wished. She simply felt freer with Jason gone.

It was several days after Jason's departure that Carolyn came up with the idea to take Laurel down to the garden. She had noticed that, despite Laurel's lack of mental powers, her senses were quite adept. She loved pretty pictures and always ran her hands over the soft textures of Carolyn's gowns. Whenever Carolyn hugged her, she breathed in the subtle fragrance of Carolyn's perfume and smiled broadly. "You know," Carolyn commented to Bonnie, "I think she would enjoy seeing the flowers, smelling them. Don't you think so?"

Bonnie gave her an odd look. "If you say so, milady."

"It seems as though she's always shut up inside these rooms."

"I take her on walks, Miss Caro!"

"I'm sure you do." Carolyn tried to sound soothing. She had seen Laurel and Bonnie on their walks, the nurse striding out briskly, eyes straight ahead, a firm grip on Laurel's arm. Laurel would stumble along beside her, her head turning from side to side, bewildered by the sudden onslaught of new sensations. It took the girl longer than most people to absorb something new, and Carolyn was sure Bonnie's walks were nothing but a rather frightening blur of unknowns to her. "But I'd like to take her with me to the garden, anyway."

"Yes, milady." Bonnie had taken quite easily to calling Carolyn "milady," though she never referred to Cynthia as anything but Miss Cynthia.

Bonnie bundled Laurel into a blue polka coat and a brushed beaver bonnet. It seemed far too warm to Carolyn, who went outside with only a shawl wrapped around her shoulders for protection. Laurel protested being dressed for outside, her eyes welling with tears, and she pulled against Bonnie's hold with all her strength. "No! No!" She pointed to Carolyn again and again as she uttered the clearest word she ever said.

Bonnie finally won the struggle and got her dressed in coat and bonnet, but by the time she did her cheeks were flushed and her breath came faster than normal. "There! She's in a tear today, milady. I warn you. She's thinking I'm trying to take her for a walk while you're here." She shot Carolyn an accusing look. "She's disrupted these days, always waiting for you to come visit her. Doesn't want to settle down to her routine."

"A routine isn't the be-all and end-all of life," Carolyn retorted sharply. She squatted down and held out her hand to Laurel, smiling. "Come here, darling. Mama just wants to take you outside. Would you like to go with me?"

Eagerly, Laurel nodded her head, slipping one hand into Carolyn's outstretched one. Carolyn led her out the door and down the stairs. They passed one of the maids polishing the bannister, and she turned to stare, forgetting politeness in her surprise. Carolyn ignored her, and Laurel, looking up at Carolyn with an expression of utter bliss, seemed aware of nothing but Carolyn. They went down the back hall and out the door to the manicured garden. Carolyn paused on the small porch to let Laurel gaze her fill. Then she went off the steps and started along the winding garden paths, trailing slowly so that Laurel could look at everything to her heart's content.

Everything was a new and wonderful delight to Laurel. Spontaneously, she reached out to touch the leaves of bushes, exploring the differences of shape and texture and size. She squatted to pick up a stick and examine it at length, then carried it clutched in her hand as she explored further. She picked up pebbles and sticks until her little hands could hold no more, and her mouth began to wobble in frustration. Carolyn solved the problem by sticking some of the excess in her pocket, and from then on Laurel was enthralled with finding more pebbles, twigs, snails, bits of colored glass—anything that caught her eye—and shoving them into Carolyn's pockets. When they reached the banks of massed chrysanthemums, Laurel's eyes opened wide and she exclaimed a sound of pure pleasure.

She ran to the flowers and thrust her hands into them, touching, squeezing. Carolyn squatted down beside her and showed her how to pick them, and she carefully followed Carolyn's example, grasping them below the head instead of clutching the flower in her fist. They spent several minutes there before Laurel was ready to move on. It was early autumn and already some of the trees were shedding their dried leaves. When Laurel stepped on them and they crunched beneath her feet, a look of amazement crossed her innocent face, and she stamped up and down delightedly, listening to the crackle of leaves beneath her feet. She scuffed them with her feet and bent to take up handfuls and scatter them in the air, giggling as they floated back down to the ground. Carolyn couldn't help but join in her happiness.

They reached the open white gazebo at the end of the garden and sat in it, looking out on the river. Laurel at first roamed about the little wooden folly, touching the carvings, posts, and rails, but finally she settled down on the bench beside Carolyn and studied the river. Soon, lulled by its even flow, she dozed against Carolyn's side. Carolyn smiled, cuddling her closer, thinking to herself that she would be content to sit this way forever.

But of course they could not. Soon a late-afternoon mist rolled up from the river, seeping through their clothes. Though Carolyn was impatient with the way Bonnie bundled Laurel up as if she were an invalid, she knew the damp could make her ill, and she must not allow that. She shook Laurel lightly, and the child opened her limpid, vague blue eyes. She seemed to feel no surprise at waking in such different surroundings. She merely smiled at Carolyn and eased her feet onto the floor. Confidently, she placed her hand in Carolyn's and they strolled toward the house, again stopping to admire the wonders on the way.

Laurel's bonnet had been pushed back and dangled by its ribbons down her back. Her hair was tangled, as was Carolyn's, and bits of leaves and flowers clung to it. Flushed and in disarray, they looked supremely carefree as they bent to examine a snail's progress along a branch.

"Cynthia!" Lord Broughton's roar interrupted their quiet study, and they jerked up guiltily. Jason hurried along the path toward them, his long strides eating up the ground. He was hatless, and the sun glinted off his crow-black hair. His eyes were narrowed almost to slits; his brows contracted so fiercely that deep lines bit into his forehead and between his eyes. His face was dark and congested with rage, his fists clenched at his sides. Laurel glanced up at Carolyn fearfully, and Carolyn put a protective arm around the girl's shoulders. When Jason drew near, he reached out and grasped Laurel's wrist, jerking her away from Carolyn's arm. His eyes remained fixed on Carolyn. "What the hell do you think you're doing?" he snapped. "I thought I warned you about this the other night."

"You did. Warnings aren't always followed, you know." She forced her voice to maintain a crisp, cool tone she didn't feel at all. "Would you mind controlling your temper? You're frightening Laurel."

Jason's eyes flamed for an instant, but he looked down at Laurel's anxious expression. "Go inside, Laurel."

Laurel turned her gaze to Carolyn for reassurance. Carolyn smiled. "Yes, Laurel. Go to your room. There's Nurse waiting for you at the door. I wager she'll give you a nice cup of hot cocoa. Don't worry. I'll join you later."

Jason turned to watch Laurel's lagging departure. When she reached the doorway, he swung back to Carolyn. "The hell you will. I've told you, I won't have you playing your games with my daughter!"

"I'm not playing games. She's my daughter, too."

"Not so as anyone would know it. You're a selfish, spoiled bitch, and you've never given a damn about anyone but yourself, least of all Laurel. You forfeited your rights to her long ago."

"I'm her mother," Carolyn insisted stubbornly. "You can't keep me from seeing her."

"Oh, no?" He loomed over her, so close she had to bend her head back to look at him. She could see the feathery brush of the dark lashes around his eyes, the bright black pinpoints of his pupils. His warm masculine scent surrounded her—a combination of horse, leather, and cologne that filled her senses. It reminded her piercingly of Kit and her father, and yet it wasn't like either of them, for it contained a subtle, seductive element that was Jason's alone. He put his hands on her shoulders, and his thumbs dug into her flesh, circling slowly. "If you want so much to be Laurel's mother, perhaps you'd like to resume your place as my wife, as well. Hmm?"

Carolyn swallowed, but refused to lower her eyes. In truth, she didn't think she could look away. He pinned her with his silver-green gaze, as hard and cold as steel. His voice was low and husky. "What if I decided to resume my marital rights? I might, you know, if you continue to see Laurel. Don't you remember how much you hated that?" Suddenly he bent his head, and his mouth was pressing hurtfully into hers, parting her lips. He pulled her against him, fitting her soft body against the full length of his, molding her into the iron of his muscles and sinews. His breath seared her flesh. Carolyn trembled, suddenly flushed all over. She raised her hands to his chest as if to ward him off, but there was no strength in her touch. His kiss deepened, his lips moving insistently over hers. He cupped his hand around one of her breasts, and even through her layers of clothing, she felt the fierce heat. His thumb sought her nipple as his tongue sought the nectar of her mouth. He traced the ridges along the roof of her mouth and lazily circled her tongue while his free hand pressed her hips up into him, rubbing her against his body suggestively.

Carolyn was lost, swirling in a world of violent sensation. Everywhere he touched her she was alive—breasts, mouth, abdomen, all responding to him with sharp desire. Suddenly, he released her, almost flung her away. "Is that what you want?" His face was as cold as his words. He watched her, his mouth curling with contempt, eyes glittering. "To be in my bed again?"

Shakily Carolyn wet her lips and tried to collect her

scattered wits. This was no time to fall apart. She must think of Laurel. That was what was important. She had to keep her mind on Laurel and on being Cynthia. Swallowing, she answered in a low voice, "You know it's not."

His faint smile was chilling. "I didn't think it was. More likely you're trying to hurt me through my daughter, to worm your way into her affections so that you could threaten me with withdrawing from her life."

"Oh! How could even you think such a thing as that!" Carolyn gasped.

"My dear, where you're concerned I can believe anything."

"Then believe that I've changed! I won't hurt Laurel. I simply want a chance to be with her. I want to be her mother."

"You couldn't stand her. You'd shudder at the sight of her. Why the difference?"

"I—I've had some experiences that showed me I had been wrong." Carolyn studied her hands. She mustn't fail now, couldn't let him overpower her or confuse her. She'd think about her feelings later. Later she'd put everything that had just happened into perspective, but right now she had to convince Jason that Cynthia's elopement had given her a change of heart where Laurel was concerned. Otherwise everything she did with Laurel would ring untrue. He would continue to doubt her intentions toward Laurel and forbid her to visit the girl—or he would realize she was a fraud and throw her out of his house. She bit her lip, barely able to restrain the trembling that seemed to have taken over her body. What could she say that he would believe? What could have changed Cynthia? "I—I saw terrible things, worse things than I had ever dreamed existed." Her eyes turned inward, remembering the horrors she had witnessed in India. "Starving children. Crippled. Mutilated. Abandoned."

Jason stared at her silently, his taut, furious face slowly relaxing in amazement. Carolyn raised her face to him, and her eyes were luminous with unshed tears, beseeching. "I realized what a fool I'd been about Laurel, how much better off I was than so many mothers. I want—I want to make up for all the years I lost. I never meant to hurt Laurel. It's just that I've always had this weakness about . . . about people who are different. Now I see how foolish, how petty it was. Please, Jason, give me another chance. Don't cut me off from my child without even a hope. Don't do that to me."

His eyes were wary, but his mouth was no longer its usual cruel slash. "Lord, but you're lovely at begging for pity. You always have been able to tear a man's guts out when you look at him like that."

"Please, Jason, do you want me on my knees to you? Do you want me to crawl and plead? Would that satisfy your pride?"

"It's not my pride I'm concerned about! God knows, I've given up all hope of that where you're concerned. It's Laurel that concerns me. She's *all* that I care about now."

"Then let her have a mother. She wants me, Jason. She's happy with me."

"She sees only how beautiful you are. She's too simple to understand how shallow that beauty is." He paused. "All right, I won't forbid you to see her, but I promise I'll keep a close eye on you. If you do anything—*anything*—to harm Laurel, I'll make you regret it till the day you die."

Seven

Though his threat shook her, Carolyn held her ground. She faced him, head high, and gave a small nod of understanding. Jason stalked off, leaving her alone in the garden, and she made her way to the stone bench beside the chrysanthemums. Jason's savage kiss had shaken her badly, not because of the hatred that lay behind it, but because of her own astonishing response to his kiss. She had actually felt a strong surge of passion, an insane desire to throw her arms around him and return his kiss. Carolyn blushed, remembering the way her skin had heated beneath his touch and her nipples had hardened. How humiliating, to have reacted that way to a kiss that Jason had meant only as a reminder to Cynthia of his brutal lovemaking!

It wasn't like her. She had known some passion with Kit, but never to the extent he had. Kit had assured her that that was perfectly natural and right in a lady of quality. He had taught her ways to please him, and she had happily performed them, but more for the happiness of bringing him joy than for any pleasure within herself. Since Kit's death, she had had no problem turning down countless suitors, feeling not even a flicker of desire for any of them. Yet she had felt a distinct flash of desire for her sister's husband . . . a man who had mistreated and abused Cynthia and who had treated Carolyn with nothing but scorn and contempt since she met him.

Carolyn was flooded with turbulent, conflicting emotions. When she was younger, she had ridden such feelings away. There was nothing like controlling a fast, temperamental mount or feeling the wind on your face to get rid of all sorts of troublesome emotions and thoughts. Carolyn glanced longingly toward the stables. If only she could do that today. . . .

But she could not, for Cynthia almost never rode, so Carolyn had stayed away from the stables since she arrived, though with her love of riding it had been a constant struggle. Riding had been her favorite pastime until she no longer had the money to pursue it. Carolyn sighed and started for the house. Once inside, however, she could not quell her restless feeling. Cynthia's bedroom, with its massive furniture and cluttered, ruffled decorations, was smothering. It was as if Cynthia's life were closing in on her, trapping her. She felt desperate for air.

Carolyn flung open the wardrobe door and searched through the row of clothes until she found a royal-blue velvet riding habit. Surely Cynthia must have ridden on occasion, or she wouldn't possess a riding habit. Carolyn quickly pulled off her clothes, not bothering to ring for Priscilla to help her undress. She threw the mass of dress, petticoat, and hoop on the bed and slipped into the slim-lined habit. The color suited her, as did the plain military style of the jacket. She tugged on a pair of slickly shining boots and searched the room for a riding crop. Finally she found it thrown far to the back of the wardrobe. Fortunately, the leather riding gloves and the jaunty blue hat that matched the habit were easier to find. She set the hat on her head and secured it with a long hatpin, then smiled at her reflection. The hat was quite becoming, with a long blue pheasant feather curling over and down to touch the opposite cheek. She pulled on her gloves, grabbed the crop, and stepped out of her bedroom.

She paused in the hall, glancing around, then hurried down the stairs and out the back door almost furtively. The fewer people who saw her, the less chance there was of word getting back to Jason. Outside, she strode across the garden and graveled drive to the stables beyond. When she stepped from the light into the semi-darkness of the stable, she hesitated, blinking to adjust her eyes. As she stood there, a stableboy hurried up, slack-jawed with surprise. He tugged the cap off his head. "Milady! I—I didn't expect to see you here."

"I was suddenly seized with the desire to ride." She smiled, dazzling him. "A very gentle horse, of course." She mustn't ask for the kind of horse she herself would choose. That would be utterly preposterous. But it was conceivable that on rare occasions Cynthia decided to get a little fresh air on the back of a nag.

The boy nodded and swallowed, crushing his hat in his hand. He ran to bring out a horse and saddle it for her. When he returned leading a fat, passive mare, Carolyn repressed a sigh and smiled at him. The boy was clearly overwhelmed by her presence, and she decided to use that to her advantage. She leaned toward him in confidence and said, "Please don't tell anyone about this. You see, I'm trying to learn to ride as a surprise for his lordship."

"Oh, yes, milady. I won't tell a soul."

"Thank you." He led the horse to the mounting block, and Carolyn mounted. She was rusty enough that it didn't take much acting to look ungraceful. She turned the nag out of the stable yard and took a track leading eastward. Her primary intent was simply to get out of sight of the house as quickly as possible. Once she was beyond a sheltering copse of trees, she relaxed and settled down to enjoy the scenery around her. She remembered that Bonnie had said the old Keep was in this direction. Since it had been a favorite spot of Cynthia's, according to Bonnie, it would be a good place to go. If Cynthia had gone there often, she ought to at least know what it looked like.

It didn't take her long to reach the old building. No doubt Cynthia usually walked the distance. Hemby Keep was one of the square Norman keeps set up in Kent hundreds of years ago to defend against attacks from across the Channel. Built of the same grayish-brown stone of Broughton Court, it had had two wings added onto it in later days. Only two walls of the original keep remained standing, and the additions were in ruins as well. Carolyn dismounted and walked over to the tower.

The door was on the level of the second floor, often the case in these old keeps built solely for war. The twins's own home, originally a pele tower for border defense, had been the same way, though later occupants had turned the high door into a stained-glass window. Entrance had been gained by a rope ladder that was pulled up when the keep was attacked, thus making it harder to invade. However, now the high door was merely ironic, for the ruins stood open on two sides. Carolyn walked around and stepped through an opening in the rubble. Looking up at the top of the shell, the effect was dizzying, for the walls seemed to tilt inward.

Carolyn glanced down hastily and edged away from the walls, entering the ruins of the later additions. Here, too, parts of the roof and walls were gone, collapsed into rubble. Yet curiously many of the inner walls remained. Bonnie said they had used the stones of Hemby Keep to build the walls of Broughton Court, which would account for the advanced deterioration of the newer wings.

It was much dimmer inside the addition than in the keep, for more and higher walls remained standing. In one or two rooms it was almost dark. Carolyn roamed through the old house, sidestepping rubble, trying to place each room. She heard a chink of stone meeting stone. It sounded as if something had fallen. She glanced around. There was nothing in the twilight of the ruins, but a frisson of fear ran down her spine. If it was a person, surely he would have called out. She tensed, listening, but there was only silence.

She was acting like someone out of a melodramatic novel; it must be the mood of the place. No doubt a small animal had dislodged a chunk of stone and sent it tumbling. A rat, perhaps—that thought sent her shooting out of the old house, holding up her trailing skirts. Outside, it was pleasantly warm and sunny, a beautiful autumn day, and Carolyn felt even more foolish for her vague apprehension. The opposite wing had evidently been burned at some point, for the inside was gutted, and here and there charred timbers lay on the ground or slanted downward from the ceiling. There was no reason to go in there, she thought with relief, so she took a peek and then she walked back to where her horse waited. She couldn't understand Cynthia's preference for the place. It was a romantic view, but it seemed gloomy, messy, and far too eerie.

Carolyn led the nag over to a tree stump to mount. As

she swung into the sidesaddle and adjusted her leg on the horn, she was conscious again of the feeling that someone was watching her. She felt exposed and nervous, and she stared into the trees lining the path to the north and east as she rode along. They were thick and clustered, the edge of a deeper wood. Someone could be hiding among the thick bushes and saplings, watching her, and she would not be able to see him. Perhaps Jason, had he seen her riding out and followed her, examining her every move to determine if she was a fraud?

That was ridiculous, she told herself, for if Jason suspected her, he'd not hide the knowledge—he'd use his disclosure and dangle it before her. Unpleasant he might be, but he was certainly not the type to sneak around in the woods to watch her. His way would be the direct attack. It seemed unlikely that there was anyone else watching her. It was simply one of those odd things that felt like intuition or prescience, but in reality meant nothing, much like the feeling she sometimes had that she had been in a place before. Firmly, Carolyn quelled her feelings of uneasiness and dug her heels into the mare.

As Gray Lady ambled forward, Carolyn couldn't help but smile. She certainly wasn't going to outrun any watcher on this nag.

She stopped in the yard in front of the stables and waited for the lad's help to dismount, though she could have done it quite easily by herself. When he helped her down and led the horse back into the stables, Carolyn followed him, drawn by curiosity and her love of horses. In one stall stood a magnificent white stallion that pricked up its ears at her approach and studied her alertly. This, she knew, was Jason's mount. She had seen him on the stallion once or twice at a distance, and she had thought him a gorgeous animal, but seeing him up close, she was even more impressed. She passed a bay and at the end of the row of stalls found a dainty black Arabian mare with a blaze of white down her face. Carolyn leaned against the wooden slats of the stall and gazed at her yearningly. She was a ladies' horse: not large, but there was a bright look to her and Carolyn suspected she was fast.

The stableboy had unsaddled Carolyn's mount and was rubbing her down before putting her in the stall. Carolyn turned toward him and asked, "What's the name of this mare?"

His eyebrows went up, but he quickly wiped the look from his face. "Why, that's Felicity, milady, the mare his lordship gave you several years ago."

Carolyn did her best to save the moment. "Yes, I thought that was the horse." She gave a delicate little shudder. "Pity, isn't it, that something so beautiful can be so fearsome."

"Yes, milady." Carolyn could almost see his mental shrug. It would seem a crazy attitude to him, but one more in keeping with Cynthia's reputation.

Back in her room, Carolyn had just stripped out of her riding clothes when Priscilla announced she had drawn her bath. After a long and soothing soak, Priscilla brushed her hair dry before the low fire, then bound it into a knot and curled the still-damp loose hairs around her finger. Carolyn dressed in a pale-lavender gown of satin, draping a delicate white lace fichu around her bare shoulders and over the deep décolleté of the neckline. A small enameled brooch fastened the ends of the scarf at her breasts. The golden glow of her skin was fading, Carolyn noticed. Her complexion more and more resembled the pale ideal of the British.

When she reached the drawing room downstairs, Jason was already there, glass in hand. Carolyn realized with dread that this would be the first night they would dine together without Selena. Jason finished his drink and turned to her, his eyes shimmering. "You're looking lovely tonight—as usual. Sherry?"

"Please." The look in his eyes unsettled her. Jason had already drunk more than his usual single glass of whisky.

Jason handed her a sherry, then poured himself another healthy glass. He sat down across from Carolyn, and they looked at one another, stiff and uncomfortable. "I trust you and Selena had a pleasant journey," Carolyn tried to begin a polite conversation.

Jason shrugged. "Well enough, I suppose."

"Did she make it in time for the dinner?"

"What dinner?"

"She had told me she was obligated to a dinner for a friend who was introducing a daughter-in-law into society."

"Oh, that." He looked vague and nonplussed. "Yes. She dragged me along with her. Damned boring affair." He took a long gulp of his drink.

"And was the daughter-in-law as awful as she feared?"

Jason took another drink. "No. Nice, quiet girl, as far as I could tell. Look, you needn't try to keep up a social chat. I'm not in the mood. There's no one here to witness your act, anyway."

"There are the servants."

"Who all know exactly how we feel about each other."

Carolyn's spine stiffened and color lit her cheeks. "I was under the impression that you wanted to keep up appearances. I thought that was why you dragged me back here."

Jason finished the rest of his drink and slammed the glass

down on the table. "Keeping up appearances does not mean that you need to pretend an interest in me or what I did in London, at least not when there's not another soul in the room."

"I see. At those times I'm supposed to keep my mouth meekly shut, is that it?"

"Exactly."

"I'll remember that. Believe me, I have no wish to carry on any kind of conversation with you, polite or not. And I have no need to ask what you did in London, since I'm sure I know exactly what it was!"

He made a harsh noise that was something between a grunt and a laugh. "Oh? Do you? Pray enlighten me."

Carolyn raised her eyebrows and pursed her lips. "I thought I wasn't supposed to carry on a conversation with you."

Jason glared and carried his glass to the sideboard to refill it. "I presume you're intimating that I went to visit my mistress."

So he did have a mistress, Carolyn thought, seething. He could chase Cynthia down and force her to return when she ran away with a man she loved, but it was perfectly all right for him to keep a permanent mistress stashed away in London. No doubt he was properly discreet about it!

"What's the matter, Cynthia? The green-eyed monster got you? I would have thought you'd welcome my taking my attentions elsewhere. And, after all, 'what's sauce for the goose,' and . . . so forth."

"I'm sure I have no interest in how you conduct your personal life."

"I'm sure."

Carolyn clamped her jaws tightly together. He was an

abominable man and a surly drunk, it seemed. She fumed in silence until the butler announced dinner. Jason rose and extended his arm to her, and she realized with a ripple of revulsion that she would have to touch his arm, now and for many nights to come. With Selena gone, it would be her he would escort to the dining table. Though her lace mitts and the layers of his jacket and shirt lay between their skins, it was too intimate a touch to suit her. She could feel the warmth of his flesh and had to stand too close to him. Her hand trembled slightly. She hoped he couldn't feel it. The last thing she wanted was for him to know she feared him.

They walked into the dining room, and he politely seated her at the table. Carolyn wondered how much he had had to drink. There was a looseness about him, and he had shown a display of emotions that she had rarely witnessed before, but his stride was even and straight. He made none of the overly careful yet clumsy movements of a drunkard in pulling out her chair. He continued to drink steadily throughout dinner. "Don't you think you've had enough?" Carolyn snapped as Jason lifted his third glass of wine.

His eyes narrowed. "Where and what and how much I drink are none of your concern," he growled.

Carolyn raised her eyebrows as if to emphasize how little concern she felt for him and turned her attention back to her plate. They didn't speak another word throughout dinner. Once Carolyn felt his gaze on her so strongly that she glanced up, and then quickly back down. She'd just as soon not face that fierce and accusing look. As soon as the dessert was laid before them, Carolyn quickly took a couple of bites, then rose. "I'll excuse myself now."

Jason shrugged slightly as Carolyn headed hastily for the stairs. When she reached the sanctuary of her bedroom she sank down onto a chair and struggled to catch her breath. Her fashionably tight stays made running almost impossible. She had to get out of these restraints. When Priscilla came, she undressed and put on one of Cynthia's long-sleeved nightgowns, slipping on a pale-pink satin dressing gown over it and securing it with a sash. Priscilla brushed out her long golden-red hair until it crackled with electricity and shone like burnished metal.

Tying her long hair back with a simple velvet ribbon, she went to Laurel's room for their bedtime visit. Bonnie fixed them cups of cocoa, as had become their custom, and they drank them seated at Laurel's child-sized table. Then Laurel sat on Carolyn's lap in the rocking chair, her face wreathed in a beatific smile as she listened to Carolyn sing. Laurel was insatiable when it came to songs, but finally the girl's head drooped, and Carolyn set her down in her bed, parting with a kiss good night. On her way back to her room, Carolyn paused at the top of the stairs, listening. The house was quiet and dark, lit in only a few rooms. The servants must have already finished in the kitchens and gone to bed. There was no sign or sound of Jason. Odd, how she had begun to actually think of herself as Lady Broughton, Jason Somerville's wife. It made her a trifle uneasy. She didn't *want* to think of Jason as her husband. He should remain a stranger who had married her sister, a man who was nothing to her.

In her room, Carolyn curled up in an easy chair to read before she went to bed. The overfurnished room was stifling, and after a few minutes she opened the door into the hall, hoping that would let in some air. It helped, but Carolyn still felt closed in, uneasy, and nervous. She laid her book aside and climbed into bed, but only stared at the ruffled blue-and-white canopy above her head. The minutes ticked away.

After a while she looked at the clock on the mantel. It was almost eleven-thirty. No doubt everyone else in the house was long since asleep, while she lay wide awake.

A splintering crash downstairs cut through the nighttime peace of the house, and Carolyn jumped out of bed. She ran out of her room, heedless of her bare feet and lack of robe, and bent over the railing at the top of the stairs, looking down. She could see nothing except a pale sliver of light in the hallway below. Her heart knocking against her ribs, she lifted the trailing nightgown and hurried down the stairs. Cautiously, she ventured through the darkened hallway, following the ribbon of light to its source, the study door left ajar, which she pushed open. She poked her head into the room.

Inside the heavily furnished study, Jason sat sprawled in a chair, his eyes closed. Directly across from him hung a large portrait of Cynthia. She was dressed in powder blue and held a bunch of nosegays in her hands as she smiled sweetly out at the observer. A huge stain covered part of her face and her shoulder and trickled down in slender streams to the bottom of the frame. A metal goblet lay on the floor in front of the picture, still wavering slightly. Jason had taken out his anger on the painting, hurling a half-filled cup of liquor at it.

At the sound of her sigh, Jason's eyes flew open. "What the hell are you doing here?" His voice was thick, and Carolyn knew he had finally reached a state of complete intoxication.

"Drinking certainly doesn't improve your temper—or your aim. You missed most of the face."

A ghost of a smile crossed his lips. "I'm lucky to have hit the damned thing at all." He sighed and closed his eyes. "If

I thought it'd blot you out of my mind, I'd have destroyed that portrait years ago."

"I'm surprised you haven't No, wait, I know the answer—appearances, again."

"Appearances. Of course." He ran a hand over his face wearily and blinked. "Oh, Lord, I'm drunk. I haven't been this way since—since the day I finally admitted to myself that you weren't shy, but simply cold as ice, at least to me." He focused on her. "Are you not that way with the others? Do your lovers know your heat? Is there any passion in you?"

A blush stained Carolyn's cheeks. "That's always a man's response, isn't it? That a woman is cold and passionless if she doesn't accept his brutish advances."

"No doubt that popinjay Bingham wasn't 'brutish,' " he remarked scornfully, his mouth twisting into a grim parody of a smile. "I'm sure he treated you with great respect—until he abandoned you."

"What a dog in the manger you are. You've told me in no uncertain terms that you don't desire me, yet you spew jealousy of a man who did."

"I am not jealous!" he roared, lurching out of his chair.

"Of course not," Carolyn retorted smoothly. "That's why you tossed a goblet at Cy—my portrait."

He frowned at her, swaying slightly. Carolyn felt no fear of him now, for she knew how to handle a drunk man. More than once she had found Kit out of control and had put him to bed. Though their moods might differ when they were drunk, by this point they were the same—hopelessly befuddled and in need of someone to tell them what to do. Carolyn walked over and grasped Jason's arm. He had taken off his jacket and only his thin shirt separated her fingers from his skin. A shock ran through her fingertips when she touched him; his skin was warm, yielding, yet with rock-hard muscle beneath. She tightened her fingers, irritated with her reaction. "Come along, I think it's time you went to bed."

She felt his muscles tense beneath her hand as if he was going to jerk his arm from her grasp, but then he relaxed. "All right. I can manage by myself, however."

"Uh-huh," Carolyn retorted disbelievingly. "I'll guide you to your room and leave you to your valet."

Carolyn took down a candle and lit it, then turned out the gaslight. He draped an arm around her shoulders, which surprised her. But she realized when they started forward that he needed that much support, and she curled an arm around his waist. He leaned heavily against her, and she could feel the sharp prominence of his hipbone, the ridged flesh of his ribcage, the muscular length of his thigh. Even worse, she knew that he could feel the soft curves of her own body, clad as it was in only a nightgown. All she could hope was that Jason was drunk enough that he wouldn't remember in the morning.

They climbed the stairs slowly. His arm weighed down her shoulders, and her arm ached from holding the candle up to light their way. She wondered why she hadn't simply left him in the study and rung for his valet to help him upstairs. Gratefully, she pushed open his bedroom door and they stumbled inside. She guided him to the nearest chair, where he plopped down and rested his elbows on his knees, covering his face with his hands. "I'll ring for your valet." Carolyn started toward the gold bellpull.

His hand lashed out and caught her nightgown. "No, don't. I'll manage by myself. I told Joseph to go to bed hours ago. No point in disturbing him."

He was now slumped in his chair, his eyes closed and

head lolling back, his forehead and upper lip dotted with perspiration. It would be all right to help him, she reasoned, since the alcohol had made him so powerless. Kneeling before him, she grasped one of his boots by the heel and toe and worked it off, dropping it onto the carpet, then similarly disposed of the other boot. She glanced up at him from her kneeling position and was startled to find his eyes open—he watched her with a look on his face she had never seen before, and had wondered if she'd ever see.

As if a cold mask of ice had melted, his features were slackened, softer. His lips were full, and his nostrils flared and tightened in hard, rapid breaths. And in his eyes, which were no longer icy at all, Carolyn recognized the curious blend of sharpness and softness that was male desire. Her breath caught in her throat, and for an instant she froze. Jason reached out and took her face between his lean, hard hands. He slid his fingers through her hair, holding her head immobile. She felt the control in his hands and realized that he wasn't as drunk as she'd thought. She swallowed convulsively.

"You seem quite competent at this." His voice was low and husky.

She couldn't say that she had done it for Kit many times. Carolyn wet her lips as she struggled to think of a reply. Quickly, she said, "I've done it for Father often enough."

His eyes were fixed on her moist lips. His thumbs began to caress her cheeks and jawline in a slow circular motion. Carolyn shivered, caught, unable to move out of his grasp or even to tear her gaze away from his. "You looked so beautiful today, spouting defiance at me. I wanted to rip open your dress and take you there in the garden. How can you still have the power to torment me? I thought to threaten you when I kissed you, and instead I entrapped myself." His hands slid down her throat and across her shoulders, gliding over her satin skin. Jason grasped her arms and, letting a barely audible groan come forth from deep in his throat, he pulled her up and buried his mouth in hers.

Greedily, hungrily, he kissed her, his tongue pressing against her lips, demanding admittance. When he fell back in the chair, he pulled her with him, so that his legs wrapped around her, pinning her against the hardening swell of his desire. Carolyn started at the feel of his insistent maleness and made a noise against his mouth. His legs relaxed and flexed in reply, moving her body fractionally against him. One arm swooped around her and his other hand dug into her hair, ripping away the ribbon that held her hair back. Her tresses tumbled around their faces like a glittering curtain.

Jason rained kisses across her lips and cheeks and buried his face in her hair. "I love your hair wild and loose like this. It looks like spun gold, yet there's that brilliant red glow to it. I want to wrap it around me, lose myself in it." He pinched her earlobe between his teeth, and as he did, his hot, rapid breath tickled her ear, sending shivers through her. He traced the shell of her ear with his tongue.

Carolyn gasped and twisted in his hold, but her movement only heightened Jason's arousal. Carolyn's fingers curled into his shirt. She knew she should be fighting him, should struggle to free herself from his embrace. He was drunk; she could easily win free. But the onslaught of sensations she felt within her had locked her in place—she was powerless in his grip. Kit was the only man who had ever kissed her, but his kisses had never been as passionate, as hungry, or as desperate as this.

Jason kissed her as though he would die if he didn't, and the response he evoked in her was new and almost frighteningly delightful. At his kiss a ripple of fire had run down the center of her body, melting her with yearning. Her nerves seemed to have risen to the surface of her skin, and she was intensely aware of every point where Jason's body touched hers. His mouth tasted of brandy, warm and drugging; his scent invaded her nostrils; she could see and hear and touch only him. There was no world, no time, nothing but this moment and the exquisite pleasure Jason awakened in her.

His legs loosened, releasing her, but only so that he could turn her in his arms until she sat in his lap, supported by his arm around her back. Carolyn let her head fall back, limp and acquiescent with pleasure, and Jason's lips feasted on her white throat. His tongue traced the vulnerable hollow of her throat. Carolyn was flooded with shimmering, eager pleasure. As his mouth explored her throat, his hand came up to cover her breast, fingers exploring. Her nipple tightened, pushing against his palm.

He cupped and caressed her breasts, teasing the nipples with his fingertips until they were hard and pebbly. She ached for him. Breasts, thighs, abdomen sought his touch. He made a strange, choked noise, and ran his hand down the plain of her stomach to the joinder of her legs. His fingers worked ecstatically between her legs: rhythmically, he pushed and rubbed, and as the gown dampened beneath his fingers, Jason closed his eyes as if in pain and a breathy laugh burst from his lips. "Cynthia, Cynthia. You never . . ."

He stopped his sweet movements and went to the buttons of her gown, which were small and difficult to unfasten. He cursed as he popped the last two from their moorings, and his hand delved inside the open gown to find her breast beneath. But with his words, she stiffened. Cynthia. Jason was Cynthia's husband, not hers. She had no right to be here. The words, the touch, the kisses, the groans of passion were not for her, but for Cynthia! The heat drained from her body, and she began to shake.

"No!" she exclaimed, pushing against his chest with her hands. "Jason, let me go! You're blind drunk and don't know what you're doing."

"Don't, don't." His face was slack with passion, softened into handsomeness, and now tinged with bewildered denial at her sudden rejection. He pushed her arms down with his and again cupped her breast in his palm. Carolyn knocked his arm aside with all her strength and scrambled from his lap. Jason grabbed her before she could reach the floor, pulling her back against him and chaining her with his arms.

"Jason, no," she pleaded, staring up at his dark face, torn between her intense desire and outrage. Looking at his sensual lips and hungry eyes, she felt herself softening inside, the treacherous warmth stealing back. He wanted her, and that want tugged at her viscerally, made her ache to fill his need. Sternly, Carolyn closed her eyes. She must not think that way, must not let him seduce her. He was a brute who had hurt Cynthia terribly; he had been rude and cruel to her. "You promised. You promised you would not. Please let me go."

"Damn you!" he bellowed. He shoved her from him, heedless as she tumbled to the floor, her wealth of hair spilling around her. He lurched to his feet and stumbled away to lean against the cool glass of the window. Stunned by the sudden, violent move, Carolyn lay still, watching him, the ache of falling beginning in her knees and side. He turned back to her, hatred flashing from his eyes. His voice grated as he spoke, "You must really enjoy that game. Does it make you feel powerful to lure me back into your clutches? To lead me on, make me desperate to have you—and then slap me down once again? It must have scalded your pride that I have paid you no attention the past few weeks. Well, now you can be proud again. Apparently, I will still play the fool for you."

His bitter words infused her with life, and Carolyn scrambled to her feet. "Lead you on! What a mass of conceit you are! I never led you on. I was trying to help you, to be kind. And you attacked me like the drunken, ravening beast you are!"

"Attacked you? Hardly. You certainly didn't protest until you knew you had me caught in your net." Carolyn drew herself up, enraged and wanting to deny his words, but she could find no answer. She *had* let him kiss and caress her without protest; she had lain willingly in his arms until his calling her "Cynthia" had finally awakened her. She looked aside. "What? No quick retort? No self-serving, sanctimonious reply?" His lip curled with contempt. "I wish to God I never had to see you again. Get out of this room. Out!"

Carolyn turned and ran, clutching the open neck of her gown, fleeing from his room as if the hounds of hell were after her.

Eight

Carolyn awoke the next morning with stiff limbs and an aching head. What a ghastly night! After that wretched scene with Jason, it had taken her hours to calm down enough to sleep, and then she had been plagued with dark, disturbing dreams. After washing her face, she rang for her morning tea and toast, then sat down to brush her hair.

Priscilla bustled in moments later, carrying a tray, which she set down on the vanity table in front of Carolyn. "Good morning, milady, how are you this morning?"

"Fine, thank you," Carolyn lied automatically. "And you?"

"Same as ever, I guess," Priscilla replied cheerfully. She took the hairbrush from the vanity and began brushing out Carolyn's tangled hair. Carolyn listlessly poured a cup of tea and watched Priscilla's movements in the mirror. "You've got such lovely hair, milady," the girl sighed. "It's like copper and gold all mixed. Oh, I nearly forgot—his lordship wants you to join him in his study as soon as you are dressed."

A blush rose up Carolyn's throat. That was all she needed—to have to face Broughton this morning. Where did he find the gall to summon her to his study . . . as if nothing had happened? She was so embarrassed she wouldn't be able to look him in the eyes—and he was far more guilty than she, despite his foul accusations, for it had been Jason who'd advanced toward her, who had kissed her and run his hands over her body.

Yet that was what was so humiliating: She despised Jason, had fought with him at every turn. Yet she longed for his touch as she never had with Kit, whom she'd loved. She had melted beneath his touch, and if he had not called her by her sister's name, there was no telling what she might have let him do. Perhaps her father was right in his prudish lectures; maybe she was weak and destined for a life of sin. Maybe she was filled with dark desires and corrupt longings that only required a satanic lover to be brought to the surface.

Carolyn sighed and rubbed her temples. Well, whatever the reason, she'd make sure it wouldn't happen again. She could control her desires; she wouldn't allow herself to be caught in such a situation again. This morning she would face him—she had no other choice, really—and she would set the pattern for the future.

But remembering the things Jason had said last night, she doubted she'd even need to control herself. There had been a hard finality in his words when he told her to leave, and Carolyn suspected he would assiduously avoid a repetition of what had happened last evening. It didn't make sense, then, that he wished to see her this morning . . . unless he had decided to live separately from her, as he had said he would do later when the gossip had died down. She could not stop her fearful thoughts as she absently had some toast and tea.

Dressed in a modest, lacy day dress, Carolyn went down the stairs to Jason's study. At the sight of the study door, her heart pounded furiously. She rapped lightly on the wood and waited for his approval before she stepped inside. Jason was seated behind his desk, scowling down at a ledger spread before him. Not looking at her, he growled, "Cynthia."

"Hello, Jason." She wondered if her voice sounded as shaky to him as it did to her. Standing before him, she felt like a criminal in the dock. Belatedly, Jason remembered his manners and rose.

"Please sit down."

"Thank you." She sank into a chair across the desk from him, and he resumed his seat. How polite and formal they were—it seemed absurd when she remembered his impassioned desire last night. Quickly she looked away—she hoped he hadn't seen her thoughts written on her face.

Jason sighed and ran his hand through his hair, resting his elbows on the desk. "I asked you to come here for two reasons. The first is that I wish to apologize for last night."

That was the last thing she had expected him to say. She noticed that the lines around his mouth and eyes were deep today, and his skin had a grayish tint. "The morning after," she thought to herself glumly, "is a little late for an apology."

"You were right," Jason continued stiffly. "I promised not to touch you, and I broke my vow. I want to assure you that it won't happen again. It's not my custom to drink immoderately, and in the future I'll make sure I don't do so, at least not when I am here."

"Fine—" she again kept her thoughts to herself—"save your drinking *and* your passion for your mistress in London. . . ." Aloud, she replied, "I accept your apology. I am reluctant to believe in your promise again, but then I haven't much choice, have I?"

She knew she had struck a nerve. "I am no ravager of unwilling women, as you should well know. God knows how many times you taunted and tormented me, then withheld your favors. I never once forced you, though it would have been within my rights as your husband. I have no taste for rape, madam."

Suddenly her blow seemed petty and Jason wished she could take it back. She couldn't imagine Cynthia actually teasing, then rejecting Jason, as he claimed. After all, Jason had accused her of leading him on last night. Apparently he considered it leading him on if a woman didn't put up a struggle.

"What—what was the other reason you summoned me here? You said there were two."

Jason drew a deep breath, returning to his usual cool demeanor. "I plan to have a hunting weekend."

Carolyn's heart leaped with excitement. How she loved the hunt—the crisp air rushing past her face, the barking of the hounds, the laughter and conviviality, and the hearty hunt breakfast afterward. But just as she almost exclaimed with joy, she caught herself in time. At all the hunts Cynthia had attended, she stayed at the back on a poor horse—the girl hated the wildness, the violence, the energy of the hunt. Carolyn put on a face of disdain. "I see. What does that have to do with me? You know I hate to hunt."

"Yes, but you are my wife, and you will perform your other wifely duties." Other than sharing his bed, Carolyn thought—and ignored the half of her that liked the thought. . . . "I want you to write and send the invitations. You can get Millicent Nelson to help you. Poor girl, she'd probably welcome the diversion."

"She'll welcome the chance to be in the same house with you," Carolyn said dryly.

Jason raised his eyebrows. "I didn't realize you'd noticed."

"I would have to be blind not to. She's as open and naive in her adoration as a puppy."

"You can't be jealous of Millicent Nelson, surely." Jason looked quite appalled, and Carolyn couldn't entirely suppress the giggle that rose in her throat. Jason cast her an odd look, and his lips twitched with the beginnings of a smile, but he quickly dispelled all signs of levity. "I was thinking of having it the last weekend in October, so the invitations will need to be posted quickly." He shuffled through the papers on his desk and finally withdrew a long sheet of notepaper. "Here is the list of guests."

Carolyn neatly folded it into a quarter its size and slid it into her skirt pocket obediently. His quick dismissal of any humor or warmth between them irritated her. He looked upon her as a servant who must be kept strictly at a distance lest she presume too much.

"Is that all? May I go now?" She stood up, and he politely rose. "Yes, if you haven't any questions."

"No. I shall see to the invitations immediately."

After she left Jason's study, Carolyn ordered the pony cart brought round and went to call on Millicent Nelson, deciding that the sooner she got the task over with, the better. If it had been left up to her, she wouldn't have enlisted Millicent's aid at all. Carolyn enjoyed parties and was always eager to prepare for them. Even the dull task of writing and addressing invitations would be a relief from the monotony of her days at Broughton Court. However, Jason had implied that Cynthia did not like such pursuits. Secretly she hoped Millicent would refuse, but she knew there wasn't much chance of that. As Jason had said, the vicar's sister had little in the way of pleasant diversions.

Millicent looked taken aback to find Carolyn on her doorstep, but as Carolyn had expected she agreed readily enough to the proposition and promised to be at Broughton Court the following afternoon. She sped home and rushed to her room, found a pad of foolscap and a pen, and sat down to practice Cynthia's handwriting. She knew Cynthia's handwriting had been similar to hers, but it had been years since she'd seen her sister's script, and though their writing had been similar, there were many nuances that could give her away. She dug out every scrap of paper she could find that Cynthia had scribbled on and studied it, then carefully copied the lines over and over until a hand much like Cynthia's emerged. It was doubtful that anyone receiving the invitations would be able to recognize Cynthia's writing, but it was best to be careful. Late that afternoon, Carolyn tried out her forgery on a few ivory parchment sheets and penned several acceptable invitations. When she had finished for the day, she gathered up all her practice sheets and failures and carefully tore them up. She really wanted to burn them, but there was no fire burning in the fireplace, for it was a pleasant day, so she laboriously burned them piece by piece over a candle and dropped the ashes in the fireplace. Then she hurried off to see Laurel, whom she had neglected that day.

Jason sent her word that he would not be there for supper that evening, so to save bother Carolyn had a tray brought to her room and ate supper there. At ten o'clock, she discarded her book and, unable to keep her eyes open, she prepared for bed. Suddenly, she felt a wrenching contraction in her stomach. She doubled over, and Priscilla dropped the dress she was hanging up and rushed to her. "Milady, what's the matter?"

Carolyn shook her head and pressed her hands more tightly around her waist. "I don't know. I feel—so sick." Priscilla quickly brought a basin and held her as Carolyn was wracked with spasms. Again and again she retched helplessly, feeling as if her insides were being torn from her, but slowly the pain lessened and the spasms stopped, leaving her with an ache in her stomach and bowels.

Priscilla wiped her face with a cool, damp cloth and helped her to bed. "There now, it's over. You'll feel better soon. My poor beautiful lady." Soothingly Priscilla talked to Carolyn as she sponged her face.

"Thank you, Priscilla," Carolyn told her weakly.

"I suspect it was that dinner. Probably Cook put something too old in it. I'll give her a right ear-ringing when I go down . . . How many times have I told her to always make sure . . ."

Carolyn heard no more of the maid's outpouring, for she slipped quietly into sleep.

A pounding headache and a foul taste in her mouth were all that Carolyn was aware of the next morning. As she slowly sat up, a wave of dizziness swept her, and she closed her eyes, fighting nausea. She lay back down. "Silly," she thought—"no need to ring for Priscilla, anyway." She slipped back into a shallow, troubled half-sleep. An hour later she awoke when Priscilla tiptoed into the room. The girl helped her to sit up, and though she forced herself to sip some of the sweet tea Priscilla had brought, the toast repulsed her. Priscilla straightened the bedclothes while she described the rousing argument she had had with the cook the evening before. "'Course, Cook says it wasn't her doing, that everything on that tray was fresh, but I told her I knew better. I said she'd better watch it, or she'd wind up poisoning you and his lordship. I can tell you, she didn't like it one bit. She said she never sends up a dish she hasn't tasted first, and that none of them were spoiled."

"No, they didn't taste spoiled," Carolyn agreed. "Perhaps I caught some illness or other. It doesn't matter. I'll be over it soon."

"I'm sorry. Is my chatter bothering you? My mum always did say I ran on about things. I'll just leave and let you sleep. You'll ring if you need something, won't you?"

"Yes, of course." She had Priscilla send a message to Millicent Nelson, letting her know that she was too ill to work on the invitations today, then she dozed on and off throughout the day. Around three o'clock, Priscilla woke her to say that Millicent had come despite the message, bringing a pot of custard with her. "She says it works wonders with sick people, milady. And she said if you'd give her the envelopes and the list, she'll be glad to get started on the addresses this afternoon, anyway."

Carolyn sighed and pointed to the little mahogany secretary in the corner of the room. "The list and all the stationery are in there. Take her whatever else she wants." She looked down glumly at the bowl of yellow custard Priscilla had set on the table beside her bed.

"You ought to eat, milady. It will make you feel better."

"I suppose you're right. Though I wouldn't put it past Millicent to poison me."

"What?" Priscilla stared at her with great, rounded eyes.

Carolyn managed a faint smile. "Merely a jest, Priscilla."

"Oh. I see. You mean because of her mooning about after the master all the time."

"Yes. It was a feeble joke, but I'm not up to my best today." Carolyn spooned up the pale custard and, steadying her lurching stomach, she ate almost a third of the bowl. "Please give Millicent my thanks for the custard," she told Priscilla as the girl headed for the door. "Be sure to tell her I ate some of it."

An hour later Bonnie bustled in the room. "What's this I hear about you being sick?"

"I'm afraid it's true. But I'm feeling better now."

"And you didn't even call me!" Bonnie scolded, ignoring her words. "Now, who do you think could take care of you better than your old nurse?"

"No one, of course." Carolyn managed a smile. "But I really didn't need much care. Priscilla's been lurking around to give me help if I needed it."

Bonnie sniffed her opinion of Carolyn's ladies' maid. "No more sense than a pea goose. She's never tended to a sick one."

"I'm feeling better, really. All I need is a little sleep. And you need to look after Laurel."

"One of the maids can do that well enough. I'm staying with you."

Carolyn sighed but gave up trying to dissuade her. It wouldn't hurt, after all, and if it would make Bonnie feel better. . . . So Bonnie stayed and tended her, bringing Carolyn a gruel of her own making for supper. Carolyn made a face at it, but ate as much as she could. However, when Bonnie offered to sit up beside her bed through the night, Carolyn firmly pointed out that there was no need. The nurse finally agreed to sleep in her own bedroom if Carolyn let her tie an extension to the bell cord so that she could ring for a servant from her bed if she awoke and needed anything.

Carolyn spent a peaceful night and awoke the next morning feeling much better, though still a trifle weak. She drank the tea and ate the toast Priscilla had brought and got out of bed to dress. "Are you sure, milady?" Priscilla asked anxiously.

"My goodness!" Carolyn exclaimed. "You'd think I was an invalid, the way everyone treats me. I'm feeling much improved, and I must work on those invitations. Lord Broughton wants them posted immediately."

She spent most of the morning writing invitations, pausing only for a brief, bland lunch of Millicent Nelson's custard and toast. By the time Millicent arrived that afternoon, Carolyn's headache was back in full force, and now and then the letters swam before her eyes. Millicent took one look at her face and pronounced, "Well, I see you really were sick yesterday."

Carolyn stared at her. "Did you think I wasn't?"

Millicent shrugged as she took off her gloves and set them down on the table beside her reticule. "There have been other times when you have been conveniently ill."

What a shrew, Carolyn thought irritably. Her attitude and Carolyn's subsequent irritation weren't helping her headache one bit. She waved the other woman to a seat, saying sharply, "Really, Miss Nelson, if you don't wish to help with the invitations, why didn't you say so? I can do them myself."

Millicent's mouth twisted slightly and she pulled out a

chair at the game table on which Carolyn had chosen to work. "Trying to muddy the water? You know I don't mind addressing the envelopes."

"Particularly since they're for Jason?" Carolyn said, knowing it was beyond the bounds of politeness, but she felt too bad to care.

"I'm always happy to help his lordship," Millicent returned smoothly. "It's the least I can do after all he's done for Thomas."

Carolyn restrained herself and turned back to her work. It took all of her concentration to conform to her sister's writing, and Millicent's presence made it even harder. With every letter, she worried that she wrote too formal a salutation. Even though she suspected the guests were largely Jason's friends, and not Cynthia's, there could be one or two whom Cynthia knew intimately enough to address by their first name. But she had no idea which ones. She vacillated over the one to Hugh St. John. It seemed very odd not to call him by his first name, so she took a chance on calling him "Cousin Hugh," praying that Cynthia had addressed him that way sometimes. Her head continued its dull throbbing, and she wished she could go back to bed.

Millicent worked with quick efficiency. She had polished off all the envelopes the afternoon before, and now she took up writing the invitations themselves. Carolyn still burned over their sharp words, but was too relieved to be done with the invitations to care. The way she felt, she would never have been able to get them all done.

They paused for tea when Barlow carried in the tray at four o'clock. Carolyn served, fixing a polite smile on her face, and offered her guest her choice from the various pastries and cakes. Nothing on the tray held much appeal for Carolyn, but she nibbled delicately on a raisin muffin. "How is your brother?" she asked to make polite conversation.

"Quite well, thank you, and hard at work on this Sunday's sermon. He wants so badly to do well here. He's very grateful to Lord Broughton."

Carolyn barely stopped herself from inquiring how long Thomas had been vicar. Her mind was far too fuzzy; it would be easy to make a drastic slip. She wet her lips. "I—I'm sure my husband is pleased with his work."

"I hope so." Millicent set her lips in prim disapproval. "Thomas was most distraught when you . . . um, left. He feared that he had not done his duty, that he should have known the, uh, state you were in. He thought his lordship might take him to task for not working to prevent what happened."

"I can't see why Jason should blame your brother for anything I did."

"Because he had been a particular friend of yours, as well as your spiritual shepherd. Lord Broughton could easily have assumed that you would confide in Thomas and that Thomas didn't inform him."

"I would think one's confidences to her 'spiritual shepherd' would be sacrosanct. A priest's role is not to spy on me and report his findings to a woman's husband." Two red spots of anger flamed on Carolyn's cheeks. "That may be Jason Somerville's way of doing things, but I hate to think a vicar would stoop to such behavior."

Millicent's resentment, never far below the surface, sprang up. "Jason Somerville is always the gentleman. He would never ask Thomas to spy on his wife."

"Then why would your brother have anything to fear?"

"Because he takes far too much upon himself; he assumes the guilt of those around him. He felt responsible for you because he thought he had been your friend and an example to you. Whereas you, of course, felt no guilt at all."

Carolyn set her cup and saucer down on the table, her hands trembling with fury and weakness. "Who are you to judge me? You have no idea what I thought or felt."

"I know what you did!" Millicent shot back, her face flushed, eyes burning. Her feelings had been restrained too long, and now they came forth in a gush of rage. "Do you honestly think anyone is fooled by the story Jason put out? You would never have gone to Italy with his mother. Oh, yes, Lady Selena covered for you admirably, cloaking you with her friendship, sanctioning your lies with her reputation. But everyone knows the truth. They only pretend to believe in order to save Jason's face. No one wants to hurt him."

"I doubt that. I imagine there are quite a few people who'd love to see his pride punctured."

"Petty, lying cowards like you, perhaps!" Millicent reached up to wipe away the fierce tears that had flooded her eyes. "You've done everything you could to ruin him. You haven't been a wife to him, a helpmate. You haven't even been a friend. He's a fine, decent man who's had all the laughter and love and happiness drained out of him. You've broken his heart, dishonored his name, and the only heir you could give him was a mindless girl!"

Carolyn's hand lashed out and cracked against the other woman's cheek. "You can belittle me all you want. I know you're a jealous, spiteful witch, and I can fight you back. But don't you ever, *ever* denigrate my daughter. If Jason feels cheated of an heir, it's his own self-centered pride at fault.

He has a wonderful, loving child, and it wouldn't be a humiliation to any man with more soul and less devotion to his family name!"

Millicent brought one hand to her burning cheek, her eyes wide with astonishment. "How—how dare you—"

"I dare anything! Don't you know that? If I can brave Jason Somerville's wrath, yours is not much to face. Now, I think it's time for you to leave, don't you?"

The woman grabbed her purse and gloves, eyes glaring out her hatred. "Thomas tells me you're to be pitied for your sinful nature, but I'm afraid I'm not Christian enough to do that. You're wicked. Wicked. And I despise you. I only hope you don't destroy Jason completely."

Millicent fled the room. Carolyn whirled and grabbed a book from a nearby end table and hurled it across the room—it hit the wall and came crashing down, knocking a glass figurine off a shelf. Her head pounded furiously, and she raised her hands to her temples, pressing against them. Her stomach was empty and sick. She sank onto the sofa, suddenly incredibly tired. Today had been too much for her. Such undiluted hate, even from that foolish girl, was too much to bear. She tugged the gold rope bellpull and, when Barlow appeared, asked him to send Priscilla to her. With her maid's arm around her waist, she climbed the stairs to her bedroom, still weeping quietly. Priscilla loosened her clothing and slipped the shoes from her feet, then left her in the room with the curtains pulled. The day's events swirling about in her mind, Carolyn fell into sleep.

She felt even worse the next day. Right after Priscilla brought her morning tea, she began to vomit, and the seizures left her sore and weak as a kitten.

Days passed, and she showed no improvement. Her head ached almost constantly, and she had never known such violent stomach pains, which kept her dizzy and nauseated. Carolyn couldn't understand it. All her life she had been the healthiest of women. Even during her pregnancy she had been as strong as a peasant.

She tried to fight the treacherous nausea and weakness by forcing herself to get up, to dress, to pick at the food Priscilla and Bonnie brought her. But she could keep very little down. She lost weight, and her eyes were huge and shadowed in her thin face. At night she cried, afraid and alone, for deep inside she knew she was desperately ill. Still she denied it, refusing to admit her fears.

Jason was out of the house much of the time. He sent word to her that he would not be home for lunch or dinner, taking his noon meals in the fields or the homes of his farmers and often spending dinner and most of the evening in the tavern in Hokely. Curiously, Carolyn wished Jason were with her; her fear and weakness cried out for his strength. But she had enough pride left not to beg him for his company. She must not expose herself to him in that powerless state.

I'm dying, she thought, I'm dying. And she knew Jason would not mourn his wife.

By the fourth day, she no longer tried to combat the demon by dressing and pretending to live her normal life. Instead, she stayed in bed, dozing and dreaming sick dreams. When she heard Carolyn was confined to her bed, Bonnie came to her, insisting that only she could adequately nurse her lady. Carolyn was glad for Bonnie's warm and familiar face, and it was a comfort to know it was all right if in her weakened state, she made a slip that would reveal to strangers who she was. Bonnie fixed her tea and weak cocoa over a spirit lamp in the room and bullied her into drinking them. Mealtimes brought a tray of food from the kitchen with every sort of treat that Cook could think of to tempt her appetite. Try as she might, she could keep nothing down. Carolyn had the awful, helpless feeling that she was slipping away from herself but didn't know how to stop it. Molten tears rolled from her eyes, but she hadn't the strength to sob.

Bonnie set up a cot in Carolyn's room and slept there at night. She would sit in a comfortable chair pulled close to the bed, knitting or sewing until Carolyn nodded off, then she would go to her narrow bed and sleep. One evening as she sat watching Carolyn and blinking her eyes, fighting off sleep, there was a soft tap on the door.

Carolyn turned her head slowly and looked over. Jason stood framed in the doorway. His eyes opened wide with amazement and panic when he saw Carolyn. "Good God!" He rushed to the side of her bed. "What on earth has happened to you?"

"I—haven't been feeling well." Carolyn looked up at him looming over her, overwhelming in his strength and health. "Didn't the servants tell you?"

"Yes, of course, they said you were feeling under the weather the past few days, but I never dreamed you were so ill! You have spells of not feeling well often, so I assumed it was another one of those—a migraine or faintness."

Carolyn closed her eyes wearily. So his wife's spells of illness didn't bother him enough to come check on her. He had probably been relieved when she didn't leave her room, because it made it easy to avoid her.

"Cynthia, why didn't you tell me? Why didn't you send word by one of the servants?"

"Why didn't you visit me?" she retorted, but her breathy voice made the words come out more pitiful than argumentative.

Silent, he picked up one of her pale hands lying on the coverlet, and then almost tenderly he laid it back down on the bed and reached over to brush a wisp of hair back from her face. "You're so thin." He didn't add that she looked like a corpse, but she knew it was what he was thinking. She'd seen herself in the mirror that afternoon.

Jason swung toward Bonnie, barking out, "Find Broaddus and tell him to put the best-riding stableboy on a horse and ride to Dr. Heywood's. No, wait. Never mind. You stay here with my wife. I'll ride to the doctor's myself. No lad could get there as quickly as I can." He turned back to Carolyn, his voice softening. "I'll be back with the doctor as soon as I can."

She nodded, embarrassed at the hot tears that rose in her eyes at his concern. A strange expression crossed Jason's face, and he reached out to catch one of the teardrops as it rolled from her eye. He swallowed and turned away, striding to the door.

It was over two hours before Jason returned with the doctor. "I'm sorry to take so long," he told Carolyn, coming to stand beside her, one hand reaching out to stroke her forehead. "He was away on business, and I had to track him down."

Carolyn smiled faintly. "He does have other patients, you know."

Jason made a disgruntled noise. The doctor sidled up to the bed. Jason stepped back to allow him room to examine her, but he did not move far away and his sharp green eyes followed the doctor's every movement. "Well, well, Lady Broughton. You don't seem to be feeling very well at the moment."

That was the understatement of the century, Carolyn thought. What was the doctor's name, which she would of course know. What had Jason said? Heyward? Heywood. Yes, that was it. "Hello, Dr. Heywood."

"Now tell me what kind of problems you've been having," he prompted, opening his bag.

Carolyn described her symptoms, with Bonnie throwing in a comment now and then. All the while she studied the doctor. He was a middle-aged man with a small pot belly. The smell of pipe smoke clung to him. He seemed good-natured enough, but rather hesitant and cautious, often casting a glance over at Jason before he asked her a question. He listened to her heart and lungs, had her cough, looked in her eyes and ears and nose, and pushed a little at her stomach and abdomen. "Ah, any reason to believe you might be, uh, in the family way?" he asked delicately.

"No!" Carolyn responded immediately. She saw Jason frown behind the doctor. All she needed was for Jason to think she was pregnant with her lover's child. "This is nothing, nothing like when I—the other time."

"Well, it seems to me to be a particularly debilitating inflammation of the stomach. I will leave you a draught that will make you feel better. Try to drink as much tea and other fluids as you can." He pulled a vial from his bag and turned to Bonnie, giving her instructions on preparing the medicine.

Jason left with the doctor. Bonnie stirred a spoonful of the medicine into a glass of water, which turned the water cloudy. Carolyn forced herself to drink the entire glass of murky liquid. It was bitter, but at least it stayed down. Her stomach stayed calm, and she relaxed a little. Her headache began to ease, and soon she felt drowsy. Jason returned. "Have you given her the medicine?" Bonnie nodded. He glanced at the cot. "Have you been sleeping here?"

"Yes, I was afraid milady wouldn't have the strength to pull the cord, or she might be unconscious."

"I'm sure you've tired yourself. Why don't you go back to your room and get some sleep? I'll stay here tonight."

Bonnie hesitated, clearly not wanting to leave, but not brave enough to defy his orders. Carolyn, despite her exhaustion, did not want to be alone with Jason. "No, please! Please, I'd like for Bonnie to stay."

Jason turned to her, his face settling into its usual cold mask. "Of course, my dear, if that's what you wish. I'll drop in tomorrow morning to see how you're doing."

After he left, Bonnie bustled over to pull the covers higher around Carolyn's shoulders. "Thank the good Lord you spoke up, miss. I wouldn't trust you with him, and that's the truth."

Carolyn wanted to cry again, but she suppressed the tears. Almost immediately she fell asleep, dropping into unconsciousness, as if she'd fallen into a black hole.

The doctor came to visit her every day. After a couple of days he gave Bonnie a different vial of medicine, this one a clear red. It, too, made her drowsy and eased the pain, but her condition did not improve. She still was unable to eat, still racked with seizures of nausea, still gripped by abdominal pain. She slept more now, and when she was awake, she felt groggy.

Jason visited her, usually several times a day. He would

stand by her bed and watch her for a while, then pace up and down the room. Oddly enough the repetitious movements soothed her, and she would watch him march back and forth ceaselessly. After the doctor's fourth visit, he burst out, "I don't think that damn fool has any idea what's wrong with you. There hasn't been any improvement, none at all! Do you feel any better?"

Carolyn was too listless to answer and merely shook her head.

"I didn't think so." He resumed his pacing. "Damn it!" He exploded, crashing one fist into the other palm. "I won't let you die!" He strode to her bedside and grasped her arms, scowling down at her. "Do you understand me? You will not die. I'm going to London to fetch a better doctor for you. You have to hang on until I get back. Will you promise me that?" Carolyn nodded sleepily and his fingers dug into her wasted flesh. He muttered almost to himself, "You can't slip away from me like that. I won't let you."

Then he released her and charged out of the room. Carolyn closed her eyes, feeling strangely warmed.

It was three days before he returned. The man who accompanied him had none of the timidity of Dr. Heywood. He spoke to Jason as to an equal. He was large and well-dressed, and his voice and manner carried a touch of authority, as he conducted the business of Carolyn's diagnosis. "Good day, Lady Broughton. I'm Dr. Wilkins. Do you remember me?"

Carolyn shook her head. "I—I don't think so."

"I saw you once in London about six or seven years ago. I believe you were pregnant at the time."

"Oh, yes."

He repeated the same tests of eyes and nose and ears that

Dr. Heywood had, then pushed with his fingers against her stomach so hard that Carolyn cried out in pain. "Have you noticed any swelling in your stomach area, Lady Broughton?"

Carolyn shook her head. "No. I've done nothing but shrink."

A smile quirked his straight mouth. "I admire your spirit, madam." Suddenly his brows drew together, and he leaned forward, touching a dark spot on her arm. "How long have you had this?"

"A day or two."

"Any other places like that?"

"I'm not sure."

He examined her other arm, her throat, and face, pausing to study another spot. His frown deepened. He picked up her hands and examined her fingernails. "If you don't mind, I'd like a cutting from one of your fingernails or a piece of hair."

"What? Well, yes, if you want.

Jason came forward quickly. "Why do you need that? Do you know what's the matter with her?"

"I hate to say until I've made the proper tests."

"Damn it, man, I won't hold you to it if the tests disprove your theory. What do you suspect?"

Dr. Wilkins sighed. "Frankly, it looks to me like chronic arsenic poisoning."

Nine

The room fell silent. The doctor's words penetrated Carolyn's hazy brain, and she began to struggle to sit up. "What? What did you say?"

"I'm not surprised your country doctor didn't recognize it," Wilkins told Jason. "But I've seen it more than once in fashionable ladies. They use it for their skin, you know. Gets rid of spots, gives it a lovely translucent quality. They take a little bit every day, not enough to kill them, of course, but sometimes they take too much. It might not kill them immediately—though I've seen that happen, too—but it's enough to make them thoroughly ill. Eventually, of course, taking too much over a period of time is deadly."

Outraged, Jason swung on Carolyn. "I told you to stop that! I even took the bottle away and locked it up in my study. Have you no sense? Is your vanity that huge?"

"But I—I didn't—" Carolyn protested faintly, too stunned and groggy to formulate her thoughts. "I never took it. I didn't."

"There's no point in lying about it, Cynthia. Did you steal it from my desk?"

"No, please."

"It's not very difficult to obtain, Lord Broughton," the

doctor spoke in a cool, clinical tone. "It can be found in almost any gardener's shed. Used to poison rats, you know."

"Bonnie, search the room," Jason ordered. "Find her supply, wherever it is, and give it to me."

"My lord, if you could have someone take me to the local chemist's . . . I need to make this test before I can give you a positive diagnosis."

"Yes, of course." In silence the doctor clipped a small lock of Carolyn's hair, then Jason escorted him out of the room.

Carolyn closed her eyes weakly, listening to the rustle of Bonnie's search. It couldn't be true. Surely the fancy London physician was wrong. She knew of women taking arsenic in small amounts for their skin, but she had never done it. Arsenic poisoning. She shivered, suddenly terrified. Jason might believe she'd done it herself, but she knew she hadn't. Which meant . . . someone had been putting it in her food or drink. Someone was trying to kill her!

When Jason returned, Bonnie had found no arsenic, so Jason himself ransacked the room, opening drawers and pulling out all their contents, sifting through linens and underclothes, even searching her shoes and all the hatboxes. He looked under all the furniture and behind the pieces that backed up to the wall. Finally even he had to admit defeat. "Where did you hide it, Cynthia? Please. It would be easier to tell me."

"I didn't. I didn't hide it." Carolyn's head ached abominably, and tears began to flow again from her eyes. "I didn't take any."

"Do you honestly expect me to believe that? Do you think Cook is poisoning you?"

"Not necessarily Cook. Anyone—anyone could put it in my food."

"For God's sake, Cynthia, who in this house would want to murder you?"

Carolyn opened her eyes and looked at him. "Only one person that I can think of."

"Me?" he growled. "Now you're accusing me of trying to kill you?" He laughed harshly. "Oh, that's rich. That's really rich. Rather than confess to your own stupid pandering to your vanity, you're going to accuse me of plotting to murder you."

"Please, leave me alone," Carolyn whispered, closing her eyes in weariness and pain.

"Gladly, my dear wife. Gladly." There was the thud of his boots across the floor, and the door slammed to behind him.

The doctor called the next morning to confirm his original suspicions. There had been traces of arsenic in her hair sample. He gave Carolyn a stern lecture on the dangers of using arsenic as a beauty aid and wrung an exasperated promise from her not to do it again. Jason came soon after the doctor left to inform Carolyn that if she did not stop the idiotic practice, he would set a servant to spy on her constantly to keep her from doing it.

"I swear to you that I will not voluntarily take arsenic," Carolyn assured him in sarcastic tones. He glared at her and stamped out of the room.

"If anybody tried to poison you, Miss Caro, it was him," Bonnie pronounced, thrusting out her chin.

"If? Don't you believe me, either?"

"I believe you," Bonnie replied flatly. "Whatever else you did, Miss Caro, you aren't a liar."

Thank you for faint praise, Carolyn thought. Bonnie had stopped giving her Dr. Heywood's medicine as soon as the London doctor announced his suspicions. She was more alert this morning, and the pain had receded a little in her head and stomach. Carolyn had refused to eat or drink anything, until Bonnie plaintively asked if she didn't trust her old nurse. After that Carolyn had given in and drunk the tea Bonnie made over the spirit lamp. Later, Bonnie declared that she would go downstairs and prepare Carolyn's food herself, never letting her eyes off of it.

Gradually, as the days passed, Carolyn began to feel better. Reasoning that whoever had tried to poison her would stop now that the poisoning had been discovered, she cautiously began to eat food directly from the kitchen again. Before long, the headaches and stomach pains were gone, but she knew it would take some time for her to gain back her strength, for she had lost so much weight.

Her mind regained its strength long before her body, and she spent many days lying in bed, thinking. She alone was positive that she hadn't taken the arsenic herself. She could sense the suspicion of the servants, and even Bonnie seemed unsure. Jason made it clear that he believed she had brought it upon herself. However, she knew she hadn't, so it followed that someone was trying to poison her and, gradually, kill her. The length of her illness would make it seem more like a stomach ailment than a quick poisoning. But it wasn't even she they wanted—someone was trying to kill Cynthia.

Carolyn sighed at the confusion of it all. Since Carolyn herself had been banished from her family, any money from Sir Neville's will would go to Cynthia—or maybe it wouldn't, now that Cynthia had disappointed her father—but that gave no reason for an attempt on her life. Who else but Jason—who hated Cynthia so—would have any reason to harm Cynthia?

Millicent Nelson had made her dislike of Cynthia clear, and she could have doctored the custard she brought Carolyn. But there was one fact that made it impossible for the culprit to be Millicent. Whoever had done it lived at Broughton Court, for Carolyn had been given a little poison in her food every day. That meant it was either Jason or the servants. It seemed preposterous that any of the servants would want to kill her.

Jason. No matter how hard she viewed it, all the evidence pointed to Jason. He had the means; he had said he'd taken Cynthia's arsenic away and locked it in his desk. He had been home during her illness. Feigning concern over what his wife was eating or drinking, he could have slipped a few tiny grains in her meal. And he had a strong motive: He despised her and would be happy to have her out of his life. Jason had to be the one who wanted her dead.

Yet she refused to let herself believe it. Why didn't she go to the authorities and tell them? She hadn't enough proof to report this crazy attempted murder. It was only her word against Jason's that she hadn't taken the arsenic freely; Jason was a nobleman, well-respected, the most influential man in the county, and she was an adulteress. It would be Jason's word they'd take. Besides, she still refused to let herself believe Jason was responsible. The crime didn't seem like him. He was blunt to the point of rudeness, direct, straightforward; it seemed more likely that he would confront her with his rage than use this sneaking, cowardly murder plot. She couldn't imagine Jason engaging in such secretive maneuvers.

There was so much Carolyn didn't know about the seven

blank years in Cynthia's past that it was possible it was someone else. Perhaps during that time she had acquired an enemy whom Carolyn knew nothing about. When she was stronger, she could look through Cynthia's possessions for letters she had written or received, diaries, notes—surely there must be something Cynthia had left behind that could give her a clue to the unknown years. Until she knew, she must not voice her suspicions. She couldn't afford to damage Jason's reputation without solid proof.

Carolyn discussed her thoughts with no one. She concentrated on getting well, taking long naps and eating every bite of her food. She was still very weak, but within two days she insisted on getting out of bed and walking to her armchair to sit for an hour. Not long after that, she began making excursions up and down the hall outside her room. It was a week before she managed to walk down the stairs, but before a fortnight ended, she had progressed to rising, dressing, and going downstairs for a fairly normal day, though she continued to pamper herself with daily naps. Carolyn was determined to be well enough to participate in the hunt weekend that was swiftly approaching.

The housekeeper, Mrs. Morely, had worked up a menu for the meals during the hunt weekend and had already set the maids to airing and cleaning the vacant bedrooms. For the first time, Carolyn saw the third-floor rooms opened up and released from their dust covers. Carolyn was left with little to do except pen the place cards for the meals and decide where to put their guests—a monumental task in itself, since she had no idea who many of the guests were. She knew she could make a ghastly faux pas by placing the wrong people beside each other at the table or giving someone a bedroom that didn't reflect his or her importance.

Carolyn inspected the bedrooms and assigned them and the table settings as best she could, guided only by the title or lack of it beside the guests' names. She took the arrangements to Jason to check, explaining that she still felt so fuzzy headed that she was afraid she might make a dreadful blunder. Jason examined the neatly penned sheets of paper without comment and suggested one or two changes. Carolyn thanked him and left to draw up a good copy for the housekeeper. Her request might have puzzled Jason, for such social things were normally in the wife's domain, but at least she felt secure in the knowledge that she hadn't made an irreparable error.

By the time the hunt weekend arrived, the house was spotless, extra help hired, the cook prepared for the ordeal, and Carolyn had recovered her strength. Once the guests started arriving, she was glad, for it didn't take much energy to stand with Jason in the drawing room, greeting the guests as Barlow escorted them in and announced them. Carolyn smiled and greeted them, listening carefully to the way her husband addressed them and generally following his lead.

Carolyn struggled to remember all the names and not confuse any of the faces, for after this it was unlikely that she would have Jason around to cue her. Her mind was active, noting the degree of friendliness each person displayed to her and striving to match it herself. None of the women appeared particularly fond of or close to her, but neither did anyone speak to her with dislike or offense.

Late in the afternoon Barlow announced the Earl and Countess of Westbridge. Jason jumped up and strode across the room toward the couple, hands outstretched. "Jack! How good to see you. And Flora, my dear, you look as radiant as ever."

The new arrivals were a handsome couple. The earl was shorter than Jason, but with the broad shoulders and well-developed arms of a horseman. Sandy haired, with a pale, lightly freckled complexion, he was not a striking man, but his wide mouth and merry blue eyes bespoke good humor. The countess was stunning. Jet-black hair framed her elegant, oval face. Her dark brows and delicate eyelashes enhanced her large, melting brown eyes. A straight patrician nose and sensual red lips completed the lovely picture. When she smiled, Carolyn saw that there was a narrow gap between her two front teeth: The slight imperfection didn't spoil her loveliness, but only gave her a vulnerability that saved her features from coldness. Jack pumped Jason's hand with a great good will, and Flora radiated a beautiful smile as Jason bent over her hand.

"La, Jason, what a flatterer you are." She glanced past him to Carolyn and held out both her hands. "There you are, Cynthia. You look quite the picture of health. Jason had written us saying you were ill."

"Thank you. I'm quite recovered now. It's so nice to see you." She gripped Flora's hands, then moved on to the earl. "Jack," she said confidently as she extended her hand.

Carolyn turned toward the other guests scattered about the drawing room. "I think you know everyone."

"Heavens, yes," Flora chuckled, turning with her to greet the others. "Stella, how are you?" She addressed a statuesque, middle-aged woman with a square face and strong, capable hands, who struck Carolyn immediately as one more interested in riding and hunting than in anything else. "How is your arm?"

Stella grimaced. "Stupid thing. I knew Solo was half-rogue, yet I wasn't firm enough. Scraped me off on a tree, you see. Ah, well, it's fine now. I'm quite ready for tomorrow."

She chatted on for a while about the prospective hunt, speculating on the weather, the disposition of the hounds, and the state of the ground they would cover. Flora and Carolyn listened, nodding and smiling when it seemed appropriate, and eased away as soon as they could.

"Nice woman," Flora murmured confidentially, "but she knows only one topic."

Carolyn grinned. She liked Flora. The woman was bright and breezy and casually fond of Cynthia. It made sense that there was a certain distance between them that indicated she and Cynthia had not been bosom friends; Jason's friends were unlikely to be Cynthia's friends. Carolyn and Flora continued around the room, greeting the other guests, which thankfully, gave Cynthia time apart from Jason.

Jason's notion that they would act as a loving, happy couple this weekend was taking its toll on Carolyn's nerves. Throughout the afternoon, he had remained by her side, taking her arm as they walked, and even smiling at her with affection. She had become used to rarely being around him the past few weeks. But this afternoon she had been constantly aware of him—feeling the heat of his body and the scrape of his clothing against hers as they stood together, hearing his voice and deep laughter, and worst of all, seeing the false expression of love on his face. She watched his eyes and mouth smile down at her, knowing that Jason meant nothing by it, that it was a masquerade for the benefit of their guests. A lie within a lie, she thought glumly. Pretending to be Jason's unloving wife was difficult enough, but it was an almost unbearable strain to mask the feelings of desire. Her skin tingled whenever he touched her, no matter how briefly. It was insane. Jason hated her. She despised him. She must remember that reality. She had to combat the rush of memories that came with his every glance, every touch—memories of the night Jason had been drunk and she had helped him to bed.

No matter how she tried to suppress them, her feelings poured forth unimpeded, unlocked by their charade of love and happiness. She remembered the sense of Jason's hands on her skin, his lips caressing hers, hot and demanding. She couldn't ignore that she had wanted him, nor could she quell the hot flush that sped through her body when she recalled his lovemaking.

It was a relief to escape him as she followed Flora from one person to the next; listening to her talk to their guests fixed each one more firmly in her mind and provided a wealth of pertinent information. At least now she would be able to chat with Lady Rutherford about her grandson, and she would know that when Colonel and Mrs. Holsby talked fondly of "Henry" they were speaking of their pet bulldog, not a child.

"Cynthia, my dear." The sudden sound of Jason's voice and his light touch upon her arm made her jump. She hadn't heard him approaching, wrapped up as she was in Flora's conversation with Claire Wells-Smythe. "The Osbornes are here."

"What? Oh." Carolyn took a deep breath and followed as Jason led the way to the new arrivals. In the elegant foyer, Carolyn met a middle-aged man and woman who were both a trifle portly, and a third man, in his mid-twenties, she imagined, and quite handsome—he had the dark look of an agonized poet. Jason greeted the older couple formally, but when he turned to the younger man, his manner turned icy.

He was not hostile, but merely curt as he gave a short nod. "Simmons."

"Milord." Simmons greeted him with equally stiff gravity, but as he bent over Carolyn's hand, his lips pressing firmly against her fingers, his eyes were warm and expressive. "Milady."

"Mr. Simmons." Who on earth was this strange young man—for he obviously was not the Osborne's son—and what was the meaning behind his searching look? He kept his hold on her hand far longer than was necessary or polite, and finally Carolyn had to pull it firmly out of his grasp.

"I'm so glad for this chance for us to chat," Mrs. Osborne said to Carolyn, breaking the awkward silence. The two women settled themselves in nearby chairs, Carolyn appearing confident but actually dreading the encounter—what could she say to this stranger? Like a puppy, Simmons followed them and stood, straight-backed, beside Carolyn's chair. "Now, now, Mark." The older woman wagged a finger at him playfully. "This is my time with Cynthia. You'll have a chance to worship at her feet later."

Simmons did his best to look dignified as he left them and stationed himself beside the mantel, leaning one elbow against it gracefully, directing his fiery gaze at Carolyn. What she was witnessing, Carolyn realized, was a pure case of infatuation. It wasn't unusual for a young gentleman to nurture an unrequited love for a married lady; it was romantic and reminiscent of the chivalric code of honor and love popularized in recent times. Its appeal lay primarily in the fact that it was a safe way for a young man to be in love while partaking of his fun with women of the demimonde. Simmons's making calf eyes at her was irritating, and she did her best to stonily ignore him. "That nephew of mine," Mrs.

Osborne said, shaking her head and chuckling. "He's simply head-over-heels in love with you. They're like that, though, young men. One week their hearts are broken, and they're sure they'll be miserable all their lives. The next they're out dancing and flirting. But no use telling him he'll be over it in a few months."

"I'm glad you don't take it seriously." She saw the nephew out of the corner of her eye, staring stonily into the roomful of laughing and chattering guests.

"Heavens, no, don't fret yourself about that. I know you haven't led the poor boy on. At least it keeps him out of trouble composing sonnets to your eyes and all that. We're hoping he will marry Eckingham's daughter in a few years. She's only sixteen now, but it will be a good match when the time comes. Their land borders ours, you know, on the south. Foster has hinted to Eckingham about it a couple of times. The old man's dense as a log, but he finally caught Foster's drift, and he approves. Mark stands to inherit all Foster's money and land, you see, since we have no children." She paused, then plunged into a long-winded diatribe on the wonders and talents of Mary Dora Eckingham.

Carolyn struggled to appear interested as the other woman prattled on. Soon it became clear why Jason had invited this tedious woman and her husband. When Sarah Osborne touched on the subjects of horses and hunting, Carolyn realized the woman disliked horses as much as Cynthia did, and no doubt she was a guest simply to keep Carolyn company on her gentle nag far behind the real hunt enthusiasts. Carolyn barely suppressed a sigh. Now even the hunt, which she had anticipated for weeks, would be a frustrating mockery of the real thing.

The endless afternoon finally drew to a close, and Carolyn escaped to her room to dress for dinner. Priscilla freshened her hairdo and helped her into a pale green dress of shimmering taffeta, then went on to help some of the women who hadn't brought along their personal maids. Carolyn dabbed a bit of lavender perfume on her wrists and at her neck and fastened a pearl circlet around her neck. Two small pearls dangled from her ears, and a creamy vellum fan painted with a rural scene and a delicate lace shawl around her shoulders completed her outfit.

Back in the drawing room, Stella Rutherford engaged Carolyn in a brisk conversation about the merits of several jumpers from which she was trying to choose. Carolyn listened distractedly as she watched the other guests trickle in. Mark entered and took up his customary position against the wall facing her. Carolyn frowned at him slightly before turning to face Lady Rutherford; he was making a cake of himself, she thought, and wondered why he didn't have more pride.

"Ah, there's Arthur Beasley," Stella exclaimed and rose suddenly. "I must see him. Lady Chester told me he'd considered buying that white gelding I was telling you about. Excuse me."

Before Carolyn knew it, Mark Simmons took Lady Rutherford's seat on the sofa beside her. "Why are you tormenting me this way?" he demanded in a low voice, his face twisted in a morose pout.

"I beg your pardon?" Carolyn raised her eyebrows coolly.

"Don't be coy with me. You know what I'm talking about. The way you called me 'Mr. Simmons,' as if I were a stranger, the way you've avoided me since we came in. Are you angry because we didn't arrive earlier? I tried to get Aunt and Uncle to leave last night, or at least at dawn this morning. You know what a long journey it is from Harneck Hill, but they would have none of it. I could have strangled Uncle Foster, particularly when he told the coachman to spare the horses. I wanted to race to you, my darling, surely you must know that." He seized one of her hands in his burst of emotion, cradling it tenderly between his.

Carolyn snatched her hand away. "Really! It is no concern to me when you arrived. And you mustn't address me that way."

"Mustn't—" He goggled at her. "Are you trying to kill me? That's what your coldness will do. Cynthia, you can't— don't tell me your affections have changed. You can't have forgotten the way it was for us. Surely you haven't forgotten that day at the hammer pond. . . ."

If only she knew what he was talking about! Carolyn floundered for a reply. "You're speaking foolishly. You mustn't take hope from that day. I am Lord Broughton's wife. I can never—"

His face cleared—he looked boyish, really, now that he'd lost his scowl—and he chuckled. "Oh, you are teasing me! You always say I'm too serious."

What would it take to get through to this man? He must have a sublime self-confidence to shrug off her rejections. "Mark, I—"

"Please, dearest, no more jesting. Tell me what I've done wrong, and I'll correct it. But don't continue to hold me off. For weeks I've done nothing but dream of your sweet white body. I'm on fire for you."

Carolyn gaped at him, stunned. "Mr. Simmons! You forget yourself!"

"I know. We're in the midst of a crowd. I must not be so obvious in my love for you. I'll leave now. But promise you'll meet me on the west porch tonight. Let's say . . . eleven o'clock."

Carolyn began to protest, but he was already gone, wending his way to the cabinet where Jason was dispensing drinks. Carolyn clenched her hands in her lap, her face suffused with anger. How dare he! Asking her to meet him, as if she were a common flirt who ignored her wedding vows and met strange men in the dark! Cynthia should have given him a thorough set down long before this, but then, she wouldn't have known how to handle a man who so far overstepped the boundaries of good taste as Mark Simmons had, which explained how the fool had concluded they were . . . "involved." But his forward manner and pig-headed assumptions outraged Carolyn—she would not stand for it if he tried it again.

She was still fuming when Jason came to escort her into dinner. Her flushed cheeks enhanced her beauty, and Jason's hard face softened a fraction. "You look very lovely tonight."

Carolyn's eyes blazed, her unspent anger bubbling out. "Tell me, did I perform to your specifications today?"

His face closed. "Yes, I think so—except for letting young Simmons slaver all over your hand."

"I didn't 'let' him! He wouldn't release my hand. I had to jerk it away from him."

"So I saw. I was . . . surprised, shall we say?"

Carolyn shot him an uncertain glance. "Surprised? What do you mean?"

"I was under the impression that you enjoyed his, er, attentions."

"He's a pig."

"Ah, well, I'm glad to know there are other men who fit in that category besides myself."

"There are far too many of you."

"Then it's the entire sex you dislike, not just your husband?"

Carolyn replied drolly, "There are a few exceptions."

Too late she realized that he had taken her remark to mean Dennis Bingham, the man for whom Cynthia had left him. Carolyn looked away, cursing her quick tongue. It had been a meaningless remark, really, an attempt to be dryly teasing. Instead, she had unthinkingly stabbed Jason's pride. He seated her and walked to his place at the opposite end of the table without exchanging another word.

Carolyn was seated between Flora and Lord Rutherford, whose conversation had one more dimension than Lady Rutherford's, since he talked about guns as well as horses. With Flora, Carolyn found it increasingly difficult to dampen her own vitality and respond in a soft, demure way, for her natural reaction was to laugh uninhibitedly at Flora's sallies and respond with her own wit and vivacity. She tempered her personality as best she could, noting that at least Jason's anger toward her had depressed her spirits a little.

After dinner the ladies retired to the drawing room while the men enjoyed their port and cigars. Later, when the men joined them, Mrs. Osborne was persuaded—without great difficulty—to play a few popular melodies on the piano, and Flora sang with her, while Carolyn sat with ease between two women so that Mark Simmons could not confront her again. Because of the early start of the hunt the next day, everyone retired by ten, leaving only a few inveterate card-players who had decided to get up a game. Jason escorted Carolyn to the door of her bedroom in best imitation of a loving husband. They said nothing on the way up the stairs, and Carolyn knew that to try to explain or apologize for her pointless remark would only make matters worse.

Priscilla waited inside Carolyn's room to help her off with her gown and brush out her hair. Alone at last, Carolyn glanced at the clock on the mantle before she turned out the gas lamp beside her bed. Twenty minutes until eleven. . . . She pictured Mark waiting expectantly on the west porch, and she hoped he would find it very, very cold.

The morning of the hunt dawned crisp and clear, a perfect day for riding, and Carolyn awoke with high spirits. She rose and washed her face, humming, and rang for Priscilla. While Carolyn sipped the deliciously hot, sweet tea the girl had brought, Priscilla pulled her hair back and braided it, winding it into a secure knot at the nape of her neck. Carolyn smiled at her reflection; this angular style suited her much better than dainty curls. Quickly she dressed in the deep-blue riding habit and pinned the matching cap to her hair. The style and color suited her, and she knew she looked her best. She could not suppress the glow of anticipation and excitement on her face.

There was no one else downstairs yet as she started down the wide stairway to the floor below. "Cynthia!" She stopped and turned inquiringly at the sound of her name, but when she saw Mark Simmons hurrying to join her, she wished she had not paused. "Good morning, Mr. Simmons."

"Damn it! Will you stop calling me that?" he hissed, seizing her arm as he reached her. "Why didn't you come last night? I waited for an hour."

"I'm surprised you didn't get chilled and come in earlier."

"Stop being flippant. It doesn't become you. What is it, why have you changed since the last time? Please *tell* me—please!" He took her other arm in his grasp and pulled her close, startling Carolyn so that she stepped off balance and had to grab the lapels of his coat to keep from stumbling. He took the gesture as encouragement and bent to kiss her.

She broke away, appalled at his daring. Automatically her hand flashed out, slapping him hard across his cheek. "How dare you! You're a rude, insolent puppy! And if you continue this abominable behavior, it will be my husband you have to deal with."

For a moment Mark gaped, then his eyes shot off sparks of their own. "What the hell is the matter with you? You've never complained about my 'forwardness' before.

"I haven't the slightest idea what you're talking about."

His mouth twisted. "I'm not a fool, Cynthia. I know a willing woman when I hold one. You used to practically purr under my caresses. You said my touch was like heaven after submitting to that bull of a husband of yours. How can you deny that now? You came to me, disgusted by Broughton's lust, and I made you happy. I treated you as you deserved. I worshiped at the shrine of your body. And now you callously cast me aside?"

"Really, I think you're a bit melodramatic, Mark. Why, in God's name, if I don't like a sexually aggressive husband, would I want a total stranger pawing me? You've gone well over the boundaries of propriety, and I'll thank you to leave me alone in the future." Carolyn hurried down the stairs and started for the front door, her heels tapping out militantly on the marble floor. Then she stopped—in the mirror she saw Jason lounging against the wall outside his study door, arms crossed, lean and indolent in his riding clothes and boots. She whirled to face him, and he bared his teeth in a mockery of a smile, bringing his hands together in a pantomime of clapping.

Carolyn marched down the hall to him. "What are you doing here? Did you hear all that?"

"Yes, of course, just as you intended, no doubt."

"Then why didn't you come forward and help me? Any normal husband would have hurried to his wife's protection."

"And spoil your noble scene? Never! It was far too good a performance to miss."

"What are you talking about?"

"Why, of a classic act of outraged virtue staged for your husband's benefit."

"You think I knew you were here?" Carolyn's voice rose indignantly. "That I pretended to be insulted? That that little worm and I—that we—" She broke off, choked with fury and frustration.

"Precisely. I'm no longer quite so naive, Cynthia."

"Oh! You are the most abominable man I've ever met. You can see the truth right in front of your eyes and still insist that it's not there."

"No. I simply don't listen to lies anymore."

Carolyn made a low noise of frustration and swung around. Mark stood at the foot of the stairs watching them. As Carolyn stalked past him, he smiled and whispered, "I understand."

He, too, believed she had been putting on a show for Jason's benefit! It was the perfect ending to this whole ridiculous farce. She stormed out the front door, wishing a thousand plagues on the heads of both her husband and her would-be lover.

Outside, in the pale, chilly light of dawn, grooms were scurrying about, bringing saddled horses out of the stables. A pack of spotted hounds milled around two servants who held them on leashes. Among a small circle of men Carolyn recognized Hugh St. John, Cousin Hugh, and she eagerly welcomed a familiar face. "Hugh!"

He turned, looking quite dashing in the misty morning light, and smiled when he saw her. "Cousin Cynthia!" He raised a hand and came over to the steps where she stood. "How early you're up! I've never known you not to be late for a hunt."

"I thought I might as well get it over with. Delaying never made it go away. Besides, it's such a lovely day, I welcome an opportunity for a little exercise."

"I see they have your usual mount." He nodded toward the hitching post where the gray horse she had ridden before stood beside an equally placid bay, both oblivious to the hubbub around them.

A giggle rose in Carolyn's throat. "Yes. And no doubt one for Mrs. Osborne as well."

"Who? Oh, yes, your companion in the back of the field." He chuckled, his hazel eyes warm.

"You're very different from your cousin," Carolyn said impulsively.

He raised an eyebrow. "You've only just noticed?"

"No, of course not. I saw it the first time I met you. But it just struck me afresh. You're kind about my lack of riding skills and merely tease me a little. Jason has been, well, rather caustic in the past."

"I'm afraid Jason doesn't know much about fear, having never experienced it."

"Nor about compassion, either."

"Come." He patted her arm. "Don't be too hard on Jason. I told you before, he's just hot-tempered. He doesn't mean to frighten people or hurt them."

"Well, he certainly does a good job of it for someone who doesn't try."

He frowned. "Have, uh, things not been going well between you since you returned?"

"It's no worse than it's ever been, I suppose," Carolyn hedged.

He sighed and looked away toward the horses. The front door opened, and several men and women filed out, among them Sarah Osborne, who made her way immediately to Carolyn. "Ah, there you are, my dear. And Mr. St. John. My, it's been a long time since we've seen you."

"Mrs. Osborne," Hugh greeted her and Carolyn almost laughed at the hunted expression in his eyes. "Uh, why don't I bring up your horses?"

"Thank you, Cousin Hugh, that sounds very nice."

Now there was a steady exodus from the house. Mr. Osborne joined them, as well as Mark, his dark eyes gazing tragically at Carolyn, and she experienced a deep desire to kick him in the shins. Hugh brought up their horses and she quickly turned to mount. As Jason emerged from the door, Carolyn glimpsed his tall, lean frame out of the corner of her eye. Hugh cupped his hands for her, but Jason intercepted, saying smoothly, "I'll help Cynthia, Hugh. Why don't you assist Mrs. Osborne?"

"Of course." Hugh fell back immediately, looking from one to the other, then turned to help the older woman.

Jason moved into Hugh's place, bent slightly, and cupped his hands. Placing her foot in his hands she acted like a nervous rider with little experience as he hoisted her onto the horse—she fumbled clumsily for the reins and gasped as she nearly lost her balance as her foot sought the stirrup. With force, Jason guided her foot into the stirrup, then reached up to position her hands correctly on the reins. The tension of impatience was in his hands, but he smiled up at her as if performing the adjustments with affection. "I'm not the one in this house who plays scenes for an audience," she hissed down at him.

"My dear, surely you can't think I'm playing a scene," he replied imperturbably. "There, now you're all settled." He ran a hand down the mount's left wither, then lifted its leg to study his hoof. "She looks completely healed," he announced, giving the horse a final pat. His false pleasantness barely concealing his arrogant sneer, he said "I hope you have a pleasant ride, my dear."

"I'm sure I will," Carolyn returned sweetly. Two could play this game.

The riders were almost all ready, laughter and enthusiastic talk filling the yard. Frisky mounts danced and blew out steam from their nostrils, shaking their heads. Carolyn's horse stood without moving except to sweep away a fly with her tail. Soon the hounds were let loose, and the riders streamed after them in a beautiful parade of red and blue jackets and shimmering horses against the green-gray of the copse of trees. Jason led the pack as they picked up speed and wound away into the countryside. A canter seemed the height of her horse's speed. Mrs. Osborne kept up a steady chatter as they rode, which didn't increase Carolyn's good humor.

It was the worst hunt she'd ever attended. Within minutes, Carolyn and Sarah Osborne were at the rear of the pack and most of the morning they weren't even in sight of the rest of the riders. Longing to dig her heels into the tired horse to move her canter to a hearty gallop, she instead had to endure Mrs. Osborne's unbearable monologue on her various ailments, and her neighbors' scandals. There was no way out of this dismal situation, she had decided, when suddenly the horse jumped, snorted, and took off running at full speed. It gave her a start, and she grabbed the reins quickly and held on, then settled down to the unexpected pleasure of a good ride.

They passed the narrow copse alongside them and emerged into an open meadow, broken only by a long hedge directly in front of them. Carolyn had not yet tested the horse's jumping ability; she prayed silently that the mare could jump, for she had no idea. With a swoosh, the horse cleared the hedge and came down jarringly on the other side. It was then that Carolyn felt her saddle turn beneath her. She struggled to regain her balance, but the saddle was loose and falling. She saw the ground rushing up at her. Kicking her foot loose from the stirrup, she jumped from the speeding horse.

Ten

One of the first things her father had taught Carolyn about riding was how to fall, and Carolyn hit the ground expertly, then rolled. But the fall stunned her, knocking the air out of her lungs. Behind her she heard Sarah let out a scream. Carolyn lay staring up at the blue sky, recovering her breath after a few moments. She moved her limbs; nothing was broken, and she struggled to her feet.

Mrs. Osborne rode toward her in a panic. If Carolyn had been capable of laughing at that moment, the sight of the pudgy middle-aged woman bouncing along on her horse, feet kicking, one hand waving in the air and the other flapping the reins would have thrown her into fits of laughter. Carolyn waved to let Sarah know she was all right, but Sarah continued to yell for help.

Carolyn dusted off her clothes and looked around for her hat. She wished Sarah would stop screeching. The last thing Carolyn wanted was to face all those horsemen and horsewomen and admit that she had fallen off the slowest, most placid horse in the country. Carolyn didn't think it would have been possible for the nag to jump and run like that, and she pondered the cause.

Sarah slid clumsily down from her horse and hurried to

Carolyn. "Cynthia! Cynthia! Are you all right? Oh, my dear, my dear!"

"I'm fine, Sarah. Really. No broken bones. Not even a sprain, I think."

"Oh, my, oh, my," Sarah kept babbling, wringing her hands as she looked at Carolyn searchingly. "Are you sure? What a shock! I nearly collapsed when I saw you running off like that. Whatever possessed you?"

"It wasn't me! It was Gray Lady up there." She nodded toward the fence where her horse now stood, head down and sides heaving from her exertion.

"Oh, my goodness. I *knew* there wasn't such a thing as a gentle mount, though Foster is always trying to convince me so."

"I'm sure something must have startled her. A hare jumping out, maybe," she said, though she would have bet a hundred pounds yesterday that Gray Lady wouldn't have even twitched at the sight of a score of hares scampering across a field. Carolyn reached up painfully to roll her braid, which had come loose and lay down her back, into the best knot she could manage without maid or mirror. Her arms ached all up and down, as did her knees, for they had taken the brunt of the fall. Her riding skirt was smeared with grass stains and dirt, and there was a small tear near the knee. She limped over to the base of a nearby tree and picked up her hat, just as Jason and several others galloped over.

Carolyn watched in grudging admiration as Jason's mount soared across the fence and thundered down upon them for he truly was an excellent rider. Sarah's screams must have brought everyone running, for all the riders poured across the field. Carolyn sighed and turned her attention to molding her hat back into something approximating its original shape. Jason leaped from his horse and ran to her, pushing others out of his way as he approached.

"What the devil happened to you?" he demanded roughly, grabbing her arms. "Where's your horse?"

Carolyn pointed silently to where her mount stood, now grazing peacefully in the grass.

"Good Lord, woman!" Jason exploded. "Can't you even stay on a rocking horse?"

Carolyn jerked out of his grasp, her pride stung. "Of course I can. Something startled Gray Lady, and she took off running."

"That horse? Never!"

"Well, she did this time. And my saddle turned!"

"Impossible. Really, Cynthia . . ."

"It did! Just look at the mare, and you'll see."

Jason ground his teeth and turned to fetch the gentle mare. Hugh was already leading her to them. "She seems to have lost her saddle," he called out cheerfully.

"There it is—on the ground," Lady Chester pointed with her whip.

"I'll be damned," Jason murmured as he examined the saddle. "The girth must have been buckled carelessly. I'll have the groom's hide for this. Sheer negligence!"

"They were rather busy this morning," Carolyn remarked, a bit unnerved at his vehemence. After all, it had been only a small riding accident, and she had taken a tumble, which she had done before.

"That's no excuse." He turned the saddle over. "There doesn't seem to be anything wrong with this saddle."

Hugh slid from his horse and joined Jason. "You're right. Probably didn't catch the tongue of the buckle, or something like that."

"It might have been all right if the mare hadn't bolted," Carolyn mused.

"Bolted?" Hugh glanced at her with astonishment. "Gray Lady bolted? She's never done a thing like that before, has she, Jason?"

"No, and I doubt she did this time."

"What?" Carolyn exploded. "I just told you—"

Jason ignored her, speaking to Hugh. "You know what a terrible horsewoman Cynthia is. The horse probably broke into a canter."

Hugh laughed. "Oh, come now, Jason, even Cousin Cynthia knows a canter from bolting. Don't you?"

"Most definitely. And Gray Lady bolted. She was frightened or hurt."

"I say," Harry Benningfield interrupted their argument. "Are we going to finish the hunt or stand about here jawing?"

"Finish, I should think. We can still catch up." Jason turned to Carolyn. "Do you want to return to the house? I'm sure Mrs. Osborne would be good enough to accompany you."

"Oh, yes, certainly," Sarah chimed in. "Mark will escort you, won't you dear?"

"No, that's all right," Carolyn put in hastily. "It was only a fall. Nothing's broken, and Gray Lady seems fine. I'd like to go on with everyone else."

"Certainly."

Jason flung the saddle on the horse and reached underneath it to pull the girth under the horse's belly. Thinking back vaguely on the morning, Carolyn remembered him reaching down to inspect one of Gray Lady's legs, a perfect opportunity to slip the girth partially out of the buckle, so that with some exertion by the mare, the saddle could come loose and turn, spilling its rider. . . .

How ridiculous it was, for a fall off a horse wasn't usually fatal. If a husband was trying to kill his wife, it was a chancy way of doing it . . . unless that wife was a notoriously poor rider. Unless she was frightened of horses and had never ridden anything but the gentlest nags. When she felt the saddle slipping, she had known enough to jump, and correctly at that. But Cynthia, she knew, would have panicked and been badly hurt . . . or killed.

Jason finished strapping on the saddle and turned to her. "There you are. Ready?"

When he cupped his hands for her to step up, she hesitated. Had he truly been so angry at the grooms for not buckling her saddle properly? Or was he acting the part of the concerned husband so that no one would suspect he was actually trying to kill her? Carolyn's head was in a whirl, but she thrust the thought aside and mounted, forgetting in her anxiety that she was supposed to be clumsy about it.

The others had ridden on, eager for the hunt, but Sarah and Jason stayed beside her. Carolyn clutched her reins, lost in thought. The combination of Jason's mysterious show of anger and Gray Lady's bolting added up to something frightening. Why had the placid horse taken off like a shot? Perhaps a small rock had hit her, or a tiny dart, or even a bee sting. Carolyn wished she could dismount and inspect her horse for a cut or bite. But that would be most unlike Cynthia. Jason would ask questions, and he in turn would become suspicious of her, which she couldn't allow.

Jason watched her. She offered a tentative smile. "Are you feeling all right?" he asked.

"Oh, yes, fine. My skirt was damaged far more than I."

"I must say, you're being rather courageous."

Carolyn froze at her error. Cynthia wouldn't have shrugged off the incident. No doubt she would have wept and seized the chance to return home. "Not courageous. Just foolish. I'm embarrassed to have fallen off a horse like this—and in front of all those excellent riders! I feel like such an idiot." Carolyn had learned to call tears to her eyes at will, for she often had to cry on the stage. She couldn't manufacture enough tears for them to spill from her eyes, but at least she could get the glimmer of unshed tears. "I spoiled everyone's fun, and they were quite angry with me." She considered setting her lower lip to quivering, but decided it would be too much.

"I see. Your pride was hurt."

"Yes," Carolyn responded truthfully enough.

"I'm relieved. I thought you might be going stalwart on me."

"How typical of you to joke about it. Why don't you catch up with the others?"

"And leave my poor, shaken wife alone?"

"Mrs. Osborne is here." Carolyn nodded at the other woman who rode a little behind them.

"But not much protection if your wild horse gets loose again, nor much comfort if you succumb to hysterics."

Carolyn glared. "Oh, go away! No one will blame you, and frankly I prefer not to have your company."

He dipped his head in a mocking bow. "Since you put it so graciously . . . I believe I'll join the others. Good day, Cynthia. Good day, Mrs. Osborne."

Carolyn watched him ride off, and as soon as he was out of sight, she pulled her horse to a halt. "Tired, dear?" Sarah asked compassionately. "Why don't we turn back now?"

"No, I'm fine. I simply want to get down a moment." She slid lithely off the horse and, running her hands over the smooth skin, checked for bruises or cuts, while Mrs. Osborne looked on.

"Cynthia, whatever are you doing?"

"I thought Gray Lady was favoring one leg a little." Nothing! There didn't seem to be a single hair out of place. "Alright, perhaps I am being overly suspicious," she told herself. Her bout with arsenic poisoning had made her see shadows everywhere. But this scheme she imagined was too complicated and risky to pull of successfully, and Jason wasn't the sort of man to gamble on uncertain results. It was an accident, nothing more.

Carolyn heaved herself onto the waiting mare, ignoring Mrs. Osborne's words of alarm. "Come along, Sarah, let's find the gate to this fence. I'm afraid Gray Lady is not much of a jumper."

Carolyn and Sarah met the rest of the party returning from the kill and rode back with them to the house for the customary massive hunt breakfast. Ignoring her bedraggled riding habit, Carolyn joined the others in the dining room, where the huge sideboards were laden with a splendid array of silver dishes. Platters of bacon, ham, and sausage were arranged in front of a huge rare roast beef and a luscious roast goose stuffed to overflowing with wild rice. There were stuffed mushrooms, at least ten different cheeses, poached eggs, and great bowls of fruit, and all kinds of bread and pastries. Only a hearty trencherman could do justice to the repast. Carolyn ate all she could of the feast, trying all the while to ignore the recounts of the chase she had missed. When the guests began to filter into the drawing room to chat and sip brandy, she slipped away to her room and changed into a more presentable dress.

"Cynthia, I must say you certainly look fresh," said Flora, upon her return downstairs.

Carolyn smiled at the vivacious countess. "Thank you. I had to change. My skirt was past redemption. I confess I seized the opportunity to lie down for a moment with a damp rag on my forehead."

"Good. You deserved it. You took a nasty tumble. I was quite proud of you for getting back on and continuing the hunt, though. I would have thought you'd have come straight back."

"Thank you." Carolyn almost winced, and inwardly her spirits sank. She was sure everyone had noticed how out of character it was for her to refuse to return to the house. This assignment was beginning to seem too much for her. . . .

Across the room, Jason smiled and nodded to her. Carolyn forced a return smile and sat down with Flora in a cushioned alcove of the bay windows. They began a little polite small talk, but were soon chatting away like the best of friends. Carolyn liked Flora far better than anyone she had met here. She was bright and droll, with a tongue that was often sharp, but with underlying kindness and compassion. Suddenly, the sound of eager footsteps made all heads turn—Laurel burst through the open double doors.

"Mama! Mama!" The pretty child skidded to a halt at the sight of so many strange faces and looked around her a trifle fearfully.

"Here I am, Laurel." Carolyn rose and moved to embrace her.

Laurel flung herself forward and wrapped her arms around Carolyn's waist. "Laurel, come back here! Laurel!"

Bonnie's voice sounded in the hallway, and then she peered into the room. "Oh, no! Milady, I'm so sorry." The nurse rushed into the room. "She got clean away from me. I had no idea . . . Come here, Laurel."

"No."

Carolyn patted the girl's back. "It's all right, Bonnie. Let her stay here for a moment. She hasn't gotten to see any of the fun."

Bonnie didn't dare contest Carolyn's decision in front of the gathered aristocrats. "Yes'm." She gave a little curtsy and scurried back out of the room.

"Why don't you come sit on my lap?" Carolyn asked Laurel. "There's a lovely lady here you'd like to see, I know."

Carolyn led her over to Flora, then sat down again and pulled the girl up on her lap. "Flora, this is Laurel. Laurel, this lady is Flora. Isn't she pretty?"

Laurel nodded and reached out to touch Flora's creamy skin. Flora smiled and went on to fascinate the child with a series of simple finger tricks. Laurel watched her with rounded eyes, and when Flora stopped, she bounced up and down enthusiastically on Carolyn's lap.

"That means she wants more," said Carolyn. "Careful, Flora, once you begin, you can't ever stop."

The murmur of conversation rose around them again. Carolyn felt Jason's eyes on her, and turned to face him. Jason's attention had wandered from the circle of men he was with; he frowned as he watched her, no doubt disapproving of Laurel's presence among his friends. What a blow to his massive pride for the others to see his simple-minded daughter. "Let him think what he wants to think," Carolyn said to herself. She refused to hide Laurel like an embarrassing mistake.

In a bit she excused herself and walked with Laurel to the nursery. Bonnie burst forth with apologies and explanations again, but Carolyn raised her hand to stop the flow of words. "It's all right, Bonnie. I'm sure Laurel's confused about why she hasn't seen as much of me the past couple of days. No one minded the little interruption." Carolyn bent down. "I have to go now, sweetheart. You stay here with Nurse, and I promise I'll come by to see you before the dance tonight."

Rising, Carolyn turned to Bonnie. "Why don't you allow her to stay up past her bedtime and watch a little of the dance? She could peek through the door into the ballroom from the servants' hall and see the dressed-up people and hear the music. I'm sure it would be a special treat for her."

"Yes'm."

"I'll be by for our usual cocoa and cookies before I go downstairs this evening."

"Very good, ma'am."

Bonnie's brief, subservient answers meant Carolyn had alienated her yet again. She found it hard to understand the woman's resentment, for if Cynthia had truly ignored the child, she would think that her own concern and help would be welcome. Yet whenever Carolyn came to be with Laurel, Bonnie's hostility was clear and unmasked as her lips thinned into a grim line. Carolyn wasn't, after all, trying to undermine Bonnie's authority in the nursery, but merely shower her love and affection on a beautiful child who'd been ignored for too long. "Yet another mystery," she said softly and returned to her guests.

After tea Carolyn bathed and dressed for the ball, which, despite the many near disasters of the weekend, she looked forward to eagerly. It would be the highlight of the weekend, especially since she loved dancing, and it had been so very long since she had had the chance. Carolyn undressed and sank into the hot tub Priscilla prepared, blissfully soaking away the soreness from her fall. When finally the water turned too cool to stay in, she gave her hair a quick scrubbing, then stepped out of the tub. She dried off with an enormous linen towel and slipped into pantalets, chemise, and stockings.

Carolyn knelt in front of the fire to dry her hair, brushing it out in the heat of the hearth. Soon her face was rosy with warmth; she stretched, and sat back on her heels. There was a sharp tap on her door, and Jason pushed it open without waiting for a reply.

His eyes riveted on her. Carolyn gasped, staring, for a moment unable to move, thinking only of her particular state of undress. Her hair spread like a red-gold cape around her shoulders and down her back. Jason's eyes traced the sweep of her hair across her white chest to the swelling top of her breasts above the chemise. He took a step forward.

She jumped up and scrambled for the satin dressing gown that lay spread across her bed. "Do you always barge into rooms without asking permission?" she asked, belting the shimmering green robe at the waist.

"I knocked," he reminded her, rocking on his heels and clasping his hands behind his back.

"You didn't wait for an answer before you opened the door and came in."

"I beg your pardon. I didn't realize formalities were required between a husband and a wife."

Carolyn's chin lifted a trifle. "We're not exactly a normal husband and wife."

"No. We aren't, are we?" He paused and glanced around the room.

"Well, why did you come? I presume you had a reason."

"I—I was puzzled this afternoon by your behavior with Laurel." Carolyn said nothing, and merely raised one eyebrow. "You seemed to be genuinely fond of her."

"She *is* my daughter."

"Come, Cynthia, let's not pretend you've been a doting parent all these years. In the past you'd have been horrified if Laurel had come barreling into a room full of guests like that." Carolyn stood silently, unable to deny his words.

"I was surprised to hear Laurel speak so clearly," Jason continued. "In the past she couldn't say 'mama,' only a sound that we knew meant the word. What's happened?"

"I've been working with her." Pride reflected in Carolyn's eyes. "I think she's capable of more than any of us ever believed. I've talked to her a great deal and tried to show her how to move her lips and tongue to say words. And we've worked on putting on her clothes, brushing her hair, feeding herself. Really, there's been a vast improvement."

"I've seen it when I visit her before supper, but I've told myself it was my imagination. It's hard to recognize change when you're with a person frequently," Jason remarked.

"Do you visit her often?"

"Almost every afternoon. Surely you know that."

"I—wasn't sure how often you saw her. I would think visiting her would remind you of the blow to your pride."

"What blow?" His eyes took on a wary aspect.

"Having a child like that in the Somerville family."

"She's my daughter, and I love her," he replied fiercely. "How can you think that I—"

"You weren't ashamed this afternoon when she burst in on your friends?"

"No! Only amazed and bewildered by your attitude toward her." He stood only inches away from her. Carolyn's heart raced and she clutched the edges of her dressing gown together with trembling fingers. She could feel his warmth, and she could not keep the memories of his kisses from rushing into her mind. Jason raised his hand and trailed a forefinger down her cheek. His eyes were stark with pain and yearning. "I can't believe you've really changed."

"No? You couldn't believe the change in Laurel, either, could you?" Her smile was a challenge. This was the only way she could explain her mistakes—by making him believe that Cynthia's experiences had changed her.

He frowned, and his hand dropped away. "Excuse me. I must dress for the dance. I'll come by your room so that we can go down together."

"I'll be ready."

He turned and walked away. Carolyn sank into the small chair in front of her vanity table. How she hated keeping up this pretense, this confining, nerve-racking game-playing. Yet now there was Laurel to consider. Carolyn didn't think she could bear to leave her, and she was sure she really *had* helped the child to learn. And Jason . . . well, she wouldn't think about Jason. She no longer knew what she should think or say or do.

But there was no time for these thoughts. She must stop dithering about and get ready. After ringing for Priscilla, she went to her wardrobe. The pale-pink velvet ball gown she had chosen for this evening awaited her, carefully ironed and ready to be worn. It was a beautiful dress, but so pale and ruffled and dainty. Sighing, Carolyn rifled through the dozens of dresses before her. The moment she saw it, she knew it was perfect: a ball gown of vivid sapphire-blue satin, far plainer than the others, with rows of black lace only on the train, but Carolyn knew it would look stunning, and she defiantly pulled it out and laid it across the bed.

When Carolyn said she'd changed her mind, Priscilla took the blue dress without comment and hurried off to rid it of any wrinkles. In Cynthia's jewelry box Carolyn found a silver chain with a pendant of a large, pear-shaped sapphire surrounded by tiny diamonds. There were also sapphire ear studs to match and a slender bracelet of linked diamonds and sapphires. Carolyn knew the set would look perfect with the dress, even though more simple jewelry was now the style. She fastened the ear studs and set out the necklace and bracelet on the vanity.

When Priscilla returned with the ironed dress, she helped her into it, then put Carolyn's hair in a heavy roll across the back. Though it was a plainer style than she usually wore, its simplicity would highlight the elegant bone structure of her face and add a vulnerable touch to her beauty. After adding the finishing touches, Priscilla clasped her hands together in awe. "Oh, milady, you're beautiful! I never saw you look so—elegant. You look like a queen, and that's the truth."

Carolyn beamed. "Why, thank you, Priscilla." She was truly radiant. The blue was a perfect foil for her skin and blazing hair. The sapphires shimmered at her ears and throat.

Carolyn took out a black lace fan and black lace mitts, fingerless above the second knuckle. Excitement rose in her throat as she imagined the look of admiration on Jason's face. "No!" she nearly cried aloud—these thoughts were dangerous.

There was a knock on the door. "Enter."

Jason stepped in, saying with a wry twist to his mouth, "You see, I waited for your answer this—" He stopped and stared at Carolyn for a long moment. His voice was curiously hushed. "How beautiful you are. I'd forgotten how regal you can be—yet infinitely alluring." He moved closer, reaching out with one hand to touch the gleaming sapphire at her throat. "You wore Gran's sapphire set. I'm glad." His face softened, and his smile was genuine and warm.

Priscilla slipped quietly out of the room, but the other two noticed her leaving no more than they had her presence. Jason placed a small box before Carolyn, and she opened it, puzzled. Inside nestled a pale lavender orchid, its creamy throat streaked with varying shades of blue and purple. Carolyn gasped. "It's lovely!"

"I had Jack bring it with them from London yesterday. Impossible to get here. I had no idea how well it would suit you."

He fastened it on her wrist, where it lay soft and cool against her skin. "It's lovely," she repeated, touching the flower with awe. "Thank you, Jason." She lifted her eyes, blue and tender, and he drew in his breath.

"Cynthia . . ." For an instant she thought he would kiss her, and Carolyn swayed forward a little. But Jason straightened, suddenly formal. "We . . . must hurry, or we shan't arrive in the ballroom before our guests."

Carolyn tried to suppress the confused emotions she felt. Picking up her fan, she spoke with confidence: "Yes, of course. I'm ready."

At one end of the ballroom there was a small stage for the musicians and the rest of the huge hall spread out before it. The hardwood floor gleamed, and the walls were painted a pale cream, with exquisite plaster moldings around the top of the walls, and suspended from the center of the ceiling was a large crystal chandelier. Sconces of gaslights on the walls added more soft, warm light. One long wall of the room was broken by three alcoves with tall bay windows and narrow, three-sided window seats below them; the curtains and cushions in the alcoves were plush red velvet, a bright splash of color in the pale room.

Carolyn had seen the room in her secret explorations of the house and had marveled then at its beauty, but now, lit up by the chandeliers and adorned with a bounty of flowers, the ballroom was breathtaking. The eight couples they had invited for the weekend would seem lost in it, so they had sent out invitations to the dance to all the neighboring gentry. Hugh would be there, and Thomas and Millicent Nelson, as well as Admiral Parker's widow and her gaggle of marriageable daughters.

Any nervousness Carolyn had about meeting this new flood of local guests fled when the dance began, for Carolyn delighted in it. She was a graceful dancer, and her dance card filled up immediately, Jason placing his name for three waltzes. Mark Simmons confronted her in front of several other guests, and she couldn't courteously do anything other than grant him one dance, though she made sure that it was a fast country set rather than a more intimate waltz.

He was obviously chagrined by her choice, but could not publicly complain. Later, when he led her out to the dance floor, he whispered bitterly, "How could you fob me off with a country set? Surely I deserve at least one waltz."

"Mr. Simmons . . ."

"Damn it, Cynthia, I won't stand for it. Do you hear? You've led me around by the nose for months. I'd have done anything for you. And now you act as if we were strangers!"

"You mean you've been making a fool of yourself for months," Carolyn tossed back tartly. "I've had nothing to do with that."

"What's happened to you? Once you loved me."

"I think you presume too much."

"Presume! You call me presumptuous to think you love me after you came to my bed?"

Carolyn's heart leaped as she swept past Mark to take her place opposite him. She went automatically through the complex dance, but her mind was far away. His words echoed in her head. ". . . *After you came to my bed?*" Cynthia had . . . been intimate with this foolish boy. . . .

Even if everything else Mark had said was rationalized by youthful exaggeration and wishful thinking, there was no way she could get around his last statement. Why should he lie about something so personal when he thought he was speaking to Cynthia, who would know it was untrue? All that he'd said was not the product of his fevered imagination nor enlargements upon Cynthia's reaction to a stolen kiss or two, but the oupourings of a fevered and impassioned lust.

Carolyn had excused her sister's unfaithfulness with Dennis Bingham, reasoning that it was the only way she could be with the man she loved, the only way to escape the brutal husband who had abused her. But now she questioned her sister's fidelity, and wondered if there had been others. She remembered Jason's vicious comment about her lovers, but she had chosen to ignore him then. But now? Now she wasn't sure what to believe.

From Jason's comments and Bonnie's story, she had gotten the impression that Cynthia had little liking for sex. She had assumed that Jason's roughness and perversions had given her a distaste for it, a distaste that Bingham had cured. But apparently Mark Simmons had already cured that dislike. It seemed impossible, but she could find no other explanation.

Bonnie had said that Dennis Bingham had given Cynthia the only love she'd known and had taken her away from Jason's perverted abuse. Carolyn had accepted that, for she could imagine nothing else that would cause her virtuous sister to run away with another man. But now she wondered how accurate Bonnie's tale had been. If Cynthia had made love with more than one man, perhaps it hadn't taken sexual abuse to drive her "moral" sister to commit adultery.

Carolyn had seen Jason in a rage, but he had never struck her, even in the middle of their most heated exchanges. He seemed to exercise a stern control over himself. And that night when she had gone to him in his study, his kisses and caresses had been passionate, arousing, but in no way brutal. Heavens, Carolyn thought, she hoped that sort of lovemaking wasn't abnormal, for she had been thoroughly stirred by it. Perhaps Cynthia had misinterpreted Jason's hot passion for roughness. His kisses had been demanding and fierce, not gentle; that was certainly true, but Carolyn knew nothing more stirring, more compelling than his passionate touch.

If Jason was not the beast Bonnie claimed . . . if Cynthia had been unfaithful to him often . . . if Cynthia had withdrawn from his passion . . . no, she mustn't start thinking like that, for she'd drive herself crazy. She was certain of only one thing: Her sister had shared intimacy with at least two men besides her husband, which meant that Carolyn didn't know Cynthia nearly as well as she had presumed. "What if," Carolyn mused, "there are other aspects of her character that I'm not aware of?" There could be many secrets in Cynthia's life, and one of them might be the reason for the attempt to murder Carolyn. There was so much she didn't know about Cynthia—there could be several people with motives to poison her besides Jason. Maybe her suspicions of the man were unfounded after all. . . .

As soon as the energetic dance ended, Mark was immediately by her side to guide her to the edge of the dance floor. Carolyn realized that whatever had happened between Mark and Cynthia, she must put a stop to his continued advances now. He was gasping for breath after the lively dance, so before he could speak, she began quickly, "Mr. Simmons, whatever we have been to each other in the past, we must end it here and now."

"What? Darling, how can you? Why are you acting this way?"

"Because I very foolishly ran away from my husband."

"People have been whispering of it, but I refused to believe it. I was certain that you loved me."

"I *don't* love you," Carolyn said bluntly. She raised a hand to stop his protestations. "No. Whatever I said in the past is over. It's no longer important or relevant. I learned something while I was away. Nothing is as important to me as my husband and child. Please, believe me, I regret that I have to be cruel. In the end, you'll see that it's the best thing for both of us."

Well, that certainly sounded pious enough, Carolyn thought.

Outrage spread across Mark's face. "You vain, deceitful bitch!"

She so disliked this melodramatic prig—she wondered what Cynthia found attractive about him and sighed. Cynthia's taste seemed questionable at best.

"Please, don't make a scene."

"Don't make a scene! That's all you care about, isn't it? Sam Fanning warned me. He said that under that angelic exterior, you were heartless and unprincipled." His eyes flashed wildly. "Just wait. Just wait, my beautiful lady. You'll regret this. I swear it!" He stalked out of the room.

Suddenly, an iron grip held her arm, and she knew without glancing up that it was Jason. "I believe I have the next dance, my dear."

His green eyes gazed down at her quizzically, almost warmly. "Oh. Yes, of course." Jason led her onto the dance floor and pulled her into his arms. Though he was not an excellent dancer, he was very good and he guided her firmly—it was easy for Carolyn to follow his lead.

"Did I overhear that pasteboard Byron threatening you?"

She spoke in a hushed voice, her lips near his ear. "I didn't realize you were nearby. Uh, yes, he threatened me after a fashion. I don't imagine it was serious, though. Rather like a child saying 'You'll be sorry.' You know the sort of thing."

"Yes, I know. But somehow I doubt it was quite that mild. I'll have a talk with him later."

Carolyn glanced up anxiously, meeting his grim smile. "Don't worry. I doubt he'll reveal anything I didn't already suspect. I take it you gave him his walking papers."

"Something like that."

"Does he no longer appeal? Don't tell me you've grown bored with boys and weaklings."

"I can't imagine what—" Carolyn barely stopped herself from saying her twin's name. She bit her lip, fearing she might cry. How she hated the mockery in Jason's voice, how she wanted to cry out that she wasn't Cynthia, that she had never been unfaithful to her husband even after he died. And how until one day ago, Mark Simmons was a stranger to her—that he meant nothing to her. Her eyes glimmered with tears. It was this man who embraced her now, Cynthia's husband, whose very touch made her shiver with longing. She looked up at him and something in her face made him draw in a hasty breath.

Jason led them to the edge of the dance floor and pulled Carolyn into one of the small, darkened alcoves. "The way you looked at me just then," he murmured. "I used to lie awake at night praying you'd look at me that way."

"I—I—what way?" Carolyn stammered.

"Heavy-lidded, your eyes deep blue, your mouth slightly open, so." He brushed his thumb across her lower lip. "As if you wanted—quite badly—to be kissed." His arms encircled her, pulling her up and into him. He kissed her deeply, his mouth feasting on hers. Carolyn trembled against him, filled with a need she had never known before. His lips were greedy, like those of a starving man at a banquet who fears that his food might be jerked away from him at any moment. His arms pulled her more and more tightly against him; through their clothes she could feel the pulse of his desire, and in response a bittersweet ache blossomed within her. Carolyn dug her fingers into his shoulders, arching up into him.

Jason groaned faintly at her action and trailed fervent kisses down her vulnerable throat. "You want me. Say you want me," he murmured.

"I do," she whispered, and his lips returned to seize her mouth, wild and triumphant.

"Oh, excuse me," A male voice exclaimed behind them, then chuckled in surprise. Jason released her and whirled. Lord Chester stood in the opening of the alcove, smiling, his face rosy with alcohol and good cheer. "I say, Broughton, still acting like honeymooners after all these years?" He chuckled again and was gone.

Jason's eyes were wild and glittering, his face imbued with passion. He wet his lips and slowly released his clenched hands. "God, Cynthia, how can you still have the power to—I must be mad!" He hurried from the alcove.

Carolyn stared after him, shaking from the onslaught of a swirl of feelings. Now she was forced to admit it—she wanted him. The truth was, she longed to feel his naked skin against hers. She desired him with a hunger she'd never felt for any man. But he was already taken—she couldn't have him, even *if* Cynthia didn't appreciate him. . . . She turned her vacant and defeated stare out to the dark night.

Eleven

$\mathcal{S}$omehow she got through the rest of the party, dancing, smiling, talking. Finally, all the guests were gone, and she could seek the safety and comfort of her room. Priscilla, tired from the extra work of the weekend, was quite content to help her undress with little comment on the ball. After the girl had gone downstairs, Carolyn crawled into bed, longing for the blissful oblivion of sleep.

But she could not sleep—the scene in the alcove replayed in her mind, over and over. Carolyn shook her head. It didn't make any difference that Cynthia had rejected Jason—it was still wrong, dreadfully wrong of her to desire this man. "Which is really all it is," she told herself, for she had no love for Jason Somerville. She couldn't, not if he was as evil as she was told. But then, she had no concrete evidence—to Carolyn, Jason seemed firm but sometimes understanding, passionate—and certainly desirable. . . .

Carolyn shoved her hands into her hair and pressed her palms against her skull, as if to control the thoughts rampaging within. What did it matter who was right or wrong or whether Jason and Cynthia were not good for each other? The fact remained that Jason was married to Cynthia, and that meant there could be nothing between him and Carolyn. Besides, Jason despised her. How could she let a man make love to her knowing that he held her in contempt even as he caressed her body? There was no love on his part, only desire, and that desire was not even for herself but for her sister.

It was a dreadful mess. She ought to go to Jason now and explain, confess the scheme, and then leave this house forever. It would be the best thing never to see Jason Somerville again, for he was far too unsettling. But her heart ached at the thought of leaving Laurel, who had come to trust and depend on her. The child was what was important, and she would have to manage the situation for Laurel's sake. She'd stay away from Jason, avoid any hint of intimacy, and she would exercise a stern control over her thoughts and emotions.

A noise of metal grating on metal cut through the still air, and Carolyn jumped. She looked at the door leading to Jason's room—he had tried to enter her room and had found the door locked. Carolyn held her breath, but there was no knock upon the door, only the faint click of his heels retreating from the door. Carolyn slid from her bed and tiptoed to the door. She leaned her ear against the wood and listened. There was the muffled sound of pacing footsteps and every now and then a clink of glass or the soft thud of a drawer closing. But the pacing continued. Carolyn shivered; the night air was cool, and she knew she should return to bed. Yet she didn't move.

The footsteps came toward the door again, but then there was only silence, then a low curse, then the pacing went on. Torn between relief and disappointment, Carolyn returned to bed and huddled beneath the covers. Her shivering soon stopped, but it was many hours before she went to sleep.

Though she was bedraggled and groggy the next morning, Jason didn't look as if he had lost any sleep the night before. Carolyn knew every minute of her sleeplessness showed in the dark shadows beneath her eyes, and she longed to return to bed to recover some of the rest she had lost listening to Jason's footsteps into the night. Jason was by her side again today as they bid farewell to their weekend guests, who left throughout the day.

When Flora and Jack came to say good-bye, Flora drew Carolyn to one side. "I can't tell you how much I've enjoyed the weekend," she began. "It's been the most pleasant time I've had at Broughton Court, I do believe. You and Jason look as if you have reached a . . . pleasant understanding. No, no need to tell me; I'm not prying, just extending my good wishes."

"Thank you, Flora. I appreciate that you care."

"Again, I may be sticking my nose in where it's not wanted, but I thought you might be interested: I know a woman in London who has done a great deal of work with children like Laurel. I met her at a tea where they were raising funds for her organization. Her name is Lucy Carlisle. I talked to her for several minutes and quite liked her. She has some new and startling ideas, and you might be interested in what she has to say."

"Oh, yes! I'd give anything for some information on what to do with Laurel. Most of the time I flounder around in the dark. I'd appreciate it if you could give me her address so I could write her."

"I don't know her address, but I'm sure I can find out. When I do, I'll send you a letter."

"Thank you." Carolyn gave the woman's hand a fervent squeeze. "You're a wonderful friend."

"Thank you for saying so. Now, good-bye, dear. Come to

London with Jason sometime, and we can get together for a nice, long gossip."

"I'd love to."

"What's this?" Jason asked softly as the other couple walked away and out the front door held open by Barlow. "You and Flora planning something?"

Carolyn shrugged. "Sort of. She asked me to visit her if I went to London with you. I guess that's not very likely."

"I'd say not, from past experience."

"She's a very dear person," Carolyn continued.

"Flora?" His eyebrows shot up. "I thought you called her 'brassy and bold.' "

Carolyn met his gaze squarely. "That doesn't mean she can't be warm and generous, too. Does it?"

"I suppose not."

"She offered to send me the address of a woman who works with children like Laurel. It could be a great help."

In response, he simply looked at her hard for a moment, then moved away to greet the couple coming toward them. "Mr. Osborne. Ma'am."

The Osbornes were the last to leave, and Carolyn sagged with relief when Barlow closed the door behind them. Well, she had survived the weekend, the hardest test yet of her masquerade as Cynthia. And yet . . . she felt more downhearted than she had any time since she had come to Broughton Court.

The next two weeks were painfully tedious. Carolyn continued to spend several hours a day with Laurel. One day she took Laurel downstairs to the music room and played several pieces on the piano. Carolyn had never been as good a pianist as Cynthia, but she could play well enough to pick out simple tunes, and the girl's eyes shone as she listened to the songs. When Carolyn suggested that she try it out herself, Laurel ran her fingers lovingly over the ivory keys. She alternated between the deep vibration of the low keys and the piercing tinkle of the upper notes, delighted with the contrast. Then to her amazement the girl jumped up, abandoning the piano, and began to march around the room, thrilled at the sound of her own feet keeping a beat.

A harp stood in one corner of the room, and Carolyn trailed her fingertips down its strings. Laurel was by her side in an instant, reaching out to pluck the strings. She lost interest in it, though, and began to march and clap again. Laughing with her, Carolyn clapped in time to the girl's noise. Suddenly, Jason barged in. "What the devil's going on here?" He saw Laurel, and his face softened. "Hello, love."

Carolyn experienced a stabbing pain in her chest at the soft words he addressed only to his daughter. Suppressing it, she answered calmly. "We are having an introduction to music."

"Really?" he commented, his voice dry. "I thought perhaps it was an introduction to riot."

"Nonsense," Carolyn told him sternly. "Laurel, show your father how you can clap."

Eagerly Laurel began to clap and march, then hurried to the harp and the piano to display her other new discoveries. She beamed with pleasure at each thing she did, and Jason couldn't help but smile back. Laurel demanded, "Mama sing."

"No, pet, not now," Carolyn demured. "Later, when we go back to your room."

Laurel pouted. "Mama sing."

"Go ahead," Jason urged. "I'd like to hear you."

Carolyn sighed. "Well, all right. It was my singing that made me first realize Laurel so enjoyed music." She began an old ballad, and Laurel happily plunked herself down in Carolyn's lap and leaned her head against Carolyn's shoulder. Jason watched them with an odd look on his face, and Carolyn wondered what his thoughts were. He looked almost sad, though Carolyn could see little reason for it.

When Carolyn finished, he clapped lightly. "Bravo! I've enjoyed listening to you both, but now I must get back to work." He leaned over to drop a kiss on Laurel's forehead, and for a moment he was so close to Carolyn she could see the individual lashes around his eyes. As he rose from the kiss, his eyes strayed to Carolyn's mouth, and Carolyn remembered clearly the touch of his lips on hers, could almost taste them again, and she wondered if he was thinking the same thing. Jason hastily left the room. Carolyn stood, setting Laurel on the floor. "I think it's time we went back up to your room."

Despite the hours she spent with the child, Laurel could not fill all Carolyn's time, and she was often bored. She had few household duties, and Jason was rarely around. She saw him only at meals and perhaps for a few minutes after supper in the evenings.

But in his every glance and movement, it was evident that he hadn't been able to cast off the desire that had been kindled the night of the ball.

Often at dinner, as they talked in a stilted manner about the weather and household happenings, his eyes would be steadily on her and his finger would circle the rim of his wine glass again and again until Carolyn was mesmerized by it. She could feel the scratch of his faintly rough fingertip gliding over her skin, and she wondered if that was what he felt, too, instead of the cool glass beneath his finger. His eyes would darken, his mouth would soften, and he would shift in his chair. Sexual tension stretched between them like a web, fragile, shimmering, but unbreakable. The sight of him tugged at her senses, and Carolyn ached to touch him, to smell his hot male scent, to hear his breath rasping in her ear.

After being with him, Carolyn was charged with nervous energy, but when he wasn't around she was unbearably bored. To fill her day, she began to ride again. She went to the stables as often as she could and rode out on the placid Gray Lady. She explored the area surrounding Broughton Court, but was always careful to keep her directions straight, for she could ill afford to get lost and have to ask someone how to return to her own house. The ruins of the old keep had given her an eerie feeling, so she usually visited the hop fields and the orchards, taking practically every country path she passed. One day she found a beautiful long pond, lazy and smooth in the early-winter sun, with an old waterwheel and a decaying wooden building at the far end. Reeds grew at the water's edge, housing coots and moorhens, and past the reeds the slim white beech trees began.

Carolyn often dismounted there and sat on a large flat rock, dreamily contemplating the still water, broken now and then by the silvery flash of a fish underwater or the plop of a kingfisher diving to catch his prey. She remembered that Mark Simmons had mentioned a hammer pond, and she wondered if this was it. Obviously the pond had once powered a now-defunct mill of some sort, but the building was too decayed to encourage any exploration of it. It was only when Priscilla mentioned her great-grandfather working in the forge that Carolyn put it together. "Oh, you mean down by the hammer pond?"

"Yes'm, that's the place. They dammed up the pond so the water would work the bellows and trip-hammers, you see. It was once a tremendous sight, they say. I never saw it myself. The iron work stopped long before I was born, you know. But me grandmother says it was a sight to behold, that peaceful pond out there and inside the bellows blowing and the fires going in the vast furnaces, looking like Hades itself."

"What happened to it? I mean, why did they stop making iron?"

Priscilla shrugged. "I don't understand it exactly, milady, but I think it was because of coal. They began using coal for the furnaces instead of charcoal, like they used here. So the forges moved north, where the coalfields are. There are abandoned forges and hammer ponds all over the country-side in the Weald."

Carolyn didn't need to ask what the Weald was, for that much she knew from her geography lessons as a child. The Weald was the fertile inner strip of Kent running between the southern and northern Chalk Downs. "How sad," she commented softly. "And yet it's a beautiful spot."

The next time she visited the pond, Carolyn went to the sagging doorway of the ramshackle building and peered in. It was still and dusty inside, boards fallen everywhere. Sun slanted through holes in the roof and walls, and dust motes danced in the beams of light. There was nothing left of the furnaces and bellows. They had been sold, she supposed, or stolen bit by bit for their metal. But she could well imagine the eerie sight of flames leaping in large furnaces while men toiled and sweated in front of them, with the ear-splitting ring of hammers sounding out.

When she wasn't riding, Carolyn pondered the identity of the person who had tried to poison her. She had already looked through Cynthia's room and found no letters or diaries or even an address book, but she searched the room again, emptying out every drawer and checking behind it for a secret compartment or something glued to the back wall. She twisted and poked at all the curliques and scrollwork of the ornate furniture and even tried to pull off the knobs atop the posters of the bed. She found nothing. Next she went to the trunks in the attic. Priscilla gave her an odd look, but obligingly led her to the gloomy attic and showed her which trunks contained Cynthia's clothes. Carolyn pawed through them without any success and investigated several other trunks and some old furniture as well. She marveled over some beautiful pieces of Tudor and Jacobean furniture, thinking how much better it suited the house than the more modern furniture, but she discovered nothing to her purpose.

The next day, when she went up to Laurel's room, she took Bonnie aside and questioned her. "Did Cynthia have any sort of safe or locked jewel box? Any hiding place that you know of?"

Bonnie stared at her. "Why, no, miss, not that I recall."

"Think," Carolyn urged. "It's important. I'm looking for any kind of letter or note or maybe even a diary of Cynthia's, anything that would give me a clue."

"A clue? Whatever are you talking about?"

"Bonnie, someone tried to poison me. I know I didn't take that arsenic myself. But since everyone thinks I'm Cynthia, that means it's someone trying to kill Cynthia. Don't you see?"

"But who would want to murder Miss Cynthia? That's sheer nonsense."

"It's not! Cynthia may have taken arsenic for her complexion, but I've never done so in my life. And the other day at the hunt, my saddle happened to come loose *and* Gray Lady, the most gentle horse in the world, suddenly bolted. You know Cynthia can't ride well. If it had been she on the horse, she could have been seriously injured or even killed—and everyone thought it was Cynthia on the horse."

Bonnie frowned. "I see what you mean, Miss Caro, but couldn't they have been accidents?"

"The horse, perhaps, but not putting arsenic in my food or drink every day, a little bit at a time."

"I saw Miss Cindy toss a bundle of letters in the fire one day before she left. My guess is she burned her personal papers or took them with her, so his lordship wouldn't find them."

Carolyn sighed in frustration. "Did you ever hear Cynthia talk about anyone who might have cause to dislike her? Who might hold a grudge against her?"

"Miss Cynthia? Not likely. Everyone loved her . . . except *him.* If you're looking for a murderer, it'd be his lordship. He'd be happy to get rid of her as long as his name didn't suffer for it. And he's one who wouldn't stop at anything to get what he wants." Bonnie nodded her head sagely. "That's who it is."

"I—I've thought of him." Carolyn looked away from Bonnie. "But I don't think it is. It isn't like him."

"What? Isn't like him! That man's capable of anything. I told you how he treated your sister, how cruel and harsh—"

"But, you see, I've found out it wasn't exactly like that," Carolyn blurted out. "I think—I think Cynthia hid some things from you."

"What are you saying? That your own sweet sister was a liar?" She grabbed Carolyn's shoulders and stared into her face, her eyes narrowed and furious. "Have you been listening to that devil's lies? Are you turning your back on your own twin?"

"No, Bonnie, of course not!" Carolyn grasped the nurse's

wrists and firmly pulled her hands away. "It was nothing Jason said to me. I'm not turning my back on Cynthia. But Mark Simmons hounded me during the hunt weekend, acting as if he and I had been lovers. I didn't believe his hints and innuendoes, of course, but finally he told me outright that he and Cynthia had been . . . well, intimate."

The color drained from Bonnie's face. She stepped back and sat down heavily in the rocker. "No," she murmured, "I don't believe it."

"Why should he lie? He thought he was talking to Cynthia, who would be the one person who'd know if he lied. It would be pointless to pretend with her."

Bonnie blinked. "There must be a mistake. Mr. Bingham was the only man she ever loved. Cynthia would never—"

Carolyn dropped down on her knees beside the woman's chair. "I don't know what Cynthia did or why. I only know that she wasn't as she seemed in at least one area of her life. Like you, I thought there could be no one who held a grudge against her or would wish to harm her, but now I'm not so sure. What if Mark Simmons had a jealous fiancée? What if Dennis Bingham jilted someone for her? What if she . . . had another lover besides Mark Simmons, and he was filled with a murderous rage when she ran off with Mr. Bingham?"

"No! You're making your sister out to be a whore. It's not true. I won't have it! I won't listen to this!" Bonnie glared at her. "You were always jealous of Miss Cindy, always. Because she was so sweet and pretty, so well-loved."

"How can you say that? It's crazy! Wrong! Yes, Cynthia was loved by many people, but I wasn't jealous of her for it. I loved her, too! I was the one who protected her, helped her. You know that."

"I know you were always trying to get Sir Neville's attention, always shoving poor little Cynthia into the background."

"Rubbish! It's true our father seemed to prefer me. We had a common interest in horses that Cynthia didn't share, and he was scornful of Cynthia's timidity and fear of animals. Because of that Cynthia often felt that he didn't love her as he did me, but I don't think that's true. As we got older, he changed and wanted me to be more like Cynthia. But I never tried to outdo Cynthia or relegate her to the background. Cynthia was retiring, and I was outgoing. I enjoyed going for a ride with Papa, and Cynthia didn't. It was as simple as that."

Bonnie sighed, and Carolyn realized suddenly how old she looked. "I'm sorry, miss. I shouldn't have said that. But I can't believe my baby has done anything wrong."

"I'm not saying Cynthia did anything wrong. No doubt there was a reason for whatever she did. I wouldn't have told you, except I want you to realize how urgent and necessary it is that I find out about Cynthia's past. There could be a person in it who's now trying to kill her—or rather, me."

"Sir Neville turned against her, just as he did against you."

"Father wouldn't harm her, no matter how irate he got."

"No, of course not."

"Who were her friends?"

"Friends? Not many came here except his lordship's friends. When they traveled to London, I expect she had friends there, but I never went with them to London. Laurel and I stayed here. She was fairly close to your Cousin Bella. At least, they used to write each other now and then. I remember she received a letter from her a week or two before she left. There was a Mrs. Willingham, I believe, who also wrote her. And she mentioned a lady named Melissa a few times when she was telling me about what she did in London. But that could have been the same person as Mrs. Willingham. I'm not sure."

"Did she never speak of anyone who was cutting to her or who disliked her?"

Bonnie frowned. "Once she told me that Miss Nelson disliked her heartily. She said Miss Nelson had a *tendre* for his lordship and was jealous of her. She had to giggle, it was so silly: Imagine anyone being jealous of her because of Lord Broughton, when they disliked each other so excessively."

"Yes, I thought of Millicent Nelson. She has been obvious in her dislike for Cynthia. And she brought me something to eat when I was first ill. But she wasn't at the hunt. Besides, she couldn't have been here every day to doctor my food."

"No one was here every day except the servants and Lord Broughton," Bonnie pointed out. "And if one of the servants had it in for milady, I'd have heard. Don't you see? It had to be his lordship."

"Someone could have paid a servant to put a little poison in my food. Or—or maybe put arsenic in a bowl of salt or sugar that Cook used to prepare my food."

"Now you're talking out of your head. How could a person poison the salt or sugar without everyone else getting sick, too? And paying someone's the surest way of getting caught. No, it was his lordship that did it, and you're doing your best to pretend it wasn't. Why? Don't tell me you've gone sweet on that monster."

"Of course not! It simply doesn't seem like him. It's too sneaky, too secretive. He's blunt and open in his anger."

"You're fooling yourself, miss, and you'll be the one who suffers because of it. He can be charming if he wants to. Heaven knows, Miss Cynthia was fooled by him at first, enough that she went and married him. She regretted it bitterly, and you will, too, if you let him win you over with sweet words and kisses."

Carolyn glanced at the woman, startled by her knowledge, then realized that she'd given herself away. Bonnie nodded, her mouth grim. "I thought so. Well, there's nothing I can say to stop you. I learned that long ago. You've always had more daring than sense, ever since you were a little girl. You'll go ahead and take the jumps. But this time it'll be the death of you."

Carolyn was overjoyed when she received a letter from Flora two weeks after the hunt. In it, she thanked Carolyn warmly for the weekend, then gave the address of Lucy Carlisle, followed by more praise of the woman's work with slow children. Carolyn immediately sent Flora back a note thanking her for the address, then began a letter to Miss Carlisle. It took her some time and several ruined pieces of stationery to give the other woman a succinct and accurate picture of Laurel and her problems. When she had finally finished, she folded and sealed the letter, then went down to Jason's study to ask him to frank it for her.

He looked surprised when she entered his study, but did as she asked. "Who is this Carlisle woman?" he asked, glancing at the address.

"A teacher Flora knows in London. You remember, I told you Flora had said she would send me her address."

"Ah, yes. She knows something about children like Laurel."

"Yes." Carolyn hesitated, aware of the subtle, persistent strain that she always felt in his presence. She longed to linger, yet was frightened to. He had such an effect on her senses, on her very reason. "Thank you. I must go now."

"Cynthia, wait." Jason rose behind her. Carolyn turned, her pulse hammering. Jason spread out his hands, bracing his fingertips against the top of his desk. His face was solemn and cool. "I will be leaving tomorrow morning."

"Oh. I see."

"I have to make a trip to Dover. I should return the following day."

"Very well. I shall tell Mrs. Morely not to expect you for dinner tomorrow."

"Thank you."

"Yes, well, good-bye. I hope you have a pleasant journey."

"Thank you. Good-bye, Cynthia."

Carolyn hurried from the study. It was amazing how it galled her when he called her by her sister's name. She wanted him to know her as herself . . . to desire her for herself. Several times during the past few weeks she had wanted to go to Jason and confess what she had done, but she couldn't bring herself to do it. For then she would have to leave, and Jason would be furious with her.

She spent the rest of the day unpleasantly mired in her confused thoughts. A good, hard gallop would help to clear away the cobwebs in her mind, but it would be impossible to get Gray Lady up to a gallop. She could explain to Jason her daily trips on Gray Lady if he should find out, but she could think of no way to justify Cynthia's galloping over the fields on a fast mount.

When she awoke the next morning, Jason was already gone, as Priscilla informed her when she brought Carolyn's breakfast in on a tray. Carolyn barely tasted the freshly baked bread slathered with pale, creamy butter or the hot, sweet tea, for her thoughts were on Jason. It was polite of him not to wake her, but she would rather he had wanted to see her before he left. She was still restless and disturbed from her thoughts of yesterday, so she decided to pit her skill and strength against a fast horse and go for a glorious ride . . . herself again, if only for an hour or two. Jason wasn't here, so he couldn't possibly catch her galloping.

Seized with haste, she jumped into her riding habit. "Just tie my hair back with a ribbon," she told Priscilla. "No need to bother with putting it up before I ride." She thrust her feet into the supple leather boots and threw on the jacket Priscilla held out to her. Waving Priscilla aside, she buttoned the large jet buttons herself. A quick jab of the hatpin secured her jaunty blue riding hat in place, and then, grabbing her thin leather gloves and riding crop, she hurried from the room.

She could have breakfast later, she thought, smelling the baking bread as she hurried past the kitchen. Right now she wanted only to go, before her courage—or stupidity—failed her. A groom glanced up, surprised, when she burst into the stables. "Oh, milady, excuse me. Were you wanting to catch his lordship? He's already gone, a good hour ago."

"I know. I've come to ride." The lad bobbed his head and started toward Gray Lady's stall. "No. This time I want Felicity."

"Felicity!" The stableboy gaped. "Oh, no, milady, you must be mistaken."

"I'm not mistaken," Carolyn told him firmly. "Felicity is my horse, is she not?"

"Yes, milady. I'll saddle her right away." Thinking she had lost her wits, he went about the business of putting a saddle and bridle on the mare. Carolyn went first to pat her nose and talk reassuringly to the mare as it was led out of the stable. She wished she had thought to get an apple or carrot from the kitchen, for that would assure the mare's trust in her. The stableboy led Felicity to the mounting block, and Carolyn climbed up expertly. This was obviously a quality horse, more nervous of temperament than the placid mare she usually rode, and Carolyn didn't want to make her uneasy by pulling at the saddle or grabbing at her mane or shifting her weight poorly.

Carolyn took the reins from the lad, getting the bit firmly in the mare's mouth, and urged on Felicity with a light tap to her ribs. Unaccustomed to this rider, Felicity danced a little, shaking her head and snorting out breath. With a toss of her head, she trotted out of the yard. Wanting to learn the horse a little better and give the mare a chance to know her, she did not put Felicity to a greater speed at once, but kept her at a pleasant gait. She seemed frisky and eager, but she was not difficult to control nor overly skittish. What a fantastic horse!

Carolyn turned her in the direction of the hammer pond, riding past the hop fields, with their lines of sweet chestnut poles, then through an orchard of apple trees. Their branches, now bare of fruit and leaves, formed a lacework canopy above her head. She emerged into a small copse of pines. A gray squirrel darted across her path and up a tree trunk. Felicity snorted but did not start at the sudden movement, confirming Carolyn's notion that she was a steady, sensible horse.

Beyond the pines lay a long, uncultivated meadow. Felicity was eager to run and, at the merest pressure of Carolyn's heels, took off across the barren soil. This was no runaway mount as Gray Lady had been the day of the hunt, but simply a healthy horse running with pleasure and firmly under the control of its rider. Carolyn laughed aloud, leaning into the mare's superb pace. The wind swept over her face and pushed through her hair, whipping off her little hat and sending it flying.

Reveling in the wonderful freedom, it was some time before she noticed the hoofbeats of another horse thundering across the meadow behind her, gaining on her steadily.

She hauled back on the reins, and Felicity slowed down. Out of the corner of her eye, she saw Jason, high upon his sleek horse, galloping parallel with her! He maneuvered the horse closer and closer to her, his face tense with concentration, until he was precariously close to her horse for the speed they were traveling. When he was riding right alongside of her, he reached for her horse's bridle, but Carolyn pulled back firmly on the reins. In frustration, Jason veered away suddenly, and Carolyn came to an urgent stop.

Jason stopped farther along the meadow and, with a sudden jerk of the reins, wheeled his white stallion back. "What the devil do you think you're doing?" he snapped, dismounting lithely and striding toward her.

Carolyn slid from her saddle to the ground and faced him, hands on her hips. "I might better ask what you think *you're* doing, grabbing at my horse's bridle like that! It frightened her; she could have unseated me."

"I was trying to stop her before you were thrown and seriously injured!" he raged back, his face thunderous.

"I wasn't about to get thrown!" Carolyn protested. "I was letting Felicity run and thoroughly enjoying it, I must say, before you came along." Carolyn's hair had come loose from its ribbon during her wild ride and it streamed around her face and shoulders like a fiery veil. Impatiently, she shoved it back and glared at Jason, her eyes sparkling with irritation. She looked wild and untamed, a challenge to the strongest man.

Jason's eyes ran over her, and when he spoke he seemed

distracted. "I thought she was running away with you. My God, Gray Lady ran away with you. How could I expect you to be able to handle Felicity?"

"Gray Lady was startled, she bolted. I wanted Felicity to run. There's a great deal of difference in the two."

"What are you doing out here on that horse, anyway?" he asked, more gently, looking through her eyes now, searching . . . .

Carolyn ignored his look and spat a question back.

"That's what you gave her to me for, isn't it? To ride?"

"Yes, of course. But you've never gone near her. She frightens you."

Carolyn shrugged. "I've ridden Gray Lady for weeks. I decided to overcome my fear of horses. It's really rather silly for a grown woman, isn't it? After the fright I got during the hunt, I realized that if I had been able to ride better I might not have been thrown. I also learned that any nag, even a gentle one, can run away with you. I've never been as safe as I thought on a placid horse." She tried to retain logic as she pieced together a believable excuse.

"So you've been practicing riding to overcome your fears?"

"Yes. I remembered all the things Papa told me when he originally taught me to ride, and I tried them over and over until I felt that I was getting the hang of it. Today I decided to graduate to Felicity."

"That's why you've ridden out each day?" His voice was soft, almost musing.

Carolyn wanted to sidetrack him before he could examine her explanation, so she turned on him indignantly and demanded, "What are *you* doing here? You rode off for Dover this morning."

Jason could not make eye contact with her—he looked off

uncomfortably toward the horizon, and Carolyn's rage was uncontrollable. "You lied to me! You never intended to go to Dover. You—you were spying on me!"

He looked up sternly. "Yes, I was spying. I wanted to discover who you met when you rode out every day."

"You thought I was meeting someone? That I was having an affair?" Carolyn was tense with fury, and she felt betrayed and hurt, not thinking of the provocation Cynthia had given Jason for believing that of her, but only feeling the deep pain of his distrust. "How dare you!"

"Don't play the virtuous, misconstrued wife with me!" Jason snapped. "What was I supposed to think when you suddenly developed this interest in riding? You? What a farce! After the scene you'd played before me with Mark Simmons, I wasn't sure whether you'd done it for my benefit and were still seeing him or had actually rejected him for another lover. It's not like you to be without a man long."

"Oh God—how I *despise* you!" In her white rage, she swung at him with her riding crop. It hardly touched him, but Jason was spurred to action. He seized her shoulders and his fingers bit into her flesh until she cried out.

"Damn you! How can you be so lovely and still so heartless? Why can't I—" He broke off, overwhelmed with anger and passion. His hands plunged into the satiny mass of her hair and held her head, while his mouth pressed hungrily into hers.

Twelve

*H*is kiss was fierce and consuming, but Carolyn met him with a wildness of her own, clinging to his mouth and wrapping her arms tightly around his neck. Their highly charged emotions of a moment earlier had broken down all restraints, and Jason was lost to reason, driven by pure animal hunger. His pent-up longing was now insatiable; he couldn't get enough of her lips, or the taste of the skin of her cheeks and chin and throat.

For Carolyn, there were no concrete thoughts, only the shimmering patterns of pleasure. She moved with him with a knowledge older than time, her body surging into this sensual realm she had never before explored. She laced her fingers through his hair, and, in a melting kiss, his tongue invaded her mouth, sending her into a spinning whirl.

Jason's hands left her hair to slide under her buttocks, and he pressed her up against him. He lifted her with his hard arms and trailed kisses down her neck. The high collar of her blouse impeded his progress, and he impatiently undid the top button, giving him access to the smooth hollow of her throat.

He let her slide down in his arms to the ground, then, in a frenzy barely kept under control, he began to unfasten her clothes. Continuing down the front of her blouse, he tore off one of the tiny flat buttons, then he pulled its ends out of her skirt, and eagerly, forcefully, removed her blouse. Her shimmering white chemise, pulled in at the top with a dainty pink ribbon, disclosed the tops of her breasts, which swelled under the satin garment.

Jason pulled the dainty pink bow loose, sending the tiny ribbon slipping through its eyelet loops, and the chemise dipped lower, drifting down to rest upon her pink-brown nipples. With his forefinger, he lowered the chemise a fraction of an inch, and he watched her steadily as he traced the brownish outside circle of her nipples with his finger, spiraling in to the very center of her breasts. Carolyn gasped with delight.

Jason smiled as he reached lower inside the chemise and pulled it down still farther, completely uncovering her breasts. The cool air made her nipples harder, and as Jason's hands spread out over her breasts, enclosing them in long, supple fingers, his eyelids fluttered half-closed in exquisite pleasure. "How beautiful you are." He bent and kissed the quivering top of one breast. "Perfection."

With a groan he lifted her and buried his face between her breasts. He carried her to the cover of a nearby oak, and Jason whipped off his riding jacket to lay it on the ground, then pulled Carolyn down beside him. She lay back on his jacket, and his eyes feasted on her until his need was too raging to permit him to linger any longer. He slid his arms beneath her back so that she arched provocatively toward him, then rested on his forearms. With a deep sigh of satisfaction, his mouth came down to capture the succulent tip of one breast.

His tongue was a hot, wet lash whipping her nipple to a

brittle point; then a softly circling seducer, laving her with soothing warmth; then a hard, teasing tip edging her nipple and tracing the line where white flesh met pink, soft skin. Carolyn writhed beneath the artistry of his mouth, alive to a hundred new and startling sensations. She had never dreamed of such glorious pleasure, such sublime frustration. A white-hot yearning bloomed in her loins, spreading, aching, overflowing, filling her with insatiable desire.

She wanted to touch him, needed to feel the searing smoothness of his skin beneath her hands. Carolyn reached up to caress his chest and arms; she unfastened the buttons of his shirt, then slid her hands beneath the material, emitting a little sigh of satisfaction. Jason lifted his head and stared down at her face while she ran her hands over him freely. Her expression was that of a woman in the throes of passion, one assaulted by pleasure. He drank it in, steeling himself to control the willful desire that raged within him, threatening to break its bounds and rush to fulfillment before he knew the full pleasure of their lovemaking.

Carolyn's hands drifted down the ridged plateau of his rib cage, her fingers separating the prickly, curling chest hairs. She found the hard nipples of his flat male breasts and circled them with her forefingers, and ran her hands around his ribs to his powerful back, exploring with fingertips and nails. Working her way back to his chest again, she traced the V of his hair and dipped down to his navel. Jason uttered a harsh groan and clenched his jaw.

He reared back, unable to wait any longer, and shoved his hands up her legs, under her skirt. Only the thin cotton cloth of her pantalets separated his hands from her skin, and he could feel the pulsing warmth of her flesh. The front of her riding skirt was bunched up around her waist from his probing caresses, and the back lay beneath her, spread out like a backdrop for the beauty of her legs. Jason caressed her through the cloth of her pantalets, then rocked back on his heels and pulled off her riding boots. He stripped off first one lacy garter, then the other, and rolled down her dark stockings. Finally, he reached up, unfastened the drawstring of her pantalets, and pulled them off her legs.

Jason's eyes were emerald fire as he gazed at her. Starting at her ankles, he slid his hands up her calves, her knees, her thighs. He spread her legs apart to caress the sensual softness of her inner thighs. Then he went to her hips, lightly caressing her skin with his fingertips, wandering down to her thighs and back to her buttocks, touching her everywhere except in that one spot, the vital, throbbing center of her desire. Carolyn ached for his touch, even arched upward to intercept his hand, but still he would not come to her. At last, he grazed the triangle of fiery hair, and his fingers slid inside her, where it was hot and damp. Carolyn moaned, and he pressed the heel of his hand against the fleshy mound as his thumb began a teasing dance of enticement.

"Yes, Jason"—she breathed, "please, yes. . . ."

Jason tore at the buttons of his trousers and jerked them down. He lifted her hips to receive him, and then he came into her, filling her, and she released a satisfied moan. He began to move within her, and her hips arched up to meet him, urging him on with circling, thrusting movements, as his desire spiraled wildly.

In an agony of pleasure and frustration, Carolyn gave into these pleasures she had never known. There was nothing else in the world, no time, no place, no thought, only this moment and this man. A tightness grew in her abdomen, spreading out heat like a fire. She was alive, bursting with sensual pleasures, and yet she was almost locked into her trance of desire. Suddenly Jason cried out, his face contorted, and thrust violently into her. The tightness within her burst, shooting waves of heat throughout her body and turning her insides to molten wax. Carolyn groaned and laughed at once in a wild whirl.

Jason slumped down on top of her, his chest slick with sweat. Carolyn slipped her arms around him under his shirt, so weak with satisfaction that she could barely move. His breathing returned to normal and he rolled off of her. "Damn!" he groaned and flung an arm across his eyes.

Carolyn moved, chilled by the touch of cool air on her body when his protection left her. Suddenly, the warm glow inside her faded. Jason's curse had not sounded like a man replete with happiness and sexual fulfillment. He stumbled to his feet, pulling on his trousers, and buttoned his shirt. "God!" he burst out and ran a hand through his hair. "You'd think I would have learned by now." He swung on her. "Do you enjoy doing this to me? Turning me into a sex-crazed animal? Does it give you some glorious feeling of power?"

Carolyn cringed before the force and evident self-disgust of his words. She struggled to a sitting position and quickly gathered her stray clothes and dressed. She was stunned and incapable of answering him, of even sorting out her own emotions. It had been so sudden, so wild, so beyond control. She fought back the stinging tears that pricked her eyelids.

Jason pointed to the meadow beyond. "Look at that. Damn! I didn't even bother to tie up the horses. We're lucky they haven't wandered off."

He strode out into the meadow, where his white stallion waited, happily munching on the leaves of a low-lying bush.

Felicity was farther afield, and Jason looped the stallion's reins around a limb of the tree before he went out to recover the mare. Carolyn watched his slow retreat as she finished tucking in her blouse and buttoning her jacket. When Jason returned, Carolyn avoided his eyes as she thrust her feet into her boots.

Mounted on their respective horses, they kept up a brisk pace back to the house. Not a word was exchanged; Jason rode beside her in silence until they were almost in sight of Broughton Court. "You'll be fine from here, won't you?" he asked.

"Yes, of course." Carolyn twisted her reins around her hands to hide their trembling.

"Good. Then I'll leave you here." He turned the stallion and cut across toward the path that ran to Hemby Keep.

Refusing to yield to the weak impulse to look after his retreating figure, Carolyn urged her horse forward. Her heart was leaden inside her chest, and she wanted desperately to cry. In the space of minutes she had vaulted to the greatest heights she'd ever known, experiencing a shattering, uncontrolled joy, then had plunged back into the dark depths of reality: It was not her love, but only her body Jason desired. Or her sister's body—it didn't seem to matter.

Jason didn't return that evening, most likely, Cynthia supposed, to carry on the pretense of having gone to Dover for the sake of the servants' gossip. Cynthia spent most of the afternoon lying in her room and had her dinner brought up on a tray. She visited Laurel, but it was an effort to sing songs and play with the child when she felt miserably weepy inside.

Why had she let everything get out of control? Her father

had always complained that she acted first and thought later, and Sir Neville had been right, it seemed to her now. This whole charade was the result of a moment's impulse, the consequences of which she should have thought of before. She had followed her heart at the expense of keeping up her role more times than she cared to remember. Arguing with Jason, mothering Laurel, riding, wearing clothes she liked— she had stepped out of character so many times it was only Jason's unawareness that kept her from exposing her true identity.

Today had been the worst, and it was no excuse that she hadn't known Jason intended to spy on her. Somehow, sooner or later, it would have gotten back to him. If she hadn't gone riding on Felicity, the whole wretched chain of events wouldn't have occurred.

Yet Carolyn had never known anything like Jason's love-making. Kit's caresses had never made her soar, but today she had known an encompassing joy she had never dreamed existed. But Jason wasn't for her, could never be for her.

With a sigh, Carolyn paced her room. It wasn't guilt over her betrayal of Cynthia that predominated her thoughts, but Jason's rejection of her that slashed her heart. He despised her so much that he was filled with self-loathing because he had made love to her, and therefore he would never willingly touch her again. That was the bitterest knowledge of all, for, no matter how much she might decry her sin, deep down she knew she wanted more than anything for Jason to make love to her again.

The night seemed endless. Carolyn passed it awake and alone with her grim thoughts. The next morning gray shadows circled under her eyes, and her skin was pasty from lack of sleep. She went through her morning routine listlessly, dressing, eating breakfast, and visiting Laurel. But after a lunch she hardly ate, she spent the afternoon napping, waking to feel more refreshed but no less confused and troubled.

Jason did not return for almost a week, and Carolyn told herself she was glad, for his absence gave her time to get her thoughts and emotions under control again. She lectured herself on the sins and insanity of what she had done and, moreover, tried to accept that his passion disgusted him. It was an impossible situation. The only thing to do was to forget him, wipe him out of her mind.

But the picture of Jason that haunted her mind's eye refused to let her forget him. She remembered his look as he took her beneath the oak tree, his eyes glittering, his mouth soft and mobile with desire. She saw him dressed in his riding clothes, trousers fitting his muscular thighs, tweed coat accenting his broad shoulders. She dreamed of his handsomeness, remembered the glory of his passion, and her insides melted with longing.

Cynthia didn't want him, Carolyn would argue. She had been unfaithful to him and run away. They were unsuited to each other, and nothing could come of their marriage. Cynthia wanted neither her husband nor her child, while Carolyn wanted both. Would it be wrong to stay, pretending to be Cynthia? To be a loving mother to Laurel, a true wife to Jason?

The only problem with her reasoning was that Jason hated her. Carolyn sighed and rubbed her forehead, feeling torn apart inside. Every tender thought of Jason, every inclination toward him seemed a betrayal of her sister, not so much because he was Cynthia's husband, but because Cynthia had left him. Carolyn found herself liking Jason, wanting him, feeling pity for the pain in his eyes. . . . Perhaps

Cynthia was the one who was wrong. Carolyn couldn't believe she could feel this way about a wicked, abusive man. Yet if Jason wasn't an evil beast, Cynthia had wronged him grievously.

To break the monotony of her dull days, she began going to Jason's study and picking out books to read. Soon she started sitting in the study to read a few pages to make certain she liked the book, and gradually she spent more and more time in the study reading. Eventually she realized that she simply wanted to be in Jason's study to feel his presence. Carolyn closed her eyes and rested her head against the high leather back of the chair, breathing in the formless aura of him.

Carolyn sat up with a start as the door opened. Jason stood on the threshold of the room, staring at her. For a moment his presence stunned her. Then she blushed and uncurled her leg from beneath her, scrambling to her feet. "I—I'm sorry. I didn't expect you back. That is, I, I borrowed a book and, well, I must have fallen asleep reading it."

"You needn't apologize," he cut her off curtly. "You are the mistress of the house, after all; none of the rooms are closed to you."

"Yes, but this is your room, and I assumed . . ." Carolyn cleared her throat. She was acting like an idiot; she must stop babbling. "Well. Welcome home. Was your trip enjoyable?"

For an answer, Jason gave an indistinguishable grunt and went to his desk to make a cursory inspection of his mail. Carolyn stood awkwardly, hating to leave, yet feeling absurd for remaining there without any encouragement from Jason. Her gaze stole to his supple hands, now casually picking up and discarding letters, and she remembered the feel of those virile hands on her breasts and legs, their heat and strength. Carolyn tore her eyes away. "I—uh, excuse me, I must go to Laurel."

She almost ran from the room and tore up the stairs to the safety of her bedroom. How could Jason have such an effect on her? As soon as he walked into the house, she started trembling and wanting him again.

She almost sent for her supper again that evening, but her pride wouldn't let her play the coward. She dressed in a lavender silk gown with a low-cut neckline filled in with sheer blond lace, refusing to acknowledge the small inner voice telling her she had chosen it for the enticement of the view it half-hid. Jason was seated on the green velvet sofa in the drawing room when she entered. He studied her without expression, then rose without a word and poured her a glass of sherry. "How is Laurel?" he asked.

"Fine. I think she improves every day. Have you seen her since you returned?"

"No. I knew you were with her—" He paused and for a moment their eyes met. Hers were dark and troubled, wounded by his words; his were bright with an intense and nameless emotion. A flicker of chagrin touched Jason's face as he realized how rude his words sounded, and he explained lamely, "I didn't want to interrupt your time with her."

"Laurel wouldn't have minded," Carolyn said, keeping her distance in their conversation. She wondered where he had really gone. Perhaps he had added a solitary truth to his lies and gone to Dover, or perhaps he had taken the train to London to spend the week with his mistress. "Where did you go this week?" she blurted out the words before she thought.

Jason looked surprised. "Why, to Dover, of course. I did

have business there. Doubtless you don't remember, but I have part ownership in a fleet of merchant ships. I consulted with the other owners about expanding the operation."

"I see. I thought perhaps you had gone to London." Why couldn't she leave the subject alone? Jason would be vastly amused if he discovered her jealousy.

"London? No. Why would I go there?"

Carolyn shrugged. "To see friends, I suppose." She struggled to hold back the words threatening to pour out despite all her resolves. But the need to know was too strong for her. "Or your mistress."

"Who?" He sounded amazed, then burst out laughing. "Ah, yes, my mistress."

Carolyn turned scarlet with humiliation. "Yes, your mistress!" she hissed. "What gall you have, to laugh about it."

"I have no mistress!"

Carolyn looked up at him disbelievingly. "When you returned from London, you said—"

"I said nothing. You said I had a mistress, and I didn't bother to deny it. You'll think whatever you want; I know that much by now."

"I don't believe you," she snapped. He smiled smugly, and Carolyn grimaced. "Well, it's patently false. A man like you, not sleeping with his wife for three years, and you haven't got a mistress?"

"Some men might be flattered by your assumption of my virility," he retorted wryly. "Fortunately, I'm not misled. I'm well aware of your opinion of my sexual appetite. To be frank, you're right; I haven't been celibate. God knows, I'm no saint. I satisfied my carnal instincts on women who were well-paid to receive them, but I had no wish to humiliate you by openly taking a lover. Of course, when I found out you had no such scruples, I considered it, but I couldn't find a woman who interested me enough. I thought you had destroyed any feeling I could have for a woman."

Carolyn's heart picked up its beat: Maybe, then, he still *could* have feelings for a woman. Maybe . . . Jason growled and slammed down his drink.

"I see triumph all over your face. You're right. No woman can drive me mad with hunger, except you!" He glared at her. "There, does that satisfy you? You still make me itch like a green lad." The air was thick with tension. Carolyn quivered, taut and expectant, her eyes fixed on Jason's stark face. He wanted her, he still wanted her, her heart sang. "But, dammit, I'm not under your spell again. I know you now, and I'll not let you suck me back in. What happened the other afternoon won't happen again. I won't permit it."

Stepping back as though struck, Carolyn looked down at the floor, fighting to regather the remnants of her dignity. What an arrogant, pompous bastard he was! As if she were trying to bewitch him, to lure him into her bed, as if she had some evil design on his precious virtue. "Of course," she murmured sarcastically, "I might taint your holy body."

"I'm not being sanctimonious, Cynthia." His voice was hard as rock. "I'm simply attempting to salvage my self-respect."

At that moment Barlow appeared in the doorway to announce supper. The meal was fraught with tension. Jason scarcely looked her way, and both were silent. Finally, to break the oppressive quiet, Carolyn asked, "What did you and your partners decide about expanding the shipping line?"

Jason glanced at her in surprise. "That's the first time I've heard you express an interest in my business dealings."

Carolyn shrugged. "Have you ever encouraged my interest?"

"Of course I have. When we were first married, I dreamed naively of us riding over the fields together, discussing the land, crops, improvements, tenants. . . . I'd hoped you would care about the people who live on my land, get to know them, help them when they're sick. Like a fool, I believed that whatever concerned me would concern you."

"Just because I was shy of people and didn't like to ride isn't enough reason to assume that I'm disinterested."

He blew out an exasperated sigh. "I shall never cease to be amazed at your ability to make excuses for yourself."

But it wasn't herself she was making excuses for, but Cynthia, as she tried desperately to cling to her vision of her twin as the wronged party in this marriage. They were hopelessly mismatched and had been from the first. If the fault lay anywhere, it was with Sir Neville, who had pushed Cynthia into marriage with a man she didn't love. Jason had loved her; he was too bitter not to have loved her once. But Cynthia hadn't been like him, hadn't shared his interests or been able to accept the pleasure of his heated lovemaking.

If only I hadn't run away to marry Kit, Carolyn thought suddenly. She would have met Jason herself, and it would have been they who had fallen in love. She would have been the woman he had loved and desired—and she would have been able to match his desire. Carolyn blushed and turned her eyes to her plate. Whatever was she thinking of? He was her sister's husband, and she was the one who was wicked and disloyal for coveting him.

What a hopeless mess she was in!

*　　*　　*

For the next few days, Jason and Carolyn successfully avoided each other. They met only at meals, and then they were careful to stick to mundane topics. But Carolyn found that their careful avoidance only heightened her desire instead of decreasing it. She thought of Jason constantly, wondering what he was doing, what he was thinking. When she lay in bed at night, she imagined him lying in the room next to hers, with only a connecting door separating them, and wondered if he thought of their lovemaking, the texture of her skin, the eager budding of her nipples in his hands, the way their bodies fit together as if sculpted for each other. Her very thoughts made her shiver with desire.

At times Carolyn reproved herself, calling her longings sheer wickedness, but her scolding couldn't stand up long against the relentless tide of her passion. Cradling her pillow, she dreamed of him and awoke pulsing with desire, aching and unfulfilled.

One night, she went to the door between their rooms and quietly unlatched the lock. She returned to bed and lay watching the door, but he didn't enter. The next day she was cross all morning, even snapping once at Laurel, who stared at her with wide amazement. Carolyn dropped down beside her at once and hugged her, begging her forgiveness.

That evening, when Carolyn retired to her room, she dug through Cynthia's drawers and chests until she found a sheer, seductive nightgown of beige satin and blond lace. She slipped it on and studied herself in her mirror. The satin torso was held up by two thin straps across her shoulders, which left most of her upper chest bare. The gown molded to her body, clearly showing the indentation of her navel and the joinder of her legs. The satin material stopped at the middle of her thighs; from there to her ankles, the gown was sheer lace that barely concealed her legs. The top of the bodice, across her breasts, was also lace and merely shadowed her bosom enticingly. It was the gown of a temptress, and Carolyn suspected Jason had bought it early in their marriage.

Biting her lip, she pulled out the matching peignoir and belted it around her. Though Priscilla had already brushed her hair, Carolyn sat down before her mirror and brushed it again until it crackled and glowed. She picked up the cologne that she liked best among Cynthia's bottles and applied a delicate drop behind each ear and in the valley between her breasts. Then she sat down to wait, for perhaps he would come to her tonight.

Every glance, every movement showed her that he desired her, and the air around them continually quivered with sexual tension. He wanted her, but was resisting. When would his resistance break down?

She could hardly believe she was doing this, dressing to entice Jason Somerville into her bed—waiting, hoping he would come to her tonight, and wanting him so much she was actually contemplating going to him. Surely, if he saw her in this nightgown, his eyes would light, and he'd reach out for her.

Sometimes she thought she would die of frustration if she didn't feel his hands on her flesh again. She wanted to see his face slacken with passion, to read the hot admiration in his eyes as they roamed her body, to feel the sweet invasion of his masculinity. She had to find out if he wanted her. She had to know, had to experience that sweet, soaring ecstasy again.

Carolyn heard Jason stride past her door. His bedroom door opened and closed. Carolyn waited, hands anxiously clasping and unclasping. Now and then she heard the faint sounds of his undressing, the scrape of a drawer then his wardrobe door. Once his footsteps came toward the connecting door, but he stopped and turned away. After that there was only silence.

Carolyn jumped up from her chair and wrapped her arms around herself. He had gone to bed, coolly in control, while she stewed in here, her passion overwhelming logic and morals. How could he remain so indifferent, so calm and unruffled?

Carolyn's hands fell back to her sides. She took three bold steps to the door and turned the handle; she opened it wide.

The room beyond was dark, lit only by moonlight and the banked, red-glowing coals in the fireplace. Carolyn stood silhouetted against the light of her own room, her body clearly outlined through the sheer gown and peignoir. Jason rose on his elbow. "What are you doing here?" His voice was startled, almost annoyed.

In the darkness, Carolyn could see the large hump of his bed and Jason's form lying in it, but she could not make out his features. Carolyn didn't answer Jason's question. Instead, she glided toward him with slow, even steps and stopped in front of him. He sat up, the covers sliding down to reveal his browned, naked chest. Carolyn's breath came faster in her throat. Her hands were icy with fear, but she acted on instinct. She grasped the ends of her sash in her hands and pulled it loose. A shrug of her shoulders sent the peignoir slithering down her arms and body to puddle on the floor. Jason drew in his breath sharply. Already accustomed to the darkness with the light streaming in from Carolyn's room, he could see her quite clearly.

Carolyn watched him. His throat jumped as he swallowed. "God, Cynthia, why do want to torment me?"

"I don't want to torment you," Carolyn answered, her voice breathy with excitement and uncertainty. "I want . . . to please you."

For a moment he was unable to speak, then he ground out, "Go away. Leave me in peace."

Deliberately, Carolyn shook her head, and her hair brushed across her shoulders. She sat down on his bed, not quite touching him. His eyes flared, and his breath rasped in the dark silence. Reaching up with both her hands to trace the bones of his face, Carolyn ran her forefingers across his brow and cheekbones and along the slanting line of his jaw to meet at his chin. Then, in tandem, she moved her fingers down his throat, skimming over the soft hollow and out the hard plane of his collarbone.

With a feather-light touch, she caressed his neck and shoulder. Jason's eyelids were almost closed, and his tongue stole out to lick his lips. Smiling, Carolyn pushed her gown up above her knees and sat down astride his lap. He groaned and moved slightly; his hands dug into the bedclothes around him, as Carolyn settled into his lap, squirming from side to side. With her every move, the muscles of his arms and neck bulged. He swore vividly.

Carolyn leaned forward and touched one of his nipples with the tip of her tongue. He bucked involuntarily, and his breath came out in a rush. She slid her tongue back and forth across the nipple with grave deliberation. She had begun the gentle dance of her tongue to arouse him, but Carolyn was lost now in the sweet hunger of her passion.

She wanted his mouth. He groaned when her agile tongue left his heated chest, but his lips and tongue received hers eagerly. Like duelists, their tongues met in their mouths, thrusting and stroking. As they kissed, Carolyn slid her satin-clothed body over his, moving up and down and side to side. Jason's breath turned to fire against her face, and he twisted his legs around her, his desire now unhidden. They kissed again and again, moving and clutching with each new frisson of pleasure.

Finally Jason seized Carolyn's shoulders and rolled over, pulling her under him. Through the lace of her gown he took one nipple and worked it between his lips. The delicate roughness of the lace and the infinite softness of his tongue were an exquisite contrast, and Carolyn gasped, arching as if to seek more of his delights. Taking the top of the lace between his teeth, he ripped it downward, exposing her breast. Softly he blew on the wet, throbbing tip, and it tautened even more. He kissed a trail across her chest to the opposite breast, working the same wonder on it. Carolyn moved wildly beneath him, lost to all reason or embarrassment.

He sat up and Carolyn cried, "No, please, don't leave me."

Jason swallowed, for a moment unable to speak. "I won't. Believe me, I won't."

He stripped the gown from her, his hands skimming over her hips and legs as he did so. Once again he covered her, and her legs opened naturally to admit him. He plunged into her dark, welcoming warmth, and Carolyn moaned softly. His powerful hips and legs moved in long, slow circles, elongating the pleasure for both of them. Carolyn rotated her hips in counterpoint to his movements, and he strained to retain control. "Cynthia," he groaned, "oh, sweet, sweet Cyn."

Carolyn kissed his neck, his shoulder, and he came to his peak, thrusting deep within her and touching off the cataclysm of her own sweeping joy. For an instant, they met in perfect oneness. Then it was a long, slow descent from the heights.

Thirteen

$\mathcal{J}$ason rolled away from her onto his back, releasing his breath in a long sigh. Carolyn, sated and sleepy, turned her head to watch him. Finally Jason lowered his arm from his eyes and turned on his side to look at her, supporting his torso on his forearm. Carolyn gazed steadily back at him. His face was bleak and lined with pain. "Who taught you that?" he rasped.

"Taught me what?"

"To please a man. To *want* to please a man. Was it Bingham?" His face twisted in a grimace. "Damn his soul! Did he teach you to enjoy love?"

Violently he sat upright, bracing his head on either side with his hands, fingertips digging into his scalp. "For seven years I tried. I'd have given anything to get even a squeak of pleasure from you; I never did. What did it take, Cynthia? How did Bingham do it?"

Carolyn stared at him in consternation. What was she to say? If she told him that she hadn't known Bingham, that no one had aroused in her what Jason had, she must confess her identity. This was the moment when she should tell him the truth, she thought. But he would label her wanton. A former actress, a woman who came eagerly to the bed of a man not her husband, a woman who seduced her sister's husband—he would despise her. He would feel he had been duped and used, and rightly so. She had to continue to be Cynthia.

"I—never felt that way with any other man," Carolyn told him truthfully.

A harsh laugh broke from his lips. "Come now, milady. You can't expect me to believe that. After seven years of hating your husband and cringing from his touch, suddenly you're inflamed by his lovemaking? I'm not a fool."

"Then believe whatever you choose to believe," Carolyn snapped. "There's no point in telling you the truth."

"How would you know? You've never tried it!"

"Oh!" Carolyn grabbed her gown and yanked it on over her head. She flung back the bedcovers and scrambled to the floor, grabbing up the pale peignoir and hurriedly thrusting her arms into it. She wrapped the filmy lace garment around her and whirled to face Jason. He watched her with grim, jaded eyes. "I came here because I wanted you. That's the plain and simple truth. I love you. Fool that I am!" Tears welled in her eyes and spilled over onto her cheeks. Derisively she rapped her knuckles against her head. "I hoped we could have something together, that we could . . . could find a bit of happiness and joy, as we did the other morning. I thought if I came here, if it was sweet and good, you'd want me. You'd love me. I should have known better! You'll never forgive! Your heart's too cold. Don't worry, I shan't bother you again."

Carolyn ran into her own bedroom, slamming the door behind her. Throwing herself across her bed, she gave way to a flood of tears.

Carolyn awoke early the next morning, cold and cramped, still atop the covers. Cautiously she stretched out her aching muscles and crawled beneath the covers, too cold and uncomfortable to sleep. Tears had dried on her face, stiff and itching; her eyes felt twice their usual size and so tender it hurt to blink.

Alone in the barely pink light of dawn, she blushed at the thought of her boldness. It had been a witless, shameless thing to do, and she should have known that even if she managed to pierce the barrier of his self-control, he would hate her for it afterward. There hadn't been a word of love from him, no soft mention of joy or happiness, but only his thoughts of Cynthia's betrayal of him.

She had actually blurted out that she loved him. But there was no need to worry about that for he would assume she lied, as he always did. Carolyn rubbed her forehead wearily. She hadn't known she loved him until she said it—or, rather, she hadn't admitted it to herself. To her, it seemed absurd, to fall in love with the man she had set out so determinedly to dislike.

It was merely lust, she reasoned, and, never having known lust before, she didn't recognize the difference. Then she thought of him bending over her as she lay in bed, poisoned, gripped with pain and weakness; his face had been lined with worry, his eyes dark and troubled. She remembered him standing in the doorway to the nursery, gazing at her and Laurel in the rocking chair. She thought of his laugh, his unexpected smile, the flicker of amusement in his gray-green eyes. She saw him squatting on the nursery floor beside Laurel, patiently rebuilding a stack of blocks, his face soft with love. She recalled the leashed power of his body, the dry wit, the hidden kindness with which he treated those around him but from which she was barred. Oh, yes, she could love him. She did.

She couldn't continue to live here after last night. She couldn't subject her heart to the laceration of being around him, loving him, and never having him. No matter how the parting hurt, no matter how much she would miss Laurel, she must go. She would get dressed and go to Jason early this morning before her resolve weakened. She would confess everything, and then she would leave.

Carolyn shoved aside the covers and climbed out of bed, ignoring the repressed sob that waited in her chest. Later, she thought, when she was far away from here, all courage expended, she would let herself think and feel—and cry.

By the time Priscilla brought her early-morning tea and toast, Carolyn was dressed in her undergarments and dressing gown, face washed and hair brushed back and twisted up into a tight knot. "Why, milady, whatever are you doing up so early?" She came closer and laid down the small tray. Her forehead knitted in concern and she leaned toward Carolyn. "Are you all right? You look—"

"Horrid," Carolyn supplied briskly. "Yes, you're right. But it's nothing to worry about. It will soon be over."

"If I can do anything for you . . ." Priscilla offered hesitantly.

Carolyn forced a smile. "Yes, I'll call on you. Thank you, Priscilla."

Priscilla helped her into her stays, tightening the laces until Carolyn's waist was tiny enough for her dress. She dropped the cage hoop over her head and tied its drawstring at Carolyn's waist. Defiantly, Carolyn chose one of the dresses that was not of Cynthia's liking, a deep rose velvet with ivory lace at the cuffs and upstanding collar. Simple, yet vibrant, it improved her color, which was sadly in need of it this morning. Carolyn looked at her image in the mirror and repressed a sigh. Her eyelids were heavy from last night's bout of crying, and her skin was sallow and drawn. She wouldn't leave Jason with an image of herself at her best, but she supposed it didn't really matter.

Feeling rather like a prisoner going to his execution, Carolyn walked down the stairs and into the dining room. Jason sat staring abstractedly out the window, an empty plate and a cup of tea before him on the table. For a moment they stared at each other without speaking. Then Jason rose, shoving back his chair, and came around to seat her. If Carolyn had been less frozen with dread and pain, she would have laughed at the absurdities of convention—after what had passed between them last night, Jason politely pulled back her chair as if nothing untoward had happened.

"Good morning, Cynthia."

"Good morning." She was appalled by the tremor in her voice.

He resumed his seat and took a sip of tea, grimacing at its coolness. He refilled his cup from the silver pot in the center of the table. Carolyn poured a cup while Jason stirred cream and sugar into his. It was unbearably awkward. Carolyn wondered how she could broach the subject of her masquerade. She glanced at him, and though his eyes were not red and swollen, he appeared little better than she. Carolyn remembered his tortured face last night as he asked who had taught her to enjoy passion, and her heart twisted. How much he must have loved Cynthia! And she had hurt him terribly. Suddenly Carolyn was seized by a hot, consuming anger at her sister.

Cynthia had rejected his love and given herself to other,

lesser men. She had married him coldly, and over the years she had crushed his love, finally deserting him and her child. There weren't enough excuses to cover that, even from a loyal sister. His lovemaking had been glorious and generous; he had given as much pleasure as he had taken. Cynthia had been wrong, so wrong to mistake his bold, feverish caresses for perversions. From what Jason had said last night, Cynthia had never touched him, never kissed and caressed his body as Carolyn had—Cynthia had never *given* to Jason. No wonder Jason fought to avoid her; he feared being caught in the web of his love for her. He dreaded having his heart broken again.

Carolyn understood his pain and his fear. She knew what it was like to withdraw to avoid anguish; she had done it when Kit died by leaving everything and everyone she knew. She knew, too, the searing pain of a broken heart; her own was splintered in her chest. She loved Jason, but whatever emotion he had, it was for Cynthia, not her.

Jason rose and crossed to the windows. Carolyn blinked the treacherous tears from her eyes and went to the sideboard to fill her plate. Automatically, she dished out a thin slice of ham and a spoonful of eggs, but when she returned to the table, she merely pushed the food around on her plate. Jason clasped his hands behind his back and stared out the window, rocking a little on his heels. He cleared his throat. Finally he turned, clearing his throat again. "I've given a great deal of thought to what happened last night." He could not look her in the eyes. "Hell, I haven't been able to think of anything else. I—want to believe you." Suddenly he strode toward her and leaned across the table, bracing his hands on it and staring into her face. "I want it more than I've ever wanted anything. You know how long I've ached for you to respond to me. But after all that's happened . . ." He slammed a palm against the wood. "Dammit, I can't! I vowed I'd never again be caught in your trap. I swore it each time you betrayed me further. I hated you; I never dreamed you could rekindle a spark of interest in me. Yet now I find myself wanting to forget it all—my woes, my hate, your infidelities." He paused, his brow twisted in a fierce frown.

Carolyn's heart felt as if it were bursting. She wanted to cry, to scream at Jason that he could trust her, could love her. Shakily she laced her fingers together in her lap. What would he think when she told him the truth? Would he hate her even more for having bared his soul to her like this? "Jason, please believe this—I don't want to hurt you. I never wanted to hurt you."

He drew back. "That sounds suspiciously like the beginning of a speech that's going to hurt like hell."

Carolyn swallowed. She had to tell him. She had to.

"Milord." Barlow appeared in the doorway, and Carolyn sagged with relief at the temporary reprieve.

Jason swung around impatiently. "Yes, what is it?"

"I'm sorry to interrupt your breakfast, but an urgent message has just arrived for you."

"A message?" Jason's annoyance abated slightly. Barlow came forward, and Jason took the folded paper from the tray. Snapping it open, he read quickly, then stopped and reread the message. Suddenly, his face was no longer etched with irritation, but with sadness. He pressed his lips together and refolded the paper. He motioned to Barlow to leave, and Carolyn felt the groping tentacles of fear enclose her stomach.

"What is it?" Instinctively she rose to her feet, her hands digging into the hard wood of the table.

Jason came around the table to her. His voice was low. "I—this is from Sir Neville's solicitor, Mr. Comstock. Your father died during the night."

Carolyn blanched. "No . . . no! I wasn't even there. I didn't get to see him before he died. He can't—" She pressed an icy hand against her cheek. "What a silly thing to say. As if he couldn't die without my seeing him. Oh, Jason." Tears flooded her eyes. "Jason. What am I to do?"

Gently he pulled her against his chest, holding her while she clung to him. All thought of telling Jason the truth and leaving Broughton Court fled before the sudden anguish of her father's death. They had fought bitterly, and she hadn't seen him in years. She wouldn't have thought that after all this time it would hurt so much.

Even after she stopped crying, Carolyn remained in the soothing warmth of Jason's embrace. For a few minutes, with his arms tightly around her and his cheek resting on her hair, she indulged in the fantasy that she was loved and protected, not alone in the world. Reluctantly she stepped out of his arms and groped for the lacy handkerchief in her skirt pocket. She wiped the tears from her already aching eyes, blew her nose, and straightened her shoulders. "When is the funeral?"

"The solicitor says they will wait for our arrival. I'll make the travel arrangements and wire him the time." He strode to the mantel and pulled the bell cord beside it.

Almost immediately Barlow entered. "Yes, milord?"

"Sir Neville Worthing has died, Barlow. Lady Broughton and I will travel to Gresham Hall as soon as possible for the funeral. Please tell Priscilla to pack her ladyship's things right away and to be ready to accompany us. Have Broaddus prepare the carriage and horses and bring them around. He will drive us to Barham, and we'll take the train from there." Jason withdrew a gold watch from his pocket and flipped open the case. "If I'm not mistaken, there's a two-ten train from Barham to London. We should be able to make that."

"Yes, milord. I shall see to it immediately." Barlow turned politely toward Carolyn. "Please accept my condolences, milady."

"Thank you, Barlow."

Jason turned to Carolyn as the servant left the room. "It's a shock, I know, even though we've expected it for months. I think you should lie down."

"Yes. But Priscilla will need to be in my room to pack."

"Then lie down on the sofa in the sitting room. I'll see that no one disturbs you."

Jason led her into the sitting room and drew the heavy drapes, plunging the room into darkness. He left, pulling the door shut behind him. Carolyn unfastened her hoop and let it drop to the floor, for it was impossible to lie down in that cage. She curled up on the sofa and tucked a small round throw pillow beneath her head. To her surprise, she was asleep within minutes. Exhausted by her last bout of crying, she slept deeply and dreamlessly, not awaking until Jason gently shook her shoulder an hour later.

"Cynthia. I'm sorry to disturb you, but we must leave now if we hope to reach Barham by two o'clock."

Groggily, Carolyn sat up. "What? Oh. Oh, yes." Her hands went to her hair, smoothing back the strands that had twisted loose in her sleep. "Of course. I'll be ready in a moment."

Jason politely retired from the room to let her dress.

Carolyn tucked the straying hairs back into place and secured them with a hairpin, pulled on her hoop and shook the dress down around it, and went out to the hall where Jason waited for her. "I must see Laurel before we go."

"Of course. I hadn't thought of that."

He accompanied her to the nursery. As they climbed the second flight of stairs leading to the third-floor nursery, Carolyn commented, "I think we should move the nursery to our floor. It's tiresome having to climb these stairs."

Jason glanced at her in surprise. "You never fail to astonish me. I thought the noise was too much for Laurel to live on the same floor with us."

"She isn't that noisy—at least, not anymore. It seems that she would feel lonely and cut-off up there."

"Certainly, if you wish it. I agree. As soon as we return, I'll have some rooms downstairs made over for the nursery."

"Thank you." Carolyn smiled at him and stepped into the nursery.

Laurel greeted them with cries of delight, throwing herself first into Carolyn's arms, then running to Jason. Carolyn told the child that she was leaving and would be gone for a few days. At first Laurel's eyes widened in fear, and she flung her arms around Carolyn's neck, shouting, "No! No!" Patiently, Carolyn explained that she would return and soothed Laurel's fears. Jason joined in, and after a few minutes Laurel released Carolyn and stepped back. She accepted the situation, albeit a little sullenly, and gave each of them a good-bye hug and kiss.

Jason escorted Carolyn downstairs and out to the carriage, a supporting arm around her waist. Although Carolyn knew she wasn't fragile enough to require such support, she was happy to accept it. When this was past, she thought, she would tell Jason the truth and leave Broughton Court. But she needed his strength now, in this overflow of emotional storms.

Jason settled her comfortably in the carriage, tucking a warm afghan around her feet and legs to ward off the chill and arranging pillows between her and the side of the carriage to ease the rough ride and enable her to nap. He sat beside her on the bench seat, with Priscilla facing them on the opposite seat. Carolyn closed her eyes and leaned against the pillows, letting her mind drift. Later, she thought numbly. Some day in the future, some other time. . . .

The trip from Broughton Court to the Lake Country was a long one, stretching diagonally across the length and breadth of Britain. At Barham, Jason purchased tickets to Lancaster and cabled their schedule to Sir Neville's attorney in Heaverthwaite. They reached London in the evening and, after only a short wait, boarded the train to Manchester. They settled down in their private compartment to sleep away the night journey to the northern industrial city. In her emotionally drained state, Carolyn only mused briefly on the idea of changing to her nightclothes and sleeping in such close quarters with Jason. But he warded off any potential awkwardness by excusing himself to have a cigar in the smoking car, leaving her to undress and crawl into her narrow bunk to sleep. By the time he returned and undressed for bed, she was sound asleep.

Waking once during the night when the train rumbled to a stop at a station, it took Carolyn a moment to recall where she was, but when she did, the first slash of pain was eased by the thought of Jason slumbering in the bunk above her. His presence warmed the room, promising rock-hard strength. Carolyn smiled to herself and slipped back to sleep.

There was a long, tedious wait in Manchester for the train to Lancaster. After eating a hearty breakfast, they left Priscilla with their luggage and strolled through the streets of the city. It was bitterly cold, and their spirits weren't lifted by the grimy buildings and noisy streets of the factory town. They soon returned to the station. At last they were able to board the train, and Carolyn sank gratefully into the plush seats of their compartment and watched the smoking sprawl of Manchester pass by. They skirted the western side of the Forest of Bowland, and in the distance Carolyn could see a dense cover of spruces and the bleak grit-stone hump that was Beacon Fell. The train rattled across stream after stream and rumbled into the Wyre Valley. Fields dotted with black-and-white cows stretched away to the east, and though the view lacked the green of summer, there was a peaceful beauty to it that tugged at Carolyn's heart. Home! She was nearing home now.

The feeling grew as they neared Lancaster, where they spent the night. Early the next morning they caught the train to Kendal, and Carolyn stayed glued to the window for hours, soaking in the familiar landscape. At Kendal, the Worthing carriage met them for the last leg of their journey to Heaverthwaite village and Gresham Hall. Despite the cold, Carolyn insisted on peering out the tiny windows at the beauty of the Lake Country unfolding around them. Hills rolled away from the valley through which they traveled, part woods and part fertile grazing land. Here and there were outcroppings of shale or the barren slash of a scree. Tiny, rushing streams poured out of the hills, bubbling and gushing on their way, continually threatening to leap from their banks. The streams fed into the lakes and ponds that gave the area its name. The lakes were dark, serene stretches of water, as beautiful in their own way as stark crags and peaks.

Carolyn knew and loved them all. They drew close to Heaverthwaite, the village below Gresham hall, and in the background she could see Hunter's Fell and Castle Crag, the two crags which sheltered Gresham Hall. The carriage passed through Heaverthwaite without stopping and trundled over the old wooden bridge across Lindale Beck, a foaming, surging creek. In the waning late-afternoon sun, she spied a glint of light on water—there it was! Shallowmere Lake, where she and Cynthia had boated, skated, and swum. The road turned north and she could see the house itself, bathed in a golden glow.

The stern stone walls were mellowed by time and sunlight; the narrow lines of the central pele tower had been broadened by additions to the sides and back. Chimneys sprouted out all over the roof, which dipped and rose with no continuity of design. Although it was a hodgepodge of styles, shooting off in all directions, there was an air of strength and dignity about it, like an aging knight who had weathered many battles. Protected on two sides by hills and guarded on another by the smooth lake, it was an impressive sight. But to Carolyn it was no grand castle, only home. Her throat tightened as she resisted tears. She was coming home after all these years, but her father would not be there to greet her.

The carriage rolled to a stop in front of the house, and the groom jumped down to open the door. Jason climbed out and turned to help Carolyn down. As they walked up the steps, the massive front doors were opened by a footman, whom Carolyn recognized as one of the Graysons, a family long in service to the Worthings, but she had no idea which Grayson he was. An aged butler hurried toward them in short, shuffling steps as they stepped inside. Carolyn held out both hands to him, memories welling up inside her. "Charles!"

"Miss Cynthia! I mean, milady." He took her hands in his, tears glistening in his eyes. His hands, knotted and withered with age, trembled on hers. Carolyn swallowed against the lump of affection and pity in her throat. "I'm ever so glad to see you, milady. And you, milord. Edward, take their wraps."

The footman collected their hats and cloaks, and Carolyn was pleased that now she could thank him by name. Charles led them to the large, formal drawing room, where other friends and family members were located. The room was draped in black, and at the far end rested a closed casket.

She recognized almost everyone in the room, which was the greatest feeling of relief and comfort since she'd begun her charade as Cynthia. The names of the people from her childhood came back to her instantly. Aunt Elizabeth was seated on a red plush sofa, her daughter Bella at her side. They were flanked by Uncle Geoffrey and a man Carolyn didn't know, but whom she assumed must be Bella's husband, Cavendar Upton. Neighbors and acquaintances were scattered about the room, chatting to each other or conveying their condolences to the family. Elizabeth glanced up as Carolyn and Jason entered the room, and she held up a theatrically weak hand. "My dearest Cynthia. Come here."

Dutifully, Carolyn went to the sofa where her aunt and cousin sat and dropped a kiss on the older woman's cheek. "Aunt Elizabeth. And Cousin Bella. How are you?"

The men exchanged greetings, shaking hands, and Carolyn kissed her uncle on the cheek and offered her hand to Upton. A stocky, ruddy fellow whom she remembered as her father's solicitor spotted them and bustled forward from the corner of the room. "Lord Broughton." He shook Jason's hand heartily. "I'm glad to see you. I'd like to discuss the arrangements with you."

Jason followed the other man to a more secluded area where they could get down to business, while Elizabeth closed in on her, trapping Carolyn into a long and boring conversation. "Geoffrey, pull up a chair for Cynthia. You must sit down, my dear. Such a long, tiring journey, and after the dreadful shock of poor Neville's death." She shook her head and dabbed a tear from the corner of one eye. Listening to her aunt drone on and on made Carolyn want to scream. All she wanted was some time alone, some time to think things out, a while by herself to pay her last respects to her father. But with the endless stream of callers and relatives, she knew it was impossible.

Aunt Elizabeth dropped her voice and leaned in toward Carolyn. "Have you heard from Carolyn? Should we notify her about Sir Neville's death, do you think?"

Carolyn was alarmed—she hadn't considered the possibility that someone in the gathering of family and friends might mention the long-lost twin sister with whom Sir Neville had fought so. She feared that someone might mention the name to Jason—as differently as she had been acting, he was bound to figure out that she was really Cynthia's twin sister. He must not hear the news from someone else; it would make her deception even worse.

"I—no, I haven't heard from her. How would we reach her?"

"We could try sending a letter to that hotel in Antigua," Bella said thoughtfully. "You know, Cynthia, the address I gave you a few months ago when you wanted to write her. Did she answer your letter?"

No letter had ever reached Carolyn, and she despaired that she had missed Cynthia's cry for help. Perhaps when she found herself entangled in the situation with Mark and Dennis Bingham, before she left Jason, she had nowhere else to turn but to her sister, who was worlds away. "No. At least, she never answered me."

Suddenly she realized that if Cynthia knew her address in Antigua, it was possible that she could have fled to her for help and then been unable to find her. Or—and anger tore through Carolyn at this thought—had she purposely misdirected her husband there, hoping he would pick up Carolyn's trail and be further misled? Maybe she hoped—guessed—that Carolyn would do exactly as she had, pretend to be Cynthia so that Jason would give up the chase. . . .

After her experiences the past few weeks, Carolyn wasn't sure she knew her sister at all, so anything was possible. Cynthia had always been a cooler, less sensual person than Carolyn; naturally she would love with less fire and passion than her sister. But maybe this seeming lack of emotion, this detached and icy demeanor, had been within Cynthia all along, but had been hidden by her naive and innocent exterior.

Looking back, Carolyn realized how hers and Sir Neville's attitude toward Cynthia had encouraged her fears, her inability to take risks. Shielding her from the harsher things of life hadn't helped her grow strong, and constantly protecting her, standing up for her, doing things for her that she didn't like to do had only added to her weakness.

It would suit Cynthia's personality to run to the person who always came to her aid. This morning Carolyn had burned with anger at the way Cynthia had treated Jason, but that had been her heart speaking. Cynthia was no villainess, only weak, and Carolyn had helped to make her that way.

"Cynthia, dear, you remember Dr. Morehouse, don't you?"

With a start, Carolyn withdrew from her heavy thoughts and turned to the aging man who stood beside Aunt Elizabeth. Tall, thin, and white-haired, he was dressed in an unfashionable black suit; he looked just as Carolyn remembered him, except a trifle older. She smiled genuinely and extended her hand to him. "Of course I do. How could I forget the man who cured all my stomachaches? How are you, Dr. Morehouse?"

He clasped her hand in his and covered it with his other hand, patting it gently. "I'm fine, my dear. You know how deeply I regret your father's death. It's a loss to all of us."

"I know. Thank you." He stayed a few more minutes, then moved on to join Squire Moore by the window. After the doctor there came a wave of callers, and for the next hour Carolyn greeted old acquaintances and received their condolences finding, to her relief, that she recalled almost every name she should.

Carolyn was tired from the long journey, and she hadn't eaten much in the past two days. The strain of greeting people combined with a constant anxiety that her name would be mentioned to Jason drained her. She was grateful when Jason appeared by her side and took her hand, pulling her up from the couch.

"It's time you rested," he commanded. "I'm sure your aunt and cousin will excuse you."

"Of course," Aunt Elizabeth agreed. "The trip must have exhausted you. We'll be happy to accept the condolence calls, won't we, Bella?"

"Yes, Mama," Bella answered dutifully, though her smile was forced.

The housekeeper waited for them in the hall, and when Carolyn saw her, she broke into a broad grin. "Mrs. Amanda!" She called her by the childhood name she and Cynthia had given her, unable to twist their tongues around her last name, Billingsley.

"Hello, my dear." The woman clasped her hands, shaking her head sadly. "I'm going to miss him so much. Sir Neville was a difficult man sometimes, but the house will be empty without him." She sniffed and pulled a handkerchief from the capacious pocket of her starched apron. "But, there, that's enough of that. Let me take you to your room so you can rest."

The two climbed the stairs and went to the room that had been Cynthia's when they were young. As soon as Mrs. Billingsley left, she slipped next door to what had been her old room, and to her surprise nothing was as she remembered it. Every personal thing that had told of her presence had been swept away, all her pictures and knicknacks, every piece of furniture replaced with thick, ornate oak furniture—dark, somber, serious. Tears sparkled in her eyes as she returned to Cynthia's room. Her father had been this mad at her; he had despised her enough to tear out everything that was hers from his life.

Priscilla was waiting for her. "There you are, milady. For a second I was afraid I'd gone to the wrong room."

"No. I decided to look at some of the other rooms to see if they are as I remember them."

"And were they?" Priscilla asked as she helped Carolyn out of her dress, stays, and hoop.

"No, I'm afraid not."

Priscilla quickly unpinned her hair and brushed it out to hang loosely over her shoulders. Then she crossed to the windows to pull the heavy drapes. "There now, you take a nice rest, milady. I've already unpacked your bags and his lordship's things, too; no one will be coming in and disturbing you."

Carolyn tried to keep her sudden consternation from showing, but as soon as Priscilla left, Carolyn rushed to the wardrobe and pulled open its doors. Jason's clothes hung there neatly beside hers. Mrs. Billingsley had put her and Jason in the same room, which was only natural since she thought they were husband and wife. It would be terribly embarrassing to explain to the housekeeper that she and Jason commonly slept apart. Besides, Bella and Aunt Elizabeth and their husbands were staying here, and Carolyn felt sure that several of the family friends who lived outside of Heaverthwaite would sleep in the house until after the funeral, thereby leaving no spare rooms so they could sleep separately.

Carolyn walked to the bed and looked down at it, her hands clenching the spindles of the bedposts. It had been bad enough sleeping in the same tiny compartment with him on the train, but at least there they had had separate beds. Here she would have to lie in the same bed with him, covered by the same sheet and blankets, warmed by his warmth, and only inches from touching him.

Carolyn closed her eyes. Perhaps Cynthia wasn't cold; maybe it was she who was unnatural. With her father only a few days dead, she was thinking of Jason's lovemaking and beginning to tremble and melt at the thought. Perhaps her father was right: There must be a wanton streak in her nature that she had not acknowledged before. Her loins ached for him even now. It would be torture to lie close to him, to want his comfort and love, knowing she couldn't have it. Even worse, what if she yielded again to the flood of desire he aroused in her and begged him to take her? The humiliation would be too much.

She sat down on the side of the bed but knew she wouldn't be able to nap now, for her mind was too busy with her predicament. By the time Priscilla returned to help her dress for dinner, Carolyn hadn't slept a wink. Nor had she figured out any solution to the problem. She slipped into the black velvet formal dress Priscilla pulled out of the wardrobe and fastened jet earrings in her ears. Priscilla styled her hair again and, bracing herself for the evening, Carolyn went downstairs.

After years of being with Sir Neville, everyone must have become accustomed to avoiding all discussion of Carolyn, for no one mentioned her throughout dinner. For the rest of the evening she endured Aunt Elizabeth's company and welcomed the continual callers. Finally, Bella and her husband retired, followed soon after by Aunt Elizabeth, leaving Carolyn and Jason alone. She walked the length of the large drawing room to stand before Sir Neville's casket, and placed her hands on the smooth, cool wood. She felt no sense of her father's presence or of communication with him, but only that he was lost to her now, utterly lost. She bent her head, and two fat teardrops rolled down her cheek and chin.

Jason's arm suddenly slid around her shoulders, and she smiled faintly in thanks. He wiped the tears from her cheeks.

"I don't feel any closeness to him," Carolyn murmured. "I thought perhaps if I was here beside him, I would sense him. But I don't."

"I'm sorry." Jason pulled her closer and encircled her with both arms. Carolyn leaned against his chest, comforted. "We'd better go to bed. Tomorrow will be a hard day, I'm afraid."

A hard knot clenched within her. "Yes, of course." With each step up the stairs, her dread grew. Jason opened the door to Cynthia's room, then gravely, formally, he took one of her hands and raised it to his lips, bowing over it. "Good night, my dear. Do you know by any chance which room I've been given?"

Carolyn wet her lips nervously. "I—apparently Mrs. Billingsley put us together in this room."

Jason looked beyond her to the large double bed in the middle of the room and frowned darkly. "I see. Damn the woman!" He stepped inside the room and closed the door behind him. "I hadn't thought of this."

Her heart was lacerated by the expression on his face, for it was obvious that Jason detested the thought of sleeping with her. "I'm sorry."

"Not your fault," he responded automatically. "Well, there's nothing to do except for me to sleep on the chaise lounge. It looks comfortable enough."

"What? Oh, yes, I guess so. I hadn't thought of that." It was the best solution to the problem, but Carolyn's wayward heart sank. Jason had decided without hesitation; he hadn't the least spark of desire for her.

Fourteen

With trembling fingers Carolyn removed her earrings and set them in the small jewelry case on the vanity table, then rang for Priscilla. Jason had not bothered to bring his valet with him for the few days they would be gone, and he began to undress behind her. In the mirror she could see him as he stripped off his coat and tossed it across a chair, then stuck each foot in the boot jack to pull off his glossy boots, the muscles of his thighs stretching and retracting with his efforts.

She ducked her head to pull the hairpins from her hair and several tumbled to the floor, for her fingers were fumbling and unsure. Glancing in the mirror again, she saw that Jason's shirt was unbuttoned and hanging open in the front, exposing his muscular chest. He peeled the shirt back and off his arms, muscles rippling beneath his smooth skin. His hands went to the buttons of his trousers, and Carolyn watched, her breath stopping in her throat. Soon he was completely naked. Lean-hipped and brown, he was utterly desirable. Realizing how she was staring, she blushed and lowered her head again to pull out the remaining hairpins.

Jason slipped into an ankle-length brocade dressing gown and belted it. Carolyn piled the hairpins in their little ceramic box and replaced the lid. She laced her fingers together in her lap, wondering when or where she should undress. If she waited for Priscilla, it might be less embarrassing to undress in front of Jason, but, on the other hand, a third party in the room might make it even worse.

Priscilla resolved the issue by tapping at the door. "Enter."

"Good evening, ma'am. Good evening, milord."

"Priscilla." Jason acknowledged her with a nod and settled into an armchair, a book in hand. Priscilla brushed out Carolyn's hair with her usual smooth strokes. With her eyes closed, Carolyn did not see Jason's attention wander from the book in his lap to her hair. It crackled like fire as Priscilla brushed it, and it had the sheen of satin in the lamplight.

Priscilla smoothed the mass of hair into a glossy fall over her shoulders. Carolyn stood up, turning her back to Priscilla so that the girl could unbutton the row of tiny buttons down her back. Jason's gaze was unswerving, and he watched as Priscilla slipped the dress over Carolyn's head. Acutely aware of the bareness of her shoulders, arms, and chest above the ruffled chemise, Carolyn snapped, "Give me my dressing gown, I'm freezing."

"Yes, milady. I'm sorry," the girl said in surprise, then hurried to pull out a pink satin dressing gown. Carolyn slipped into it quickly, belting it. She kept her face turned from Jason, wanting to avoid the contempt in his eyes. Priscilla knelt to unhook Carolyn's high kid boots and pull them off. After that her hose, hoop, and petticoats came off in swift succession. Carolyn was forced to remove the loose dressing gown in order to take off the thin cotton chemise, then she thrust her head and arms into the long nightgown and peeled off her pantalets beneath its protection. Once more wrapping the robe around her, she waited while Priscilla put away the undergarments, neatly turned down the covers of the bed, and departed quietly.

Drawing a deep breath, Carolyn climbed onto the small stool and slipped under the sheets, which were cozy from the warming pan. She pulled the covers high around her shoulders and nestled into her pillow. Jason's book closed with a thud. "Good night, Cynthia."

"Good night."

From the trunk at the foot of the bed he pulled out a couple of blankets, then wrapped the blankets around him and lay down on the chaise lounge. Carolyn squinted at him from the bed. The lounging chair was obviously too short for him, and he wouldn't spend a comfortable night. But she wouldn't ask him to share the bed, for it would be too humiliating if he refused. There was the sound of the lamp being blown out, then some sighs and grunts as Jason squirmed and shifted on the narrow bed. Carolyn swallowed and stared at the dark ceiling. It was going to be a long, long night.

As Jason had predicted, the following day was long and difficult. When Carolyn awoke, Jason was already up, dressed, and gone from the room. Carolyn dressed in a high-necked, long-sleeved wool day dress. The only relief to its severity were tiny lace-edged ruffles around the throat and cuffs. She had been amazed at the number of black dresses Cynthia owned, which must have been left from her mourning for Jason's father a few years earlier. They were handsome in style and material, and black looked good on her, emphasizing her pale complexion and bright hair. Still, Carolyn hated the dark dresses; they didn't suit her spirit.

The funeral was held in the small, dim village church in Heaverthwaite. The aging pastor read his eulogy in a thin, quavering voice, and Carolyn hardly listened. Beside her Aunt Elizabeth sniffled into her handkerchief, but Carolyn had cried out all her tears: she felt only drained. On the other side of her in the Worthing family pew was Jason, whose mere presence had the power to warm and support her.

Sir Neville was laid to rest in the Worthing tomb. The wind was bitterly cold and cut right through Carolyn's thick coat and wool dress. She had forgotten how much colder it was in the north. For a moment she remembered Antigua's scorching heat with longing. Jason escorted her to the carriage and put her in with her aunt, Bella, and a distant female cousin. The men rode on their mounts alongside the carriage. Carolyn longed to be by herself for a while.

But she wasn't to have her wish. There was a long, tiring buffet meal after the funeral, and once again she had to speak to those who came to express their grief and sorrow. With each passing moment she grew more and more restless. In the middle of the afternoon, when she thought she could stand it no longer, she rose to leave the room. Jason started after her, catching up just as she ran into Mr. Comstock, her father's solicitor.

"Lady Broughton," Comstock greeted her solemnly. "I was looking for you. It's time we gathered to read the will."

"What? Oh." Jason's hand slid under her elbow, supporting her unobtrusively. Carolyn turned toward him, her face pleading. "Would you go in my stead? I'm so tired, and, really, I don't care about the will." She swung her head back to the solicitor. "Wouldn't it be enough if my husband was there?"

Mr. Comstock nodded eagerly. "Yes, yes, of course. Lord Broughton?" Carolyn suspected he was far happier to deal with a man instead of a poor, weak female who might very well go into hysterics in front of him.

"Naturally, I'll represent my wife's interests," Jason replied smoothly, covering his initial surprise. "If that's really what you wish, my dear?"

"Yes, please." Carolyn smiled at him gratefully. "I'd appreciate it so much. I'd like to take a little walk."

Jason frowned. "It's terribly cold out there. Are you sure?"

Carolyn nodded. "Yes. I'll wrap up warmly."

She did as she promised, pulling out an old, long cloak of Cynthia's, which had a hood and was lined with warm fur. With her hands tucked into a compact fur muff, she would be amply protected from the cold. Carolyn slipped out the back door and set off briskly up the barren slope of Castle Crag, which lay immediately behind Gresham Hall. She climbed a track to the top of the crag; though it was narrow, its incline was gradual. At the top she passed a large outcropping of rock and turned to look down on Gresham Hall.

Her home sprawled before her, all stone and foreshortened chimneys from up here. Beyond it lay the long oval of Shallowmere Lake, the small island in its center a dark mass of pines. Breathing in the sharp air, she walked across the flat top of the crag. In the middle lay Blackbow Tarn, a small, dark pond shaped like a half-moon. The bare trunks of larches and copper beeches clustered at the far edge of the tarn. On Carolyn's side were huge humps of rhododendron bushes and green conifers. In summer the rhododendrons were a beautiful blaze of color, the slender trees a cool blend of white and green.

Carolyn sat down at the edge of the tarn on a large, flat rock. She huddled her knees up against her body for warmth and gazed into the dark, fathomless water. Local legend had it that the pond was bottomless, and no one ever swam in it. Once, when she was twelve, Cynthia had dared her to try it, and Carolyn had. But her swim had been short, and she had never tried it again, for its darkness bothered her. When she peered about underwater, she had seen no sign of a bottom, and it gave her an eerie, shivery feeling.

The sun started down, and reluctantly Carolyn rose to leave. It was safer to traverse the narrow path during the daylight, though she had once or twice traveled it in the dark. Twilight had fallen by the time she reached Gresham Hall, and she hurried inside. She would be late for dinner if she didn't rush to get dressed, and Aunt Elizabeth would be most vocal about that social slip. Jason waited in her room, his brow creased. "Where the devil have you been?" he exclaimed, jumping up. "I could throttle you."

"I went for a walk. I told you that."

"For three hours? I was worried sick for fear you'd fallen and hurt yourself and couldn't get home."

Carolyn laughed. "I'm perfectly safe on the crag. I've been up and down it a million times in my life."

"Well, I'm glad you find it amusing. I was about to go search for you, though I had no idea where you'd gone."

"I climbed the crag, that's all. I like to sit by Blackbow Tarn. It helps me think, makes me feel . . . I don't know. At peace, I guess. I needed some of that today."

Jason stared at her, and she felt uneasy. She turned away

and began to unfasten the buttons at the neck of her dress. "Where's Priscilla?"

"I sent her away. The way she kept jumping up to look out the window was driving me mad. Here, I'll help you dress tonight." Brushing her fumbling fingers aside, he efficiently opened the long line of jet buttons. Carolyn stood still under his hands, afraid to move for fear his hands might brush her body. When he had finished, he spread apart the sides of her dress and for a long moment gazed at her back.

Carolyn felt the warm, unexpected pressure of his lips upon the skin of her back, and she jumped, heart fluttering wildly. Jason raised his head. His finger traced the narrow seam of flesh he had kissed. "How did you get that scar?"

Carolyn swallowed. "I don't remember," she lied. It had happened long ago, when she was a child. She had been riding at full tilt, bent over, and a branch had jabbed through her habit, scratching her deeply. At one time it had been a long scar, but as she grew older and bigger, it had seemed to shrink. Now it was only a fine white line about an inch long on one shoulder blade.

"It looks old."

"I must have gotten it as a child. You know how children are, always bumping into things and falling down."

"Odd. I don't remember seeing it before."

Carolyn struggled to steady her breath. She couldn't tell him. She needed his comfort and strength, no matter how falsely obtained, for a while longer. The truth would be the same next week. "I—uh, wasn't aware that you were that familiar with every inch of my body."

"Unfortunately not." He put his hands on her shoulders and turned her around to face him. His earlier anger seemed to have fled, and there was a strange expression on his face—not quite amused nor irritated nor even desirous, but a peculiar mixture of all three.

"Jason? Is there something wrong?"

Slowly he drew her dress down over her arms, baring her arms. "I'm not sure. For the past hour, I've been furious with you. But now it doesn't seem important." He spread out his hands on her collarbone, his thumbs casually caressing her neck. "Tell me, dear wife, do you enjoy this?"

"What?"

He smiled and lightly teased her skin. "This. My touch. Your eyes turn deep blue, almost smoky, and your lips part a little, so that I can see the tips of your teeth and tongue." His hands moved up, and one thumb traced her lips, slipping in to touch the sharp edge of her teeth, the wet warmth of her tongue. Carolyn closed her eyes at the sharp stab of desire in her loins.

"What do you want of me?" she whispered. "My humiliation? Must I admit how much I—"

"I want only a kiss. Kiss me, Cynthia."

Carolyn could not resist his entreaty. Going up on her toes, she curled her arms around Jason's neck and kissed him long and lovingly. He wrapped his arms around her, but did not deepen the kiss, demanding nothing, only taking what she gave. Carolyn tasted his mouth leisurely. After a long, long moment of pleasure, she sank back flat on her feet and leaned her head against his chest. His chest rose and fell rapidly, and the flesh of his arms was searing.

"Thank you," he whispered hoarsely. "You told me what I want to know."

"What's that?" She raised her head, puzzled.

"I'll tell you another time." A crooked, almost boyish grin touched his lips. "Now, we better get you dressed for dinner, or your aunt will give us a proper tongue-lashing."

Efficiently he helped her into the black velvet evening dress, and Carolyn smoothed her hair into place. Throughout dinner Carolyn felt Jason's eyes on her again and again, sometimes thoughtful and pondering, at other times soft and burning. She paid scant attention to the others' conversation; her mind was busy with the sudden change in Jason's attitude. When she first came in, he had been blazing with anger, as furious as a worried parent with a stray child, but after he calmed down, he seemed pleased, loving, desirous. He had asked her to kiss him! He had seemed to desire her without his usual self-disgust. Why?

Perhaps her kiss had been proof of a change within her—or within *him.* But Carolyn couldn't imagine what had happened to melt the ice around his heart. She told herself not to worry about it. Just accept it, her heart counseled. Take it and be glad.

That evening was incredibly long, and her eyes turned frequently to the tall grandfather clock against the wall, which she willed to speed up. Shortly after nine, she rose and excused herself, confessing that she was rather tired. Jason took her arm and walked with her from the room.

Priscilla waited for Carolyn in the bedroom. As the maid helped her undress, Carolyn again felt Jason's eyes on her. But tonight they lingered and caressed her almost tangibly. Where last night his glances had been short and almost involuntary, tonight he gave her disrobing his full attention. He wanted her, and he was making no effort to hide the fact. Carolyn's heart raced. Would he come to her bed tonight?

When Priscilla left the room, Jason rose from his chair and began to undress. Carolyn climbed into bed and pulled the covers up to her waist, but remained sitting up, watching him. He pulled off his shoes and stockings without haste, and, with the same leisurely movements, he removed his cravat and coat and unfastened his shirt buttons. As he removed his clothes, his gaze remained on Carolyn. He saw her heightened color, the flicker of her tongue as it sneaked out to wet her dry lips, the pointing of her nipples beneath the silky gown. Carolyn couldn't tear her eyes away from him, and swallowed, excitement building painfully, wonderfully, within her.

Jason threw aside the remainder of his clothing and stood before her naked and unashamed, his desire clear and strong. He padded noiselessly to the side of her bed, stopping only inches from her. Carolyn was scarcely able to breathe. "I want to sleep with you tonight." She stared, wide-eyed; her voice deserted her. "Tonight and every night," he continued, reaching out to lift a strand of her hair and curl it around one finger. "You see, I want to discard our old agreement and make a new one. No more separate beds. No more pretense of marriage. I want your body and your love. I want you to be my wife in truth. Will you agree to my new bargain?"

The slight tremor of his finger against her hair sent waves of longing through her. He was anxious about her reply, a trifle frightened. "Yes." Her word came out barely a whisper. She swallowed and spoke more firmly. "Yes, I agree."

His nostrils flared, and he took her hand and brought it to his face, cupping her palm against his cheek. He kissed the pads of each of her fingers and returned again to the palm; his hot breath grazed her skin, sending tremors through her. Jason closed his eyes. "I want to please you tonight. Please you past anything you've ever known. Will you let me?"

Carolyn nodded. "You needn't ask. I am yours."

He buried his mouth in her hand again, eyes closed, and his body was still with concentration. Then he reached down and flipped back the elegant covers of the bed. Inching up her gown over legs and hips, he finally whisked it off over her head. Jason's eyes roamed her naked body. He lay down beside her and cupped one lush breast in his hand, which he explored leisurely, then drifted to the other, all the while keeping his gaze on his hand and her response to it. There was no hiding the flush of desire that rose in her throat or the eager prickling of her nipples.

He left her breasts to move over her entire body, seeking the tender flesh of her inner thighs, the sensitive skin behind her knees, caressing even the faintly roughened soles of her feet. "Turn over," he told her hoarsely, and she did as he asked. His hands worked their wonders on her back, tracing the knobby column of her spine and curving over her rounded buttocks. The sound of his heavy breathing stirred Carolyn almost as much as his expert hands, and she groaned softly and moved her legs, restless with longing. Jason took the opportunity to slip his fingers between her legs from behind, sighing with pleasure at the feel of the most intimate part of her desire. "That's right," he breathed. "That's good. Ah, my sweet girl."

Carolyn groaned in frustration, biting the sheet beneath her. "Jason, please, I can't—oh, oh, yes. Jason, please, kiss me."

He turned her over, pulling her beneath him. He kissed her lips, her eyes, her cheeks, and throat, as sweet and languid as honey. He kissed her all over, his tongue and lips caressing her chest and breasts and stomach as his fingers continued their breathtaking exploration at the joinder of her legs. Carolyn writhed beneath his ministrations, panting, unable to think or speak. She wanted him, all of him; her hands moved frantically over his body, caressing his flesh wherever she could touch.

With infinite slowness, Jason slid down her body until he lay between her legs. His head lowered, and Carolyn gasped.

"No! What are you doing?"

"Pleasing you," he answered huskily. "Trust me. Relax. I won't do anything you don't enjoy."

Carolyn forced her limbs to loosen and gave herself up to the exquisite pleasure of his mouth. She had never imagined such shattering, sizzling joy as his lips and tongue evoked from her now. Every feeling in her body coalesced in the center of her body. She was hot and pulsating under the moist seal of his mouth. His tongue teased the hard bud of joy at her very core until it swelled and throbbed. A multitude of sparkling lights danced behind her eyelids, gathering in force and speed until the pleasure was so great it almost hurt. Carolyn sobbed Jason's name, her head rolling from side to side, and then the deep, nameless something inside her exploded, smashing through her with waves of electrifying joy. She tensed, her hips rising from the bed, as the pleasure rocked her. With a heavy groan, she relaxed.

Her eyelids fluttered open; there was a vulnerable look to her eyes, the expression of a woman fulfilled past her dreams. Jason smiled at the blush that stained her cheeks. There was no soft, satisfied, dreamy-eyed look about him. He was coiled tight as a spring, rigid with sexual tension. Carolyn brushed her fingertips over his taut flanks. "Come into me now," she whispered, and his eyes shot fire. "I want to feel you inside me."

Jason growled deep in his throat and slowly he thrust into

her, burying himself within her. Just as slowly he pulled back, almost withdrawing, then plunged in again. Sweat dotted his forehead and upper lip as he began to stroke rhythmically within her, rebuilding her desire as he pushed his to its highest point. At last he shuddered, straining against her, and his hips churned in a cataclysm of passion. The explosion of his wild desire sparked her to her own shattering peak again, and they vaulted to the heights together, for a moment lost in each other and their joy.

Jason collapsed against her, his breath heavy. "I love you," he whispered against her ear and kissed the lobe.

Carolyn's eyes widened, and for a single instant she knew a burst of inexpressible happiness. "I love you," she confessed softly. Then pain seared her chest. Oh, yes, he loved, all right. How desperately she wished she were the object of his love. But it wasn't her Jason loved, but Cynthia!

During their remaining two days at Gresham Hall and all the way back to Kent, Carolyn was in awe of Jason's behavior. Whereas before he had avoided her at every opportunity, now he was almost constantly by her side, often gazing at her with warmth and affection. He took her hand or draped his arms around her shoulders, now and then pausing in what he was doing to drop a kiss on her cheek or lips. At night in the privacy of their bedroom, he made love to her, often waking her again in the middle of the night by raining kisses over her face and body. He took her tenderly, forcefully, eagerly, happily exploring her body and finding all the spots that brought her pleasure.

In their cramped train compartment going back to London, he slept with Carolyn in her narrow bed. In the anonymous privacy of their railway room, he brought them both to a glorious pleasure again and again. He couldn't get enough of her, and Carolyn was happy to comply with his wishes. He taught her the things that brought him pleasure, delighted by her eagerness to learn. They experimented freely, and when they were drained of passion, they laughed and talked together of mundane things. Carolyn successfully banished any thought of the future from her mind. She refused to contemplate what would happen when they reached home, how she would tell Jason the truth, and what she would do afterward. Instead, she lived only in the joy of the moment.

They made a stopover in London to visit Jason's mother. Carolyn was happy to see Selena, and Selena greeted her with equal delight. She cast a wondering look at her son, who was strangely relaxed, almost carefree, and openly affectionate to his wife, but she said nothing about the remarkable change in his behavior.

On the second day they were at his mother's house, Jason went out to attend to some business. As soon as he left, Selena turned to Carolyn, smiling. "My dear, whatever has happened to Jason?"

"I don't know," Carolyn answered truthfully. She could not understand the change in their relationship, though she was too happy to question it too much.

"You've wrought a remarkable change, I'll say that. I haven't seen him this happy since, well, since he became engaged to you. No, I take it back; he's even happier now than he was then. He seems . . . almost at peace." Selena's eyes gleamed with love. "I'm so grateful to you."

"I—don't know that I did anything."

"You changed, that's what you did. I'll tell you honestly,

there have been times when I bitterly regretted your entrance into this family."

Carolyn's head snapped up and she stared at the woman, astonished, for she had never imagined that Selena disliked Cynthia. "But you—I, I didn't know."

"Please, don't be hurt. And don't imagine that Jason tattled to his mother about what went on between you two. But I could see how desperately unhappy he was almost from the time he married you. Why, when you returned from your honeymoon on the Continent, he looked more like a man who'd been on the rack. I knew something was very wrong, but I thought it best not to interfere. Mothers-in-law can be such pests, and I vowed I would never be like that. Don't think I blamed you entirely. As I said, I didn't know the facts. No doubt Jason was as much at fault as you; he is a headstrong, forceful man. He can be tender, but he can hurt without thinking, too. Whatever the reasons, he was unhappy. He turned taciturn and bitter. His life lacked joy."

"I'm so sorry," Carolyn murmured, moved by Selena's description of Jason's pain. "It was my fault."

Selena patted her hand and smiled. "There, there, don't fuss. It's in the past. Jason's happy now, and I'm grateful to you." She paused, studying her daughter-in-law shrewdly. "I feared that you didn't love Jason, that you married him for your father's sake."

Carolyn stared at her in surprise. "How did you—" She stopped, biting her lower lip in chagrin. She had just admitted Selena's words.

"I saw you with Jason; I saw the things he was too blinded by love to notice. I also saw you with your father. One hears rumors; it's said you had a sister who died young and you tried to make up to Sir Neville for her. And it was common knowledge that Sir Neville wanted to marry his daughter to a family of long and distinguished lineage."

"I suppose the latter is true," Carolyn admitted. "Papa's family was in trade less than two centuries ago. He thought the stigma hadn't been completely blotted out."

"But the part about the sister isn't true?" Selena pursued.

"Noooo, not exactly." Carolyn looked away from the woman's too-knowing eyes. She wanted suddenly, desperately to confess the whole story to this kind woman.

Selena waited patiently, not pressing for an explanation of Carolyn's statement. Carolyn swallowed and studied her hands. She couldn't tell her. No matter how understanding Selena was, she wouldn't accept an actress masquerading as her daughter-in-law, sleeping with her son without benefit of marriage, lying to him about her identity. Tears clogged her throat. "I—I love Jason. I want you to believe that."

"I do believe it, my dear. I can see it in your eyes, in the way you turn toward him every time he enters the room, like a plant toward the sun. And it's mutual, that's obvious."

But it isn't, Carolyn thought miserably. If he found out how Carolyn had deceived him, he would hate her. She remembered the contempt in his voice when he asked her if she had stooped so low as to become an actress. Just the knowledge that she had been in an acting troupe for five years would be enough to condemn her in his eyes. But, beyond that, she had lied to him, tricked him. It would wound his pride; he would think she had made a fool of him. He would be humiliated for telling her he loved her, and he would hate her for rekindling the spark of his love for Cynthia. His heart would be lacerated once again when he found out that Cynthia hadn't changed and didn't love him. He'd be more furious with her now than he would have been if she had told him before her father died. If she revealed the truth, he would cast her off immediately.

Yet she must tell him! She despised the deception she had been living. The fact that he made love to her and told her he loved her, all the while believing she was Cynthia, was a constant wound to her heart. She wondered how long she could stand the torture of continuing her deception.

Carolyn pressed her lips together and swallowed the confession that was pushing up her throat. Selena, watching her with a faint, worried frown, quickly changed the subject. "My dear, did I tell you about Lady Abernathy's fete?"

Carolyn smiled gratefully. "No, I don't think you did. What happened?"

Selena plunged into a lightly humorous account of that worthy woman's party. The subject of Jason's change and their marriage never came up again.

They left London after only a few days, both of them anxious to return to Laurel and Broughton Court. Carolyn was surprised at how her heart lifted in pleasure and anticipation when Broughton Court came into view, graceful and unobtrusively lovely. She smiled and exclaimed, "Oh, how good it feels to be home!"

Jason glanced at her and smiled. "That's how I've always felt. The Court has woven its spell around you, too."

"Yes, I suppose it has. I only wish—"

"Wish what? Go on."

Carolyn hadn't meant to broach the subject for fear it might offend Jason, but now that she had, she went on, "Well, I saw some beautiful furniture in the attic one day. I thought of putting it in one or two of the rooms. My bedroom and the upstairs sitting room, perhaps."

His eyes glittered with amusement. "But, dear, you refurnished the whole house yourself. Now you want to put it back the way it was?"

So it was Cynthia who had decorated Broughton Court in the latest styles, leaving it too perfect and somehow hollow. It would seem peculiar that now she wanted to replace the old furniture. "I didn't mean the whole house, of course," Carolyn explained quickly. "Just a couple of rooms. I've outgrown the style of my bedroom, I think. Something a little more simple and—and graceful would appeal to me. It's a shame for the furniture in the attic to go to waste, especially when it suits the period of the house. We could move the furniture in my bedroom to one of the empty rooms on the third floor."

"Of course. Feel free to redo any rooms you wish. I'm used to redecorating; my mother does it incessantly."

The carriage rolled to a stop. Again, they had to run the gauntlet of the servants who had lined up to greet them. Carolyn was pleased and rather proud of herself when she greeted each one of them with their name and a personal comment, remembering how hesitantly she had faced them before. As soon as they finished, Jason and Carolyn went upstairs to the nursery.

Laurel ran to fling her arms around their necks, doing her best to hug and kiss both of them at once. Carolyn, who knelt to hug her, was pushed off balance by the exuberance of Laurel's greeting and tumbled to the floor. Laughing, she sat up, and Laurel plunked herself down in her lap. Carolyn looked across at Jason, and the smile that passed between them was warm and meaningful. Carolyn thought that she had never seen him look so happy and relaxed; the deep lines around his mouth and eyes had softened and, with the upturning of his lips, were no longer bitter, but laughing. Passionately Carolyn wished that he could remain this way forever, that they could stop this moment in time and make it last the rest of their lives.

She ignored the swell of emotion in her throat and glanced away. Her gaze met Bonnie's, whose mouth was clamped into a disapproving line, scorn and anger within the nurse's eyes. Carolyn knew Bonnie was thinking that she had abandoned her sister and become Jason's devoted slave. It wasn't true, for she loved Cynthia and would never abandon her. But the clash of warring loyalties broke the moment of closeness and warmth. Her life couldn't remain like this forever. With one excuse or another, she had put off the moment of truth, seizing the joy of Jason's love and passion. But she couldn't avoid it much longer. For Jason's sake, as well as her own, she had to tell him of her deception.

Hot tears stabbed her eyes, and Carolyn bent her head to hide them. Soon it would all be over. She would tell Jason and go off to somehow spend the rest of her life without the essential center of her existence. Two weeks, she told herself. She would give herself two weeks to taste the sweet fruit of Jason's love, and then she would tell him. She would have a last fortnight of pleasure before it was over.

Fifteen

$\mathcal{D}$uring her absence Carolyn had received a letter from Lucy Carlisle. In a cramped, hurried hand, Miss Carlisle thanked Lady Broughton for her interest in her work and invited Carolyn to drop by the Carlisle school the next time she was in London. She went on to say that she would be pleased to meet Laurel and would do her best to analyze what the child needed and was capable of learning, should Carolyn wish her to. In the meanwhile, she offered several suggestions of things Carolyn herself could do with Laurel.

Carolyn read the letter through hurriedly and scampered down the stairs to Jason's study. He glanced up at her swift entry and smiled. "Something's pleased you, I see."

"Yes, Jason, look. This is a letter from Miss Carlisle."

"She's already responded? Excellent."

"See? She invited me to London to visit her and her school."

"Would you like to go?"

"Very much," Carolyn returned promptly, remembering momentarily that she would not be at Broughton Court long enough to plan for a visit to London. "She's interested in seeing Laurel. Perhaps she could be of real help to us."

Jason carefully aligned his fingertips. "Dearest, I hope you won't get too hopeful that Miss Carlisle will be able to change Laurel."

"I don't want her changed. I mean, I love her as she is. I simply want her to have every opportunity to grow. I want to do everything I can to help her. I don't expect her to suddenly talk a blue streak or act like other children. But if her horizons could be expanded a little, if I knew she had been given every chance to learn and develop . . ."

"I know." He reached out and took one of her hands in his. "We'll see that she's given every chance. But, please, don't break your heart over it."

"I won't, I promise. But do you think we could invite Miss Carlisle to come here? She could meet Laurel, and I could watch and learn from her so I could help Laurel myself. Even in this letter she's given me several practical things to do." Carolyn turned to the second page and ran her fingers down the lines. "For instance, she says that to help Laurel talk I should try putting her hand in front of my mouth as I say words, so that Laurel can feel the way the air comes out with certain sounds. Then Laurel can practice the sounds and feel with her own hand whether she's doing it correctly. She mentions several rhyming games and songs to help with the sounds of different letters."

Jason bent over the letter. " 'Above all,' " he read, " 'patience and persistence are necessary. Sometimes it will seem you take a step forward only to slide back the next day. Keep in mind that your work isn't wasted. But you must stay at it.' It sounds like a heavy load."

"I suppose it is," Carolyn admitted. "But it's such a thrill when Laurel makes a bit of progress. You can't imagine how proud I was of her the other day when she held out her cup to Nurse and said, 'More.' She can put on her little pantalets and chemise all by herself now. Priscilla is sewing up a cloth with different sizes and shapes of buttons and buttonholes on it, so that we can practice doing and undoing her buttons. Miss Carlisle had some ideas about that, too. She suggested that I make up some simple dresses with loose sleeves and large buttons. They would be easier for Laurel to put on by herself. Then I could teach her to dress herself."

Jason squeezed her hand and released it reluctantly. "Invite her if you wish. I'd welcome anything that would help Laurel, you know that. Even if she can't do anything for Laurel, it'll be well worth having her here if she brings that sparkle to your eyes."

"Good. I'll invite her to come as soon as she can."

"All right."

Carolyn bent impulsively and kissed his cheek, then whirled and left the study. Sometimes she thought it would be more than she could stand to have to leave this house and Jason and Laurel. If she could arrange for Miss Carlisle's visit, at least she could feel that she had done something for Laurel and her father. She would know that she had given something, not just taken.

Carolyn penned a note to Lucy Carlisle immediately, thanking her for her letter and promising to visit her school when she was next in London. She ended the brief letter with an earnest invitation to visit at Broughton Court at her earliest possible convenience, offering the weekend after the next as a possible date. So that Miss Carlisle would not need to worry about the cost of a train ticket nor have to swallow her pride and accept Carolyn's paying for it, she added that the Broughton carriage would be at Miss Carlisle's disposal to bring her from London and carry her back again. She had

Jason frank the letter and posted it immediately, hoping Lucy Carlisle would be able to come the weekend she had suggested. She wanted to meet the woman and talk to her. If only she could do that, she would know whether Laurel would prosper with Miss Carlisle's help. Then she wouldn't feel as guilty about leaving the child, only saddened.

The next few days were the most pleasant Carolyn could remember, despite her lingering sorrow for her father's death. She rode with Jason every day, and once he took her around his fields, discussing the various tenants, the crops, and his ambitions for the land. The third day after their return dawned clear and unseasonably warm. There was only a hint of chill in the air, as in early autumn, even though it was now December. Christmas would be celebrated at Broughton Court without her, Carolyn thought, then sternly dismissed the treacherous thought from her mind. She would leave when she planned; this time there'd be no excuse-making or side-stepping. She had to keep her thoughts off the future and all the events she would never see here; she must think only about today. And today was perfect for a picnic!

She didn't know why the idea popped into her head, but the more she thought about it, the better she liked it. First she informed Cook of her plans, then went up to the nursery to gather Laurel. They met Jason as they were leaving, and he immediately invited himself along. He folded his long legs into the little pony cart, and both Carolyn and Laurel collapsed into giggles. They drove to the hammer pond and spread out their blanket beside it.

The food was delicious, the air warmed by the sun, and everything full of life and the merriest good cheer. Carolyn pointed out to Laurel the various forms of life around the pond, and the child gasped with delight at the silvery flash of a fish beneath the surface of the water, giggled and clapped her hands at the waddling moorhens, and shrieked at the swift dive of the kingfisher. By the time they returned to Broughton Court, all three were tired, their hair wind-whipped, and their clothes dirtied and snagged, but they agreed that it had been a marvelous time. One look at Laurel's beaming face told everything that her limited words could not.

Jason and Carolyn left Laurel in the nursery, where Bonnie clucked over her messy state and hustled her off for a bath. Jason took Carolyn's hand, and they trailed down the stairs toward their rooms. Jason glanced ruefully down at his clothes. There was a small rent in the thigh of his trousers where a bramble bush had caught him during a rambunctious game of tag; bits of grass and dirt clung to his jacket from rolling down the hillside with Laurel. "I rather think a bath and a change of clothes are due me, too."

Carolyn smiled, her blue eyes darkening with promise. "And shall I be your valet, milord?"

"I can think of nothing better."

She helped him undress, now playful, now seductive, as she unbuttoned his clothes and slid them from his body. As she worked, his hands were busy exploring the curves of her clothed body, and he stopped her now and again to kiss her mouth or ears or neck. When he was completely naked, Carolyn started toward his dresser to take out a new set of clothes, but he reached out to stop her. "Turnabout's fair play, don't you think?"

Carolyn didn't answer, merely smiled. Jason discarded her garments one by one and carried her to his large, high-canopied bed. There they made sweet, slow love, coming together in a cataclysm of excitement and love.

They lay twined in each other's arms, relaxed and sated. Quietly they talked and laughed, their hands drifting over each other in tender caresses. Carolyn stored the moment away in her treasury of memories, to be taken out and cherished after she had left Broughton Court and her world had turned gray and lonely. Jason yawned and stretched. "I must see to some accounts down in my study." Carolyn made a little pout of disappointment, and he laughed, leaning over to kiss her deliciously sulky lips. "I thought you were going to dress me."

Carolyn lowered her lashes flirtingly. "Milord had more pressing tasks for his servant." She hopped out of bed and walked across the room naked, while Jason propped his arms behind his head and watched her appreciatively. Carolyn brought his undergarments and shirt, helpfully buttoning his shirt and snapping in the studs of his cuffs. Jason reached out to curve a hand over her temptingly bare hips, but she swerved and walked away from him with a saucy twist of her head. She pulled out fawn trousers and a dark-brown waistcoat. "Will these suit your lordship?"

"Perfectly." Jason took the trousers from her hands. Carolyn laid the waistcoat on a chair and inspected the row of jackets in front of her. There was one in the back that caught her eye, a dark chocolate-brown broadcloth the same shade as the waistcoat. She pulled it out and held it up in front of her, posing. "And this, milord?"

Jason, shrugging into his waistcoat, glanced at her and smiled. "I'll take the model, but not the garment." Carelessly he flicked a sleeve of the coat. "This one's missing a cuff button. Fetch me that tweed there."

Carolyn hung up the jacket, lifting the offending sleeve to inspect it. There was obviously a button missing, for broken thread protruded from the cloth half an inch below a single gold button. Suddenly Carolyn stopped; all the air seemed to have been sucked from her lungs. With trembling fingers she brought the sleeve closer to her eyes and stared at the lone remaining button. Its design was pressed in gold, a shield with an animal lying before it, of the same design as the button that now lay in her black lacquer box, the button she had torn off her attacker's coat in her hotel in Antigua!

Black dots danced before her eyes, and she leaned against the center post of the wardrobe cabinet for support. Numbly she hung up the jacket and pulled out the tweed coat Jason had mentioned. Still too stunned to speak or even think coherently, she handed Jason the jacket and stepped back. Suddenly very aware of her nakedness, she hurried to pull on her garments. As she tied on the unwieldy cage of her hoop, her fingers began to tremble, and she realized that she was trembling all over.

It simply couldn't be! There must be hundreds of buttons like those on jackets all over England and the colonies. There was no proof that this particular button came from Jason's coat. "Why—why didn't you have it sewn back on?"

"Have what sewn on—oh, the button. Because I'd lost it, you see. I couldn't find it anywhere, and I hadn't an extra one like it."

"Why not purchase one?"

"I couldn't. It was a set made especially for me. Did you see the design on it? That's the coat of arms of the Hemby family. They owned this land originally—you know, Hemby Keep? Their last descendent, a woman, married into the

Broughtons. For a time, the Broughton crest carried the Hemby one beside it, but later it was dropped. I rather liked it and had the set of buttons made from it for this coat. But as it turned out, I never liked the jacket, really. When I lost the button, it didn't seem worth it to have another set made."

"Oh." There was no mistake, no possibility of another button like this at large somewhere in the world. Only Jason would own a jacket with those buttons.

She knew she was pale and trembling, and she hoped Jason wouldn't look at her closely. "I—I must put up my hair," she whispered and started for the connecting door between their rooms.

"Of course, my love." Jason stopped her on the way out and planted a light kiss on her lips. "Though I much prefer you this way."

Carolyn managed a tremulous smile. "A bit casual for dining, don't you think?"

He grinned as she slipped from his arms and went through the open door. Though she longed to shut the door that separated their rooms, she refrained. She went to the vanity table and fumbled with her hair, making an attempt to roll it into a neat bun. Out of the corner of her eye she watched the other room through the door. Jason crossed her line of sight, and an instant later, she heard his bedroom door close. There was the faint thud of his feet trotting down the stairs. Carolyn pulled out the black lacquer box, almost dropping it in her haste, and set it on top of the dresser. After wiping her sweating palms across her skirt, she lifted the box and looked in. The gold button lay on top; Carolyn reached in cautiously and pulled it out. Closing it in her palm, she ran into Jason's room and across to the looming wardrobe. She found the brown coat and stretched out its sleeve to the light, then held up the button she had found in her hotel room against the broken knot of threads. It was identical to the other button: same size, shape, color, and design.

Carolyn closed her eyes, curling her hand around the button until it bit cruelly into her palm. There was no denying it. The button she had found came from Jason's jacket, for it was Jason who had attacked her in Antigua. And it was Jason who had tried to kill her!

Carolyn spent the rest of the day in her room, pacing and thinking. No matter how much evidence there was against Jason, she couldn't believe he had tried to kill her. Thinking back to the morning she had found the button, she tried to find another explanation. She had never actually felt the button tear off during the struggle, and she had only assumed that it had come from her assailant's coat. It was possible that Jason, thinking he had discovered his wife, had come to her room during the day, perhaps waited for her or looked around the room. A loose button could have fallen off his jacket then. Her attacker that night could have been someone else, not the owner of the button.

He'd had many opportunities to kill her since that night in the West Indies and yet he had not. Perhaps he'd wanted to kill her once in his jealous rage, but after his anger cooled, he had regretted the attempt. Why, he hadn't even been able to finish the job; he had fled. Now, having recovered his love for Cynthia, he wouldn't try to harm her.

Carolyn sighed and ran a hand through her hair. Fool! She must not let herself be blinded by her love; her very life was at stake. Trying to look at the matter clearly and reasonably, she thought of the arsenic poisoning and the saddle that had come loose at the same time her placid horse bolted. If she stretched her credulity, she'd say the saddle incident could have been an accident, but there was no getting around arsenic poisoning, and someone had tried to kill her at least twice, in all likelihood, three times. Who else could try two or three times to kill her besides Jason? The button was proof that Jason was in Antigua at the time of the first attack. Jason had been at the hunt, had even stood beside her saddle and bent down to inspect her horse, which was the moment he loosened the girth. He had been at Broughton Court during her arsenic-induced illness, and only he had a motive for killing her.

But why would Jason want her dead? He said often that he loved Cynthia. But, her mind argued insistently, that could be part of his plan to appear to be a loving couple so that when she died, the finger of suspicion would not point to him. "Oh, no," the servants would say, "his lordship loved her very much. They were always together, cooing like lovebirds." Jason had suddenly changed his reluctance to make love to her, right after her father's funeral—after the reading of the will. That very night, for the first time, he had told her he loved her, and since then he had been a tender, loving husband, very much at odds with the way he had acted toward her before. Carolyn had been too happy in his lovemaking, too jealous of his feeling for Cynthia, to even wonder what had brought about the sudden change.

Jason must have discovered something at Gresham Hall in the reading of her father's will. He had never told her what was in the will, and now that very question seemed weighted with evil purpose. Carolyn had never asked him anything about it, never spoken to Sir Neville's solicitor about it. Perhaps Jason had been afraid that since her father no long approved of Cynthia, he would have cut her out of the will. Perhaps he had waited for the reading of the will for assurance that Cynthia had indeed inherited Sir Neville's estate. If she had, then her husband would naturally inherit it when she died.

It would seem strange to ask Jason about the will after all this time had elapsed. And if there was something in it that would hint at Jason's guilt, he wasn't likely to tell her, anyway. She could write the solicitor, but by the time he received her letter and replied, she could very well be dead.

She wanted to pack a few things and slip away secretly in the night. But there was no place she could run that Jason would not eventually seek her out. She could confess that she was not Cynthia, but if he wanted to kill her that would do her little good. Everyone thought she was Cynthia, and if she died, everyone would think Cynthia had died. It would serve Jason's purpose just as well, and she would accomplish nothing except a swift death, for he would doubtless kill her before she could leave or tell anyone else the truth.

In an agony of indecision, Carolyn worried away the afternoon without coming up with any solution. She dressed and went down to supper, her heart pounding with fright. How could she face Jason and act normally, as if nothing had happened? Surely he would see her suspicion written all over her face.

The drawing room was empty, so she settled into a chair to wait for Jason, schooling her expression to one of pleasant expectation. When Jason strode into the room and saw her, his face split in a wide grin. Carolyn was torn within herself, filled with love as she always was when she saw him, yet also frozen and uncertain, fearing her own feelings for him.

Searching his face for a sign of duplicity and finding nothing but open affection, Carolyn rose and went to him. He pulled her into his arms and kissed her. Carolyn tried in vain to relax, and for the first time, she did not respond to his kiss.

Jason released her and stepped back, his forehead wrinkling in puzzlement. "Sweetheart? Is something the matter?"

Carolyn wet her lips and turned away to avoid his eyes. "I—uh, haven't felt well this afternoon. A headache. I think I got too much sun at the picnic."

He smiled and murmured, "As long as it wasn't too much loving. . . ."

His hand caressed her hair, and Carolyn smiled weakly. "Is it possible to get too much of that?"

"Not for me."

They ate dinner in comparative silence, and afterward Carolyn excused herself to return to her bedroom. Only concern showed on Jason's face, not suspicion. "Have you taken a headache powder? Perhaps you should."

"Yes, I will. No doubt I'll feel better after a rest."

Carolyn hoped the excuse would hold him off for the whole night. Upstairs in her room, she dressed in an unrevealing nightgown. Priscilla brought her a glass of water, milky with dissolved headache powder, which Carolyn poured out in the ornate, cabineted chamberpot as soon as the maid left. Blowing out the lights, she crawled under the covers. When she heard Jason's bedroom door open, she quickly closed her eyes, feigning a deep sleep. Jason's footsteps came to the open connecting door and stopped. Carefully Carolyn regulated her breathing to a slow, even pace. He walked away, and she relaxed.

She listened to him undress in the other room. After his lights went out, his footsteps neared her room again, and he did not pause at the door, but walked quietly to her bed. The mattress sank beneath his weight as he lay down beside her. Involuntarily Carolyn turned, her eyes flying open, remembering too late that she was pretending to be asleep. She blinked groggily and rubbed her face. "Jason?"

"Yes, love. I'm sorry. I didn't mean to disturb you. I started to sleep in my bed, but it was lonely." He slipped an arm beneath her shoulders, pulling her to him, and Carolyn forced herself to snuggle against him, feeling split in half between her love and her suspicion.

He kissed her chastely on the forehead, demanding nothing of her, and drifted to sleep. As soon as she could, Carolyn extracted herself from his embrace and rolled to the other side of the bed. Several hours passed before she finally fell asleep.

Jason was gone the next morning when she awakened. There was a folded square of paper atop her vanity table, and she picked it up curiously and opened it. The note read, "Meet me at ten o'clock at the old Keep, inside the burned wing. Jason." Carolyn frowned. It seemed absurd. Carolyn reread the note several times and still couldn't make sense of it. She replaced the note on the vanity table, slipping it partly under the corner of her jewelry box. When Priscilla came, she bade her take out her riding habit and prepare her hair in a simple style. She couldn't imagine what Jason had in mind, but she couldn't fail to show up without arousing his suspicion.

After a light breakfast, she rode out on Felicity, purposely arriving a few minutes late. She didn't want to spend any more time than was necessary in the old ruins. However, she saw no sign of Jason's powerful white stallion. Carolyn dismounted and tied the mare to the low-hanging branches of a tree. She glanced toward the thick cluster of trees, dense even in winter because of the tangled bushes and evergreens. It was somewhat cooler than the day before, but not enough to account for the shiver that ran down her spine.

She was almost to the entrance of the burned addition of the Keep when she stopped, suddenly aware of the feeling that she was being watched just like the first time she came to this place. Carolyn turned in a slow circle, but spotted nothing.

Carolyn stepped tentatively inside the ruined shell and peered into the dimness. Most of the roof had caved in long ago, but the high, charred walls darkened the interior. At one time the building must have been at least two or three stories high. "Jason?" Carolyn held up her skirts off the debris-strewn floor as she walked. It smelled of damp, decay, and charcoal. Carolyn skirted a beam lying propped between wall and ground.

Something rustled in the inner recesses, beyond the great stone lump of the fireplace, and Carolyn stopped, icy with fear. Someone—something had moved in there. Just a rat, she told herself, then shivered at the thought. She began to pick her way back to the entrance, when there was a loud, long groan beside her. The smoked stone wall seemed to move, to collapse in on her, as she had fancied that day in the remains of the old Keep. But it wasn't her imagination; the stones were moving!

Carolyn jumped sideways and crashed into the slanting beam. She bounced off it and tumbled to the floor, just as the mighty rumble of crashing stones sounded in her ears. The earth exploded around her as heavy chunks of rock hit the earth and bounced, crashing into each other, the debris, and the earth. The air was filled with dust and pale ash and the powder of wood and stone. Carolyn curled instinctively into a ball, her arms covering her head. Something hit her leg, and several piercing pains beat on her back. The air and earth vibrated. Slowly the reverberations died away. Carolyn choked from the dust and dirt.

Unthinkingly, she tried to sit up, and her back rammed into a heavy plank of wood. Wincing, she collapsed again, and looked up to find that the wooden beam she had run into had saved her life. Two other beams had fallen from the ceiling as the old wall caved in, and they had crashed into her beam, settling slowly to the floor. The ends of the beams had come to rest on a pile of debris, so that the three logs together had formed a kind of low tent across Carolyn. By curling up, she had brought practically her whole body beneath their protection. Squares of stone lay all around her.

On her stomach, Carolyn edged out from beneath the beams and slithered atop the neighboring jumble of rock, fearing with each movement that the beams would be jarred loose and crash down upon her. Jagged pieces of rocks tore her sleeves and slashed her forearms as she crawled out inch by inch. When she was free of the beams, she rose painfully and worked her way across the broken ground to the gaping entrance. Once she was clear of the fallen rock, she broke into a run, bursting out of the ruin into the sunlight. She didn't stop running until she reached her horse. Felicity danced and snorted, frightened first by the loud crash and now by the sudden appearance of a woman running straight at her. She collapsed against the mare's side, grasping the saddle with her hands and burying her face into Felicity's coarse mane.

She continued to cough, her lungs struggling for air, and she shivered uncontrollably. Knowing only that she must reach safety, Carolyn somehow clambered into her saddle without a step up, and the frightened mare turned and dashed for home. Carolyn didn't bother going to the stables. She rode straight to the front of the house and stumbled up the steps to the door.

Inside, a footman lounged on a hallway bench. He jumped up, then gasped. "Milady?"

Carolyn caught a glimpse of her reflection in the mirror. She was covered with dust and grayish powder; her hair was loose and tangled; her habit was torn in several places, and her sleeves were in shreds, her arms cut and bleeding. She stared at herself with wide, dark eyes, and suddenly she began to laugh and cry at the same time, her shoulders heaving as she sank slowly to the floor.

What happened after she collapsed in hysterics on the entry floor of Broughton Court was afterward very vague in Carolyn's mind. Barlow had come running at the footman's frightened shout, and then Mrs. Morely and Priscilla had appeared, exclaiming and questioning. Someone—the footman, she thought—had carried Carolyn to her bed chamber, where he had left her in the women's care. Priscilla had taken off Carolyn's blood-stained clothes, then dressed the deep scratches on her forearms and slipped a nightgown gingerly over her head. The maid had tucked her into bed and stayed by her side while Mrs. Morely appeared with a steaming cup of tea.

Finally Carolyn had stopped shivering and slid into sleep. When she awoke two hours later, she started to stretch, but found the soreness all over her body too unbearable. The memory of what had happened flooded back to her. Tugging off her nightgown, she climbed out of bed and inspected the damages in the mirror. There was a huge purple bruise on one leg and several tiny ones over her back, where she must have been hit by flying pebbles. Her elbows and forearms were covered with white gauze bandages. She had scraped off a lot of skin crawling out of the rubble.

Carolyn put on the long flannel gown and eased back into bed, drained of energy. A shudder shook her frame as she recalled the terrifying instant when she saw the stone wall sway in upon her.

The door opened, and Jason strode in. His skin was pale and taut across the bones of his face. "What happened?" he demanded harshly as he crossed the room to her bedside.

"A wall fell on me. I was nearly killed!"

"A wall! Where? What happened?"

"At Hemby Keep, of course. In the wing that was damaged by fire. One of the walls collapsed."

"My God! I never thought! I should have had the place torn down years ago, but it never occurred to me that any of the walls were so weak."

"Why did you want me to meet you there, of all places?" Carolyn cried out.

He paused and stared at her. "You aren't making sense. What are you talking about?"

"I'm talking about Hemby Keep!" Carolyn snapped, sore and exasperated. "Where you asked me to meet you this morning!"

His eyebrows vaulted up. "Where I what?"

"Jason! Why do you make me repeat myself? You asked me to meet you at the Keep this morning. While I was there, one of the walls collapsed."

"I didn't ask you to meet me there."

Now it was Carolyn's turn to stare at him. "In your note! The note you left for me this morning."

"I left you no note." His brows drew together. "My dear, Mrs. Morely said you were rather hysterical when you returned to the house."

"Well, wouldn't anyone be if they'd just had a wall fall on them?"

"Of course, of course," he replied soothingly. "However, I'm not sure if you should still be—I mean—were you struck on the head?"

"No, I was not struck on the head! Why won't you admit you wrote me that note?" Carolyn scrambled out of bed, her stomach cramping with fear. "I'll show you. I left it here, under the edge of my jewelry box." Carolyn hurried to the vanity table and stopped, gaping at the table in dismay.

Her jewelry box sat on the table, but there was no folded white sheet of paper stuck underneath it. Jason's note had vanished.

Sixteen

$\mathcal{C}$arolyn swung to Jason, her eyes wide and confused. "But I—it was here this morning. I stuck it there before I went to meet you."

"What did it say?"

"I don't remember exactly. Something like: Meet me at ten o'clock in the old Keep. No, wait, it specifically mentioned the burned-out wing."

"I didn't write you a note." Jason said slowly and gravely. "I woke up early and decided to ride over to Mrs. Beacom's. Her husband was one of my tenants. He died last Thursday."

"It took you this long?"

"Of course not. I rode through the orchards and stopped to chat with Fred Hastings. Norah invited me to stay and eat with them. I couldn't get out of it without seeming rude." He paused, and one hand gently brushed her hair. "Sweetheart, you can't think that I—"

Carolyn flinched away from him. "No! Don't touch me!"

Jason froze, his eyes darkened and his mouth thinned, and for an instant he looked just as he had when Carolyn first met him. His eyes glittered with an elemental emotion, but Carolyn wasn't sure whether it was hurt or hatred. He straightened. "I'm sorry to have disturbed you. You need to rest. I'll leave now." His words were jerky and wooden, as expressionless as his face. He strode out of the room, and Carolyn returned to her bed, her heart twisting within her.

There was only one reason Jason would deny leaving that note, only one reason why he would have taken it away after she left—so no one would know that he had asked her to meet him at the Keep at ten o'clock, precisely the time and place where a stretch of wall happened to collapse on her. By all rights, she should have been dead by now, and without her statement, without the note, no one would have known she hadn't gone to the Keep by chance. It would have appeared accidental.

Jason must have arranged it. It was too coincidental that the wall collapsed at the exact time he told her to meet him there. He must have somehow weakened the wall or found its weakness. He could have tethered his horse in the woods where no one would see it and hidden there until she rode up. While she was inside the building, he had sneaked up to the wall, listening until she walked past the right section of wall and then pushed it in. What would it take? A heavy log? A tool? Perhaps just his hands and brute strength if he had weakened it enough.

A sob escaped her, and Carolyn's hands flew up to cover her face. No! He couldn't have! Yet his very denial of the note was damning. Unless . . . unless someone else wrote it.

Carolyn sprang out of bed and ran to the small secretary. Jerking out the shallow center drawer, she pawed through it until she found the list of guests Jason had given her for the hunt weekend. She stared at the bold, precise letters until they swam before her eyes. Tears seeped over her lower lid and trickled down her cheeks. It was the same handwriting as that on her note this morning. She was sure of it.

Carolyn spent the rest of the day and most of the next in bed, paralyzed by fear and indecision. She couldn't stay; she couldn't leave. She feared Jason; she couldn't bear to believe he wanted to kill her, and she had nowhere to go, no family to turn to. She dithered and cried and trembled. No days had ever been so long.

Late the next afternoon, Jason called her into his study.

Carolyn didn't want to go, but she knew she must. She had to face things, had to arrive at some decision. Jason had seen the fear in her eyes the other day; it was important that she let him see that she was strong and unafraid, able to deal with her danger—no matter how untrue that was.

Jason bounced out of his chair when she entered the study, as if he had been waiting on tenterhooks. "Good, you're here," he began without preamble, clasping his hands behind his back.

How could this man want to hurt her, Carolyn wailed inside. The instant she saw him, her heart leapt with love, not fear. She noticed the tired lines around his eyes and wondered if he had been sleeping poorly. He hadn't come to her bed since they'd quarreled over his note; he hadn't even visited her to inquire after her health. Carolyn wanted to touch his brow with her fingertips and smooth away the lines.

"I wanted to let you know that I'll be out of the house for the next few days." He perched awkwardly on the corner of his desk.

Her impulse was to grab him and beg him not to go. She felt scared and defenseless without him. "Oh." She clamped her teeth against the protest forming in her mouth. "How—how long will you be gone?"

He shrugged. "A few days. A week, perhaps. Does it matter?" His eyes glinted cynically. "I have no reason to stay here, have I?"

"No, no, of course not."

"Besides, I should think you'd feel better with me gone. Safer." Carolyn kept her head lowered and made no reply. "I want you to promise me one thing—and I mean it. Promise you won't ride out without a groom along. Don't set foot outside this house without taking a groom."

"Yes, of course." She couldn't understand it. Jason was leaving; he was taking precautions for her safety. Surely he wouldn't do that if he planned to kill her—unless it was protective coloration.

"I've hired a man from London to protect you."

"What?"

"I've hired a guard. His name is Wilson, and he's posing as a groom. He's the one who will ride out with you. He'll also keep watch on the house. He's an expert, good with his fists, and a crack shot as well. He can protect you, if you'll let him."

"Of course. Why would I oppose protection?" Her stomach curled queasily. No doubt this Wilson was expert. But Carolyn wondered if he was hired to protect her, or to kill her while Jason was safely away in another city?

"Where—where are you going?"

"London. I have business there. Now, do I have your promise?"

"Yes. I won't go out without Wilson."

"Good. Barlow has promised that he personally will serve

you every bit of your food, and he'll test it on one of the kitchen cats before you eat it."

"Really, Jason, don't you think that's a trifle melo-dramatic?"

"Yes, but then so is arsenic poisoning."

Her head flew up. "Then you believe me?" What did it matter? Of course he believed her if he was the one who had dropped arsenic in her food.

"A few too many 'accidents' have happened around you. It begins to strain one's credulity." He paused, and for an instant his eyes darkened, tinged with such pain that Caro-lyn longed to throw herself in his arms and hold him until the pain went away.

"I love you," she said jerkily, surprising even herself.

Jason's eyebrows rose. "Do you?" A reluctant smile twitched at one corner of his mouth.

"Yes. Amazingly, I do."

Jason sighed and stood up. "I hope you don't stop." He made no move to touch or kiss her. "I'll be leaving tomor-row morning. I shan't wake you to say good-bye."

He rose dismissively, and Carolyn stood up also. "Well, then, good-bye, Jason."

"Good-bye."

Carolyn left the study quickly, not daring to look back at him, or show him her tears of frustration.

Carolyn was slow to dress and drink her wake-up tea the next morning. She realized that her dawdling was a con-certed effort not to leave her room, and sternly she rebuked herself. Nothing could happen to her in the rest of the house that couldn't happen right here.

She marched down to breakfast and ate it in solitary

splendor. There were no dishes of food warming on the sideboard this morning. Barlow appeared and gravely asked what she wished to eat, then left to relay her order to Cook. When he brought her ham and eggs a few minutes later, his face carefully blank, Carolyn wondered whether he had in fact fed a small portion of everything to a cat. The idea of the dignified Barlow stooping to feed a cat tidbits from her plate brought a smile to her still face.

Now there was an element of the ridiculous in the whole matter. Her spirits lifted, and she did justice to Cook's food for the first time in days. Afterward, she went upstairs to play with Laurel. Jason wouldn't do anything to harm her when she was with Laurel. Carolyn knew she couldn't be wrong about the love in his eyes when he looked at Laurel. But, she thought guiltily, she must not use Laurel as a shield against her husband—against Jason, rather.

She made her plans to get away.

Cynthia had eluded Jason; surely Carolyn could, too, employing the tricks of makeup and dress she had learned in her years of acting. She had met all types of Englishmen during her travels: cockneys, clerks, former milkmaids, and factory workers. She could adopt a lifestyle and speech and literally fade into the background. Money wasn't a problem, since Jason had given her a generous allowance over the months she'd been here, and she had spent little of it, using it only to buy gifts and trinkets for Laurel. She was uneasy at using Jason's money to escape him, but, on the other hand, it was only fair, wasn't it, since he was trying to take her life?

She would stay another day or two with Laurel, gathering memories of the child to last her the rest of her life. Then she would sneak away during the night. On Felicity, she could ride to Barham in one night and buy a ticket for Dover, not disguising herself. After that, she'd check into a room in an inn, and she'd leave a new woman on the first train to London. Jason would never expect her to run straight toward where he was, and London would be the easiest place to lose oneself. She would get herself a cheap little room and take an anonymous little job, something unrelated to the theater. That should keep her safe while she made up her mind what she would do with her life.

The problem was sneaking Felicity out of the stables. Carolyn could saddle and bridle the mare herself, but she would have to be very quiet in order not to wake the grooms. And she had yet to figure out how to slip out without Wilson. Carolyn didn't relish the thought of being caught by Jason's henchman. She needed to discover as much as she could about the stables and Wilson. Tomorrow she'd go riding, and she'd check around for the grooms' rooms. She'd at least learn what Wilson looked like, and if she was lucky, perhaps she could worm something about his night schedule out of him.

She retired early and carefully locked both the hall door and the connecting door to Jason's bedroom. Feeling relatively secure, she climbed into bed and blew out the light. But her mind was too active to sleep right away. It was over an hour before she finally drifted off.

A snap penetrated her consciousness, and Carolyn's eyes flew open. For a moment she lay frozen in her bed, rigid with fear. Slowly she relaxed and let her eyes dart around the room. There was enough moonlight streaming in the window for her to see, but no one lurked in the shadows. She sat up a little, reclining on her elbows, thinking of what had awakened her. No doubt her fears had infected her dreams, and a nightmare had brought her awake, quivering with terror.

Suddenly, she thought she heard a noise behind the connecting door. As she watched, the handle on the door turned slowly, noiselessly, and stopped with a click. Just as slowly the handle returned to its original position. For a long moment, Carolyn stared, her heart tripping around in fast, skittering strokes. Finally she forced herself to leave the bed and tiptoe across the room to the door. She bent and peered through the keyhole, but saw nothing of the room beyond but darkness. He wasn't going to loiter around in Jason's room after he found he couldn't open the door, she thought, not even knowing who "he" was supposed to be.

She returned to bed, and she could only lie there beneath the covers, cold and still, reliving the sensations of her fear. A scrape sounded above her head, and Carolyn dug her hands into the sheets. She scrambled out of bed and looked up. There was nothing atop the canopy of her bed.

There was another noise above her, this time, a step. Carolyn swallowed and stared at the ceiling. She had heard it; it wasn't her imagination. First there had been a sound like—like a chair scraping across the floor, then the double beat of a footstep. Someone was in the room above hers on the third floor. But no one lived on that floor except Laurel and Bonnie. The nursery was at the opposite end of the hall, and Carolyn was sure that neither one would have ventured that far down the dark, spooky corridor.

Carolyn sat down in the closest chair, pulling up her cold feet and wrapping her arms around her quaking knees. Indefinable horror swept her as she thought of stories of mad relatives stashed away in attics, of escaped convicts hiding from the authorities. For a few moments Carolyn shivered in the armchair, unable to combat the shrieking, mindless terror of a hidden stalker. But finally she clenched her fists and willed herself to stop. Though her fingers still shook slightly, she managed to light the lamp by her bedside. With light banishing the far shadows of her room, it was easier to quell the racing fear.

There couldn't be a person living on the third floor and plotting to kill her, for surely she would have heard gossip about a mad, caged relative. It was ridiculous to think anyone could evade notice for weeks in this house, she told herself. Why, think of the way it had been cleaned out and filled with guests the weekend of the hunt. No lurking oddball could have survived that. Silly, what one could think of in the middle of the night.

Carolyn climbed back into bed and pulled the covers over her shoulders. She turned the wick down to a dim glow, but didn't turn it out completely. Even with the light on and her thoughts aimed sternly toward the positive, it was several hours before she was able to sleep.

Daylight streaming through the windows awakened her the next morning. She wished she had let Priscilla draw the drapes last night, but at the time she hadn't wanted to cut out the moonlight. She sat up groggily and rubbed her face, and her eyelids felt leaden this morning. It had seemed an interminable time that she had lain awake last night.

She rang the bellpull, then blew out the flickering lamp. That had been a dangerous thing to do, going to sleep with a lamp burning. Imagine thinking there was someone on the third floor! It seemed absurd by daylight.

After she dressed and had breakfast, she went up to see Laurel. At the top of the stairs, she cast a glance down the long, dim hall. The doors along the way were firmly closed, so that the only light came from the window at either end of the hall. Carolyn hesitated for an instant, then continued into the nursery. Laurel was as happy to see her as ever, and Carolyn knew she had made great progress with the child. Usually Carolyn felt great pride and satisfaction as she worked with Laurel, but this morning she had difficulty keeping her mind on the games and lessons. Glancing out the nursery windows, she realized it had been several days since she had even been out of the house. It galled her pride that she had been so cowardly. She should ride today. That way she could see Wilson and get a clue as to the nearness of the grooms to the horses at night.

Leaving Laurel's room shortly before noon, she walked across to the stairs and paused. Could there have been someone up here last night? If she opened each door and peered in, she could look for any signs of disturbance. Carolyn straightened her shoulders and started down the corridor, and opened the first door. Several ghostly humps of furniture covered with white sheets sat about the chilly room. Carolyn withdrew, rubbing her arms for warmth. She went on. The next room was much the same: heavy drapes drawn, dark and chill, with lumps of covered chairs, dresser, and bed. Carolyn closed that door and moved on.

The closer she came to the center of the house, the darker the hallway was, since the only light came from the windows at either end. It seemed to get colder, too. Her footsteps slowed as she neared the area corresponding to her bedroom below. Carolyn faltered and stopped. Only a door or two more, and she would reach the room above hers. Her legs began to tremble, and the low, dark corridor closed in on her. Icy sweat trickled down her back. She couldn't do it. Fear froze her, and she couldn't open that door.

Carolyn broke and fled, running through the hall and skimming down the stairs. She was seized with an urgent need to be outdoors, to feel the wind and the openness, to have the sun caress her face. Bursting into her room, she startled the maid making up her bed. The girl jumped. "Oh, milady, you gave me a turn."

"I'm sorry, Louise. I was in a hurry. Help me change, would you?"

"Yes, milady. Of course." The girl beamed, obviously proud to be given a chance to be a ladies' maid, even if for only a few minutes. She lacked Priscilla's competence, but she managed to unfasten the buttons and the corset laces, which were Carolyn's primary blocks to dressing herself.

Soon Carolyn was ready. As she crossed the yard to the stables, Jack, the groom who usually saddled her horse, saw her and doffed his cap, grinning. "You'll be wanting Felicity, milady?"

"Yes, please." Carolyn stepped inside the stable and looked for an area where the grooms might sleep. She saw only stalls for the horses and a loft where the hay was stored. She was relatively sure it wasn't in the house with the other servants. They would be closer to the horses. She stepped outside. On one side of the barn was the tack room, and she thought that behind it was Broaddus's quarters. Casually she strolled to the other side and found a door here leading into another side room. That must be a dormitory for the stable lads. They would be awfully near, but if she could keep Felicity from making noise as she saddled her . . .

"Here you go, milady," Jack's cheerful voice broke in on her thoughts, and she jumped. "Sorry, ma'am. I guess we're all a little nervy these days, what with that scare you had the other day and him wandering about all the time." A slight nod of his head indicated the man walking toward them from the garden.

"Who is that?"

"New groom. Or so Broaddus says. But I ain't seen him working in the stables yet. Always snooping around." Jack helped her onto her horse and handed her the reins.

"Is that Wilson?"

"Yes'm. The master says he's to ride out with you whenever you go. That's why I saddled the other horse."

"Yes, Lord Broughton told me about him."

Wilson came within speaking range and pulled off his cap. "Milady. I'm George Wilson, at your service. Lord Broughton asked me to look after you while he was gone."

"Yes, I know. I promised Jason not to leave Broughton Court without you."

Wilson set his cap back on his head and took the reins of his horse from the lad. He was a thick, sturdy man with a square face. His features were blunt and heavy, his eyebrows a single thick line above his eyes. He looked thoroughly hard and tough, and Carolyn thought she would feel quite safe with him around to protect her—if that was truly what he had been hired to do.

He mounted the horse awkwardly, and Carolyn noticed that he held the reins like a novice. She sighed inwardly. If she let him keep up with her, there would be no galloping today. She set off at a steady pace, and he followed a respectful distance behind her. Once or twice she twisted her head to look back at him and each time she found him studying the terrain. Carolyn had no particular place in mind to go, and at first she simply let Felicity wander down the lanes as she would.

Felicity headed in the general direction of the village, and

Carolyn decided to go to Hokely. She could buy Laurel a toy or pretty ribbons for her hair, a present to remember Carolyn by, after she had gone. She started along a path that wound through a wood of oaks and chestnuts and down a low hill to the village. As it neared the village, the lane became a little larger and entered Hokely from the back side.

They emerged from the woods onto the crest of the hill. Carolyn stopped, as she always did, to admire the view. The small town lay spread out before, with the quaint old church and rectory the closest buildings. A magnificent white horse stood tethered beside Reverend Nelson's house. Jason's horse! There was no other like it for miles around.

Carolyn wheeled her horse around and started back. Wilson was, as all through the ride, several paces behind her. She must not let him draw even with her and get a good look at what she'd seen. He probably wouldn't recognize Jason's horse, but he'd certainly recognize Jason if he happened to walk out of the house. Carolyn didn't want Wilson to know she had found out the truth. That one bit of knowledge was the only weapon she had, though she wasn't sure how she could use it.

Meeting Wilson on the path, she smiled woodenly. "Let's start back, shall we?" The man shrugged and let Carolyn pass him, then began his awkward maneuvering to turn his mount around and follow her.

Why had Jason lied to her? She figured he wanted to be in London with a good alibi while Wilson did the dirty work of killing her. Perhaps Wilson wasn't involved; perhaps Jason had hired Wilson to make himself look concerned and then had hidden at the Nelsons with plans of killing her himself. Or maybe it required two of them to stage the accident. Or Jason was arranging something with Millicent that would set Carolyn's death in motion, and then he would rush to London for his alibi.

She didn't know what to think. Nothing was certain except the fact that if Jason was here, it made her escape far riskier. She had counted on Jason being in London when Barlow notified him that she had gone and having to return from there before he could begin his search. But now she knew he would be on her trail immediately. His presence meant she better leave Broughton Court without further delay. She didn't know his plans, but his secretive movements couldn't bode anything but ill for her health.

She had to escape tonight. Carolyn tapped Felicity lightly with her heels, and the horse broke into a canter. Glancing back at her guard, Carolyn had to smother a smile. Wilson bounced along on his horse, his face grim with concentration. Whatever skills Wilson might possess, riding was definitely not one of them. At least she could be sure he couldn't catch her once she was on Felicity's back.

As soon as she reached the stables, Carolyn slid off her horse and handed the reins to the stableboy. Giving a nod to Wilson, she strode toward the house, her mind busy with plans for her getaway that night. As she walked in the back door, she was intercepted by Barlow. "Milady."

"Yes?"

"Master Hugh is here, milady."

"What? Oh. Where is he?"

"I put him in the sitting room."

"Very well. Thank you."

Carolyn detoured to the downstairs sitting room. What a bother. Why had Hugh had to pick today to come calling? With a forced smile on her face, she stepped through the door. "Cousin Hugh, what a pleasant surprise. I'm sorry I was out."

Hugh sprang up from the comfortable chair in which he'd been lounging. "Cousin Cynthia." He bent gracefully over her hand. "When they told me you were riding, I could hardly believe it." His eyes twinkled merrily at her. "But I reasoned that if *that* was what you were doing, you wouldn't be gone long. So I decided to wait for you to return."

"I'm glad you did. I hope you weren't too bored."

"Not at all. I've been here only a few minutes."

"I'll have to impose on your kindness once again. I really must change." Carolyn glanced down ruefully at her riding habit. "Will you excuse me?"

"No, please. Don't trouble yourself. You're lovely just as you are. I shan't be here but a few minutes."

"But you must stay for luncheon," Carolyn pleaded politely. Frankly, she wished he'd be gone straight away. She had more than enough to deal with, knowing Jason was hiding in the area while his employee waited in the stables to follow her wherever she went. She needed to do some serious planning, and a polite social visit with Hugh St. John would be a frustrating delay. However, she couldn't arouse his suspicions by being rude.

Looking at Hugh's open, pleasant face, Carolyn wondered for an instant if she should pour out her story to him and ask for his aid. He seemed to like Cynthia well enough, and he might help her get away if she could convince him that Jason was actually dangerous.

But that was the problem: Jason's friends and relatives were very loyal to him, and Hugh would never believe his cousin had tried to kill her. No, she must not confide in Hugh. She would rely only on her own wits, as always.

Hugh smiled agreeably, but shook his head. "No. I regret it, but I can't lunch with you. I have an appointment for which I mustn't be late. I merely wanted to stop by and make sure you were feeling all right. Jason told me what happened to you the other day."

"Oh? I wasn't aware you'd seen Jason since then." Carolyn meant nothing particular by her words. They were only another line of idle conversation. But Hugh's eyes shifted away from her, and a faint blush rose up his throat. Carolyn realized she had caught him in a lie, and in the next instant she understood why he was here. Jason must have gone to Hugh after he left Broughton Court. It would be the logical place for him to stay if he wanted to remain in the area without being at Broughton Court. No doubt he had sent Hugh here this morning to see what she was doing. Carolyn doubted that Hugh had any idea what Jason was up to, but he would have gone along with his cousin's request simply because he was fond of Jason.

Carolyn cut into Hugh's mumbled explanation. "Well, as you can see, I'm perfectly all right. Why, I even went out riding this morning. Of course, I took a groom with me, as Jason asked me to." She supposed that was what Jason had sent Hugh to find out, doubtless under the guise of husbandly concern. She wondered what sort of story he had spun for Hugh to explain his lying about the trip to London.

"Oh, yes. You look splendid. Splendid." Hugh made a few more awkward efforts at conversation, but Carolyn did little to help him, and before long he took his leave. Carolyn watched him mount his bay gelding in the driveway, a rueful smile forming on her lips. Hugh St. John wouldn't make much of a spy.

She started purposefully up the stairs. She must change

into a day dress and eat luncheon, then get down to business. When she reached her door, Bonnie was just turning away from it. "Oh! Milady! I was looking for you. I must speak to you," Bonnie began without preamble, opening the door for Carolyn.

What now? Carolyn's nerves were already overloaded. "Is it important, Bonnie?"

"Milady, I saw her!"

"Who?" For the first time Carolyn noticed the excitement in Bonnie's usually dour face. The woman's eyes were shining. Carolyn grabbed her arm, her heart leaping. "Cynthia? Do you mean Cynthia?"

"Yes! Miss Cindy. I was taking Laurel on her walk this morning, and all of a sudden, past the big pine tree down the drive, Miss Cynthia appears! I was never so flabbergasted in my life."

"What did she say? Where is she?"

"She's waiting for you, Miss Caro. She wants you to meet her down by the hammer pond."

"When?"

"As soon as you can. She said she'd go straight there and be waiting for you. I told her about that man in the stables, the one his lordship set to spy on you, and she said you must get away without him."

"Yes, yes, I'll manage. Thank you, Bonnie." Thankful she hadn't changed yet, Carolyn turned and hurried back down the stairs, hoping she wouldn't meet Barlow announcing luncheon. They'd just have to hold the meal until she returned.

Carolyn reached the stables without incident, and Jack, the stableboy, came out to meet her, looking surprised and confused. "Jack, saddle Felicity for me again. I just remembered that I forgot an errand while I was out."

"Yes, milady." He made no comment on the vagaries of the nobility, though his face was expressive enough. "But I have to tell that fellow."

"Wilson? Yes, of course. But do get on with it."

Jack disappeared and returned shortly leading two horses, as he had before. Wilson emerged from the tack room, his face disgruntled. Carolyn suspected she had pulled him away from his meal. She mounted calmly and moved Felicity aside. As Wilson grasped his reins and started to mount, Carolyn kicked her mare in the sides and tapped her hindquarters with her crop. Felicity leaped forward, racing through the open gate and along the path to Hemby Keep.

The stableboy gaped in amazement, and Wilson yelled furiously after her, "Wait!" Carolyn curved lower over the horse's neck and urged her to greater speed. The path was well-trodden and fairly wide, quite safe for Felicity to run on. As soon as she was well out of sight of the stables, Carolyn pulled back on the reins and slowed Felicity to a trot. She turned her aside into the apple orchard. She had no desire to visit the old Keep, only to throw off Wilson when he managed to get on his horse and follow her.

She made a wide sweep around Broughton Court and emerged far west of the house on the way to the hammer pond. Not wanting to tire Felicity, she slowed the mare to a walk. She was certain she had eluded Wilson, and she needed the mare fresh tonight for her escape. Her thoughts turned to Cynthia. At first she had felt only pleasure at the idea of seeing her twin again, but now she began to wonder why Cynthia had returned. Would she want to resume her role as Lady Broughton?

Carolyn thought of her sister with Jason and Laurel, and an unaccustomed flash of jealousy tore through her. No! Cynthia couldn't simply waltz back into their lives. She'd ruin everything Carolyn had built up the past few months. Laurel would think Cynthia was the woman who had loved her, and it would break her heart when Cynthia rejected her. It wasn't fair!

Sternly Carolyn stemmed the flood of her emotions. This was preposterous, for she had already decided to flee Broughton Court that night. It would be she herself who broke Laurel's heart. Besides, Cynthia could no more resume her position as Lady Broughton than Carolyn could stay here. If Jason was trying to kill Cynthia, she would have to run away with her, too.

But maybe Cynthia could shed some light on the killer. With Cynthia's help Carolyn could solve the mystery, and then . . . well, she'd cross that bridge later. The important thing was to get some answers out of Cynthia.

Her sister wasn't in sight when Carolyn stopped beside the hammer pond. Carolyn dismounted and tied Felicity's reins around a low branch. She wandered back to the pond and stood gazing at it. It was mellow here in the sunlight, and with her cloak around her, she was quite warm. Just as she wondered if Bonnie had Cynthia's directions right, something moved among the beech trees across the pond. There was a glimmer of pink, and a woman stepped out. She wore a dark cloak with the hood thrown back. Her red-gold hair caught and held the pale sunlight. As she walked, a pink dress showed between the edges of her cloak. Carolyn started toward her, her heart thudding, and tears burned at her eyes. It had been so long. How strange after all these years, to see her mirror image walking toward her. "Cynthia?"

The woman's steps quickened, and a smile began on her face. "Caro!"

Carolyn lifted her skirts and ran, skirting the pond to meet her. Her arms flew wide, and in the next moment, Cynthia threw herself into Carolyn's arms. "Oh, Cynthia."

Carolyn broke away first. "Here, let me look at you." Cynthia's vivid blue eyes sparkled; her cheeks were flushed. "I saw you riding. You're as graceful as ever. How did you get away with riding that awful horse when you're supposed to be me?"

"I got caught red-handed," Carolyn confessed, chuckling. "Oh, Cindy, it's so good to see you! Tell me everything. Everything. Where have you been? What happened? Why did you leave Jason? Why—"

"Whoa! Slow down." Cynthia curled an arm around Carolyn's waist, and they began to stroll along the pond's edge. "I can't answer everything at once. I was miserable, Caro. Jason hates me. I was never good enough for him. He was forever after me to learn to ride, to stop being such a coward. I hated it!" Her eyes darkened. "I had to get away from him. And I—I fell in love."

"With Dennis Bingham?" Cynthia nodded. "What about Mark Simmons? Did you love him, too?"

Carolyn shot her a surprised glance. "Mark!"

"Yes, I met him. I know that you were having an affair with him. Why, Cynthia, why?"

Her sister turned away slightly, the petulant droop of her lips spoiling her mouth. Carolyn watched her twin pout sulkily. "You wouldn't understand. You're so sure of everything. Everyone loves you. You never had to wonder. You were never second best."

"What are you talking about? I'm very often unsure of myself, and everyone didn't love me. I was constantly being scolded, remember?"

"Papa loved you best," Cynthia insisted stubbornly. "After you left, I thought I'd have a chance. I thought he'd love *me* best, but it was always you. Always. You were more important in your absence than I was being there."

"Is that why you married Jason? To please Papa?"

"Of course." Cynthia shuddered. "Jason repulsed me. He was so . . . so forceful, so full of energy. I thought I could stand it, but I couldn't. After we married, he would kiss me and maul me. I hated it. He's disgusting."

Carolyn stared. "How can you say that? Jason's so—" She stopped and blushed fierily.

Cynthia's eyes narrowed. "So it's true. You have fallen in love with him. I should have known. He told me, but I didn't believe him."

"He?" Carolyn repeated, bewildered. "Who? Who told you I loved Jason?"

"Hugh."

"Hugh! Do you mean he knew where you were?"

"But of course I did." Hugh's voice sounded behind her. Carolyn whirled, and the blood in her veins turned icy. Hugh St. John stood at the edge of the trees a few feet away from her. In one hand he held a pistol pointed levelly at her.

Seventeen

*C*arolyn stared at him, open-mouthed. "You?" Her voice rose incredulously. "It was you who tried to kill me?"

Hugh smiled. "Of course. Surely you didn't think it was our sterling Jason."

Carolyn knew a rush of fierce delight. Jason hadn't tried to kill her! He was just as she thought him.

"No," Hugh drawled, "but it will appear that he is the killer." He sighed affectedly. "Poor Jason. He always had everything. The money, the title, even the woman I wanted. But now it seems he'll lose it all."

Carolyn thought longingly of the guard she had left behind at the stables. Jason had done his best to protect her, and she had foolishly thrown away that protection. No one knew where she was except Bonnie, and she would never tell Jason or Wilson. With her impulsive flight Carolyn had effectively cut herself off from help. Impulse again. Would she never learn? Well, it looked now as if she wouldn't have the chance to. Still, it was best to stall for time. After all, there were two of them, both her and Cynthia against Hugh. Carolyn turned toward her sister and saw that Cynthia had stepped away. Arms crossed, she stared across the lake, ignoring the scene behind her. The truth soaked in, creeping like acid through Carolyn's veins. Cynthia had lured Carolyn here to be killed by Hugh. Cynthia wanted her dead! "Why? Cynthia, why?" Her voice broke on a note of grief and pain. Half of the foundation of her life had been ripped away in one brief moment, as if a part of herself had turned against her.

Cynthia kept her head averted, refusing to answer. Carolyn swung back to Hugh. "Why? Why do you want to kill me?"

"Oh, no, not you. Cynthia. It won't be Carolyn Mabry they find her on the ground. It will be Lady Broughton. Lady Broughton's clothes, her horse, her hairstyle. Any of the servants will be able to identify you. 'She looks just as she did when she left the house,' they'll say."

"And that will free Cynthia? Keep Jason from chasing her?"

Hugh sneered and uttered an ugly laugh. "Dear Jason will be too busy to chase anyone. He'll be in the dock fighting not to be hanged." With a leisurely movement he cocked the hammer of the pistol. "You'll be shot with Jason's dueling pistol, you see. The other one of the set is lying in its open case on Jason's desk—right beside a love note from Mark Simmons to you, asking you to rendezvous with him at the hammer pond."

"You put it there when you called on me this morning!"

"Clever girl."

"And that note from Jason asking me to meet him at the Keep—did you write it?"

"Of course. I've been able to copy Jason's handwriting since we were children. It's come in handy a few times.

They'll find that note hidden in his desk, also. More evidence, you see."

Carolyn's lip curled. "You're unspeakable."

"Probably so," he agreed cheerfully and took careful aim.

"Wait!" Cynthia whirled and walked toward him. "No, Hugh, you promised. You said you'd wait until I left."

"Turning squeamish, my love?" His smile was chilling, and Carolyn wondered how she could ever have thought he resembled Jason. Suddenly, a picture floated up out of the mists of memory. A man's face, Hugh's face. The admirer who had stopped her outside the theater in Antigua and handed her a bouquet of flowers. The incident had been so routine she'd barely noticed him, and the events that had followed had so overshadowed him that she had forgotten the man entirely. But now she remembered. No wonder he had looked vaguely familiar to Carolyn when she first met him. She *had* seen him before. And even then he had been planting clues to lead to Jason, leaving Jason's button on the floor of her lodgings.

"You know I can't bear such things," Cynthia fretted. "Hugh, let me leave."

"No, I don't think so. What if you should turn more squeamish in the future? Maybe even decide to tell the court the truth, that it was I, not Jason, who killed your sister? No, I want you as deep in this thing as I am. If I go down, you will, too. You're staying right here."

"No! I won't. I'm leaving!"

Hugh's free hand lashed out, catching her by the wrist. "Oh, no, you're not!" This was her moment, Carolyn knew. Quarreling, their attention was on each other, not her. Cautiously Carolyn slid a step backwards. Hugh didn't glance in her direction. "Need I remind you that I don't need you for this scheme? With both sisters dead, I'd get all the money as Laurel's guardian." Step by step, Carolyn edged toward Felicity, tied up at the edge of the trees. Her only hope was to make a run for the horse. "Damn it!" His head snapped toward Carolyn. Carolyn broke and ran for the black mare. Felicity snorted and danced.

Hugh aimed the pistol. Cynthia leaped forward, grabbing his wrist and jerking the gun down. They struggled, Cynthia a poor match for St. John's strength. Just as Carolyn reached the mare, she heard the shot. She whirled and saw Cynthia and Hugh staring at each other in surprise, gun clasped between them. Slowly Cynthia crumpled to the ground. Carolyn froze. Cynthia! For the first time in the whole episode, she screamed, a high, piercing shriek of rage and loss.

Without thinking, Carolyn ran, not to safety, but straight at Hugh. She leaped upon him, sobbing with fury, clawing, hitting, kicking like a wild creature. "You killed her! You killed her!"

Startled, Hugh staggered backward under her onslaught, flinging up his arms to ward her off. It took him only a second to recover, however, and Carolyn was no match for his superior strength. He hurled her to the ground. She bounded up, hands scrabbling for a stick, a rock, any weapon. But Hugh reached her first. His hands clamped around her throat, fingers digging into her delicate flesh. Carolyn flailed wildly with her hands and feet, but his arms were too long—she couldn't reach him. Frantically she clawed at his fingers. He didn't release her. Hugh's face contorted as he shoved her to the ground. Carolyn's struggles weakened, and tiny dots buzzed before her eyes. There was a low roaring in her ears, a sound like thundering hoof-beats.

Hugh's head jerked up, and his fingers relaxed involuntarily. Dirt and mud sprayed the air as a white stallion skidded to a halt beside them. Carolyn saw the horse's enormously long legs, the huge hoofs close to her face, and then a man launched himself off the horse and flew across her vision, taking Hugh to the ground beneath him. Jason!

Carolyn, released, crawled away feebly, sucking in precious air. She staggered to her feet. Her throat was on fire; every breath pained her. Jason was atop his cousin, his fists smashing into the other man's face. "Jason!" Carolyn reeled over to him and tugged at his jacket. "Jason, he's out. Stop. You'll kill him."

Her words broke his diabolic trance. His hands dropped away, and he eased his weight off the inert form. He stood up, stumbling slightly, and jerked Carolyn against him. "Oh, my love, my love. I almost didn't make it. If he'd killed you . . ." He couldn't go on and buried his face in her tumbled hair.

"Jason." She was unable to say anything but his name. That seemed to be enough for him. They held each other for a long moment, then Carolyn remembered her sister. "Cynthia! He shot her, Jason. She's over there."

She rushed toward the body, but Jason stopped her with one hand. "Let me." He walked across to Cynthia's crumpled form and knelt beside it. Gently he turned her over, and Carolyn saw the bright red stain covering the front of her dress. Jason pressed his fingers against her throat. After a moment he looked back at Carolyn and shook his head. "I'm sorry, love. She's gone."

For the first time she could remember, Carolyn fainted.

* * *

There was a cool cloth on her forehead. She heard voices. Now she was being carried. Carolyn smiled a little. Papa was carrying her to bed. "Papa? Cindy?" Her eyes fluttered open, and a man's stern face floated above her. She realized that he was carrying her. "Jason."

The face smiled down at her, its severity waning. "Hush. No need to talk. I'm taking you home now."

He lifted her onto his horse and swung up after her, encircling her with his arms and taking the reins in his hands. A man stood on the ground beside them, and Carolyn looked down curiously at him. "Don't you fear, milord," he was saying. "I'll stay with 'em till the doctor and the constable get here. He won't be getting up while I'm around."

"Thank you, Wilson," Jason answered.

Carolyn leaned against Jason's chest, lulled by the warmth of his body and the heavy rhythm of his heart. She closed her eyes, but the vision of Cynthia's body was etched on her eyelids. Tears seeped out beneath her eyelids, and she began to cry. "She saved my life," she gulped. "In the end she couldn't let him do it. She grabbed his gun, and he shot her." Jason's arms tightened around Carolyn, and his chin pressed sharply into the top of her head. Carolyn cried until she could cry no longer, mourning for her sister's death and for all the years of trust and closeness that had been lies.

When they reached the house, Jason carried her up to her room, though Carolyn protested feebly that she could walk. Priscilla tucked her into bed, dirt, shoes, and all, and rushed off to get her a cup of hot tea. The warmth of the bed was soothing, like a cocoon. Jason left the room, and she ached for the loss of him. But the pull of shock and the comfort of the bed were too much for her, and Carolyn drifted into sleep.

"Milady?" Priscilla touched her shoulder gingerly. "Milady?"

"Yes? What?" She was momentarily groggy and confused. Then she remembered what had happened, and her heart sank. It was over, Cynthia was dead, and Jason must know who she was. If not, he would soon. She had lost her sister, and now she would lose Jason and Laurel.

Priscilla's mouth trembled in sympathy at the look of sorrow in Carolyn's eyes. "I'm sorry to wake you up, ma'am. I wouldn't have, but that constable insisted that he talk to you. Even his lordship couldn't persuade him to wait till tomorrow."

"It's all right, Priscilla." Carolyn sat up and slipped out of bed. "I can talk to him." She caught sight of herself in the mirror over the dresser. "Good heavens. I look a fright." She was covered with dirt and splotches of mud, and her hair stuck out in all directions, making her pale face look almost sickly. "I don't suppose he'll allow me time to bathe and change.

"He said he wanted to see you as you are, milady."

Carolyn shakily descended the stairs. She dreaded telling the whole awful story in front of the constable and Jason, for it wasn't at all the way she would have wanted Jason to learn the truth, coldly, in front of a stranger. Carolyn shivered. But there was no other way. She had to tell the truth now.

There were three men in the study when she opened the door, and all sprang up at her entrance. Jason took her hand and brought her into the room; the other two stared, taken aback by her disheveled appearance. One of the men began to stammer apologetically, and Jason smiled. "I told you, Ned; you'll have to face the wrath of a lady forced to appear in disarray."

"Mrs. Mabry," the one Jason had addressed began tentatively. "I'm terribly sorry to put you out like this. I—uh—"

"It's quite all right, Constable. Shall we get on with it?"

"Of course, ma'am."

He had called her Mrs. Mabry. Did that mean Jason knew her identity? She glanced surreptitiously at him. She could see no damning knowledge in his eyes. Jason patted her hand and seated her in a cushioned chair. "My dear, this is Constable Ned Waters, and this is his assistant, Alfred Jones."

Carolyn gave the men a regal nod. The constable sat down behind Jason's desk and rested his elbows on the desk. "Mr. Jones will be taking notes while you talk. I hope it won't bother you."

"Not at all. Shall I begin at the very first?"

"Yes, please."

"Well . . . I'm Carolyn Worthing Mabry, Lady Broughton's twin sister."

"Yes, I see. You're very alike."

"Identical. That's why I could pass for Lady Broughton." Carolyn kept her eyes carefully averted from Jason as she poured out the whole story, beginning with the admirer who had stopped her after the show and given her a bouquet and continuing straight through to Cynthia's death. She left out only what had passed between her and Jason personally. She felt sure the constable was dying to hear that, too, but she wasn't about to satisfy his curiosity unless he asked her directly. The youthful Mr. Jones scribbled away on his tablet while she talked, and Ned Waters nodded thoughtfully now and again. When she was finished, he asked her a few questions to clarify some of the things she had said. Jason said nothing the whole time.

When she finished, the constable made a gesture toward his assistant and stood up. "I think that does it, ma'am. Your brother-in-law and the servants have all given their accounts, and with Master Hugh's confession . . ." He shook his head sadly. "Nasty business. I never would have thought it of Hugh St. John if I hadn't heard it with my own ears."

"But, please, won't you tell me what happened? I mean, why? I can't understand why they wanted to kill me."

"For money," Jason replied grimly. "Money and lifelong envy." His face was lined with sadness, and Carolyn's heart ached to see it. "I'll tell you about it. I heard Hugh's confession."

The constable and his assistant left. Jason rose and went to a cabinet on the far wall. "I could use something to drink. Shall I pour you one as well?" Carolyn shook her head. "No? Well, I'm going to, anyway. You need it. You've had quite a shock today."

"Was it Hugh every time? How did he do it?"

"When Cynthia left with Dennis Bingham, who was nothing but a dupe in this whole affair, Hugh had already sailed to the West Indies and located you. Cynthia purposely left a trail a blind man could have followed and then booked passage on the ship in Bingham's name. They didn't go, of course. If I hadn't been so furious and so used to Cynthia's eternal show of incompetence, I would have suspected something. Following them was too easy. When I arrived on the island, Hugh must have attacked you. He failed and I whisked you off, so he had no choice but to come home and try again."

"How did he manage to put the arsenic in my food?"
Jason frowned. "Bonnie did it for him."

"Bonnie!" Carolyn gasped. "No!"

"Apparently, over the years her love for Cynthia grew into an obsession. I blame myself for not taking enough notice of her. I should never have let a woman who was so unbalanced care for Laurel. But Cynthia wanted her badly, and she was so distressed at the time. I thought if she had her old nurse from home, it might somehow help her to accept Laurel." He shrugged. "Bonnie had been fired by Sir Neville and was slavishly grateful to Cynthia for taking her on. She believed everything Cynthia told her, and somehow or other Hugh and Cynthia twisted her thinking around to where she thought poisoning you was the righteous thing to do. It would help her Miss Cindy, you see, and that made it all right in her mind."

"It's so hard to believe." Carolyn shook her head. "I was so sure it was you. I didn't want to believe it, yet the evidence was plainly against you. When I saw your horse this morning at the vicarage, I nearly died."

"At the vicarage?" Jason sighed. "I handled it badly all around. I played right into Hugh's hands. You see, I knew someone was trying to kill you, but I wasn't sure who it was. You suspected me. Logically, I could understand that, but emotionally it hurt. I had to find out what was going on, so I devised this scheme to force the killer to show his hand. I pretended to go to London so the killer would think you were unprotected, but I hired Wilson to keep you safe. I waited, out of sight, to catch him red-handed. I spent the night in the unused room above yours, so I could be nearby if you needed help.

"That was you!" Carolyn laughed, a trifle hysterically.

"You can't imagine what I envisioned—mad relatives and all sorts of things."

"You heard me?"

She nodded. "Someone tried my door, and it woke me up. Later I heard a noise above my head, and I suspected there was someone on the third floor."

"I was checking to make sure you had locked your doors." Jason made a disgusted sound. "I made a complete muddle of it. Like an idiot, the first thing I did was go to Hugh's and explain my plan. Of course, he seized on it; it was perfect for his purposes. I had lied about going to London; both he and the Nelsons could testify that I was really here during that time. He called on you and sneaked into the study, stole my dueling pistol and planted an old love note from Mark Simmons on my study desk."

Jason sighed and shook his head. "All these years, I thought he was my friend as well as my cousin. Never for an instant did I dream that he was having an affair with my wife, envying me, and plotting for my death. He hated me from childhood. He even said that he lost me on purpose that time in the maze when we were children. I was so young at the time that I don't even remember the incident."

"But why do it this way? Why not just kill you?"

"Hugh's mind was more complex than that. He wanted to humiliate me as well. Besides, they wanted to get rid of you, too. The title and Broughton Court, being entailed, would have gone to Hugh, but not the bulk of my fortune. That would have gone partly to my wife, but primarily to Laurel. Because I didn't want Cynthia to have any control of my money if I should die, I had set up a trust fund for Laurel if Cynthia was her guardian. It was to be managed by three people: a bank officer, my solicitor, and Hugh. But if

Cynthia was dead, I appointed Hugh Laurel's guardian, without any trust. I trusted him, you see. I never feared that he would waste Laurel's money. They wanted your money as well."

"My money?" Carolyn echoed. "But I don't have any money."

"Ah, but you do. Sir Neville had a falling out with Cynthia several months ago. Somehow or other he found out about her adulteries, and he was incensed. He cut her out of his will and left all his money to you instead. He told Cynthia, and that was when she and Hugh cooked up this scheme. They had already been using Cynthia's affairs with Mark and Bingham and others as a smokescreen for their own affair. So they decided to use Bingham again. She ran away with him and later cast him off in Germany. There she took on your name and lived while you were here pretending to be her. After Sir Neville's death, she came to England to collect her money. They were desperate to kill you as soon as your father died. They feared you would figure out their plot once you heard that you, not Cynthia, was to inherit the fortune. Like many venal people, they overestimated your greed. They didn't know you had so little interest in the money that you never even inquired about the terms of your father's will."

Carolyn's head snapped up, and her heart began to pound. "But you knew the terms of the will. You learned *then* that Cynthia had a twin?"

"Yes." His grin was filled with emotion. "You'd torn me apart until then. I couldn't believe I was fool enough to fall in love with Cynthia again, knowing what a manipulative, deceptive bitch she was. Yet I was on fire for you constantly; I had to stay out of the house in order to keep my hands off you. You weren't like Cynthia; I saw all the differences. But, not knowing Cynthia had a twin, it never occurred to me that you might be a different person. I couldn't believe she'd changed that much, so I presumed Cynthia was scheming to make me fall in love with her again and use me in some way. At the reading of the will the solicitor said Cynthia's sister Carolyn received the bulk of the estate. I was totally in the dark. But Elizabeth was there, and she was happy to inform me about the scapegrace of the family. The wild young girl who'd thrown away family and fortune for love. Then I knew who you were."

"Oh, Jason!" Carolyn swallowed hot tears. "I'm so sorry for deceiving you. At first I thought I was justified. Later I felt terribly guilty. But I couldn't bring myself to tell you."

"Why not?" Jason crossed to her and dropped down onto one knee beside her chair. Earnestly he took her hands. "Why didn't you tell me? I kept waiting and hoping that you'd reveal the truth to me. I thought, if she isn't lying about her love, if she really cares for me, she'll tell me the truth."

"I was scared to! I was afraid you'd hate me. You had been disgusted I was an actress when I first met you. You despised Cynthia for her morals. Truly, Jason, I've never known another man but you and my husband, but everyone considers actresses only glorified prostitutes. I thought you'd despise me for sleeping with you, knowing I wasn't your wife; for being an actress. I was certain you'd throw me out of the house as soon as you learned who I was. And I couldn't bear to leave."

"Why not?"

"You must know why. I love you!"

"Didn't you realize that I loved you just as much? I don't

give a damn that you were an actress. Your being in my bed was heaven, not something I'd condemn you for. I love you, Carolyn."

"No. You loved Cynthia! Not me. It nearly killed me, knowing that every moan, every sigh, every loving word was meant for Cynthia."

"I lost my love for Cynthia long ago—if, indeed, I ever had it. Sometimes I think I fell in love with a dream of my own making. From the very first, she wasn't what I'd been longing for, dreaming of. Perhaps I was really searching for you and just didn't know it. I fell in love with the woman who came back with me from the West Indies, fell in love despite my best efforts not to. I wouldn't admit it, wouldn't let myself feel it or express it, until I realized you weren't Cynthia. Don't you remember the first time I told you I love you?"

"Of course," Carolyn answered quickly. "The night of Papa's funeral." She stopped, his point dawning on her. "Right after the reading of his will."

"Exactly. When I realized you were Carolyn, I was deliriously happy, not upset. It was Carolyn I made love to, not Cynthia."

"Oh, Jason!" Carolyn flung herself into his arms, clinging to him. "I love you so."

For a long time there was nothing but the soft kisses and caresses of lovers, the gentle, timeless murmurs of a man and woman who had at last found their soul's desire. Finally they pulled apart, and Carolyn rested her head against Jason's broad chest. "What are we going to do?" she sighed.

"What do you mean? We'll get married, of course. It will all come out at Hugh's trial. We can't go on pretending you're Cynthia. Besides, I want to call you by your real name."

"But, Jason, think of the scandal. Everyone will know I've been living here pretending to be your wife when I wasn't. It'll come out about my eloping with Kit and then becoming an actress after he died."

"Yes, the scandalmongers will have a field day. But our true friends, like Jack and Flora, will stick by us. Do you care so much?"

"I? Hardly. The thought of scandal didn't keep me from becoming an actress after Kit died instead of taking a more genteel path of poverty. It's you I'm thinking of. You're a proud man, and you love the Somerville name. Think of what it would do to you name! To your mother."

"Mother has weathered other storms; she'll manage this one. I don't care about the name. I clung to my pride and my name when I had nothing else. But with you—all that counts is your love and respect. The rest of the world be damned! I intend to marry you, Carolyn Worthing Mabry, and no pious appeals to family name are going to put me off. Not only that, I plan to marry you indecently soon. I have no intentions of spending a year living apart from you just to observe the conventions."

Carolyn's smile was dazzling. "Really? Do you mean it?"

"More than I've ever meant anything. I love you. You're all that matters."

She laughed shakily. "You must love me, to say that when I'm all splattered with mud and my hair sticking out every which way."

"You never looked more desirable."

"Oh, Jason." She melted into his arms again.

"My love." His mouth came down on hers hungrily.